TARAN MATHARU

SUMM★NER

— THE BATTLEMAGE —

Hodder
Children's
Books

HODDER CHILDREN'S BOOKS

First published in Great Britain in hardback in 2017
First published in Great Britain in paperback in 2018
This edition published in 2020

1

Text copyright © 2017 Taran Matharu Ltd.
Cover illustration copyright © 2017 Małgorzata Gruszka
Demonology illustrations Copyright © 2018 David North

The moral rights of the author and illustrators have been asserted.

A CIP catalogue record for this book is available from the British Library.

ISBN: 978 1 444 95827 0

Typeset in Garamond by Avon DataSet Ltd, Bidford-on-Avon, Warwickshire

Printed and bound by Clays Ltd, Elcograf S.p.A.

The paper and board used in this book are made from wood from responsible sources.

Hodder Children's Books
An imprint of Hachette Children's Group
Part of Hodder and Stoughton
Carmelite House
50 Victoria Embankment
London EC4Y 0DZ

An Hachette UK Company

www.hachette.co.uk

SUMM☆NER

To my father, for giving me the tools to write
And to my brother and sister, for their lifelong friendship

Map of Hominum

Elven Lands

Pelt

Beartooth Mountains

Faversham Forest

Boreas

Corcillum

Antioch

Vesanian Sea

Vocans Academy

Raleighshire

Orc Jungle

The Pyramid

The Warren

The Waterfall

The Swamps

The Battlemage: Character List

Lord Fletcher Raleigh — summoner, lord of Raleighshire

Pelt Villagers/Raleighshire Colonists

Berdon Wulf — Fletcher's adoptive father, blacksmith
Janet — trader and leatherworker
Rotherham 'Rotter' — soldier, Fletcher's friend
Sergeant Jakov — guardsperson, a member of Didric's Wardens

The Nobles

Old King Alfric — former king of Hominum, founder of
the Inquisition, leader of the Pinkertons, overseer of Judges
King Harold — king of Hominum
Lady Alice Raleigh — the lady of Raleighshire, Fletcher's mother,
Josephine Forsyth's twin sister
Lord Edmund Raleigh — the late lord of Raleighshire,
Fletcher's father
Lord Zacharias Forsyth —Tarquin and Isadora's father
Lady Ophelia Faversham — old King Alfric's cousin,
Lord Faversham's wife
Triumvirate — an alliance between the Cavells, Forsyths and
Faversham as a unit

The Inquisition

Inquisitor Damian Rook

Others

The Pinkertons — lawmakers from the city

Teachers

Captain Arcturus – officer, battlemage, spellcraft teacher, commoner

Captain Elaine Lovett – summoning teacher, noble

Sir Caulder – weapons master, commoner

Major Goodwin – demonology teacher, noble

The Dwarves

Othello Thorsager – Fletcher's friend and fellow student at Vocans

Cress Freya – first year student at Vocans

Briss Thorsager – Othello's mother

Atilla Thorsager – Othello's twin brother

Uhtred Thorsager – Othello's father, blacksmith

Thaissa Thorsager – Othello's sister

Millo – blacksmith, Thaissa's husband

Athol – Uhtred the blacksmith's apprentice

Gallo – Raleighshire colonist

The Elves

Sylva Arkenia – Fletcher's friend and heir to an Elven chieftainship

Dalia – wood elf, Raleighshire guard volunteer

Guides

Jeffrey – Vocans Academy servant, Fletcher's team guide

Mason – former Orc slave and member of the Forsyth Furies

The Gremlins

Half-ear

Blue

The Orcs
Khan – leader
Mother

Students
Tarquin Forsyth – lieutenant, noble
Isadora Forsyth – lieutenant, noble
Lord Didric Cavell – first year, noble
Seraph Pasha – second year, noble
Rory Cooper – second year, commoner
Genevieve Leatherby – second year, commoner

The Barracks
Staff Clerk Murray
Squeems – Clerk helper

Raleighshire Guard Volunteers
Kobe – former slave
Logan – troublemaker

Demons
Ignatius – Fletcher's demon (Drake)
Athena – Fletcher's demon (Gryphowl)
Lysander – Captain Lovett/Sylva's demon (Griffin)
Solomon – Othello's demon (Golem)
Sheldon – ether demon (Zaratan)
Tosk – Cress's demon (Raiju)
Pria – Othello's demon (Pyrausta)
Kongamato – Khan's demon (Ahool)
Sacharissa – Captain Arcturus's demon (Canid)
Bucephalus/Buck – Captain Lovett's demon (Alicorn)
Aeschylus – Captain Arcturus's demon (Hippalectryon)

Aeschylus – Captain Arcturus's demon (Hippalectryon)
Malachi – Rory's demon (Mite)
Holver – Atilla's demon (Caladrius)
Zomok – Khan's demon (Dragon)
Stoorn – Ophelia Faversham's demon (Peryton)

1

A kaleidoscope of violet seared across Fletcher's vision. Then he was in an abyss, dark water flooding his mouth and nose.

Something rubbery knocked against his ankle as he kicked, fighting the inexorable drag down into the black emptiness. His lungs burned ice cold as he choked on the brackish liquid.

Consciousness faded, seeping from him with the warmth from his body. He was numb, weightless.

With each moment, flashes of memory darted across his air-starved brain. Sariel, crushed beneath the shattered masonry of the pyramid. Jeffrey's smirking face, stepping over the paralysed bodies of his friends, a blowpipe in his hands. The portal, spinning. His mother.

He hung in the void.

But thick fingers grasped his outstretched wrist and drew him up. He gagged as cool air hit his face, then felt the meaty thump of a fist on his back as he vomited up the liquid he had swallowed.

'That's it, get it all out,' Othello murmured, as Fletcher blinked the water away and saw the new world around them.

They were on a small, craggy island, shaped like an upturned bowl and coated in a thick layer of green algae.

He could see they were in the middle of a channel of inky water, with submerged, mangrove-like trees forming a thick barrier on either side. The sky above was a dim, sullen blue, like dusk in winter.

Cress, Sylva and his mother were also there, shivering wet and pressed up close to Lysander's side, while Tosk nestled in his master's lap. Ignatius was busy tongue-drying a bedraggled-looking Athena, and Solomon lay face down, hugging the island for dear life, panting with the herculean effort it must have taken to haul himself and the paralysed Griffin out of the water.

'It's moving,' Sylva said, pointing at the contracting portal, ten feet from the island. It was half submerged in the placid water. 'That's why you were all the way over there when you came through from the chamber.' As Fletcher watched, the shrinking portal seemed to get further away, before disappearing with a faint pop.

'No,' Othello said, nodding at the shifting trees beside them. 'We're the ones that are moving.'

It was true. They were slowly but surely edging down the dark river. It was almost as if the island was . . . floating.

Fletcher crawled to the edge of the rocks. In the murky water below, a reptilian head turned to the side, revealing a gold-flecked iris that blinked up at him.

'It's not an island,' Fletcher whispered, watching as a webbed claw drifted beneath the surface. 'We're on a Zaratan.'

He backed away slowly, careful not to slip on the shell's surface. For that is what it was – a shell. The demon they rode could have been described as a giant, amphibious turtle. He guessed this one was fairly young, for the species could grow many times larger than the specimen they were perched on.

Looking at the sunken trees beside them, Fletcher considered their options. With no land in sight, they were stuck until they found something better.

Blue light flashed on the trees around them, and he turned to see that the craggy form of Solomon was gone, infused using Othello's sodden summoning leather.

'Solomon would sink like a stone if our ride here decides to dive,' Othello said, eyeing the black water with trepidation.

'Good idea,' Fletcher replied, feeling a pang of fear for Lysander. The Griffin was still paralysed from the darts Jeffrey had shot him with, and would likely have drowned had the Zaratan not been passing by.

As for Ignatius, he had curled around Athena, using his natural heat to warm her, while she in turn settled her wings over him like a blanket. Fletcher let them stay. It would do the two demons good to bond. He needed them to be a team, now more than ever.

The group sat in silence, the only sound being the creaking of trees in the wind. With each gust, the placid surface of the water shivered like a living creature.

'The only question is, what do we do now?' Cress finally asked, squinting at the dim sky above.

'We wait,' Sylva said, resting her head on Cress's shoulder. 'Wait for dry land, or somewhere to hide. Let's just hope the Zaratan gets us out of here quickly.'

'Why do we need to hide?' Othello asked.

'You think the orcs won't guess where we've gone?' Sylva said, gesturing around them. 'They'll see the blood pattern on the floor, and know we've escaped through a portal into their part of the ether. Of course the keys don't transport us to a precise location, so they won't know exactly where we are, but they'll know we're in the area.'

'Maybe they'll let us go,' Cress whispered, half to herself.

'We just walked into the heart of their holiest place and destroyed half an army that's taken them years to build,' Sylva replied, shaking her head. 'They won't let us get away that easily. The Wyvern riders will be hunting us in a matter of hours, entering the ether as soon as they're back from chasing the other teams. We're just lucky Fletcher buried so many of the nearest shamans' demons. They will be in disarray, for a while at least.'

'She's right,' Fletcher agreed. 'We wait for land and the cover of the forest. We're too exposed out here.'

He shuffled back and pressed himself against his mother. It felt strange, to touch her. He could hardly believe she was real. Was it truly her . . . after all this time?

All those years, searching the faces of the women he met, thinking of the heartless person that could have left him naked in the snow. And now, to know that she had loved him, and had been kept from him all this time.

As he lay his head on her shoulder, Fletcher realised she was shivering – her frame was so emaciated that it provided no protection from the cold, and the filthy rags she wore were soaked.

'Cress, where are the satchels?' Fletcher asked.

'Erm . . . about that,' Cress murmured, twisting her hands in

4

her lap. 'We landed in the water. I needed my hands to stay afloat. I only managed to keep hold of two satchels and one of the petal bags. Yours and Jeffrey's. Here.'

She pushed Fletcher's sodden bag over. At the thought of the loss of their precious petals, a pulse of fear spread across Fletcher's chest – they were their only source of immunity from the ether's atmosphere's natural poison – but he pushed that worry aside for the moment. Instead, he opened the satchel and was relieved to find the tight leather casing had kept most of the water out. Rummaging at the very bottom, he dug out the jacket Berdon had given him for his birthday and wrapped it tightly around his mother's shoulders, pulling the hood over her head. She rubbed her cheek against the soft down of the rabbit fur.

For the first time, he met his mother's eyes. The swamp water had washed most of the dirt from her face, and Fletcher marvelled at the striking resemblance to her twin, Josephine, the woman he had seen by Zacharias Forsyth's side at his trial. However, she was by no means identical, not in her current state. Her eyes were sunken, staring blankly past him. He brushed a stray hair from her cheek, which was so gaunt that it bordered on skeletal. Who knew what she had suffered in the seventeen years of her captivity?

'Alice, can you hear me?' Fletcher said. He tried to hold her gaze, but there was no light behind her stare. 'Mother?'

'Mother?' Othello repeated gently. 'Fletcher . . . are you OK? This is Lady Cavendish.'

'No,' Fletcher replied, helping the woman get her skinny arms into the jacket. 'Lady Cavendish died in her fall; the prisoner was never her. This woman had been there for far

5

longer . . . my whole life. She recognised Athena, and called for her baby, and I remember her face from my dream. This is my mother. The orcs took her when I was a child.'

Othello creased his brow, then understanding dawned upon him. But, even as he opened his mouth to speak, his eyes flicked to the murky waters behind them.

'Get back!' Othello yelled, diving across the shell. Fletcher was tackled to the ground, and he heard the hollow snap of jaws above his head. Fetid, fish-laden breath washed over him, then the creature was gone, slipping back into the dark waters around them with barely a sound.

Fletcher caught a glimpse of a reptilian head, and for a panicked moment he thought the Wyverns had caught up with them. But then he saw the humped, log-like shapes in the water around them, and his lessons at Vocans flashed unbidden to his mind.

Sobeks. Great bipedal crocodile-like creatures that used their claws and jaws to tear apart their opponents, if their large tails didn't batter them to death first. Hunched over at five feet tall, the Sobek was a level nine demon.

And now they were surrounded by dozens of them.

2

Fletcher scrambled back, dragging his mother with him. They pressed against Lysander's side with the others, but they were still no more than a few feet from the water – and the humped shapes lurking beneath the surface.

'Where did they come from?' Cress gasped, drawing her seax from its scabbard.

'They must have sensed the Zaratan,' Sylva said. 'Sobeks prey on smaller ones like ours.'

The shell shook beneath them, and Fletcher saw that they had stopped their slow passage down the waterway. There was a splash as the nearest Sobek thrashed its tail with excitement. They had their prey cornered.

'Our ride's going to dive,' Othello warned, struggling on to his knees. 'Has Lysander recovered? He'll drown!'

Another tremor rocked them, but they didn't sink. Instead the Zaratan held its ground, even as the Sobeks began to circle, their ridged, leathery backs barely breaking the surface.

'Why isn't it diving?' Fletcher murmured. He peered into the water and the golden eyes of the Zaratan stared back at him.

'It's . . . protecting us,' he whispered. 'It knows we'd die in the water.'

'Well, it'll just die with us if we don't do something,' Sylva snarled, tugging her bow from her shoulders. She reached for an arrow, but her quiver was empty, its contents lost to the swamp.

A Sobek lunged at the Zaratan. The turtle demon jerked, dipping his shell to one side, and Lysander slid down the surface. He struggled weakly to climb back up, but as he clawed at the gentle incline, the nearest Sobeks saw their chance. The water foamed white as two separated from the pack, their thick tails lashing back and forth as they homed in on the powerless Griffin. The others hung back: they were more patient than their siblings.

'No!' Fletcher yelled, drawing his khopesh and leaping over Lysander's inert body. Sylva followed, her curved falx held high as the two monsters sped towards them. Yellow-green eyes flashed, then the first leaped from the water. It crouched low on its two legs and scraped its claws along the shell, leaving furrows in the algae coating. The long snout opened, revealing a cavernous yellow mouth filled with jagged teeth.

It lashed out, so fast that Fletcher barely had time to parry it, meeting the five sickle-shaped claws in the curve of his khopesh. The power in the Sobek's arms was immense and Fletcher could barely keep the needlepoints from hooking into his face. He heaved his sword with both hands, in desperation.

The demon's second arm swung up, and only a frantic swipe from Sylva's falx deflected the blow. Even as she did so, the other Sobek sprang from the water and she had to turn and meet it.

Teeth snapped over Fletcher's blade, forcing him to lean

back, teetering on the slippery coating of the shell. Then the Sobek broke away and spun low. Its heavy tail whipped around, knocking Fletcher's feet from under him. His head cracked against the shell beneath, and his vision bruised. The khopesh fell from his nerveless fingers.

The yellow jaws of the Sobek flashed down, but even as its hot breath wafted over him, a ball of flame blasted the demon into the water, leaving the scent of scorched flesh in Fletcher's nostrils.

Ignatius had come to the rescue.

In his concussed haze, Fletcher scrambled to his knees and saw Othello, Cress and Sylva advance together, hacking and parrying the remaining Sobek. Seeing its partner defeated, it dived back in with an angry bellow, leaving the trio panting by the water's edge.

'We can't fight them all,' Fletcher gasped, snatching back his khopesh as Ignatius scampered on to his shoulder. Athena remained with his mother, keeping the confused woman from leaving the relative safety of the centre of the shell.

The burned Sobek seemed none the worse for Ignatius's attack, but it slipped away into the network of trees opposite them. Its retreat did not deter the others – already they were circling closer, perhaps encouraged by the pitiful resistance from the stranded team. It would not be long now.

'Fire won't work, not in the water, anyway,' Othello wheezed. 'Kinetic blasts won't do it either.'

'Lightning,' Cress said, and suddenly Tosk was on her shoulder, his furry tail crackling with electric sparks.

'No,' Fletcher shouted, holding up his hand. 'The spell would

9

fan out in the water and hit the Zaratan too. We'll sink.'

'We can cross that bridge when we come to it,' Cress replied. 'It's the only spell that'll work.'

'Don't waste your mana,' Sylva said, gesturing at the circling Sobeks. 'It won't be powerful enough to kill them all.'

Lysander groaned behind them, fighting the vestiges of the paralytic poison. A level-ten Griffin battling beside them might help even the odds, but Lysander was barely able to crawl up the gentle incline of the shell.

Another Sobek broke from the pack, gliding closer to test their defences. There was a spray of water as a webbed foot erupted from the river, sending the reptile tumbling in the air. It splashed back down in a deluge, floundering, half-stunned among its brethren. The Zaratan was fighting back.

'*Think*,' Fletcher muttered to himself. He ran through the spells he knew. Shield spells were useless against demons; the demonic energy tore through them like rice paper. There were spells to numb pain, open and close locks, pull moisture from the air. Spells that amplified and deadened sound, spells that allowed the caster to detect nearby movement. All useless.

But then, as he stared out at the marshes around him, he remembered another swamp, back in the orc jungles. And Malik, testing Jeffrey's ice spell on its inky pools, turning the black water into solid ice. Sobeks would freeze in just the same way.

He etched in the air, trying to remember the pattern that Jeffrey had shown them. It was a complex glyph, in the shape of a snowflake.

'Wait . . .' Othello said, his eyes widening. 'That might just work.'

The pattern sizzled, but Fletcher's year of training in Pelt's dungeons came to the fore, his mind easily maintaining the pulses of mana both to and through his finger. As if galvanised by the symbol's blue light, a pack broke off from the circling Sobeks. Three of them, powering through the water in a V-shaped formation.

A bead of sweat trickled down Fletcher's brow. His finger darted back and forth, its pad burning and freezing as the last line was formed in the air. The Sobeks were so close he could see their slitted pupils focused on him, with malevolent intent. A bolt from Cress's crossbow whipped past his shoulder, but it missed, disappearing into the dark water with barely a ripple.

'Fletcher, hurry!' Sylva cried, and he felt the Zaratan shudder beneath them.

Then, as the first Sobek hurled itself out of the river, a long streak of white gusted from Fletcher's fingers, blasting ice crystals into the water. He could feel the mana draining from him, but he redoubled his efforts, sending pulse after pulse at the approaching demons until the air was filled with a blizzard of snowflakes. It was only when half of his mana had been expended that he stopped, collapsing to his knees and panting with exertion.

Slowly, the flakes settled on the water, revealing the full extent of Fletcher's efforts.

The Sobek hung motionless in a jagged lump of crystal, its jaws half open, claws outstretched for Fletcher's throat. Only its tail and back legs remained uncovered, hanging limply from the back of the floating iceberg. The other two demons could be seen half submerged in the water, their bodies frozen solid, while a sheet of ice crackled and snapped around them on the swamp's surface.

'Bloody hell,' Cress murmured. 'That worked like a charm.'

'Is the Zaratan OK?' Fletcher asked, worried at how close he had blasted the ice spell.

As if in answer, the shell beneath them shuddered as the Zaratan began to swim. Fletcher kept the ice symbol fixed in the air, but already the remaining Sobeks were breaking away at the sight of their stricken companions, one by one at first, but soon in twos and threes as the Zaratan neared the edge of the circling pack.

Soon they were alone once again in the swamps, the silence disturbed only by the gentle rattle of tree branches, as a chill wind wafted over them. They had survived.

For now.

3

The Zaratan swam on as the sky began to darken, pausing only to chew on the occasional patch of river weed that floated by. It swam with new purpose, and they ate up the distance quickly, even if their surroundings looked much the same. Every minute that ticked by was a blessing, for it meant they were going further and further away from the orcish part of the ether, where the orc shamans and the Wyverns they rode would undoubtedly have already begun their pursuit.

As they waited for the swamps to end, cold became their greatest enemy; the damp air sucking the heat from their bodies to leave them shivering against the faint warmth of Lysander's downy sides. Fletcher left Ignatius draped around his mother's shoulders, while Athena curled up in her lap. Alice twisted her fingers absently through Athena's fur, a distant smile playing across her lips as the Gryphowl purred and chirruped.

A dull lethargy began to take hold of them as time passed by – and Fletcher could barely muster the energy to move at all. He wondered if it was the after-effects of Jeffrey's darts . . . or the ether's poison slowly taking hold.

When night fell, they produced a small wyrdlight and ate the last of their supplies from the mission – salted pork from Briss's kitchen and bruised bananas harvested from the jungle. It was simple fare, but Alice wolfed down the pork with feral jerks of her head, as if she had not tasted meat in years. Fletcher gave her his own portion, and he didn't know whether to laugh or cry as she sat back with a mindless groan, clutching her distended belly. Moments later she was almost asleep, her head resting on Fletcher's shoulder.

Fletcher's vision of his mother, for the brief time he had known her as Alice Raleigh, had been of a gentle, beautiful woman, full of love for her only child. Now, he found himself the caretaker of a lost soul with a broken mind and no memory of even herself, let alone her son. Yet, as he gently wiped the oily stains from the corners of Alice's mouth, he found his heart breaking for her. How could he hold his disappointment against her, after all she had endured? He loved her just the same.

They used the last light of dusk – if you could call it that in this alien world – to check their supplies. They even had some spare dry clothing, which they changed into surreptitiously, using Lysander's body as a makeshift wall between boys and girls.

To Fletcher's surprise, they discovered that they had kept all of their weapons, though most of the gunpowder had become soaked in the water. Sylva's arrows had all been lost, but Fletcher had some to share, and Cress had seven remaining crossbow bolts too. Yet, in this environment, they all knew that it was their demons that would be their most useful tools, and Fletcher felt a pang of pity for Sylva. She had no demon or mana any more.

As they sheathed their weapons and settled for the night, Fletcher turned his mind to the petals. There were roughly one hundred in the sack Cress had managed to save, though in the dark it was hard to tell. And even as he sorted through them and counted them under his breath, Fletcher could sense their effects waning, the strange lethargy they were all feeling building with every minute. Soon each breath became laboured, until it felt like he had just climbed Vocans' west staircase. He was alarmed at how quickly the protective power of the petals seemed to be wearing off, and suddenly the diminished supply in this sack seemed a pitiful protection against the deadly ether air.

Seeing the others dozing, Fletcher realised it was too dangerous to sleep – he might never wake up if the effects wore off in the night.

'I need another petal,' he panted.

'I didn't want to be the first to say it,' Cress sighed, cracking open her eyes and plucking one from the sack.

Sylva and Othello followed suit, and even Alice allowed Fletcher to place a petal in her mouth without complaint, swallowing it down when Fletcher gently rubbed her throat.

'What was that, five hours?' Fletcher asked, instantly feeling strength returning to his body.

'More or less,' Othello agreed. 'That's almost five petals a day, each. At least in our world's time – I know the cycles of night and day vary in the ether.'

'Do they? I should have paid more attention in class,' Cress grumbled.

'Don't worry, we learned this in second year,' Othello continued. 'The ether's days are around ten hours in winter and forty hours in the summer, but our years and seasons are the same length. That's how we're able to predict the migrations that pass through Hominum's part of the ether. It's winter now so . . . we should probably get some shut-eye; it'll be light in five hours or so.'

Fletcher listened intently. He was a year behind Othello, and with his focus on the Tournament, he had forgotten much of what he had learned in his demonology and etherwork lessons.

'You're missing the big picture,' Sylva snapped, her voice cutting through the darkness and making Fletcher jump. 'We'll go through five petals every five hours. How long before we run out and are slowly poisoned to death? There can't be more than a hundred petals in that bag. That's one hundred hours each. Ten day-night cycles in the ether.'

Fletcher's mind raced. That came to a little over four days in Hominum-time. Four days until they lost the use of their bodies, and, eventually . . . died.

'Well, surely there will be some of those flowers around here,' Fletcher suggested, but already his heart was sinking.

'Do you see any?' Sylva asked, motioning at the submerged bushes around them. 'I'm sure the flowers exist in the orcish part of the ether somewhere – it's the only way they would have so many of them. But not here. These swamplands must be on the very edge of their territory – that's probably the only reason the orcs haven't found us yet.'

'Well, does it really matter?' Cress muttered.

'What the hell do you mean? Of course it bloody does,' Sylva retorted.

Fletcher frowned. It wasn't like Sylva to curse.

'Guys, take it easy,' Othello said nervously.

'No, I want to know,' Sylva growled, shaking off Othello's hand as he tried to calm her. 'I want to know why she thinks the only thing that's keeping us from keeling over, foaming at the mouth and spasming and twitching to our deaths doesn't *matter*.'

'It doesn't matter because we're all going to die here anyway!' Cress shouted. And then, to Fletcher's astonishment, she burst into tears.

'One hundred hours, two hundred hours. Who cares,' she sobbed, hiding her face in her hands. 'There's no way back.'

Sylva froze, her angry retort dying on her lips.

'Hey,' Sylva said, shuffling closer to her. 'I just . . . with Sariel dead and now the petals . . . I was lashing out. I'm sorry.'

She wrapped her arms around Cress and buried her head in the dwarf's shoulder.

Despite their circumstances, Fletcher and Othello smiled at each other. After all of Sylva's suspicion and distrust, it seemed that she and Cress could finally let their defences down and see each other for who they truly were.

Fletcher let them hug it out a few beats longer, but knew he could not leave it at that. They needed a plan, or even just a sliver of hope. He cleared his throat.

'It's not a hundred hours until we die,' he said, lacing his voice with confidence he did not feel. Sylva pulled away from Cress, and he saw her face was also damp with tears.

'What do you mean?' she said.

'We just have to find some more petals,' Fletcher continued. 'That's all. Think about it – the flowers must exist in both Hominum's and the orcs' part of the ether, so it's got to be a common plant. I bet Jeffrey's journal has all the information we need on what they look like and where they grow.'

'OK,' Cress said, her voice barely above a whisper. 'So we search for them. But . . . what about getting home?'

'We aren't able to create a portal back to our world from here, or even another part of the ether, not without some sort of new keys,' Othello said quickly. 'It's been tried before.'

'Great,' Sylva said despondently.

'But . . . we can go back through a portal that someone in *our* world has already created.'

'So what are you suggesting?' Cress muttered. 'That we somehow turn this Zaratan around, make our way back to where we started, avoid the Wyverns and shamans, find a portal they've just opened, jump through, fight our way out of wherever we end up and then hightail it through the jungle to the Hominum border with half of orcdom in pursuit? No thanks.'

'You're right,' Fletcher said, holding up his hands in surrender. 'We're definitely not doing that. We're going to get as far from the orcish part of the ether as possible.'

'Then what?' Othello asked. He and Cress looked confused, but Fletcher could see the beginnings of a smile playing across Sylva's face. He took a deep breath.

'We're going to get out of these swamps and traverse the ether – until we find Hominum's part of it.'

4

Fletcher woke. He heard a soft thud and rocked to the side. Another followed, and he rolled against Lysander's belly.

'Wuh—' he managed, cracking open his eyes.

There were trees around him. Real trees, with dangling branches like willows, shading him from the pale skies. Cress's face swam into view, a bright grin plastered across it.

'Sheldon's walking,' she said, tugging at his jacket. 'We're heading out of the swamps.'

Fletcher sat up, wincing as his back twinged with pain. It had not been a comfortable sleep, and far less than he would have liked.

His first thought was of Alice. She was awake and chewing on a petal, sitting near the Zaratan's tail and staring vacantly at the trees above.

There was a flake of yellow resting on her upper lip. Fletcher wiped it away gently and tugged the jacket close about her shoulders, taking care not to disturb the still sleeping Ignatius. Athena was alert, but had not moved from Alice's lap. He could sense a great melancholy from the Gryphowl and knew that she loved Alice as much as his father had. He rubbed her head and left the two together.

'Sheldon?' he asked, Cress's words catching up with him.

'Our Zaratan – we decided to name him,' Sylva said, holding out a petal for Fletcher to eat. 'Eat up – it's been five hours, or at least that's what Cress's pocket watch says.'

As he munched on the tart garnish, he saw Sylva was busy counting the petals in the sack, stacking them carefully between her thighs.

'How do you know it's a him?' Othello said, still sprawled across the front half of the shell, his eyes closed.

'I checked,' Cress said, her cheeks flushing red.

Fletcher chuckled and crawled to the front of the Zaratan. Sheldon turned to look back at him, blinking his golden eyes ponderously. He was a handsome creature, with a smooth yellow beak and a long, agile neck. His pace, though deliberate, was faster than it seemed, the long strides eating up the ground beneath his splayed, claw-tipped feet.

For a moment Fletcher considered whether the demon might be worth harnessing. But a Zaratan was a level-fifteen demon – far too high for Sylva.

'Ninety petals,' Sylva announced, interrupting his thoughts. 'Just as I thought. Ninety hours left.'

Fletcher's eyes flicked to the ground around them, searching for even a hint of yellow. Yet it was all a mess of greens and browns, with nary a demon or blossom in sight.

'We should stay with Sheldon,' Fletcher suggested, looking ahead where the ground was still swampy but already beginning to dry out, with even the occasional patch of coarse grass making an appearance. Beyond, the trees became taller, though the area was obscured by the deepening shadow of the canopy.

'I agree; he's faster than we would be on foot,' Sylva said. 'Plus he's not completely defenceless – his claws and beak look sharp enough.'

'We can stay on the move while we're sleeping too, if one of us keeps watch,' Cress agreed, scrambling over to join Fletcher.

She reached out to pet Sheldon, and Fletcher grinned when the Zaratan rumbled with pleasure as she scratched the root of his neck. The gentle giant would be a formidable ally in the coming days.

A squawk cut through the air, followed by a cry from Sylva. Fletcher turned to see Lysander had finally recovered – but he was advancing on Tosk with his hackles raised, stalking him like a lion would a gazelle. His eyes were different somehow, the pupils dilated and empty of the intelligence that had shone there before.

'Lysander, what are you doing?' Fletcher shouted. He knew Lysander hadn't eaten since being paralysed but this was more than hunger.

'His bond with Lovett was broken when the portal closed,' Sylva said, horrified. 'He's becoming wild again.'

Lysander took another step closer to the terrified Raiju, whose blue fur was standing on end. Tosk's squirrel-like tail arched, crackling with lightning. In response, the Griffin opened his beak wide and unleashed a roar, the timbre rising until it ended in a screech.

'We need to do something,' Othello shouted, half obscured

by the prowling Griffin. 'He's going to kill him!'

Fletcher's mind raced. Lysander's summoning scroll was stuffed down the side of his pack. The only problem was, the pack was underneath the Griffin's belly.

'I'm not letting him hurt Tosk,' Cress said, and suddenly her crossbow was armed, the tip centred on Lysander's head.

'Fletcher, any ideas?' Sylva yelled.

Sylva. Without Sariel, she might be capable of harnessing a level-ten demon like Lysander. Two years ago, she had a summoning level of seven.

'Get ready,' he said, lowering himself into a crouch.

'What's that supposed to mean?' Sylva hissed. But there was no time to explain.

'Athena, now!' Fletcher shouted, sprinting up the incline of the Zaratan's shell. He skidded beneath Lysander's belly and thrust his hand into the side pocket of his satchel. The world above brightened as Lysander leaped for Tosk, only to find his prey snatched away by the swooping Gryphowl.

'Read it!' Fletcher bellowed, hurling the scroll into Sylva's bewildered hands.

'What . . . ?' Sylva began, but then, '*Lo ro di mai si lo.*'

Lysander screeched and spun, his talons scraping on the surface of the shell. His eyes bore into Fletcher's with a deep, animal hunger. It was all Fletcher could do not to scramble away.

Ignatius was circling the pair, woken from Alice's neck by Sylva's scream. He waited for an opportunity to strike, but Fletcher ordered him to hold off. They needed time; an attack from Ignatius would just force a confrontation too soon.

As if Sheldon could sense the commotion, the shell shuddered beneath them. The tremors gave the Griffin pause, and he widened his stance, spreading himself like a bear crossing a frozen lake. Already white threads were beginning to appear between him and Sylva, twisting together to form a cord of glowing light.

'Hurry up . . .' Fletcher whispered under his breath, willing Sylva's chanting on as it swirled around them.

Lysander took a faltering step, his fierce beak hanging open to reveal a pink maw within. He was struggling, his bond with Sylva growing with every word that she spoke. Fletcher remained still, knowing that any sudden movement might set the Griffin off.

Another step, and now Fletcher could feel the panting Griffin's hot breaths, moist from the demon's gullet. He closed his eyes.

The cold, hard beak grazed his cheek, and then he felt the soft ruffle of feathers as the demon nuzzled him, burying his great head against Fletcher's chest. Sylva's chanting had stopped . . . Lysander was back.

Fletcher wrapped his arms around the Griffin's neck, but seconds later they were empty. He opened his eyes and saw the Griffin dissolving in a haze of white light, with Sylva holding a summoning leather beneath him.

As the last of the luminescence flowed into her, she sat back with her fists clenched, shuddering with the euphoria of infusing a new demon for the first time. Finally she lay down, a gentle smile playing across her lips.

Fletcher collapsed on to the shell beside her, and then Ignatius knocked him on to his back, chirping with relief. It was strange, but the demon seemed heavier somehow. He gave Fletcher a remonstrative nip on the ear for scaring him and promptly enveloped Fletcher's neck.

'Right, someone has to tell me what the hell just happened,' Cress growled.

Fletcher turned to see her stomping across the shell towards them, Tosk's round, black eyes peering out from where he had hidden within her jacket.

'It happens when demons lose their masters,' Othello explained, rubbing the back of his neck. 'I should have remembered, we learned about it in second year. Demons only become truly sentient when they are captured and harnessed by a summoner – before that they're no more intelligent than any other animal. Without the bond, they return to that state until they bond with a new master and remember who they are. We're lucky that Lysander was paralysed for so long – it usually happens very quickly.'

'It's true,' Fletcher said, his mind flashing back to Athena's memory of the night he was left outside Pelt's gates. How she had felt the wild call of the ether, tugging at her very essence.

'Well, you could have bloody warned us,' Cress grumbled.

Fletcher stood and tried to extricate himself from Ignatius's embrace, but the demon refused to budge. He sighed and scooted down the shell's incline to Alice, who was sitting cross-legged, staring vacantly ahead. She had not moved, not even when Lysander had roared. It was only the occasional stroke of her hand across Athena's back that gave him any hope that she might one day recover.

Fletcher had lost his birth father, Edmund. But he would not lose his mother again. Not now, when they had spent so little time together. There had to be a way.

He gazed out at the wasteland, searching for some semblance of hope. But there was no food, no flowers, just mud and drab plants.

'Don't worry, Ali— Mum,' Fletcher murmured, the word sitting strangely in his mouth. 'We'll get you home. I promise.'

5

The light of the sky changed quickly in the ether, going from golden morning sun to clear grey sky in the space of an hour. The area around them remained desolate, the only sign of life coming from a lone Kappa: a scrawny, green-skinned humanoid that slipped into a pool of murky water as soon as they neared. Fletcher had just enough time to identify it, and see the strange, bowl-like indent on the top of its head, where it stored water when it travelled on land.

In a way, he was glad of the lack of demons nearby – for it made the occasional need to relieve themselves safer. Cress had taken on the role of minder for his mother, guiding her ahead of Sheldon to the bushes at regular intervals, after Tosk had scouted them for safety first. She told Fletcher that she had cared for her grandmother in the same way, when she had become too old to look after herself. He was immensely grateful; he knew he could not bring himself to take that on just yet.

As the hours went by, Fletcher felt oddly drowsy, as if his body could not recognise the rhythms of this new world.

He supposed they had spent more time in the ether than any human, elf or dwarf ever had.

He was not the only one who was feeling the effects – Cress and Othello were snoozing, propping themselves up against each other in the centre of the shell. Sylva sat below the Zaratan's neck, her back to him. Her head was tilted forward, as if she were staring at her lap.

Curious, Fletcher settled down beside her.

'What are you reading?' Fletcher asked, seeing an open book resting on her calves. It was not unlike James Baker's, with sketches of small, insectile demons in the margins.

'That traitor Jeffrey's journal,' Sylva spat, and Fletcher could almost feel the anger radiating from her like a furnace.

'Sorry,' he said, not wanting to intrude.

He began to get up, but Sylva caught his expression and grasped his wrist.

'No, I'm sorry,' she whispered, her face softening. 'For blaming you . . . when Sariel died. If you hadn't acted, none of us would be alive right now.'

She lowered her head and looked into his eyes. There was sincerity there and . . . something else.

For a moment Fletcher's mind flashed to the moment he had buried Sariel beneath the rubble of the pyramid, along with the enemy demons that were bearing down on them. He'd had no choice . . . had he?

'There's nothing to apologise for,' Fletcher said, feeling a pang of guilt, despite her words. 'I don't know what I would have done if I had lost Ignatius.'

He paused, searching for a subject to get her mind off Sariel.

Sadly, his first thought was not much cheerier.

'Still, I can't help but think that all I've done is delay the inevitable,' he said. 'We're no closer to finding those yellow flowers than yesterday.'

Fletcher half expected Sylva to grow more despondent, but to his surprise she broke into a grin.

'That's where you're wrong,' she said, flipping forward a few pages and running her finger over the yellow paper. 'Look.'

There was a sketch of a flower there, with a delicate stem and large petals that curved around each other in the shape of a conch shell. Below it, Fletcher could read a short passage, written in Jeffrey's surprisingly neat handwriting.

Experiment 786 – The Three Sister Flowers

Captain Jacoby's search of the ether bore fruit today – or should I say, plants. A trio of flowering plants, each appearing near identical but for the colouring of their petals – red, blue and yellow. Clearly, they are related to each other somehow.

From what Jacoby tells us, the red flowers (genus: Medusa) tend to grow near the similarly coloured sands of the deadlands – perhaps a camouflage mechanism of sorts.

The blue flowers (genus: Stheno) grow near saltwater, which is a shame, as other than the occasional small, brackish marsh, the nearest saltwater is a sea, some distance from Hominum's part of the ether. I imagine he may have used a charging stone to keep the portal open long enough for his Chamrosh to travel there and back. Impressive.

Finally, the yellow flowers (genus: Euryale). Apparently

they only grow near lava. The batch he brought us was found in the crater of a nearby volcano. It is a good thing those are common near our part of the ether.

Though our dissection of the plants yielded poor results, Captain Lovett has volunteered to consume them in order to determine if they have any medicinal properties. The chances of poisoning are far higher than any positive results but I say we roll the dice. After all, what else is she good for?

Fletcher clenched his fists as he read the final sentence. How had he judged Jeffrey so poorly? He had pitied the sickly servant boy, had even seen some of himself in him. But appearances could be deceiving. Jeffrey had been as heartless as the Forsyths were.

'Don't you see?' Sylva asked, interrupting his thoughts. 'The flower we're looking for grows near lava.'

She was beaming from ear to ear, but Fletcher wasn't hopeful.

'I mean, have you seen any volcanoes?' he asked, gesturing at the lifeless bayou surrounding them. 'I know there are some near Hominum's part of the ether but we're probably miles away from there, and might not even be heading in the right direction.'

'Well, send Athena out to have a look!' she said, exasperated. 'We need a plan, Fletcher. Look around you. Do you really think sitting back and hoping for the best is the right thing to do? I know you've just found your mother, but you're still our leader. So, lead.'

Fletcher knew she spoke sense, but the thought of sending Athena to scout filled him with dread. He was scared of what he might see. An empty skyline, void of the telltale columns of volcanic smoke? A sea of green, with no end in sight? He didn't want to know the answer. Not yet.

He looked at Alice, and the gentle stroking of her hand across Athena's back. His mother looked almost content. Why not stay on the shell, wait it out and let fate decide? He was tired of making decisions, rolling the dice. They were safe here.

As if she could sense his doubt, Sylva lay her hand on his, her palm cool and smooth to the touch. He lifted his head and met her gaze.

'You've got us this far,' she whispered. 'Lysander's too big . . . you're the only one that can do this.' Her eyes were filled with hope, and he felt disgusted with himself, at his fear, his doubt.

'I don't want to risk it,' he said, hating himself with every word. 'She might be seen. We should wait, at least until we're further away . . . we still have time. I don't want to make any hasty decisions.'

Sylva lowered her gaze and pulled away from him, stashing the book inside her jacket.

'Doing nothing is as much a choice as doing something, Fletcher,' she said. 'It might be the greatest risk of all.'

She stood up, swaying slightly as the shell tilted with each of Sheldon's ponderous steps.

'Think it over,' she said, walking away from him.

To Fletcher's surprise, she went to sit beside his mother. As he watched, she tugged an ivory-coloured object from the coil of her braided hair, letting her tresses fall loose around her shoulders in a wave of white-gold.

It was a comb made from carved deer-bone, and Sylva lifted it and gently pulled it through Alice's hair. Fletcher's heart leaped as a smile played across his mother's lips, and she closed her eyes and tilted her head back, enjoying the sensation.

Sylva did not seem to notice, instead teasing Alice's hair with long, careful strokes until it hung straight down his mother's back, free of the muck that had coated it, the dirty yellow soon a burnished flaxen sheet, peppered with white at the roots. Pocketing the comb, Sylva lifted her hands, and soon her nimble fingers were dancing back and forth, twisting and braiding it.

'There,' Sylva said, tugging Alice's hair one final time. It had been braided to fall in a thick plait down his mother's back, and Fletcher smiled. Gone was the wild woman, leaving a frail, elegant beauty in her place.

'Thank you,' Fletcher breathed, hurrying over to them. 'She needed it. And the braid, it's beautiful.'

'Just something my mother taught me,' Sylva said, shrugging shyly.

Fletcher smiled again.

'I wish I'd had time to meet her after the council meeting,' Fletcher said.

Sylva looked down at her hands.

'She died when I was very young,' she said.

Fletcher kicked himself. Of course. How had he never asked about her mother?

He suddenly realised that he knew far less about Sylva than any other of his friends. Ever since they met, she had never spoken about her home, and rarely mentioned her family. But when she had it had always been about her father.

'I'm sorry,' he said. 'I should have known.'

'No . . . I never talk about her,' Sylva said, her voice taut with pain.

Fletcher said nothing. He didn't want to press her. The silence stretched on, until Sylva finally spoke again.

'Maybe I should,' she said, her voice barely more than a breath. 'You would have liked her. She was brave, and loyal. But she trusted too much. She was poisoned and . . . we couldn't save her.'

She turned her head away and wiped a tear from her eye.

'I . . . that's awful, Sylva,' Fletcher said. It was all beginning to make sense now. How hard it was for her to trust, to care about others. Her constant suspicion of his motives. It all came down to this.

'Why would someone do such a thing?' Fletcher whispered.

'It was my sister,' Sylva said, and her face turned hard once more. 'She was older. Wanted to be chieftain, and knew that she was next in line. When they found hemlock in her room, we knew it was her. But we couldn't prove it, so she was banished from our lands. I haven't seen her in eight years.'

Fletcher shook his head, horrified. Somehow, he had imagined elves to be above such evils.

'So . . . why aren't you chieftain then?' Fletcher asked, hoping to change the subject.

'I wasn't old enough, and I'm not even now. My father took her position. Our society passes chieftainship through the mother to the eldest daughter, or if there are none, the eldest son.'

So that was why most of the Elven Chieftains had been female. It was a stark contrast to Hominum's society.

'Anyway, enough of that,' Sylva said, getting to her knees.

'I'm glad you have a chance to know your own mother. She's a sweetheart.'

Sylva leaned forward and kissed the top of Alice's head. And then something amazing happened. Alice lifted her hand and pressed it against Sylva's cheek.

'Mum?' Fletcher asked, his pulse quickening. 'Can you hear me?'

He leaned forward and peered into her eyes. For the briefest of moments, his mother met his gaze. Then her hand dropped to her lap and she peered vacantly out at the thickening groves around them.

Hope flooded Fletcher.

Perhaps his mother could be saved. She needed normality, comfort and care. And he knew they wouldn't find that out here, in this sullen wasteland. Sylva was right, he needed to act.

'Athena,' Fletcher said, pulling the Gryphowl from his mother's lap. She gave him a disgruntled yowl, but reluctantly unfurled her wings and looked at him expectantly.

'How would you like to do some scouting?'

6

Green leaves blurred as Athena whipped through the canopy, searching for a tall tree to perch on. She didn't want to breach into open air, at least, not yet. Instead, she found a tall, pine-like conifer, with gnarled bark and sharp, pin-like leaves. It towered above the trees around it and she landed with outstretched claws. Careful to avoid detection, she crawled up its trunk and inserted herself among the needles at the top.

A few hundred feet back and even further below, Fletcher and his team peered at Verity's tablet, which Cress unashamedly confessed to having 'borrowed' when the young noble was not looking.

'I can't see a thing,' Othello murmured, leaning closer to the tablet. 'There are branches in the way.'

Fletcher nudged Athena forward with a thought. Strangely, she did not seem afraid at all. Instead, he sensed exhilaration and knew she was in her element among the treetops. Gryphowls were solitary rovers by nature; never staying in one place for too long, so the unfamiliar territory did not intimidate her.

Within the branches, Athena used her claws to push aside the green needles, then poked her head through to survey the landscape around her. Using her flexible, owl-like neck, she slowly turned to give them a panoramic view of the skyline.

'Bloody hell,' Cress breathed.

Mountains stretched into the heavens ahead, rust red against the pale yellow of the dimming sky. They curved east, half encircling them in a sierra of jagged peaks, towering so high that the Beartooth Mountains were mere hills in comparison. To the west, a sparkling sea glimmered, with emerald green shallows that slowly darkened into the dusky blue of fathomless depths.

The skies were almost devoid of life, except for a few moving specks too far away to discern. A pall of clouds hung low, blocking the view directly above. A low-flying Ropen half a mile away was the only identifiable creature – a large, featherless hybrid of bat and bird, with wings of stretched membrane, a pelican-like beak full of teeth and an elongated crest on the back of its head.

'We're trapped,' Sylva stated, tracing her finger along the mountaintops. 'Sea to the left, mountains straight ahead and to the right. We can't get through and see what's beyond. So we have to go back. Take our chances in the orcs' part of the ether.'

'Aye,' Othello agreed, shaking his head.

Fletcher gritted his teeth; his heart was pumping with disappointment. They had lost fifteen hours since their arrival – and their way back was through desolate swamps and Sobek-infested waters. Not to mention the fact that Sheldon was needed to get through the water: he hadn't once deviated from his course, even when the way had been snarled with fallen tree branches.

'Sheldon,' Fletcher said, thinking aloud. 'He hasn't turned once.'

'What are you talking about?' Sylva asked, prying a clump of lichen from the shell and hurling it angrily into the trees.

'Sheldon's heading straight for those mountains,' Fletcher said, standing up and looking at the Zaratan's direction. As if he recognised his name, Sheldon swung his ponderous head at them and blinked slowly, before returning to his lumbering across the soggy land.

'So what?' Sylva said, though her eyes had brightened.

'He's heading somewhere, and he's not built for climbing. There must be a way through. Guys, what do you remember about Zaratans? Are they good at navigating?' Fletcher asked.

He had never really thought his demonology lessons would be important or, at least, not the lessons about obscure demons such as the one they rode now.

'They can grow pretty big, maybe three or four times Sheldon's size,' Cress said. 'But I think that's only the really ancient ones. Sheldon's probably in his prime.'

'They migrate annually, as do many other species of demon,' Othello said, scratching at his beard, 'congregating to breed and lay their eggs – though where wasn't specified.'

'When?' Fletcher asked. 'When do they do it?'

'Winter time,' Othello said, a half-smile slowly spreading across his face. 'Like . . . right now.'

'So unless he's never made this journey before, he probably knows exactly where he's going.' Fletcher grinned, and it suddenly felt as if a great weight had lifted from his shoulders. 'If we stay on him long enough, he'll take us through the mountains.'

'You horny devil, you,' Cress said, slapping Sheldon's shell. 'You're off to find a missus, aren't you?'

Fletcher burst out laughing. It felt good to laugh, and the others joined in, until their sides hurt and Fletcher was struggling for breath. Even Ignatius seemed to be happier, barking and spinning around. Athena rejoined them and settled back in Alice's lap. For a time, at least, they were happy.

But soon the light began to fade, and their happiness with it. Their stomachs rumbled and their flasks sloshed half empty. Despite the apparent lifelessness of their surroundings, strange noises echoed through the treetops and they could hear nocturnal creatures prowling close by. They had left the swamplands now, and the trees were becoming so congested that Sheldon struggled to pass between them.

Tosk was on night watch, but with every snap and rustle Fletcher found himself sitting up and gazing into the gloom. He saw nothing but shadow upon shadow. Still, Tosk seemed unperturbed, even when he heard a low snarling from what felt like a few yards away.

A moment later, in the dim darkness, a blue glow appeared, the chill light matching the icy fear that took hold of him.

'Guys, wake up,' Fletcher whispered, shaking the others.

'You thought I was sleeping?' Othello said, turning over and rubbing his spine. 'It's bloody impossible, with this pineapple of a shell and that racket—'

'Quiet!' Fletcher hissed, clamping his hand over Othello's mouth.

Sylva was silent, but rolled into a low crouch, her falx half drawn from its scabbard on her back.

'Wyrdlight – over there,' Fletcher whispered, pointing at the glow. It was growing stronger by the second, and Fletcher could see dark shapes skittering past them – tiny demons escaping the unnatural light.

Fletcher heard the creak of wood and metal as Cress slowly cranked her crossbow, and his heart hammered in his chest as he peered into the gloom.

'Shamans?' Sylva hissed.

The first speck appeared clearly now, glowing an electric blue in the darkness. Soon others followed. They were small, perhaps smaller than a normal wyrdlight, but brighter and more numerous, with hundreds of them spread out in a line across the forest as far as the eye could see. Stranger still, their movement seemed purposeful and co-ordinated.

Then they saw it. Figures, following behind the swarm of lights, walking with the slow pace of sleepwalkers.

'They're combing the forest for us,' Cress gasped, edging away as the halo of light turned Sheldon's shell a dull blue. 'We should climb into the trees!'

'No, wait,' Othello growled, holding up his hand. 'Look.'

The dark shapes were demons. At first they confirmed Fletcher's suspicions that shamans were nearby, for there was a mishmash of species that would rarely be seen together. A shaggy-haired Canid stumbled over a tree root, its eyes fixed on the lights above. Three Lavellans, ratty rodents with poisonous fangs, followed in a line nearby. A dozen lesser Mites of varying colours trundled along the ground beside them, ranging in size from that of a weevil to a stag beetle.

There was even a Baku, a rare, pig-sized demon with an elephantine trunk and tusks, and the striped orange fur of a tiger. But all walked like the zombies of legend, mesmerised by the lights above.

'Will-o'-the-wisps,' Othello said, his brow creased in consternation. 'We needn't worry.'

'What do you mean?' Fletcher asked, shuffling back as the glowing specks of blue light neared the shell.

'They fill their translucent abdomens with wyrdlight and use it to move around, like tiny, limbless glow-worms.'

Even as Othello replied, Fletcher could see tiny motes of black beneath the lights.

'What are they doing?' Sylva whispered, waving her hand at one as it floated past.

'They're leading them to their deaths,' Othello murmured.

The Canid knocked against Sheldon's trunk-like leg, but it seemed not to notice, merely continuing on beneath the Zaratan's belly.

'They mesmerise demons with their lights and lead them into swamps, or quicksand, or anywhere their victims will die. Then they feed on the corpses and lay their eggs in them. It's probably why this area is so lifeless – it must be infested with them. Luckily, it only works on smaller, wild demons.'

Fletcher shuddered and drew his coat closer around him. They had seemed so beautiful, yet their true purpose left a cold feeling in the pit of his stomach.

He realised that Othello was the only one of the group to have had two years at Vocans, and the dwarf's knowledge would be useful in the coming days. He only hoped that they would avoid the more dangerous demons of the ether.

The group watched in silence as the blue light faded, and the mesmerised demons disappeared into the gloom. Fletcher shuffled closer to his mother, but saw she was sleeping, curled up with Ignatius and Athena nestling beside her.

'We should have killed it,' Sylva murmured, so low that Fletcher could barely hear her over the dull thuds of Sheldon's footsteps.

'Killed what?' he asked.

'The Baku,' she replied, pointing the way the demons had gone. 'It's a prey demon – low on the food chain. Plenty of meat on it too.'

'You want to eat demons?' Cress gasped, overhearing.

'You've been eating them since you got here – hell, even *before* you got here,' Sylva said, pointing at their dwindling supplies of petals. 'Didn't Electra say plants from the ether are technically demons too?'

'Yeah, but . . . it feels wrong,' Cress said, pulling Tosk to her chest and cuddling him protectively.

'Well, it's either that or starve,' Sylva replied. 'Unless Hominum's part of the ether is around the corner – which it isn't, by the look of those mountains – we're going to need to feed ourselves at some point.'

'I've never heard of anyone eating a demon before, although I hear shamans do it during some of their ceremonies,' Cress mused.

The thought of eating a demon had never crossed Fletcher's mind. It repulsed him in some ways, but then, demons ate meat from his dimension. Why could he not do so in theirs?

'Fletcher, what do you reckon?' Othello said, watching his face as he mulled it over.

Fletcher grinned and shook his head ruefully, suddenly acutely aware of the hollowness in his empty stomach.

'Get some sleep,' he said, scooting over to his mother and laying himself out beside her. 'Tomorrow, we hunt.'

7

The sky was already darkening and Fletcher's stomach was cramping and gurgling, digesting nothing but the petal he had eaten a few hours ago. The team had been hunting all day, having been dropped off by Lysander several miles ahead of Sheldon's path, but had found nothing. Now they had separated to cover more ground.

Fletcher had known hunger like this before, when winter had come early to Pelt and the mountain paths had been too icy for the traders to travel. Starvation had been staved off by hunting. Then and now, his senses were sharp, honed of desperation, but he was weaker and slower too. The difference was that in Pelt's forests, a failed attempt meant another day of hunger. Here, it meant death.

Crouched in the shadow of a gnarled bush, Fletcher heard the thud of hooves in the damp soil nearby. Then a deep snort, and the soft rhythmic squelching of tissue being chewed to pulp. It was the first sign of life he had come across.

Fletcher dared to tread closer, placing one foot after another with care born of long practice. He dared not pull on his bow, for the creak of the string might give him away. Another step, and he pressed the arrow against the bow's stock in case of clattering. Behind the thinning screen of the bush's leaves, Fletcher saw his prey.

It was a hulking beast, as large as a buffalo and shaped like one too, with powerful shoulders, between which grew a mane not unlike a wild horse's. It had a tufted tail that switched back and forth, a sign of agitation that left Fletcher uneasy.

As if it sensed it was being watched, the beast swung its head low and to the side, snorting and sniffing, misting the air with its mucus.

Protected by no more than a few leaves and twigs, Fletcher froze, hoping desperately that the beast had poor eyesight. It had small red eyes, after all, with a piggish head resembling that of a warthog, but with a pair of curving horns on its brow and tusks that were far more prominent. Its snout was stained with green around the edges and Fletcher could see a pile of nettles that it had been busy chewing on.

In that moment, he knew what he faced. This was no easy prey, though more high-level carnivores did hunt and eat them. But a human would be mad to attack one, even if he was starving and desperate. It was a Catoblepas.

The species ate only poisonous plants which few other demons would consume, and so their fodder was plentiful. It could gore an attacker with tusk or horn, whichever came first, but even these were not the demon's most potent weapons. No, it was the green-tinged saliva of the demon itself where the natural toxins of the plants would concentrate. A bite was as good as a death sentence and its misty breath was so poisonous that it would blind any attacker, or kill any that inhaled it. And now it was staring at Fletcher with its red, piggish eyes, and was turning slowly, its muscled haunches bunching and flexing with every slow, deliberate step.

A screech from above echoed through the trees – Athena, attempting to distract it. The noise did little more than stimulate a flick of the Catoblepas's ears. Ignatius had been left with Sheldon to protect Alice, half a mile back. The others were hunting even further afield. He and Athena were on their own.

The demon grunted, spraying a gout of steam from its nose. The moisture sizzled on the mulch of browning leaves that coated the ground.

Spells were not as effective against demons, and shields even less so, for the demonic energy that formed demons' bodies was able to pass through them with ease. He thought of his pistols – they were both loaded, but the crash of gunfire might alert nearby shamans, searching in the skies above, of their presence. It would have to be the bow.

Ever so slowly, he eased back on his bowstring, taking the strain with his weakened muscles. He was bone tired, so much so that the arrowhead seemed to swim in and out of focus, twitching as the tendons in his arm clenched and locked. Inch by inch, the bow creaked back, until it was at full draw. Still, he did not fire, even as the monster scraped the ground with a hoof, its hunched back a round silhouette against the fading dusk light.

The beast's head was enormous, but Fletcher had a decision to make. The skull was too thick to penetrate – only a direct hit in the soft tissue of its eyes would kill the beast. A difficult shot – even for the most practised archer.

Beneath, the broad chest presented an even larger target. The chances of an arrow passing its ribcage were better, but the beast might not die quickly. It could be enraged, charging him and goring his body to shreds before it collapsed. Then, as if it sensed his indecision, the Catoblepas bellowed and stampeded towards him.

Fletcher loosed the arrow, and the shaft jarred against his hand in flight. Cursing, he dived aside, landing painfully among the roots of a nearby tree. It was not a moment too soon, for the monster tore through the thin screen of branches a half-second later, snapping its jaws with fierce abandon.

There was blood on the soil; the arrow had lodged deeply in the demon's belly, hanging from it like a macabre umbilical cord. It was a gut wound, the kind that would take hours to kill.

With a guttural roar of pain the demon spun around, seeking its tormentor. Fletcher froze, still as a millpond. The beast snuffled the ground, a long tongue lapping at the soil as if to taste his path. It could not see him, for he was deep in the tree's shadow and the last light of the sky was almost gone.

Fletcher reached for another arrow, but his hands met air. He looked over his shoulder to see the ammunition scattered out of reach behind him, his desperate dive having unseated his quiver from his back.

He allowed his hand to stray to the handle of his khopesh. He did not draw it – the scrape of the blade in the scabbard would alert the beast. It would have to be in one motion, an all or nothing attack that would mean death for one or the other.

A hoot from above reminded him Athena was still there. He sensed her frantic desperation, and he knew Ignatius could too. Fletcher could feel that the little Salamander was running, but Fletcher had roamed too far ahead of Sheldon for rescue to arrive in time. Already the Catoblepas's snout was finding his scent, slobbering and grunting over the damp ground in his direction.

He needed to turn it away from him. One breath, one fleck of saliva, could kill him in an instant. Athena could . . . no, it was too risky.

But the Gryphowl sensed his idea and suddenly she was gliding towards them. Fletcher ordered her to turn aside – he strained so hard that his eyes rolled into his head, but even as he wrested back control to turn her aside, Athena did the unthinkable. She folded her wings and dropped like a stone. There was a moment of blind panic, then she crashed into the beast's side and flopped on to the ground. Fletcher's mind received an order from Athena's. Run.

The Catoblepas spun, spraying flecks of spit with a guttural bellow. They passed over Athena's head, for she was flat on the ground, stunned by the collision with the beast's barrel-like side.

Fletcher's vision filled with the demon's rear, its long tail whipping to and fro. He leaped to his feet and sprinted at the monster, drawing the khopesh from his scabbard mid-vault.

With a scream of anger he buried the blade deep into the Catoblepas's spine and into the vitals beneath. His breath gusted out of him as he thudded on to the demon's back. Only his grip on the sword's handle kept him from falling off.

He could smell the raw, animal scent of the monstrosity

below him as it bucked in agony. The wiry hair along its spine scraped against his hands as he twisted the blade, lurching to one side with every kick of the Catoblepas's legs. A gout of toxic vapour was spewed into the air, but Fletcher was out of reach. He leaned on the blade with desperate abandon, until even the handle was buried halfway into the demon's spine.

Then, with a soft, almost mournful lowing, the creature collapsed in a heap, and gusted its last, poison breath.

'Athena!' Fletcher yelled, sliding off the Catoblepas's back on to the ground beside his fallen demon. One of her wings was crushed beneath the dead monster's belly, but her eyes were open and full of life. With a snarl, he heaved against the corpse, spittle flecking from his mouth with the strain.

Athena managed to withdraw her wing, but Fletcher could feel her agony as she moved the delicate bones within, which had been fractured by the beast's great weight. He released the body with a thud and kneeled to gather her into his arms.

'Why?' he asked, cradling her broken body.

She gazed back at him, the love in her blue eyes telling him the answer.

8

When the others eventually found him, he was still holding Athena in his arms. As Lysander helped drag the Catoblepas's body to Sheldon's shell, Fletcher began ministering to Athena's wounds. He was glad to see she was not mortally injured, even if she would not be able to fly for a long while. Ignatius did all he could to comfort her, nuzzling her with his beak and lapping ineffectually at her injured wing, but his healing saliva could do nothing for broken bones and Fletcher could not risk the healing spell for fear of her bones setting crookedly.

He was tempted to infuse her and allow her to heal within him, but knew that her night vision would be needed soon – with the bloody carcass on the shell this would be the most dangerous night so far. No, they would have to do this the old-fashioned way.

With little hardwood nearby, he splinted her broken wing with the straight shaft from one of his arrows and strapped her wing to her side. She hobbled lopsidedly around the shell, miserable to be relegated to the ground. But she was not

48

downhearted for long, as their days of starvation were over and a feast was appearing before her eyes.

The carcass was butchered with their blades, separated into enormous haunches, cuts of dark flesh and piles of quivering organs. The intestines and other poisonous inedibles were removed carefully and buried some distance from their path, for the stench was dreadful and it would help prevent carrion eaters following in Sheldon's wake.

The rest was carefully spread on the skinned pelt, which stretched so large that they could have made a tent from it.

Cooking the meat was essential, but they did not wish to start a fire directly on the Zaratan's shell, for fear of hurting him. So, they piled earth high on the shell to insulate it and used the dry, punky branches that were scattered about the forest floor to start a serviceable fire.

The edible organs were eaten first, roasted over the flames on spits of greenwood that Fletcher had cut and shaved with his khopesh. Each had a different flavour; the liver dry and smooth, the kidneys rich and filling, even the heart was chewy but not unpleasant.

Herbivores Solomon and Tosk made do with foraging shoots from the forest around them, but meat-eaters Lysander, Athena and Ignatius were ravenous and ate the lungs raw, even nibbling at the brain as they waited for their turn at the cooked meat. The sight of their bloodied beaks gorging on the unsightly flesh was almost enough to ruin Fletcher's appetite. Almost.

The cuts of meat were devoured next, spitted in great lumps hacked hastily from the pile. The dark flesh was marbled with veins of butter-yellow fat that dripped sizzling into the cooking fire. Fletcher, Othello, Sylva, Cress and even Alice ate it while piping hot and chewed with overfilled mouths, tilting their heads and tearing at it with their teeth.

It was the best meal Fletcher had ever eaten. There were cuts from the legs and sides, back and rump. They dined like the finest nobles of Hominum, sampling each piece and marvelling at the variance in texture and taste.

They revelled in the glow and heat from their small fire, for they had decided that this was the only night they would allow themselves one in case it was seen from above. They ate in satisfied silence, filling it with the slurps and mastication that sounded more like dogs lapping at a bowl than civilised people at a meal.

Othello was the first to speak.

'Still think eating demons is wrong?' he mumbled, his mouth full.

Cress chewed thoughtfully for a moment.

'Nah, this thing is bloody delicious,' she said, continuing to gnaw at an enormous femur.

Fletcher collapsed on his back, groaning at his full stomach. He turned his head and surveyed the mountain of meat they still had left over.

'What a waste,' Cress said, hurling the bone into the darkness and lying back beside him. 'If we're lucky we might get breakfast in the morning before it goes bad.'

'Aye,' Othello said, overhearing them. 'That's why I'm filling my belly. After what happened to Athena, I don't want to hunt again until we have to. Feast and famine, that's how it'll have to be.'

They sat quietly for a time longer, then Sylva spoke.

'I wish we had a wood elf here,' she sighed, tugging off her boots and socks and wiggling her toes near the fire.

Fletcher grinned, remembering Othello doing the exact same thing, long ago, when they had sheltered from the rain in a shed after Sylva's attempted assassination. There was a time when she might have turned her nose up at such behaviour. How things had changed.

'Why's that then?' Cress asked. 'And what's the difference?'

'The wood elves are natural hunters, spending most of their lives on the Great Forest's floor, tending our herds of deer and ranging many miles from our homeland. They would know how to preserve the meat, even the hide.'

'Fletcher, didn't you do a bit of hunting back home?' Othello asked.

But Fletcher's mind was already at work. He was no expert at tanning furs, for he had simply provided them to the leatherworkers before the process began. But he knew how to dry the meat into jerky. He had done it at home, by Berdon's hearth and furnace. Somehow the whole thing had seemed impossible out here, in the damp, alien forest, but suddenly Fletcher decided to give it a go.

'We'll need more wood for the fire,' Fletcher said, sitting up. 'But I think I can do both. It won't be perfect – hell, it might not work at all, but I reckon it's worth a shot.'

So, Fletcher set to work. It was tough in the darkness, for there was only the fire for guidance, but Fletcher had everything he needed nearby. He cut sturdy branches from low-hanging trees and constructed a teepee-like structure, using the Catoblepas's tendons for binding. Then he latticed it with thin branches, to make a rack where strips of meat could be hung to dry.

While the others set to trimming the meat into thin strips, he began to flense the enormous fur, using Cress's seax to scrape away the excess flesh. Soon he had a taut membrane of skin, pinky-white on one side and hairy on the other.

The most gruesome part came next. Lacking a pot, Fletcher was forced to cut away the skull from the Catoblepas's head and use it instead.

'What the hell are you doing?' Othello moaned, watching as Fletcher cut and mashed the Catoblepas's brain into a gooey paste.

'With my seax!' Cress exclaimed.

'It helps tan the hide,' Fletcher said, grimacing as he stirred the disgusting mixture. 'Hunters have been doing this for centuries.'

Soon he was reluctantly spreading the liquid on the hide's skin with his hands, while Ignatius blew toasty air to dry it. The fire had almost gone out by the time they had finished their work.

'We're down to coals now, and I've put some logs of dry wood on top that will smoulder and smoke all night. Now, help me with the skin,' Fletcher ordered.

The others took a corner each and they heaved it up. Together they staggered to the fire and wrapped it around the meat-laden frame, where it was stitched in place by puncturing the edges with Sylva's stiletto blade, threading them with the last of the sinew and using the tighten spell to keep it secure.

Finally, they stood back and admired their handiwork. A steaming cloud of smoke blew from the top of the structure like a chimney. Fortunately, the smoke seemed thin enough to disappear into the air before it broke the canopy.

'We'll stoke the fire with green leaves and more wood throughout the night,' Fletcher said. 'It should tan the hide and smoke the meat at the same time. Just remember, we're not cooking it, we're drying it out. So keep the heat low and constant – don't pile up the fire too high. With any luck, it should all be ready in six hours from now. The fur will make a useful covering if it rains, or at least make the shell more comfortable for Othello's back.'

'Aye,' Othello said, rubbing his tailbone surreptitiously.

'I'll take first watch,' Sylva said.

'Wake me in two hours,' Fletcher replied, gathering Athena and Ignatius into his arms and laying down next to his mother.

It was good to have full bellies, and with any luck they would have dried meat for days. But even so, Fletcher found that sleep eluded him.

He tried not to think about the time ticking by, ignoring the twinges of frustration at their slow, pondering pace through the murky forest. Yet with each breath he took, he knew that the air poisoned him, sucking the life from his body. There was nothing they could do – only wait, and hope.

He tossed and turned on the hard shell, listening to the creak of branches, and the strange night noises of the woodland.

And finally, even as the sky began to turn bright once again, Fletcher slept.

9

The team peered into the canopy above, munching on their petals. Their stomachs were already full – the jerky had made a good appetiser, and Fletcher had cooked some of the Catoblepas's enormous bones over their small fire then cracked them open so they could eat the nutritious jelly of marrow within. He only wished they had some bread to eat it with – that was how he had eaten deer marrow when food was scarce in Pelt.

Their water had been replenished by a brief shower of rain that morning, which they had funnelled into their flasks by stretching the tanned Catoblepas's skin and catching it. The liquid tasted smoky, but was far fresher than the water from the occasional puddle they had come across in the forest.

They had to put out the fire after their meal, for its smoke and smell might alert their hunters to their presence. Strangely, Fletcher had woken to find Ignatius curled up in the flames, slumbering among the glowing coals. Fletcher supposed that after swimming in molten lava, a fire must be child's play, but

54

he was concerned – Ignatius had never done that before. Othello's voice broke into his thoughts.

'We need a new scout, especially for when we get to the other side of the mountains,' he argued, picking his teeth with a sharpened twig. 'Athena can't fly. Tosk or Ignatius might climb up one of the larger trees and get a look at the horizon, but we need to see what's ahead.'

'Lysander's too large. He might be spotted,' Sylva said quickly, but nobody was in disagreement.

'We need a Mite,' Cress mumbled, scraping the inside of a bone with her seax. 'Or something like it.'

Fletcher knew they were right. They were nearly halfway through their supply of petals and the mountains were looming above them. Sheldon had not deviated from his path, but it would be best to know what awaited them at the foot of the range.

'We should send the demons out to hunt on their own. They can avoid anything too big, but capture any small flying demons for one of us to harness,' Fletcher said.

Then he realised that he, and Sylva for that matter, had no experience with hunting or capturing demons from the ether – Rook had never allowed the commoners to hunt during their first and only year at Vocans.

'Did you do much hunting in the ether, Cress?' Fletcher asked.

'First years were banned from going into the ether when I joined,' Cress said, shrugging her shoulders. 'Something to do with what happened to Captain Lovett. I was so happy with Tosk, I didn't really mind. Othello did some though, being a second year.'

'Aye, that I did,' Othello said, scratching his head wistfully. 'Solomon was bloody useless though. His great galumphing hands couldn't hold on to anything small and he's too slow and loud to catch much anyway.'

'Well, I reckon all of us but Sylva might have a spare summoning level for a Mite,' Fletcher said, grinning. 'You might as well let Solomon stretch his legs, however useless he is; he's been infused far too long.'

So, Solomon and Lysander were summoned and sent with the other demons to hunt in the woods, which were becoming thicker and more tropical with every step that Sheldon took. In fact, he was now forced off his straight path to follow a natural trail in the forest, so overgrown was the vegetation around them.

Soon they were seated in a circle, and Fletcher strapped on his scrying lens as the others stared at their crystals. Even Alice came to join them, though whether it was because of the smell of the meat or a desire to be close to them, Fletcher couldn't tell.

Of all the demons, only Athena remained, nursing her broken wing while nestled in Alice's lap. Both seemed contented to rest together, so Fletcher focused on his scrying crystal to watch Ignatius's progress.

The Salamander was nimble in the forest, haring through the brambles and fallen logs with eyes to the sky. His excitement was infectious and Fletcher's heart quickened with every leap that took Ignatius deeper into the woods, away from the crashing tumult that Lysander and Solomon inevitably made as they fought their way through the thickets.

Lesser Mites buzzed here and there, but Ignatius ignored them. They would not do for a summoner – taking up a whole fulfilment level like a Scarab Mite would, but lacking the mandibles, stinger and intelligence of their larger cousins.

Instead, Ignatius listened intently to the air around him. Fletcher knew that the Salamander could tell the difference between demons just by the frequency and timbre of wingbeats, his hundreds of years of hunting in the ether having finely attuned his senses. Still, nothing. The Will-o'-the-wisps had stripped the forest bare of all but the lowest demons in the food chain. The only other demon he saw was a single Coatl hanging from a branch above – a snake-like demon that was coated in the gaudy, layered feathers of an exotic bird. But it was far too slow and conspicuous to be of any use.

As they waited, Fletcher explored his demon's mind, hoping to hear the sound of prey. But . . . there was something different about Ignatius – and Fletcher was really noticing it now, while focused so intently. The Salamander's consciousness was larger in his mind. It even felt as if the levels of mana contained within the little demon had grown too. In fact, *little* was hardly a descriptor he should use, as he realised that Ignatius seemed to have grown since they had entered the ether. His weight had been noticeable when Fletcher carried him that morning, and his backside had hung from Fletcher's shoulders.

A jolt of excitement flared in Ignatius's consciousness, dragging Fletcher from his thoughts. The Salamander was at the base of a tree, crawling up the hoary bark with deliberate care. Above, the wingbeats of a new demon had caught his attention. Fletcher could hear them too, a dull throb in the air that intensified intermittently as the hidden demon flew to and fro.

Then he saw it, catching the iridescent gleam of its strange body. It was as if a winged lizard had been constructed from the body parts of insects. Its wings, though shaped like a Wyvern's, were made from the same fragile material as a butterfly's, with a webbed translucent patch in the centre surrounded by the vivid blue-green mix of a shallow lagoon. Its body was marbled with the same colour, and appeared much like a beetle's carapace that segmented at the joints. There were only four legs, but each one was covered in the finest hairs and ended in a small-pronged claw. A tail with a tiny but potent sting on its end acted as a rudder and counterweight.

But the eyes . . . the eyes were the most insectile of all: black spheres made of thousands of smaller shapes, sitting beneath a pair of ant-like antennae. Only its mouth remained reptilian, revealing a long, chameleonic tongue that whipped out to snatch a Lesser Mite from the air.

It was a Pyrausta – so rare that there were no records of its capture, only scribbled descriptions from summoners who had recorded the infusion memories of their demons. It was a poor fighter, but it was known for two particular talents, which it demonstrated as it alighted on a large leaf near Ignatius to consume its prey.

Instantly, the body turned the same bright green as the leaf, blending in so perfectly that it even mimicked the veins beneath it. The Pyrausta gulped down the Mite with the help of its front claws.

Even as Fletcher squinted at his lens, its antennae twitched – then it was darting away in a sudden burst of speed. The antennae were its second unique skill, allowing it senses that other demons could only dream of.

Ignatius was already in midair, predicting the sudden movement. Even so, he barely managed to touch it with one claw, hooking into the tail and dragging it with him as he tumbled to the ground. It thudded beside him and immediately Ignatius had ensnared it with his own tail, holding it aloft with its wings and sting trapped by its side.

It was neatly done. Fletcher sent Ignatius a congratulatory pulse of pride and the Salamander yipped in excitement before scampering back towards the shell.

'We've caught something,' Fletcher announced. 'Bring the hunters home, we've got a demon to harness.'

10

The Pyrausta had turned the same intense burgundy that coloured Ignatius's skin by the time the Salamander arrived, victoriously holding his captive aloft. Already Othello's summoning leather had been placed beside the fire, the only one they had left after the supplies had been lost in the swamp.

'Bloody hell, a Pyrausta,' Othello grumbled, a hint of jealousy in his voice. 'That'll do perfectly.'

Fletcher kneeled and rubbed Ignatius's head, then stepped back and looked at his palm in astonishment. The Salamander's skin was cool to the touch.

'He's cold,' Fletcher said, furrowing his brow. 'He's never cold.'

'Weird,' Sylva said, crouching beside him. 'May I?'

It was usually taboo to touch another summoner's demon; at least, on purpose, anyway. Fletcher nodded and she stroked her hand along Ignatius's spine. Fletcher felt an involuntary pulse of pleasure and his face blushed with heat. He turned away and busily tucked his leather jacket around his mother's shoulders, hoping that Sylva wouldn't notice.

'That *is* strange,' the elf murmured, straightening. 'But lucky – it's probably why he was able to capture the Pyrausta.'

'What do you mean?' Fletcher asked.

'Well, most summoners theorise that Pyraustas are able to detect a great deal with their antennae. Heat is perhaps the most obvious indicator for them. Some say they can also feel the most minor air vibrations, even detect humidity. Most agree that their hearing, taste and smell is as good or better than a Canid's. Ignatius's heatless body must have confused it. I bet there aren't many cold-blooded demons out here.'

Fletcher grinned and looked at the Pyrausta. A lucky catch indeed.

'Do you think Ignatius is able to change his temperature at will, or was it something else?' he asked.

Fletcher pondered Ignatius's tail, which seemed even longer than before. Were his shoulder blades more prominent too, like Khan's black Salamander's had been?

'Sylva, do you think he's getting bigger?'

Sylva didn't hear him, busy inspecting the beautiful Pyrausta demon. 'Huh?' she asked, looking up at Ignatius. 'I suppose so. He did just have a big meal.'

Fletcher couldn't understand. Perhaps it was a strange reaction to what had happened in the pit of lava beneath the pyramid. Or was it his return to the ether? Eating the flesh of a demon? There was so little known about Salamanders, it could be one or a combination of all factors.

'Who's harnessing it then?' Cress asked eagerly.

'Not me,' Sylva said, tousling Lysander's head. 'This beautiful Griffin is a level ten. I doubt I have enough fulfilment levels left

61

to capture a Pyrausta, however many levels it is.'

'The species is level two, I reckon,' Othello said, kneeling and inspecting the captured demon. 'Maybe three. Who has fulfilment levels to spare? I checked myself on the fulfilmeter before the Tournament – I'm level fourteen now.'

'I'm still ten – five left for me,' Cress said, sounding hopeful.

'Finders keepers, right, Fletcher?' Sylva said, shaking her head.

But Fletcher was not so sure. Othello needed a demon like a Pyrausta, something fast and light and useful. Solomon, powerful though he was, was not a versatile demon. The Golem was a sledgehammer to the Pyrausta's scalpel.

Othello was his best friend, his ally in all things. He owed the dwarf and his family so much. And what did Fletcher need with a Pyrausta? It was little use in battle with a weapon that appeared to be similar to a Mite's sting, and Athena, though injured, was already a great scout. He didn't need another. No. It had to be Othello.

'It's yours, Othello,' Fletcher said, grinning. 'You need it more than I do, and I don't even know if my fulfilment level's high enough anyway. I was nine last year and that's all used up.'

'I went up by three since then,' Sylva interjected, exasperated at Fletcher's generosity. 'Othello's gone up by four. Have a go.'

'It's all right, Sylva,' Fletcher said. 'He needs it. Solomon's slower than a herd of turtles.'

'You mean it?' Othello said, his eyes lighting up with excitement.

'Yeah, it's yours. Go on, Ignatius will hold it over the pentacle for you.'

Othello needed no further persuasion, kneeling beside the

pentacle and smiling ruefully as Cress moaned in jealous disgust.

'I'll gift it back to him later, if he changes his mind,' Othello said, noticing Sylva's raised eyebrows. Fletcher thought of another reason and spoke quickly before Sylva could say anything.

'Now if we get split up, everyone will have demons that can fly or climb up high to find each other again. It makes sense.'

Sylva sighed and waved them on, shaking her head at Fletcher. She seemed disappointed in him somehow. Maybe he was being too nice, but he didn't care.

Ignatius strutted proudly to the summoning leather and held the Pyrausta over it. A second later and the pentacle glowed violet as Othello powered it up. Capturing a demon was much like infusing one, only much harder. Holding it in place was usually the tricky part.

Othello's jaws clenched and unclenched. A vein throbbed in his forehead and he allowed his breath to slowly whistle through his teeth as he strained, his stubby fingers pressing deep into the leather.

'Go on, you can do it,' Cress said, shuffling closer and peering at the Pyrausta. Slowly, ever so slowly, the demon began to dissolve into slivers of white light. Othello groaned aloud, his face flushing as he strained to harness the demon. Finally, when he had turned so red that Fletcher began to worry, the last of the translucent light disappeared into the mat.

Othello fell back, his chest heaving with exertion. Then a blissful look plastered across his face as the euphoria of infusing a new demon took hold of him.

'Well done,' Fletcher said, patting Othello on the shoulder.

'You know, you're the first of us that's actually captured a wild demon.'

'Half-captured, anyway,' Sylva said, but she grudgingly gave Othello a smile.

It took a few moments for Othello to recover, and then the Pyrausta was summoned again. It sat in the centre of the mat as soon as it materialised, trembling.

'It's so weird,' Othello murmured. 'My mind feels so . . . full.'

'Tell me about it,' Fletcher said. 'You'll get used to it though. Do you think you can control it enough to send it scouting?'

'Aye,' Othello said, holding out a hand. The Pyrausta fluttered up and landed on his fingers, looking up at him with its strange eyes.

'And it's a she by the way,' Othello continued, lifting the demon to his face and peering at it in wonder. 'I'll call her Pria.'

11

Pria flitted back and forth, her belly turning grey-blue to blend with the sky and her top half a mix of broken greens to blend with the canopy – ideal should any predators flying above look down.

When Othello brushed the large scrying stone against her tail, she shot into the sky, much faster than Fletcher had expected. He had been lucky to catch her.

At first they saw a crystal-clear picture of the forest, then Othello grunted and the image flickered in shades of red, yellow and orange as the Pyrausta glided on the wind, high above the trees.

'She can see heat,' Othello said proudly. 'It's like a switch in her mind. Hang on, let's see . . .'

The stone changed again. The forest turned ghostly, replaced by a strange mass of rippling black and white shapes.

'Sound and air movement, like that bat demon.' Othello scrunched up his face as he tried to remember the name. 'What's it called . . . ?'

Fletcher remembered the giant, hairy bats that some shamans would use as mounts, and shuddered.

'It doesn't matter. Be quick,' Fletcher said. 'A Pyrausta would rarely venture above the safety of the trees. If she's spotted, it might look suspicious.'

Othello nodded and soon Pria was skimming just above the tree line, occasionally flipping her vision to check for predators. Above, the red mountain range stretched into the horizon, devouring the greying sky. Fletcher found himself searching for a sun that he knew would not be there – the ether's light source was yet to be determined.

'What's that?' Othello murmured, slowing Pria as the base of the mountain neared. The trees stopped abruptly where the red rock began, as if the rusty sediment repelled them. Up close, it looked like sandstone – rough and covered in a thin layer of dust. It reminded Fletcher of the ether's deadlands. But that was not what had caught Othello's attention.

There was a crack in the rock, so narrow that they had not seen it in the distance. It appeared as if an earthquake had once split the impenetrable sierra down the centre, leaving a thin trail into the heart of the range. It was barely wide enough for Sheldon to pass through, but it appeared well used; generations of hooves, claws and feet had worn a clear path along the ground towards it.

'I told y—' Fletcher began, but suddenly Othello held up his hand, his eyes widening with panic.

'There's something coming,' he whispered, as if he were there with Pria.

The screen flashed red as the Pyrausta darted on to a nearby boulder, the largest and tallest in a pile of rubble that lay scattered around the crack in the mountains. She flipped her vision to the strange, shadowy view of the world and turned her eyes to the horizon above the trees. There were ripples high in the air, as if there was a great disturbance in the sky.

Her view returned to normal, revealing a V-shaped flock of black shadows in the distance, still too far off to make out. At first, Fletcher thought they were bird demons, perhaps Shrikes. But as they drew closer he realised they were too large for that.

Wyverns. Fletcher could count seven of them – great, reptilian beasts with jointed wings and horned heads – that spiralled down towards the mountain pass. They were as large as a stack of three horses and they landed in deep, juddering thuds that made the boulder tremble and the image on the crystal shake. Furrows were scored in the ground as they skidded to a stop, the hooked claws of their feet and wings tearing through the earth.

Othello shuddered as their riders came into view: orc shamans, resplendent in gaudy, feathered headdresses, their chests and limbs painted in whorls of bright colours. Each was armed with a quiver-full of javelins and a macana, a flat war-club with shards of obsidian embedded along the sides.

Other demons landed among them, lagging behind the Wyverns. Vesps – bee-wasp hybrids as large as pigeons. Strixs – four-legged owl-demons with red-tipped feathers and fearsome beaks. But it was another demon that caught Fletcher's eye, still circling above as if reluctant to give up the search. It was smaller than a Wyvern, but his heart seized as the beast finally descended. It loomed large in the crystal as it landed on the boulder above Pria. The Pyrausta remained perfectly still.

'Crap,' Cress muttered.

It was an Ahool – the name Othello had been searching for earlier coming, unbidden, to Fletcher's mind. It was much like an overgrown bat with the musculature, fur and wide mouth of a silverback gorilla, snorting at the air through a piggish snout and twitching its pointed ears. Twin fangs poked from either side of its mouth, sharper than hypodermic needles but long enough to skewer a human through the chest and out the other side.

Then its rider leaped from its back to land in a crouch on the ground below.

The white orc. Khan.

'Heaven help us,' Cress breathed.

Khan seemed to be shouting, his pearlescent skin bright against the grey sky. His long mane of hair tossed in the air as he strode back and forth, ordering the shamans down from their mounts in what Fletcher knew would be the guttural barks of the orc language.

The shamans were soon prowling about the clearing, examining the ground by the mountain pass. It did not take long for the orcs to determine there were no footprints, though they did seem excited by the hoof marks left along the dust. The white orc clapped his hands at the sight of them, then shooed the shamans away to examine them himself. They returned to their Wyverns and fed them red slabs of meat from baskets strapped to the demons' backs.

'Hey . . . they're not leaving,' Cress said, pointing at the crystal.

The shamans were not setting up tents, but instead sheltering beneath the wings of their Wyverns and starting small campfires with the fire-spell symbols tattooed on their fingertips. Khan joined one of them, crouching on his long haunches and warming his hands by the flames.

'Why is Khan here?' Sylva shuddered, horrified at the sight of the tall, white orc. 'There's a war on in our dimension and he's wasting his time hunting us here. It doesn't make sense!'

Khan wore nothing but a plain loincloth, a stark contrast to the colourful shamans, with their multicoloured feathers and garish body paint. His body was composed of lean, athletic muscle and his long hair seemed almost feminine alongside the shamans' cropped mix of topknots, shaved patches and bowl tops.

'What do I do?' Othello whispered, pointing at the image of the Ahool on the crystal. It was standing sentry, its head swinging slowly left and right. 'As soon as Pria moves, it'll sense her. Hell, I'm surprised it hasn't smelled her yet.'

'Ahools have poor eyesight,' Sylva said. 'It probably can smell her but can't see where she is.'

'We need her there anyway,' Fletcher suggested. 'If they're still there by morning we could run right into them. She can keep watch.'

'Aye,' Othello said, wiping sweat from his forehead.

The group sat in horrified silence as the sky began to dim and the smaller orc demons settled on the edges of the forest, watching for danger.

12

By morning the orcs were gone. Pria saw them leave at first light, flying low through the mountain pass. It had been fortunate timing, as Sheldon arrived at the entrance an hour later. Once there, the Zaratan stopped to graze at the edge of the forest, as if he knew that there would be little vegetation to feed on during the journey ahead.

The team leaped to the ground and spread out, wary of any orc demons left to keep watch. The ashes of the fires were still warm to the touch and the dung from their Wyverns left a thick, pungent stench in the air.

'They must know we're going this way,' Fletcher said, shaking his head. 'The Ahool must have tracked our scent. We're just lucky they thought we're faster than we are – they've overshot us.'

'If we were walking, we would still be in the swamplands,' Othello said, rubbing the sleep from his eyes. 'If we were riding anything but a Zaratan, say Kirins or Hippalectryons, we would be well beyond this point. They must think we're mounted, like the Dragoon Corps.'

'That's why they were so excited by these hoof prints,' Sylva guessed, crouching near the indentations the shamans had examined. 'Lucky for us, a wild herd of some demon or other must have passed this way recently.'

'Aye,' Cress agreed. She prodded a pile of Wyvern dung with a twig. 'They must think we've got large, high-level demons we can ride – it's not like they'd send a bunch of students with one or two years' experience into the belly of the beast, is it?'

Fletcher grinned at her sarcasm, even if inside he was in turmoil. It didn't hurt that their pursuers overestimated their power, but at some point they might reconsider and retrace their steps. Worse still, the crew had lost the cover of the trees and would be stuck on the only path for miles around. Migrating demons would be funnelled through the pass, from packs of wild Canids to roaming Manticores, looking for a mate. He didn't like it, but they had no choice. They were running out of time.

As if Sheldon could read his mind, the Zaratan swallowed the last of the pulped leaves he had been stripping from the forest edge and began to plod into the narrow gully, ignoring the high, sheer walls of the mountain on either side. The team hurried to heave themselves on to the shell, their feet dangling above the ground as it juddered, tilting to and fro.

Soon they had all returned to Sheldon's back, with Alice, who now had Tosk joining the pile of demons that draped themselves over her, as if they took solace in her calm demeanour. Ignatius even brought her scraps of jerky when the team ate, and spent most of his time in her lap – now that the fire was out, his temperature had gone back to normal.

Cress did not seem to mind her demon's new sleeping

companion – she spent most of her time behind Sheldon's neck, giving him the occasional scratch and holding one-sided conversations. She had become quite attached to the gentle giant, and often bemoaned the fact that he was too high a level to make her own.

Fletcher smiled at the affectionate pile of demons and kissed his mother on the forehead. As he walked to the front of the shell, he wondered if it was strange to show such tenderness towards her. But it felt natural, and right.

'It's the perfect place for an ambush,' Sylva said, interrupting his thoughts as she came to stand beside him.

She was right. They were in a winding chasm that followed the natural strata of the rock, with jagged turns that prevented them from seeing more than a dozen yards ahead. Above, deformations in the cliff walls created ledges and crevices, ideal for Wyverns hidden in wait.

'We'll have Pria keep watch,' Fletcher said. 'That will give us some warning at least.'

Only Pria would be unknown as one of their demons, for the others might have been identified by the Nanaues or goblins they had fought in the pyramid. Othello brushed her with the large scrying stone and handed it to Fletcher. The dwarf was reluctant to be away from her; he had spent the past hour experimenting with her transformations, amazed at the myriad patterns she could produce on her carapace.

As Pria hovered before them, Fletcher found it strange to see himself mirrored in the crystal, and he was struck by the change in his appearance.

His clothes and face were stained with a mess of soil, blood and dried sweat – he had not washed in days, limited to a brief splashing of water from the acrid puddles that Sheldon passed by. What wasn't stained was torn from being caught on the spiky branches of the orc jungles and the ether's forests. His hair was greasy, plastered to his forehead as if dipped in tar.

He smoothed his hair back, then wiped at his cheeks surreptitiously, until he earned himself an amused glance from Sylva. She had somehow managed to keep herself presentable. Her face was clean and fresh, while her hair was carefully braided, even if her clothes were only in marginally better condition than his own.

'Come here,' she said, pulling Fletcher to sit cross-legged beside her. She poured a splash of water on to a scrap of reasonably clean cloth and dabbed at his face with it, peering at him with her tongue poking from the corner of her lips as she worked.

'You know, we won't have many options if there's no volcano on the other side of these mountains,' she said in a low voice.

'I didn't think we had *any* options,' Fletcher replied, unsure where to look as she leaned in and wiped his cheeks. He noticed her skin, usually pale and smooth, was lightly bronzed with a dusting of freckles, tanned from her days in the orc jungles.

'We'll have to risk flying to search for one,' she murmured, shuffling closer so the others couldn't hear. 'Take some petals for the journey.'

'Abandon the others?' Fletcher asked, horrified.

'We'd bring the flowers back once we've found a volcano,' Sylva said, shaking her head. 'It's our only chance, and theirs. We split up to go hunting when we needed food the other day, this is just a little longer.'

'How will we find each other again?' Fletcher asked. 'We won't be a few hundred yards apart this time.'

'We'll find a way,' Sylva said, furrowing her brow.

Fletcher shook his head. He didn't want to leave his mother. But perhaps it was the only way.

'Well, let's hope it doesn't come to that,' he said.

As he spoke, he realised that he had been ignoring the crystal in his lap and glanced down. What he saw churned his stomach.

'Guys, you need to see this,' he said, his heart pounding.

Even as he said it, he knew it was too late – Sheldon had just stomped around a curve in their path and the walls of the ravine fell away, revealing what Pria had seen moments ago.

A canyon. A huge, empty space, widening the ravine and then narrowing again, far in the distance on the opposite side. But that was not what had alarmed him.

Giant bones towered above, scattered about like the ruined pillars of a forgotten temple. They were thick and tall as tree trunks, each one bleached a glaring white by years of exposure to light.

'What is this place?' Sylva breathed, her neck tilting as they passed beneath a ribcage. The bones curved around them like the spars of a grounded frigate, casting bars of shadow over the group.

Ahead, a leering skull greeted them, the lower jaw missing to leave its ridged teeth buried in the sand. It was as wide and tall as Sheldon's entire body, with eye sockets large enough for Lysander to fly through without touching the sides. Other skulls littered the way, revealing that scores of demons had died in the huge ravine.

'It's like an elephants' graveyard,' Othello said. He leaned out

74

and knocked one of the bones, the hollow sound of it echoing around the canyon.

'These are no elephants,' Cress said.

Indeed, they were not. These demons were many times an elephant's size. Fletcher couldn't imagine how they had arrived in this place, for they could hardly have fitted through the ravine. Pria, still travelling ahead, had reached the other side of the chasm, and he saw the answer to his question. The path was far wider there, large enough to sail a fleet of ships through.

'There was nothing this large described in our demonology lessons,' Sylva said, still horrified by the size of the enormous skeletons.

'I know what these could be,' Othello volunteered, hesitantly. 'There are legends about creatures this size, but never any confirmed sightings. Some people say they're extinct. I read about them in an old book in the library, when we were studying for the exams last year.'

He looked closer at the skull as they passed it by.

'The teeth are a herbivore's, flat and ridged,' he said, thinking aloud. 'Look at its shinbones. From its size, it would be tall enough to graze on the tree canopy. They're the tree-eaters. Behemoths.'

'Whatever they are, it's creepy as hell here.' Cress shuddered and went to sit beside Alice, who seemed completely unperturbed by the macabre graveyard.

They spent the next half hour on edge, but the land was as dead and motionless as the bones that surrounded them. Even so, it was a relief when they passed out of the silent boneyard and into the wide ravine on the other side.

Sheldon was quickening his pace, as if eager to reach the edge of the mountains. He would be dehydrated, for though the others were able to drink from their flasks, his last taste of water had been from a stagnant puddle in the forest that morning. To add to this, the weather had changed – the sky had become brighter and hotter with each passing minute.

The shell swayed beneath them and the cliffs on either side were now too wide apart to provide cover from the oppressive heat that beat down from the glowing sky above. Soon they had lapsed into silence, crouched together under the Catoblepas's pelt to take advantage of its meagre shade. It seemed that different parts of the ether had vastly different climates, despite being only miles apart.

Then they saw it, shining bright like a sheet of glass, rippling and swirling in the scrying stone as Pria flew out of the wide mountain pass.

It was a lagoon, with leagues of azure waters that were surrounded by pure white sand and rocky, vine-laden cliffs. Green jungles bordered its edges and a winding waterway stretched to their left towards the faraway ocean, running beside the mountain range until it merged with the distant waters. To the right, trickling waterfalls fell from jutting outcrops of black rock, feeding the calm pools that surrounded them.

Even as Sheldon hastened towards the water, the air began to turn humid, so much so that Cress's loose red hair began to frizz before Fletcher's eyes. Sheldon unleashed a groan of happiness and the shell bounced as he lumbered ahead, the walls of the mountain falling away on either side.

'I think we've arrived at his destination,' Cress said happily, ducking out of the cover of the pelt and crawling to the front of the shell. She patted his neck happily and then laughed aloud as he splashed into the water, spraying her. The Zaratan languished there, burying his head beneath the surface. His neck pulsed as he gulped.

Cress scooped her hand over the edge and cupped it to her lips.

'It's sweet! We can drink it.'

Fletcher didn't need more encouragement than that. He ran and leaped into the water, for it was so clear that he could see the bottom. There was a shock of cold, but soon the cool liquid was heavenly on his skin, bathing his greasy scalp to leave his hair floating weightlessly.

The water was disturbed nearby as Sylva dived in beside him, a streak of white cloth and bubbles in the water. She had stripped to her undershirt and the short, knee-length pantalettes she wore beneath her breeches.

Fletcher came up for air, only to find himself splashed in the face by the laughing elf.

'You look like a drowned rat!' She grinned, splashing him again.

On the other side of the shell, Cress and Othello had entered the water, their happy cries out of sight. He knew they should be searching the horizon for a volcano, but at that moment he didn't care. It could wait. All he saw were Sylva's sparkling blue eyes. He splashed her back – and the look of incredulous outrage on her face as she spluttered made him laugh aloud.

'Right, now you're in for it,' Sylva said in mock anger.

She ducked Fletcher's head under the surface, only to find he had tugged her feet out from under her, dragging her beneath the water with him. They wrestled there, pressed chest to chest, her lean limbs wrapping around his own as they vied for position. Fletcher's heart pounded as they tumbled on the soft sand of the lagoon bed, until the need to breathe brought them back to the surface.

They burst from the water and parted, catching their breaths as they took in the splendour of their surroundings once again. The sky was shining so that the water glittered like a handful of diamonds. Just for a moment, the fears of the past few days seemed insignificant in the face of such beauty.

Fletcher splashed Sylva again for good measure, then swam towards a gushing waterfall in the dark rock nearby. For a brief moment he revelled in the drumming of the water on his tired back. Then Sylva tackled him into the hollow cove beneath the ledge of pouring water.

He fell back on to a flat boulder, worn smooth and round by the water. She straddled his chest and pinned back his arms, the flowing water behind her like a wall that cut them off from the rest of the world, a glowing, undulating curtain that echoed in the dim chamber. The only sound was the rush of water and the ring of droplets falling from half-formed stalactites above.

She raised her eyebrows triumphantly and then, as Fletcher began to heave her off him, she leaned down . . . and the room darkened. Othello emerged through the waterfalls, shaking his head like a wet dog.

'Hey, Sheldon's on the move,' he said, sprinkling them with water from his long hair and beard.

Sylva sat up.

And, just like that, the moment was gone.

13

It was night now, and they sat, miserable, on the centre of the shell, wrapped in the Catoblepas's pelt. Their clothes were still damp from their swim, for the light of day had not been long enough to dry them. The only sounds were the gentle splashes as Sheldon swam through the lagoon. It was a slow, lazy pace, with no clear direction. He seemed to be waiting for something.

With no sign of a volcano, the mood had turned sombre, even though they were clean once again. Even his mother was fresh-faced – Cress had discreetly bathed her in the dim light of the evening while the others surveyed the landscape.

In the distance ahead of them, the jungles dwindled into red sand, revealing the deadlands, a desert wasteland of reddish sand. Beyond, the land fell away into darkness over the curved rim, where the disc that was the ether ended, and the Abyss began.

'I'm leaving with Lysander,' Sylva said, breaking the subdued calm. 'If I fly far enough I may spot a column of smoke from a volcano.'

She pushed her way out from the cloak of the pelt and stood, stretching. Lysander looked up as he heard his name and cawed mournfully. He had sensed Sylva's intentions, and didn't want to leave the group.

'What . . . now?' Cress asked, alarmed at the sudden decision. 'Right this minute?'

'We know the orcs don't travel at night. It's the best time to move. I'll hide below the tree line when day breaks.'

'How will you navigate in the dark?' Othello asked. 'Griffins have poor night vision. You'll never be able to find it, let alone make your way back to us.'

'Fletcher . . .' Sylva paused, as if she wasn't sure any more. 'Fletcher will come with me. Lysander can carry the two of us and we'll use Athena to see through the darkness. Her night vision is better than any of the other demons, even your Pyrausta.'

'We'll find you by following the mountain range until we see the lagoon again,' Fletcher added. 'Sheldon won't be leaving any time soon. It looks like he's waiting for something.'

As the others mulled over their words, Fletcher couldn't help but wonder: why had Sylva hesitated? Surely she wouldn't want to go out alone.

Was it about what had happened in the waterfall? Or rather, what hadn't happened? Fletcher felt a pang of regret in his chest.

Whatever the reason, she was already taking her share of petals from their dwindling supply, dividing it into equal piles of five. Fletcher stuffed handfuls of jerky into his backpack and refilled his flask from the lagoon.

Having secured his sword, bow and guns, he hugged his mother tightly, wishing the limp arms at her sides would wrap around him.

'We'll get you home, Mum,' he whispered, kissing her on her forehead.

An awkward handshake with Othello turned into a bear hug. Cress bussed him on both cheeks, and he felt the wet of tears on her face. It was all too quick, a decision made without warning. Their time was running out.

He brushed Athena with his scrying crystal and affixed it to his eye, his view tingeing purple as she scampered on to his shoulder. After a moment's hesitation, he pointed his palm at Ignatius and the Salamander dissolved into his palm in a flush of white light.

Then Fletcher was hauling himself up Lysander's side, the ridged spine and feathered fur sliding uncomfortably beneath his thighs as the Griffin's musculature shifted and flexed.

'Petals, water, food, weapons,' Sylva muttered under her breath. She ran her fingers along the bow and falx scabbarded on her back. The sword's handle blocked Fletcher's view, so Athena leaped into Sylva's lap, jarring with pain as her wing-splint knocked against the elf's shoulder. Her vision was bright in the pink-tinged crystal, as if the world was lit by the light of a dozen moons.

'We'll be back,' Sylva said, though she spoke so quietly that Fletcher wasn't sure if she was talking to herself.

Then, as Othello began to speak, Lysander leaped. The dwarf's words were lost as they hurled themselves into the sky, ascending in great thrusts from his powerful wings.

Fletcher's hands were wrapped around Sylva's midriff, but it did little to anchor him; she was balanced as precariously as he was. He tilted left and right with every wingbeat, and his thigh muscles ached as he desperately gripped Lysander's sides. It was only when the Griffin glided on the wind, high above the jungle, that Fletcher's heart left his mouth.

Beneath, the lagoon had shrunk to the size of a silver shilling, with a thin line denoting the wending river that poured into the vast ocean to their west. The mountain range behind them curled in a quarter circle, with the dark stain to the south where the swamplands began. Fletcher knew that the orcs' territory lay somewhere beyond and there was likely a source of Euryale flowers there. Even though the Wyverns had already gone past them, it felt wrong to backtrack so far and enter a territory where other shamans may still be searching for them.

'We head east,' Sylva said, her voice barely discernible against the gusting wind.

So Lysander turned, his wings tilting and they with them in a stomach-churning swoop. Soon they were following the rough arc of the sierra, the world beneath rolling away in a rough carpet of treetops.

Fletcher scanned the horizon, desperate for the telltale pinnacle of rock in the distance. He even watched the mountain range, hoping against hope that a column of smoke would appear. Instead, they flew on into the night, the range curving away behind them until it faded into the distance. Below, the jungles seemed endless, broken only by the red-sanded desert of the deadlands on their left and the Abyss looming on the far side of it.

Fletcher shuddered at the sight of the endless dark in the distance, remembering the tortured, tentacled creatures that lurked there. The Ceteans.

'Anything at all?' Sylva shouted, her words whipping over Fletcher's shoulder.

Nothing. Nothing but the steady brightening of the sky above. He yelled his answer in her ear and he half heard her growl with frustration.

On they went, with Lysander climbing higher and higher in a bid to see further afield. The temperature fell until the air misted with every breath, puffs of white that were snatched away by the wind. Still they flew, shivering together as they scanned the landscape. Fletcher wished he had Cress's pocket watch – only the light above told him how long they had searched. Two hours? Three?

Sylva kept on until the last vestiges of the dark sky had turned to the honey glow of dawn. Then, finally, they began to spiral down into the wet heat of the jungles below.

'There,' Fletcher called, pointing as Athena's sharp eyes focused on a gap in the canopy. It felt better to choose a clearing, where they would have a line of sight in case of approaching predators, when they landed. It was not unknown for hunters to lie in ambush within undergrowth.

Yet, as the hot air wafted over them and their destination neared, Fletcher saw a flash of white in the glade they were headed for. White stone, bright in the morning light.

'What the hell is that?' Sylva said, as Lysander swooped towards it. He landed in a skitter of scraping claws, slipping over smooth marble.

Fletcher tumbled to the ground with a hard thud, the flat rock bruising his knees. He struggled to his feet and looked around him.

Pale stone pillars stretched up to hold a roof that was no longer there, turned into humps of shattered rubble on the cracked marble floors. Broken statues, worn by years of neglect, stood arrayed in a crescent before them. Creeping vines cascaded from the edges of the jungle, curling around the columns and ruined walls towards the meagre light that filtered through the broken ceiling. There were sweeping symbols engraved upon an arch that curved between two pillars, but they looked like nothing he had seen before.

'Who built this place?' Sylva whispered. 'The orcs couldn't have done this. Could they?'

Her voice echoed around them. It was deathly quiet, the walls seeming to block the noise from the jungle. It felt like a sanctum, built for long-forgotten gods.

Feeling vulnerable, Fletcher summoned Ignatius. The violet light flashed eerily in the dim temple, and the Salamander appeared on the ground.

Ever curious, Ignatius scampered ahead of him to explore. Fletcher followed him, until they neared the half-moon line of statues. The light streamed in from the canopy to illuminate them, acting as a natural skylight.

There were ten statues, standing upon pedestals. Each was a different size and shape. Fletcher approached the five on the far left. All had the upper bodies of a human – two women and three men. Instead of legs, the first man had a finned tail of a fish, complete with carved scales and barbs. The woman beside him was similar, but with the flippers and lower body of a seal. They were beautiful to look at, and each had a crown of shells on their heads.

A slit-nostrilled female followed, her legs like a snake's tail that curved around its pedestal. She wore a crown in the shape of a coiled serpent, and the hair beneath was thick and lustrous. Her steely gaze made Fletcher shudder and move on to the next.

It was a man with the horns of a goat poking from his head, with cloven feet and hairy, strangely jointed legs. Beside, a long-haired male with the lower body of a horse, and a human torso erupting from above the animal's front legs. Both had crowns of thorned branches.

'Are they . . . demons?' Fletcher whispered.

There was a huge statue beside a tiny one in the centre, the first the great, hulking figure of a giant with a misshapen, ogre-like face. His arm had broken off, lying on the floor like a felled tree trunk. Beside, a tiny woman stood proudly on the pedestal, with minuscule features and the wings of a butterfly.

'I know what these are,' Sylva breathed, pointing along the line of the statues Fletcher had examined. 'A Merman, a Selkie, a Lamia, a Satyr and a Centaur.'

'That's a Giant, and a Fairy,' Fletcher added, nodding at the two in the centre, though he had never heard of the creatures Sylva had just named. The two he knew were from Berdon's childhood stories. What were they doing here, in the depths of the ether?

'They're from my people's folklore. My mother used to tell me about them, but they were never supposed to be real,' Sylva said, her eyes wide with surprise. 'Do you know what that is?'

She pointed at a large humanoid, standing as tall as an orc. It appeared as a long-haired gorilla that could stand with the posture of a man. The creature's eyes were gentle and it wore no crown.

'No . . . but that . . . that's an Angel, right?' Fletcher said, peering at a statue on the second-to-last pedestal. It was a man, but this one wore a skirt and breastplate. His crown was studded with what might have been jewels. But what stood out were the enormous wings that erupted from his back, with long, elegant feathers like those of a swan.

'From the creation story of your religion,' Sylva said, raising an eyebrow at Fletcher.

'Nobody remembers that stuff any more,' Fletcher said.

Indeed, the religion of Hominum was little more than a shadow of its former self, the old stories faded from memory to leave a vague concept of heaven and hell. The priests preached and the old flocked to their congregations, but the intricacies of the sins and covenants that the holy men laid out were beyond Fletcher's comprehension.

There was little that remained of the final pedestal. All had gone but the misshapen lumps of what must have been two feet. Something or someone had hacked at the statue, and the fragments that lay on the floor had been broken again into gravel.

'If we ever get back home, you can bet Dame Fairhaven would want to know about these,' Fletcher said, thinking of the kind-hearted librarian.

'I think everyone would,' Sylva replied, tracing her fingers along the carved fairy. Though wind and rain had worn it away, the detailing was still fine enough to see her tiny fingers. She was so small, barely taller than a hand breadth.

'I say we rest here,' Fletcher suggested, pointing at the corner of the temple, where a piece of roof and the two walls still remained and the light was dim from their shadow. 'It doesn't look like any demons shelter in this place – there's no leavings or bones on the ground. It'll be safe.'

Sylva nodded absently, still unable to take her eyes off the statues in front of her.

'Do you think they existed?' she asked, nodding at them.

'Maybe. But this place hasn't been touched in hundreds, maybe thousands of years,' Fletcher said, thinking aloud. 'Whoever built this place, they're long gone now.'

They walked together to the corner and settled down, using the backpack as a makeshift pillow and draping their jackets over themselves like blankets. Lysander curled up at their feet, his large frame cocooning them in. Athena kept watch, her broken wing too painful for her to sleep.

For a moment Fletcher thought Ignatius would try and curl his now larger body around his neck, but then the demon burrowed between him and Sylva, which annoyed Fletcher more than he would like to admit. He was keen to be close to Sylva, even if she was not as warm as the growing imp.

It was quiet and still in the temple, and Fletcher was glad for a sleep without the strange calls and hoots from the wild demons in the jungle, even if it was in the middle of the day.

The minutes ticked by. They lay there in a comfortable silence, warm and content. Or at least, in what Fletcher had thought was a comfortable silence. Sylva cleared her throat.

'Fletcher. You know, about yesterday,' she stammered, then paused awkwardly.

'Hmm?' Fletcher mumbled. He was half asleep, but as his memory of their time in the waterfall swam to the surface, he found himself quickly awake.

Sylva seemed to think for a moment, then spoke again.

'In my culture . . . when a . . . if a high elf and wood elf marry, they're cast out. Shunned by their people, even their own family. They're asked to leave the Great Forest. Then told to leave. Then made to leave.' She spoke in quick bursts, as if it was a struggle to get the words out.

'OK,' Fletcher said.

'They don't like the castes to mix,' Sylva said, and Fletcher could hear the shame in her voice.

'They sound like Jeffrey,' Fletcher said. 'He didn't want any mixing either.'

In the corner of his eye he saw Sylva's face wince at the traitor's name.

'Yes, like Jeffrey,' she said softly.

'Why are you telling me this?' Fletcher asked.

Silence.

'They don't like mixing . . .' Fletcher murmured.

He left his sentence unfinished. Realisation sat like a cold stone in his stomach.

'I just . . . I can't,' Sylva whispered, so quietly that Fletcher wasn't sure if he was supposed to hear it.

Being with him could ruin her. That was what she was saying.

She turned on her side, so he couldn't see her face. He felt so stupid.

'I thought that's what we were fighting against,' he said, and he couldn't keep the bitterness from his voice.

She didn't reply. It was too painful to talk about it. He wanted to pretend that she had just been telling him about her culture, that it didn't mean what he knew it did. But the words left unsaid seemed even louder than if they had been spoken.

He gathered Ignatius into his arms, leaving a gap between himself and Sylva.

It was a long time before he fell asleep.

14

Night fell, and as they flew into the dark skies, the cold and the wind became a blessing in disguise – they had an excuse not to talk. It felt awkward now, to clasp Sylva round her midriff. He hated it. Hated it so much that he almost missed the smoke.

A wisp of black, far in the distance, appeared in the overlay of the scrying stone. Was that the shadowy outline of a mountain beneath? He spoke for the first time in several hours.

'There,' he said, pointing.

He knew Sylva couldn't see it, but his stomach lurched as Lysander corrected their course. Minutes passed as they flew on, staring into the darkness. Already, the first tinge of light above signalled the approach of dawn. They were cutting it close.

'My god,' Fletcher whispered, hope flooding through him like a drug. 'I think we did it.'

The wisp had turned into a column of black smoke, widening as it rose into a mushroom of grey that was lost in the ether's skies. Beneath it was a single peak, jutting from the ground like a vast pyramid, layered with a topping of green forest and dark volcanic soil. The orange glow from the zenith became visible as they neared, the molten lava illuminating an enormous caldera. The lava lake was as large as Vocans' atrium, and the bowl of earth in which it was centred was twice that size again.

As Lysander swooped down towards the crater's edge, the heat hit them like a wave. The hairs on Fletcher's forearms shrivelled as they landed and, then, *boom*: Fletcher turned his head away as a fresh blast radiated from the volcano, beating his face with its force.

There was a thick band of steaming soil around the lip that their boots could barely stand, strewn with boulders that sported surfaces like candlewax. The red-orange pool of lava bubbled and popped, flinging droplets of molten rock that sizzled on the earth. The ground they stood on leaned in an incline towards the deadly lake, and Fletcher's mind reeled with the irrational fear that they were being sucked in towards the incandescent centre.

'How could anything grow in a place like this?' Sylva said, raising her voice so it could be heard over the roiling roar of the lava.

'We need to spread out,' Fletcher said, summoning Ignatius. He knew it was a risk, after what had happened last time the little demon had been near lava.

Still, the Salamander was made for this search, able to approach the hottest areas that they could not reach. He guessed, if it came to it, he could yank the demon out again using a kinetic lasso, as he had done the last time.

Lysander's claws could not take the soil's temperature, nor could Athena's, so the two demons settled on the rim for a well-deserved respite. The Griffin was dead on his feet, the gruelling nights of hard flying and intermittent sleep leaving him sprawled on the cooler soil, his eyes closed with exhaustion.

Ignatius ran ahead of Fletcher as he and Sylva parted ways. They were forced to shelter behind boulders as they rounded the edges of the caldera, darting from rock to rock to protect themselves from the radiating heat as they hunted for the elusive flowers. Nothing could be seen but raw, fuming earth.

Despair began to set in as Fletcher slowly surveyed the volcano's caldera. Nothing. Just dirt, and rock, and fire. They were going to die in this world, choking on the poisonous air as their paralysed lungs lay stricken in their chests.

Sylva must have yelled, but the tumult of the lava meant he realised it only when he glanced up and saw her waving from the other side of the lava pool. It took him five minutes to work his way around; hissing with pain each time he braved the space between boulders to shelter behind.

His heart dropped when he saw what Sylva had found, the image blurred as his eyes teared up from the oppressive dryness. A patch of broken stalks were all she had discovered, growing in the lee of a large boulder. The buds had been removed, torn roughly from their seats. A fragment of yellow petal remained here and there, torn and insubstantial, but enough to confirm these were the plants they were looking for.

'I tried healing them,' Sylva yelled, her face stricken. 'It didn't work.'

'There might be another patch nearby,' Fletcher replied, looking around in desperation. Ignatius was approaching them from the other side, having searched the area he and Sylva had not. The demon yapped, and Fletcher could sense the demon's frustration. Nothing there either.

He fell to his knees and scrunched his eyes tight. They had been so close.

'I thought Jeffrey's journal was going to save us,' Sylva growled, her voice barely discernible over the roar of the volcano. 'All it's done is waste the little time we had left.'

She picked at the remaining fragments of yellow, arranging them in her palm until they were in the shape of one intact petal. Then she brought them to her mouth and chewed slowly.

'This is Euryale all right,' she said, shaking her head with disappointment. 'Five hours' worth.'

Her low voice was barely audible over the volcano's noise, but Fletcher wasn't listening. Jeffrey . . . his name had sparked a memory. In a perverse way, the traitor had helped them get this far. Now, he would unwittingly aid them again, with the spell he'd taught them on their first day in the orc jungles. The growth spell.

'Wait.' Fletcher raised his soil-stained hand and etched in the air.

A symbol gradually formed, shaped like an oval leaf, complete with the webbing of veins through the line bisecting the centre. Fletcher fixed it in place, then aimed it at the patch of withered stalks.

'I hope this works,' he prayed, filling his body with mana.

A stream of green-tinged light flowed from his hand, making a beeline for the broken stalks. His mana drained from him faster than ever before, but the effect was nearly instantaneous. The stalks erupted into bloom: fat, waxy petals unfurling and twisting into a conch-like bud.

'Fletcher, you genius!' Sylva screamed, wrapping him in a fierce hug. For a moment she forgot herself and clung to him, and it was only Fletcher's hesitantly returned embrace that made her pull away.

Embarrassed, she avoided his eyes and plucked a bud from a stem. Detached from its base, the petals separated into a pile on her hand. There was a dozen of them. Looking at the twenty-odd flowers, Fletcher calculated that they had bought another—

'Ten days,' he said, thinking aloud. 'That's not enough.'

'No, Fletcher, don't you get it?' Sylva said, grinning from ear to ear.

She had already removed most of the flowers, stuffing them into her pockets. Fletcher joined in, mystified.

She lifted her own fingers as the last of the petals were poured into Fletcher's satchel. This time, she etched the growth spell in the air herself, pointing it at the plants they had just deflowered. Understanding dawned on Fletcher as another flash of green made them bloom once more.

'Twenty days.' She winked, bending to harvest them again.

Fletcher stuffed a few more bunches into his pocket. Then he froze . . . something was wrong.

'Ignatius.'

He spun, only to see the mischievous Salamander haring towards the lava, wading through puddles on the borders of the main pool. Fletcher leaped to his feet and sprinted after him, ignoring the blast of heat that enveloped his body as he left the shelter of the boulder.

'Stop!' he yelled, his voice hoarse with the dry air.

He whipped out a kinetic lasso, but the Salamander was already too far away. Ignatius hurled himself aside, easily evading the translucent line of shimmering mana. Fletcher skidded to his knees. This was the second time one of his demons had disobeyed him. They didn't have time for this.

He closed his eyes and concentrated, grasping his mind's connection with Ignatius and ordering him to stop. But the demon's consciousness was as slippery as an eel, evading his mental grasp.

'Fletcher, what are you doing?' Sylva shouted.

Ignatius was in the very centre of the lava pit now – Fletcher could see the demon's burgundy head bobbing along, like an otter swimming in a lake. He'd never be able to reach that small, distant target with a kinetic lasso.

Worse still, he couldn't move any closer – it was too hot, his feet were burning, even through the leather, and he could barely keep his eyes open as the dry heat crashed over him.

Perhaps the shield spell, to protect himself from the heat? Then, to his surprise, the head disappeared. Ignatius had dived.

There was nothing Fletcher could do for him now. All he could do was wait.

He staggered to his feet and turned back, the oppressive temperature so powerful that he felt as if his eyebrows were being burned from his face. Cursing, he ran back to the shelter of the boulder and collapsed in its shadow.

'Goddamn mischievous little imp,' he growled. 'He's gone for a swim in the lava again.'

Sylva was stuffing petals back into her pack. Strangely, she had dug out each plant, unearthing the stems and clods of soil with their root networks exposed. She caught his expression and shrugged.

'I'm out of mana, but we've got thirty more days in the ether now,' she said. Then she pointed at the plants. 'If we take these with us, maybe we can regrow them later.'

'Won't they die without the volcano's heat?' Fletcher asked. 'Maybe I should use up my mana to regrow them again too; Ignatius is just going to drain it all anyway.'

But he never heard Sylva's answer.

Fear. Sudden and all-encompassing, filling his body. Athena had seen something, and the pink overlay of his crystal came into stark focus as he sought the source. He froze.

Wyverns. They were heading straight for the volcano, already so close that Fletcher could make out the colourful riders on their backs and the long tails that lashed behind them. Leading the pack was the pale form of the white orc, astride the smaller Ahool.

'Sylva, they've found us,' Fletcher said, frantically scooping the plants and petals into their satchel. 'We have to leave, now!'

It was all so obvious. The stripped flowers – few demons would brave the heat and height of the volcano to eat them. It had been the orcs. They had come here to harvest and lie in wait, knowing the fugitives would need them eventually.

There was a thud as Lysander landed beside them, hunching in the shelter of the boulder. His plumage was singed and smoking – he had flown directly over the centre of the volcano.

Athena leaped down from his back, and Fletcher swiftly infused her. Her added weight would do them little good. Weight . . .

'Get on,' Sylva yelled, mounting Lysander with the satchel slung over her shoulder. 'We'll come back for Ignatius later.'

But Fletcher couldn't. On a good day, Lysander was faster than the Wyverns, maybe even the Ahool and the dozens of lesser demons in the Wyvern's entourage too. But with their combined weights on his back, in his current, exhausted state? Not a chance.

'We'll never make it,' Fletcher said, the words like stones in his mouth. 'Not the two of us. He's dead on his feet.'

Fletcher saw the understanding in Sylva's eyes, but she shook her head, as if to dislodge the truth of his words.

'You're wrong,' she said, and Fletcher could see a tear cutting a trail through her soot-stained face. She glared at him defiantly.

'I can't leave Ignatius,' Fletcher said, almost gently.

At that moment he knew. Perhaps he had always known, deep down. Khan would never personally lead his entire air force on a dangerous mission into the ether for a mere five fugitives. Or, at least, not for this long, nor this far.

He was here for a prophecy. For the Salamander that had been seen in the battle in the pyramid, the same one that was engraved on the walls of their most sacred place. He was here for Ignatius.

The Wyverns would arrive any minute. He slapped Lysander on the rump and the Griffin leaped into the air like a startled horse.

'Look after my mother,' he yelled.

'I'll come back for you,' Sylva shouted, her words half lost in the air.

Then they were gone.

15

Fletcher didn't bother hiding. Instead, he moved further from the lava, where the air was cooler and he could hear himself think. If he was lucky, the orcs would stop here, instead of following Sylva. She needed as much time as he could get her.

He could feel Athena struggling within him. She wanted to be summoned, to fight alongside him. He refused – better to keep the injured demon safe within him.

As for Ignatius, this time the Salamander was using up Fletcher's mana as swiftly as he had in the lava pit beneath the pyramid, but somehow gaining it even faster from some unknown source. It was as if the demon was converting the volcano's heat into mana.

Fletcher loosened his khopesh in his scabbard and pulled his pistols from their holsters. Three shots – relatively useless against the armoured skin of the Wyverns, but they might take out a shaman, if he aimed well. Perhaps even Khan himself.

He'd save Blaze for that one – the longer, rifled barrel would give him a more accurate shot. Then his death wouldn't be for nothing.

At the thought of his death, Fletcher felt a tight knot of fear in the pit of his stomach. He fought to ignore it, even as it seemed to swell within him.

The first Wyverns swooped in on the other side of the lava pool, their dark shapes shimmering in the hot air. They must have been able to see him, yet none approached. Instead, the shamans dismounted and spread in a half circle on the other side of the bubbling lake, giving Fletcher a wide berth. Too bad they were out of pistol range.

It did not take long for Khan to arrive. He had only been waiting for them to secure the perimeter. Fletcher watched him land, his pale form stark against the black volcanic soil.

To his dismay, a single Wyvern and what looked like the entire flock of Shrikes, Vesps and Strixs flew on overhead, high above him. They had spotted Sylva – he only hoped she had enough of a head start to lose them.

Fletcher tried to power up his shield spell, but the pull of mana from Ignatius was too strong, so much so that even Athena's supply had already been drained. Spellcraft would not help Fletcher now.

He heard Khan bark an order, and saw something strange happening across the lava. White light was streaming from the shamans, twisting across the earth and around the pit towards him. It was like a flood of opaque water, flowing a few inches above the ground. Shield spells.

Fletcher retreated, but in seconds it had reached him. For a moment he thought the wave was going to engulf his body, but then it reared up a few feet away and wrapped around him like a bubble, leaving him contained in a sphere of translucent light. He was trapped.

Athena would be able to break through it – the energy that demons were composed of tore shields apart – but it would take a few seconds for a demon of her size to get through one so thick. He sheathed Gale, his double-barrelled, shorter pistol, and curled his hand into a fist, so that his pentacle tattoo was hidden. It was the one card he had left to play.

It was only when the shield completely encompassed Fletcher that Khan began his approach, walking casually along the outer rim, his skirt fluttering in the hot air. He was holding the largest macana war club Fletcher had ever seen.

It was almost as tall as a man, but thinner than the broad clubs the orcs normally used, a single hand breadth wide rather than two. Instead of the usual rectangular shards of obsidian embedded intermittently along the sides, this club's shards were aligned to leave a single sharp edge all the way around. It was a deadly weapon, and the orc handled it with practised ease, resting it on his shoulder as his long legs carried him onwards.

Fletcher's breath caught in his throat, and he forced each one down in tight gulps of air. This was his enemy. His nemesis.

This was it.

The gun was slippery in his hands, though whether the sweat was from the heat or his nerves he could not tell. All he knew was that the shield that surrounded him was too thick to penetrate with a gunshot. He leaned his forehead against its wall, feeling the slippery cool of the spell on his skin.

All eight feet of the albino orc stopped beside the shield. He towered so high that Fletcher had to crane his neck to see his face. The red, baleful eyes stared down at him, with the twin tusks on either side of his mouth framing a cruel smile.

To Fletcher's surprise, Khan dropped to one knee, so that the orc's face was but a few inches from his own. Then, the orc spoke.

'Just a boy,' he growled, the words guttural in his mouth.

Fletcher gaped, and the orc unleashed a deep, throaty laugh at his captive's expression.

'Yes, I speak your tongue,' Khan chuckled.

His speech was clearer than the matronly Mother's had been; the smaller tusks he sported were less of an impediment.

'How?' Fletcher asked, the question leaving his mouth before he could bite it back.

'The woman *you* stole from us,' Khan said, pointing a finger accusingly at Fletcher. 'A useful teacher,' the orc continued, scratching his chin. 'She thought we had her baby, so I said I would kill it if she refused. That was enough. Of course, when she outlived her usefulness, I told her we had killed it anyway. I'm sure you've seen what that did to her.'

He laughed again, but Fletcher noticed that he never broke eye contact. The orc was goading him. The words cut Fletcher to his very soul, but he forced down the anger. He needed the orc to lose his temper, lower the shield. Just long enough for him to get off a shot.

'My name is Fletcher Raleigh and I *am* that child,' Fletcher said, defiantly. 'I slaughtered your goblins and buried your shamans' demons in the rubble of your most holy place. I copied your keys to the ether and stole your slaves. Me. Just a boy.'

It was his turn to laugh, though it felt fake and forced.

Khan's face was expressionless, but Fletcher could see he had struck a nerve, for the orc's hand had tightened on his macana. Fletcher pressed on.

'You brought all of your Wyverns to hunt me down. I bet our forces have been running rampant across your homeland, while we've led you on a merry chase across the face of another world. I bet—'

'Enough!' Khan slammed his fist into the side of the shield. It cracked ever so slightly. 'Your mother was a dog that we fed on scraps,' he hissed through the shield, spittle spraying from his mouth. 'She barked for us and slept in her own filth. We beat her for the joy of it until she lost her senses, then we beat her some more. I piss on her memory.'

Fletcher recoiled from the sudden torrent of hatred, all pretence of his bravado forgotten.

As if surprised by his own outburst, Khan smoothed back his long hair and stepped back. There was a mad gleam in his eye and he broke into a smile.

'Where is your demon?' he asked.

'Dead,' Fletcher replied, his mind racing. 'And she took many of your demons with her.'

It made sense too: that Fletcher was alone and had no mana to create a shield of his own.

'The Canid, yes?' Khan mused. 'A shame, I was hoping . . .'

He paused, then asked, 'Which of you has the Salamander? Is it your friend?'

He motioned in the direction that Sylva had flown. His question was casual, but he was watching Fletcher too closely.

It was all Fletcher could do not to flick his eyes to the pool of lava. Ignatius was still pulsing with mana. It was hard to think, for the demon's consciousness was growing so large that Fletcher thought his mind would burst.

'Well?' Khan asked.

Fletcher didn't answer, simply meeting Khan's gaze as confidently as he could.

'No matter, I shall find it soon enough,' the orc declared.

'Why do you care? You want another of them?' Fletcher asked.

This time it was Khan's turn to look surprised.

'We saw you with it, in the central chamber. We were hidden in the beams above you.'

Khan wrinkled his nose with irritation.

'Salamanders are my property, by birthright,' Khan growled. 'It is written on the walls of our temple.'

Fletcher eyed the crack in the shield. Another blow might allow Athena to break through fast enough. The hole would be sufficient for him to shoot Blaze through. He kept the pistol still by his side and went back on the offensive.

'I have seen these carvings,' Fletcher said, layering his voice with disdain. 'From what I saw, a Salamander could belong to a freak like you *or* a human. Not that there's anything special about Salamanders anyway. Powerful for a level-five demon, but a Wyvern would eat one for breakfast. Or a Canid for that matter.'

'Do not speak of things you do not understand,' Khan snarled. 'The significance is not what a Salamander is, but what it can become.'

103

'You're talking out of your arse,' Fletcher said, shrugging. 'The heathen beliefs of savages.'

Khan bellowed with anger.

'Do you know what a Drake is, boy? Or a Dragon?' Khan asked, his eyes wild. 'A human might be allowed to dream of controlling a Drake, the first stage in a Salamander's metamorphosis. But the next – a Dragon. No, only one of *my* kind, a "freak" with my summoning level could do that. This is why the prophecy foretells a Salamander as the key to victory. And now I will take them both.'

Khan was babbling, the mask of reason gone to leave only raw insanity behind his red eyes.

'I was born to destroy your kind. We will burn your cities to the ground and salt the earth behind us. Blood will run in the streets. None shall be spared, not the infants nor the elders. We will leave Hominum a wasteland. In a hundred years, nobody will remember your race even existed.'

Fletcher ignored him. Drakes? Dragons? He had never heard those words before. They were probably the orc's ancient gods, or some such rubbish.

It was so hard to think. Ignatius's consciousness was huge, as if the heat of the volcano had inflated the demon's presence. Thankfully, it had stopped growing, having filled the constraints of Fletcher's mind. Together, they had reached some milestone, but there was another one that Fletcher could feel Ignatius desiring, far beyond what he had already achieved. Fletcher felt like his mind would shatter if they continued on.

Not that it mattered. All that mattered was that he kill Khan. Perhaps if he tried to take mana from Ignatius again, or weakened the crack with two shots from Gale first . . .

As Fletcher tried to grasp his connection with Ignatius, Khan stood and sighed, his angry tirade seeming to have exhausted him. Then he grinned slyly as Fletcher's hand strayed to his holstered pistol.

'Perhaps you would like me to widen that crack for you, Fletcher,' the orc said.

Fletcher's eyes flicked guiltily away from the shield's fissure, and Khan's smile broadened. A stream of white light flowed from his long fingers, spreading another layer over the shield, until the surface was clouded white with the thickness of the sphere.

Fletcher watched Khan lift his curled fingers and slowly clench his fist. To Fletcher's horror, the shield began to shrink, constricting and thickening as the white walls moved closer and closer. He smashed Blaze against the side, but it was as much use as punching a brick wall.

Then, something stirred in the recesses of Fletcher's mind. Ignatius had sensed Fletcher's panic – Athena's consciousness seemed to be screaming, pulsing signals down her own connection with the Salamander. Ignatius was coming.

'Wait!' Fletcher shouted, pounding the slippery shield with his fists. 'I'll tell you who owns the Salamander.'

The shield stopped contracting, though Fletcher had to hunch to stop his head from scraping the top. He could sense Ignatius swimming towards the surface, powering through the lava with furious abandon. The demon would be on them in seconds.

'Tell me,' Khan growled, his baleful eyes shining ruby red through the opaque surface. 'And I'll make your death a quick one.'

Fletcher leaned in close until his face was inches from the orc's own.

'Me,' Fletcher whispered.

Ignatius breached the lava in a burst of molten orange. Fletcher saw a flash of burgundy as the shield was slashed apart, felt a sinuous neck slip under his legs and heave him on to broad shoulders.

He swivelled and fired Blaze, saw the white orc jerked back by the impact of the bullet.

Then he was over the edge of the caldera and falling into empty space.

16

No. Not falling. Flying.

There were wings on either side, gliding through the air, and he could see Ignatius's amber eyes gazing back at him. But to Fletcher's amazement, it was an Ignatius he no longer recognised.

The demon had grown to be as large as Lysander. He had the same turtle-like beak, four legs and spiked tail as before, but his neck was longer now and he had grown two short, back-facing horns on his head. Most striking of all were the huge, leathery wings erupting from his shoulders and down his back. He was a Salamander no longer.

In shock, Fletcher turned to see the albino orc standing on the edge of the volcano's rim, clutching a wounded shoulder as his long hair streamed behind him. Khan bellowed with hatred and raised his arm, waving on the demons that followed. The Wyverns sailed above, their mouths gaping wide with anticipation of the meal to come.

'Get us out of here!' Fletcher yelled, sheathing Blaze and tugging Gale from his holster.

The world tilted as Ignatius angled his wings upwards, beating the air to drive them higher into the sky. He was aiming for a bank of clouds above them, an insubstantial haze that might hide them from their pursuers. Far below, the rolling jungles seemed to shrink and merge into a smear of green, ringed by the red band of the deadlands beyond.

But they were slow. Fletcher could sense Ignatius's exhaustion from the transformation, and the confusion at the changes that the volcano had wrought on his body. He was unco-ordinated, unused to navigating the eddies of the wind that buffeted them.

The Wyverns were gaining, slowly but surely. Each was twice as large as Ignatius, with serrated claws and mouths full of fearsome teeth. There were eleven of them, but just one could easily tear them to shreds. Worse still, Fletcher could tell Ignatius was drained of mana – it had all been used up in his transformation. There was no more than a trickle left, barely enough for a weak shield from Fletcher or a single gout of Ignatius's flame.

Even as that realisation hit him, the first fireballs buzzed past, streaking the air with smoking trails. He turned as a javelin whistled above his head, disappearing into the cloud bank. The shamans were crouching on the backs of their Wyverns, balancing precariously while they hurled their spells and projectiles.

He pointed Gale at the nearest pursuer, but his aim was spoiled by the frantic beat of Ignatius's wings. Then, before he could fire, they were in the mist, surrounded by a fog of white. Fletcher tentatively grasped his connection with Ignatius. It felt stronger than before. He used it to change Ignatius's trajectory, to better lose their pursuers in the fog. Soon they were gliding through the white cloud, listening to the whistle of the breeze, the guttural barks of the shamans and the low roars of their Wyverns as they hunted through the mist.

The wind tore at Fletcher's hair and the mist coated his body with dew, drawing the heat away and leaving his exposed skin prickled with gooseflesh. He pressed himself against Ignatius, whose body was still piping hot from the pool of lava. The closeness helped steady Fletcher's frazzled nerves, for his heart was hammering within his chest.

It was different to riding Lysander; Fletcher felt secure in the natural hollow of Ignatius's back, the cloth of his breeches finding easy purchase against the burgundy skin beneath. He gripped the demon's neck, revelling in the powerful muscles that flexed beneath. This had to be the Drake demon that Khan had spoken of.

Ignatius stretched his neck, and Fletcher could feel his exhilaration as Ignatius tested the limits of his new body. The demon lashed his tail, cutting a score through the cloudbanks. His confusion was fading fast. Now . . . determination. Purpose.

A shadow loomed beneath them. The rasp of orcish speech, louder this time. More dark forms, above and on either side; murky, but growing larger. The shamans knew they were close. In seconds the Wyverns would be upon them.

So they would do the unthinkable. Fletcher sent his orders, wrapping one arm around Ignatius's neck and gripping the double-barrelled pistol with his free hand. It was time to fight back.

Now.

Ignatius folded his wings and Fletcher's stomach somersaulted as they hurtled downwards, then there was a bone-juddering thud as Ignatius crashed into the Wyvern beneath. The world spun in a kaleidoscope of whites and greens as two demons grappled in the air, plummeting out of the clouds. A leathery wing slammed against Fletcher's face, but Ignatius had caught the Wyvern from above and the demon could not turn to slash with its claws. Blood sprayed from Ignatius's beak as he snapped at the exposed neck, lacerating the scaly hide to expose the raw flesh beneath. The Wyvern's roars of pain and fury were so loud that Fletcher's eardrums throbbed, then popped as their altitude dropped at stomach-churning speeds.

A vice-like grip took hold of Fletcher's ankle, dragging him down. He fired blindly over his shoulder, felt the kick nearly pluck the gun from his hand, heard the grunt of pain before it was snatched away by the wind. The world flipped again and the body of the shaman tumbled past, a blur of grey tinged with red and yellow warpaint.

Green jungle came into focus beyond, rushing up to meet them.

'Break!' Fletcher screamed, and Ignatius released the Wyvern with a reluctant roar. His wings unfurled and Fletcher was thrown forward with the impetus, his head thudding into the burgundy back, half knocking him unconscious. A gut-churning swoop – so desperate and low that Fletcher heard the crackle of the tree canopy as Ignatius's claws tore through it – followed by the sickening thud of the Wyvern smashing into the earth below.

The nosedive had given them a boost of speed so that they streaked over the treetops, but Fletcher knew from his studies that they would actually cover far less ground at such a low altitude. He shook his head to gather his scrambled thoughts, cursing. There hadn't been time to plan this far ahead.

He looked up and his breath caught in his throat. The other Wyverns were already diving towards them, claws outstretched and mouths yawning, revealing the pink maws within. They had one choice.

Fletcher closed his eyes, holstered his pistol and gripped Ignatius's neck with both arms. He could feel Ignatius's fear as the Drake sensed his intentions, but there was no other way. Fletcher lowered his head and gave the order.

His stomach flipped once more and then leaves were slapping at his face. Gnarled trunks flashed by as Ignatius jinked left and right, flinging Fletcher about like a rag doll. Above, the Wyverns roared in frustration, their greater size preventing them from penetrating the maze of trees. Ignatius slowed, gliding through the jungle as Fletcher listened to the bellows above. The Wyverns were tracking them, soaring above their position and waiting for an opening.

A voice echoed down, tight with fury.

'This only ends one way, Fletcher Raleigh,' Khan bellowed.

So, the albino orc had caught up – there was still a chance to kill him. Fletcher almost wished that Ignatius had attacked instead of fleeing from the scene – but they would have had only seconds before the Wyverns were upon them.

Still, the orc was right. The tangle of branches and trees were all that protected him from the Wyverns above – a break in the canopy would permit the monsters to get at them.

'Why don't you come down and face me then?' Fletcher

yelled, goading the wounded orc. 'Your Ahool against my Drake.'

Silence. Then: 'When you're dead, I will make him my own,' the orc barked. 'My Ahool can smell your fear from here. She will track you to the ends of the ether.'

The ends of the ether. The shadow of an idea formed in Fletcher's mind. Again, Ignatius's mind filled with fear at Fletcher's intent. Even Athena was against it. It would be like running through a hail of bullets and hoping they hit his pursuers instead.

'This way,' Fletcher murmured in Ignatius's ear, coaxing him in a new direction. The loyal Drake turned without hesitation, trusting his master's judgement. Fletcher only wished that he trusted himself as much as Ignatius did. It was madness – but it was the only idea he had.

On they flew. A herd of Indrik gazed at them as they passed by, great giraffe-like creatures with mottled grey fur, thick elephantine legs and heads more akin to horses. A pack of mangy Canids prowled in their wake, waiting for a youngster to separate from the herd. The jungle was alive with sounds: the buzzing of lesser Mites close by, and in the distance, the deep lowing of a Gunni – a strange creature that Fletcher knew looked much like a bear-sized wombat with antlers.

But Fletcher could barely take it in, for he had to thread Ignatius through the thicker parts of the forest, where the Wyverns would struggle to follow. He felt a pang of guilt at his good fortune in one respect – the shaman's smaller demons had followed Sylva. Only the Ahool could make a proper pursuit, but Fletcher knew that Khan was too smart for that. Even so, he drew Gale out of its holster in case he was wrong.

112

Ignatius saw it before he did, jolting a warning through Fletcher's mind. A flash of red sand ahead, where the trees began to thin. The deadlands.

Now.

Ignatius picked up speed, hurling himself through the air with haste borne of desperation. They shot out of the jungle like a musket ball, half blinded by the bright desert sky as they left the shadowy confines of the trees.

The Wyverns roared, but Fletcher knew he had caught them by surprise – they had not thought he would leave the safety of the undergrowth. They had a slim head start. A chance.

The red dust of the deadlands hung in the air above the dry landscape, coating Fletcher's cloud-wetted skin in a fine layer of red. He squinted through the haze as Ignatius soared over the rust-coloured sands. The ground below was littered with boulders, funnelling the wind into whirling cyclones of dust that stretched into the sky, trundling across the barren terrain.

Behind, a fireball sizzled the air, slamming into Ignatius's side. His haunch shook like a horse shooing a fly – the fire would do little damage to a Drake. Fletcher was not so lucky; the next singed his hair and baked his face as it crackled past his left ear.

He turned and saw that the nearest Wyvern was so close it was snapping at Ignatius's lashing tail, its teeth gnashing in dangerous proximity. The shaman stood with a javelin poised, but Fletcher levelled his pistol and the Wyvern veered away to protect its master. It thudded into the Wyvern behind and the two tangled in the air, buying them precious seconds.

'Faster,' Fletcher cried, pressing himself down to make a

smaller target. Ignatius's wings thrummed the air in the final stretch towards their destination. The Abyss.

It yawned before them, endless darkness beyond the sheer cliffs that made up the disc's edge. They shot into the depths. This was where he would find out if his bet had paid off.

The orc territory was several days' flight from the ether's edge and separated by a mountain range. He had guessed that the orcs rarely roamed here; their knowledge of the creatures that lurked in the Abyss would be limited.

Behind, the Wyverns baulked. Fletcher knew that the demons would be filled with fear, yet unable to communicate why to their masters. He could see the shamans urging on their demons, until the first five swooped into the veiled recesses over the cliff line.

Ignatius flew deeper still, for the Wyverns hesitated, circling where the light still reached them. Fletcher raised his sword in fake triumph, as if he were escaping into the gloom. He tried to ignore the yawning darkness beneath him, and the extreme danger he had put himself in.

Even as Khan hung back, his Ahool refusing to go over the edge, his bellows urged the remainder on, until the entire squadron of ten was soaring over the bottomless expanse beneath, leaving their leader behind.

The sky above was dark as pitch, and Fletcher could see the Wyverns silhouetted against the ring of light from the rim beyond. Ignatius slowed and turned to face them, even as the inky depths stirred beneath. This was it.

A tentacle whipped out of the void, snatching a Wyvern from the air and dragging it screaming into the Abyss. More followed, flailing at the panicked Wyverns. Fireballs streaked at random as the demons scattered in panic.

Then the first Ceteans rose from the gloom. Fletcher froze in terror as he saw the clustered eyes that blinked at random, and gaping maws filled with serrated teeth. A mess of pincers and tentacles grew from their tortured bodies – none looked exactly alike but all were a nightmarish mishmash of organs and limbs. He could hear the monsters' high-pitched squeals of agony all around him, and felt a strange mix of pity and horror.

Ignatius was already moving, spinning in the air as the first tentacles reached towards them. Fletcher's world flipped again and again as Ignatius flitted to and fro. It was out of his hands now. All he could do was hold on, trying not to scream as the tentacles whipped by.

Already three Wyverns were gone, and another flew riderless towards the rim, its purpose forgotten. Six remained, swooping desperately to avoid the grasping Ceteans. Far away, the black dot of Khan's Ahool hung in the air, watching half his air force disappear in a matter of seconds.

A jerk wracked Ignatius's body, nearly throwing Fletcher from his perch. A tentacle had ensnared Ignatius's midriff. The Drake roared in panic as they were dragged down, beating his wings desperately to slow the inexorable pull towards the massed monsters waiting below.

Fletcher turned and fired Gale's second barrel into the tentacle, but it held fast, the octopus-like suckers rooted to Ignatius's skin. He cursed and tugged free his khopesh, hacking desperately at the rubbery appendage. The wounds spurted a putrid white liquid with every strike, near blinding him. Still they fell, and Fletcher thought that any minute they would be torn apart by tooth-lined gullets.

Another tentacle lashed towards them, but a blast from the last of Ignatius's fire-breath sent it writhing away. Then the tentacle parted with a final chop from the khopesh, and Ignatius propelled them back into the sky.

The severed tip fell away, only to be fought over by the slavering monsters below. All around them, the corpses of the fallen Wyverns created similar battles for sustenance, and the frenzy gave Ignatius a brief respite. Fletcher looked back at their pursuers.

The Wyverns were fleeing – Fletcher could see six forms floating above the rim; five remaining Wyverns and the smaller Ahool. Khan watched from the relative safety of the deadlands, where only the longest tentacles could reach him.

Fletcher grinned and waved, knowing he had struck a blow for Hominum that would cripple the orcish air force. In one fell stroke, Fletcher had taken out half of the flying shamans' primary demons. Far in the distance, he heard Khan's bellow of rage, echoing faintly above the slobbering squeals of the monstrosities below.

But Fletcher was not safe yet. He could not return; the Wyverns would be waiting for him. Nor could he stay, for the Ceteans would soon turn their attention back to him.

It was time to test a theory that had been debated by Vocans' scholars for hundreds of years. That Ceteans did not live beyond the borders of the ether. The theory had never been proven, as no summoner's demon had ever made the attempt. But the distraction of the Wyverns had given Fletcher the chance to try.

So, Ignatius turned away and flew on, into the Abyss.

17

Hours had passed – at least ten, for Fletcher had been forced to eat two petals from his pockets. Ignatius's wingbeats slowed, until they were gliding. It was as if the whole universe had disappeared, for the black of night engulfed them from every side. All was darkness, but for the band of light from the ether, far, far away. And it was cold . . . a cold that Fletcher did not believe possible.

Fletcher would have long frozen to death, were it not for the warmth of Ignatius's back. Even so, as the minutes ticked by and the light in the distance grew gradually larger, he wondered if he had left it too late to turn back. His teeth chattered endlessly and gouts of steam poured from his mouth.

The orcs would think him long dead, but in case they remained, he had taken Ignatius in a long curve that would bring him around to the part of the Abyss near the lagoon, saving him time on their journey back.

His hunch had been right, the theory proven. There were no Ceteans this deep into the Abyss – for there was no food, nor light, nor warmth. The monsters always gathered around the edges of the ether's disc, hoping for unwary demons to snatch from the clifftops, hibernating or cannibalising each other while they waited.

There was now one problem; crossing back into the ether. He had two things to his advantage. The first was the element of surprise; the Ceteans would never expect prey to come from behind – their eyes would be firmly focused on the cliff's edge.

Second, the frenzy that he had witnessed might have attracted Ceteans from all around to join in the feast, pulling their numbers away from the border he was approaching. Wyverns were enormous demons; five of them at once would be more food than the rabid monstrosities had ever seen in the same place. If they were lucky, there would be no Ceteans near their crossing point at all.

He could see the rim now, cliffs of red stone topped by the arid desert of the deadlands. Ignatius, tired though he was, increased the tempo of his wingbeats. All Fletcher could do was stare into the depths below, hoping against hope that the Ceteans were feasting, far away.

He held his breath. Nothing. Still nothing.

Then warmth, the glow of the sky washing over him like a hot bath, wicking away the chill that had sunk into his very bones. Relief, and a chirr of joy from Ignatius. Red sand, sweeping beneath them. They were safe now.

It would be so easy to close his eyes. To sleep.

Green, rushing below him. Warm breeze. The heady scent of vegetation, like fresh cut grass, thick in his nostrils.

He sat up, wincing as his stiff, bruised body ached. Somehow, he had fallen asleep. Or passed out. But it didn't matter, all he knew was that the monstrous creatures were far behind, even if they would haunt his dreams for years to come.

Ignatius was flying low, just above the canopy, where the rays from the fading light above drenched them in warmth. The Drake, drained of the mana that helped heat his body, had suffered in the cold expanse of the Abyss as much as he had.

He leaned forward and patted Ignatius on the neck. The demon had saved him, risking life and limb in the process.

Fletcher could sense Ignatius's exhaustion, and knew that they could not keep it up for much longer. But the demon was also filled with anticipation, as if they were nearing something. Fletcher looked up.

The lagoon. It shone like a silver platter, sparkling as the gentle waves shivered to and fro. He was thirsty, covered in soot, soil and the effluent from the Ceteans. It would be heaven, to dive in and take it all in. He could sense Ignatius had the same intention.

But something was wrong. Ignatius could hear something – already the demon was changing his path, beating his wings in a sudden urgency. A feeling of anger, of protectiveness. Then Fletcher heard it too. A roar, then a scream. Sylva?

'Come on!' Fletcher yelled, willing the exhausted demon onwards. He was bone tired, out of ammunition and had barely a trickle of mana left. But he was going into battle once more.

He was angry now. They had not come this far for it to end like this, his friends slaughtered, his mother dead. He snarled through his teeth, tugging his khopesh from its scabbard. Already he could see fireballs streaking into the sky, the demons battling on a long stretch of white beach, sandwiched by jungle and azure water.

A lone Wyvern, slashing at Lysander, the Griffin staggering, his feathers slick with blood. The corpses of lesser demons inert on the sand, others flapping and tearing at three figures, fighting back to back. Another hunched in their midst. His mother.

The wind ripped at his hair as they shot headlong into the mêlée, roaring their hatred.

Ignatius struck the Wyvern with the speed of a runaway carriage, his beak ripping into the great beast. Fletcher was hurled through the air in the tumult of claws and wings. He landed in a tangle of limbs on the sand. He lay, motionless, his strength almost gone.

'Fletcher, watch out!' Sylva screamed, and he rolled instinctively aside. There was a thud as something thumped into the sand beside him.

He leaped to his feet and slashed blindly; he felt the jar of his blade striking, saw the shaman fall to his knees, the blade halfway through his neck. Fletcher kicked the corpse from his sword, the rage taking him running towards the Wyvern.

Pain pulsed in his mind. Ignatius flew through the air, blood spraying the sand crimson as he landed in the shallows. He lay there, motionless.

Lysander limped forward as if to fight once more, but he collapsed after a few paces. A furrow of red had been clawed down his side.

The Wyvern turned, its eyes focused on Fletcher, and he suddenly realised how puny his sword was against the monstrosity before him. He backed away, slowly. His knees trembled with exhaustion, barely able to bear his weight. He could hardly stand, let alone run.

The Wyvern took a step forward, winged forearms outstretched, blood dripping from its snout and a deep wound in its chest. The shaman's control had gone, but the wild beast was in pain, confused and angry. They were vicious beasts by nature, and this one would still remember its master's intentions.

Fletcher froze, hoping it would give up.

But it was no use. The Wyvern did not hesitate, leaping across the sand. He fell back, saw the flash of the reddened mouth gaping wide. Then something bowled out of the jungle, thudding into the Wyvern's side to take it, screeching, into the water.

Sheldon.

The Zaratan had the Wyvern by the throat, his beak clamped on either side of its scaled neck as he dragged it into the shallows and beyond. Together, the two demons disappeared into the lagoon, dark shapes beneath the surface. Blood clouded the water red, then frothed white as the demons struggled below.

Fletcher turned, just in time to see Tosk blast the last of their assailants from the sky with a streak of lightning – a bee-striped Vesp that landed with a splash in the shallows.

He collapsed to his knees as the others rushed towards him – Sylva, Othello, Cress. Their faces crowded in, but he ignored them, looking for Ignatius. He sighed with relief as the Drake crawled on to the beach and used his tongue to lather healing saliva on a nasty gash in the burgundy flesh of his side.

'Lysander. Look after Lysander,' Fletcher managed, waving the others on to the injured demon behind him. There was a flash of white as the trio dashed past him and blasted the healing spell. He let out a long breath, as if he had been holding it in for a long time. The Griffin would live.

And so would his friends.

18

Sheldon was dying. The Zaratan had surfaced from the bloodied water a few minutes later, beside the drowned corpse of the Wyvern. But the battle had taken a terrible toll on the poor demon.

He was wounded horrifically, for the savage beast had slashed frantically at his head, neck and limbs while he held it beneath the surface. They watched helplessly as he dragged himself up the beach and collapsed in the crimson sand, breathing shallowly in the dim dusk light.

The team did their best to heal him with the last of their mana, but to no avail. The Zaratan had lost too much blood, something the healing spell could do nothing about.

Cress took it the hardest, lying beside him and stroking his head through the night. Sylva stayed with her in silent solidarity, reading Jeffrey's journal by firelight.

As they waited for the inevitable, Fletcher spoke into the growing darkness, telling them of his conversation with Khan, Ignatius's transformation and his escape from the Wyverns. In turn, Sylva told of the desperate chase she had endured across the ether, how she had thought she had lost them, only to be ambushed on the beach but a few hours after finding the others, just before Fletcher had arrived.

Then, as the night began to wane, Othello explained how Sheldon had left them on the land and disappeared soon after Fletcher and Sylva had left, and of his surprise that the Zaratan had returned.

And finally, as the pink light of dawn began to tinge the sky, sleep took hold of them.

Fletcher woke to find that Sheldon had passed while he slept. Cress, heartbroken, was sobbing into Sylva's shoulder, the pair clutching each other like sailors in a storm. Othello sat dejectedly nearby, his hand pressed against Sheldon's shell.

Feeling empty, Fletcher went to sit beside the demon's body, searching for words that would not come. The Zaratan had saved them a thousand times over and given his life in the process. He had no loyalty to them, no connection like a summoner and his demon might have. That he was not harnessed as other demons were, and had protected them regardless, was testament to Sheldon's great intelligence and compassion. They mourned him as they would a friend.

'I thought he might make it,' Sylva sniffed, her usual composure gone.

'He didn't seem to be in pain,' Fletcher said, trying to keep his voice steady.

Cress was dry-eyed, her tears used up through the night.

'I hope he found a nice lady friend while he was away.'

She glared at the others as if daring them to laugh.

'No, you're right,' Othello said gently, hugging Cress around her shoulders. 'It's why he came here. I bet he did. I bet there will be little Sheldons running around some day soon.'

'Aye,' Cress said, giving the demon another stroke on his head.

They were silent for a time, listening to the gentle swash of the lagoon's shoreline.

'We should leave soon,' Fletcher said, hating himself for hurrying them. 'There's a chance that one of the remaining shamans had a scrying crystal and watched the battle through a lesser demon. They might know we're somewhere by the lagoon; they could be heading this way.'

He nodded towards the pile of demon corpses, a mix of dead Shrikes, Strixs and Vesps.

'You're right,' Cress said, standing up and nodding firmly. She wiped the tear stains from her cheeks and began to gather their things. Othello trudged behind her.

Sylva stood beside Fletcher for a moment longer.

'Fletcher, before we go, I need to talk to you. After yesterday . . . if something happens to me, I want you to know something.'

Fletcher's heart leaped, but the grim look on Sylva's face told him it was not about her feelings for him. She sat and patted the sand beside her. He joined her, and was surprised to find she was leafing through Jeffrey's journal again.

'I've been reading this,' she said, flicking to the final pages. 'I hadn't got to the end until last night. Look.'

The pages towards the back of the journal were filled with numbers and dates. Strangest of all, there was a letter, slotted in among the pages. The seal was broken, but Fletcher recognised the Forsyth Crest embossed in the red wax – the three intertwined heads of a Hydra.

'Read it,' she said, handing it to him.

Jeffrey,

You have struck a blow for the safety of humanity that will be felt through the ages. It will be remembered in the years to come by the unsullied children of our descendants. Know that what you do is righteous and good. The blood of the innocent is a necessary sacrifice to protect the purity of our race.

The next blow must be struck in three days hence. Rook will have placed the barrel in the storage cupboard with the cards in a sealed envelope on top. Scatter them on your way out.

Memorise and burn this letter once you have read it.

Be well,

Zacharias

Of course, Fletcher had known that the Forsyths and their allies were involved in the Anvil bombings; Jeffrey had confessed it.

The bombs that had been killing humans around Corcillum had all been planted by the Triumvirate to frame the dwarves and their supporters for the attacks, to turn the people of Hominum against them.

But this was different. It was evidence!

'And there's more,' Sylva went on. 'There're records of payments Zacharias made to him, dates of the exact places and times the bombings took place, fuse length and blast radius calculations. He was keeping all this for some reason – to protect himself, to extort money from the Forsyths . . . or something.'

'We have them now,' Fletcher said with triumph. Finally, something was going their way.

'No,' Sylva said, shaking her head. 'We don't.'

'Why not?' Fletcher asked.

'Don't you remember what Jeffrey said?' Sylva's voice was taut with frustration. 'Back in the pyramid Jeffrey said that even *King Alfric* is involved in this. Read the letter. It mentions Rook, an *Inquisitor*.'

'So?' Fletcher asked, but his heart was already sinking.

'Who do we take it to? The Pinkertons? They're in Alfric's pocket. The Inquisition? Not likely. They'd get rid of it as soon as we handed it in, or claim it's a forgery, or kill us there and then. We can't take it to the authorities . . . they *are* the authorities!'

'So we take it to King Harold!' Fletcher exclaimed. 'He'll know what to do with it.'

'I hope you're right, Fletcher,' Sylva said, biting her lip. 'Anyway, I'll keep it safe. I just wanted you to know it exists.'

Fletcher sighed and rubbed his eyes. The few hours of sleep had done little to help with his exhaustion.

'Sorry, it's just that I thought we had something for a minute there. Thank you. I mean it.'

He squeezed her on the shoulder and stood up, just as Othello and Cress arrived, their weapons secure and bags packed.

'I'll ride with Othello,' Sylva said, taking the rolled-up Catoblepas pelt from Cress. 'You should carry your mother and Cress – I reckon Ignatius is a bit bigger than Lysander.'

She paused and stared at the Drake, and a gentle smile played across her lips.

'Who'd have thought,' she murmured, looking the demon up and down from beak to tail. 'He'll be the envy of all at Vocans.'

Shaking her head, she slung the pelt over Lysander's back, folding it so that it made a secure and comfortable seat on his spine. Fletcher grinned jealously at her ingenuity, glad that they would be taking the fur with them. He had earned it.

'Come on,' Cress murmured, coaxing Alice on to Ignatius's back. 'I know he looks a bit different, but he's the same old Ignatius, don't you worry.'

The Salamander flattened himself on the sand to make it easier for the frail lady to mount him, and purred with pleasure when she did so, glad that she trusted him. Fletcher sat in the front and Cress squeezed behind Alice, so as to be sure that the older woman did not fall. Fletcher smiled as Alice instinctively put her arms around his waist. Her first hug? Well, not really, but he'd take it.

Both dwarves were looking apprehensive.

'I bloody hate flying,' Cress groaned. 'Especially on a demon that grew his wings only a few hours ago.'

She patted Ignatius's neck apprehensively, and the Drake unleashed a deep bark of encouragement, making her flinch.

'Let's decide exactly where we're going first,' Othello said, giving Lysander and Ignatius a wide berth. 'I'd rather not have a debate up there, where the Wyverns might spot us. Plus I'd rather spend as little time in the air as possible.'

'Now we have an ample supply of petals, we need to find Hominum's part of the ether,' Fletcher said, more to himself than anyone else. 'And hope to heavens we spot a portal when we do.'

'Of course,' Othello said, nodding grimly, 'but there's no way of knowing which direction we should go in, and even if we did, we could fly right over it and not know it.'

'Well, we know that, unlike the orcish part of the ether, ours is near the ether's edge, bordering the deadlands,' Sylva mused. 'There are volcanoes near ours too. I think our best bet is to go back towards where we found the petals. There were more volcanoes that way.'

'Back towards the Wyverns?' Cress groaned. 'We just got away from them.'

'Well, volcanoes are the only thing I can think of, unless anyone has any better ideas,' Sylva replied.

'We also know there isn't an ocean near Hominum's part of the ether,' Fletcher added. 'Another reason to go Sylva's way.'

'And it's not like heading over the ocean is a good idea: we have no idea how large it is – it could go on for days,' Sylva said, motioning towards the lagoon. There was a wide outlet where she was pointing, and Fletcher knew that it led out to the vast body of water they had seen before.

'Well, it can't be that big, what with the Shrikes,' Othello said. 'Not that we'd want to follow them anyway.'

'Shrikes?' Sylva asked.

'Didn't I mention it?' Othello said, surprised. 'We saw a bloody great big flock of Shrikes the day after you and Fletcher went looking for the Euryale petals. Luckily they flew right by us and headed over the ocean.'

'I'd rather not follow in their footsteps, as it were – especially not on these deathtraps,' Cress added, looking pointedly at Lysander and Ignatius.

Sylva narrowed her eyes.

'Sorry, just a joke,' Cress said, holding up her hands in apology.

'No, it's not that,' Sylva said. 'I'm thinking.'

She chewed on her lip, then closed her eyes completely.

'How soon after the Tournament does the next year start at Vocans?' Sylva asked, her head bowed with concentration.

'What does that have to do with anything?' Cress exclaimed.

'There's not much of a break really,' Othello answered, ignoring Cress. 'What with the war on, they time it so that the next year of teaching starts almost immediately. Maybe a week or two? Only, our Tournament was delayed this year because of the Anvil attacks, so Cress should technically have started her second year a few weeks ago.'

'Even better. When Captain Lovett took us into the ether, we were just a few weeks into the academic year too, correct?' Sylva said, holding up a finger. 'We'd only had a few lessons with her.'

'Right . . .' Fletcher agreed, still unsure about the point she was trying to make.

'And Valens was attacked by a Shrike. Didn't we learn in our demonology lessons that Shrikes migrate across our part of the ether around that time? As in, the time of year we're also in *right now*?'

It hit Fletcher like a ton of bricks. The Shrikes. They could be heading towards Hominum's part of the ether.

'Sylva, you're a bloody genius,' Fletcher yelled, grinning from ear to ear.

Because they were going home.

19

The ocean seemed endless, so vast that after an hour of flying all sight of land had disappeared. There was no sun to navigate from; their only guide was the strange inner compass that all demons possessed, which pulled the creatures instinctively towards the centre of the ether.

Ignatius and Lysander flew as high and fast as they dared, wary of exhausting themselves but eager to catch up with the Shrikes. Too fast and they might tire swiftly, then drown in the ocean before they found land. Too slow and their only chance of reaching Hominum's part of the ether would be gone for ever . . . or at least, until the next year. Fletcher didn't even want to contemplate that.

Instead, he tried to live in the moment and enjoy the exhilaration of flying. His world had become filled with the tang of sea salt, the crash of waves and the dull thrum of Ignatius's beating wings.

The riders began a game to pass the time, attempting to be the first to spot demons in the dark-blue expanse. Fletcher had started it when he pointed out a pod of Encantados, leaping in the waves. They were pink, dolphin-like creatures with webbed claws on their four legs. Their appearance as quadrupedal dolphins was the same as a Nanaue's similarity to a shark, or the rare Akhlut's resemblance to a killer whale. Cress had groaned with frustration when she saw the Encantados, for they were beautiful creatures and immensely rare. But there was no time to stop.

They scanned the sea and horizon endlessly as the hours ticked by, but only saw one other demon. Even then, it was just the faint outline of a lone Trunko, a species that had the body of a white whale, except for the long trunk on its snout. It poked it out of the water to take in air, and they had learned in their demonology lessons that the appendage was designed to protect the demons from the flying predators of the ether, so that they did not expose their backs by breaching the surface.

Still they flew, even as the light faded. This was a different sort of darkness, accompanied by the gentle crash of the waves below and tempered by the warm embrace of his mother's arms. Sleep, apparently so easy in the deepest, darkest Abyss, was difficult now, for he was suddenly beset by the irrational fear of falling. This was compounded by a sudden lurch in the air, as Ignatius briefly nodded off mid-flight.

So Fletcher dozed and woke in fits and starts, until the sky filled with pink light and morning had returned once more. In the new glow, the Shrikes were nowhere to be seen, but the shadow of a distant land bruised the skyline. It grew larger with every hour, for Lysander and Ignatius beat the air with new purpose, desperate for rest.

But as they neared, Fletcher's hope faded. This land was not filled with the jungles of Hominum's territory. It was a desert, stretching out so far that it almost met the horizon, broken only by the thinnest line of green, where the sand ended and the jungle began. In the far distance, a sandstorm billowed across the blue heavens, staining them a muddy orange.

It felt to Fletcher as if they had left one ocean and entered another, for the land beneath was undulated in dunes that appeared as static waves of fine, cinnamon dust. The sky above was so oppressively bright and hot so that Fletcher's arms itched with prickles of sweat.

Then, when Fletcher began to think the desert would never end, the green edge of the jungle swam into view, at first a thin strip of green, then an unbroken swathe that extended into the horizon.

They saw no Shrikes, but swarms of Mites flew by here and there, and there was even a moment of panic as the shadow of a large demon passed above them. Luckily, it was nothing but a pelican-like Ropen, the leathery-winged, tooth-beaked beast appearing almost comical with a pointy, elongated crest at the back of its head.

Fletcher was pleased to see the telltale columns of smoke in the distance as they made their descent. Volcanoes, just like in Hominum's territory. He was tempted to hope they had reached their journey's end, but remembered that there was no desert or ocean near Hominum's part of the ether. It would be another day at least before they got there.

When the team landed, Ignatius and Lysander collapsed in a heap – there was no chance of travelling further, though there was still daylight left. Instead, they set up camp, cutting branches from the trees, then sharpening and staking them in the soil around their camp. It would do little to deter a predator, but it might be enough to keep smaller, more curious demons from approaching them in the night. As such, Athena was summoned to keep watch on a high branch, for the Gryphowl was well rested after being so long infused within Fletcher.

The jerky supply was still plentiful, though it was greying around the edges and tasted like sour, chewy leather. They ate it regardless, toasting it on the campfire on green twigs to give it a better flavour.

Ignatius and Lysander had gone to sleep together, their tired bodies draped over each other like newborn puppies. It was a well-deserved rest, and the demons had been given the lion's share of the remaining jerky before they passed out. Fletcher only hoped that the two demons would recover by morning.

'We'll have to move on, first thing tomorrow,' Fletcher murmured, poking the fire moodily. 'There's been no sign of the Shrike flock – it must be further ahead.'

'Aye, they were definitely travelling in this direction though, and we know they tend to keep along the ether's edges, which is roughly where we are.' Othello's words were positive, but his tone was dull and listless.

'It could be a different flock,' Sylva said.

'What?' Cress asked, looking up as if she had only just caught Sylva's words.

'Another flock to the one that passes through Hominum's territory. We have no idea if there are different flocks with different migration patterns around the ether. The ether is

134

massive, and Shrikes appear to be relatively common.'

'Why didn't you say this yesterday?' Othello groaned, burying his head in his hands.

'Did you have a better idea?' Sylva snapped back. 'At least we have a direction to go in!'

'Guys, this isn't helping,' Fletcher said, holding up his hands. 'It might not be the same flock, but it might very well be too. We'll keep following them for now.'

'Following what?' Cress grumbled. 'We don't even know where they are.'

'Sorry it didn't turn out the way you hoped,' Sylva said, her voice tinged with sarcasm. She stood and went over to the satchel beside Ignatius's sleeping form.

'I'm going to see if the growth spell still works on these flowers,' she said over her shoulder.

There was a glow of green and a gasp of joy from Sylva. She turned and held up a freshly bloomed plant, which she plucked showing the others the petals in her hand.

'Well, if we are going to be here a while, you lot might as well grow the rest of them before they wither and die,' Sylva said to the others. 'I'd rather not take another trip to a volcano. Come on, chop chop!'

Fletcher and the others reluctantly went to join her, and soon the camp flashed green again, the spells draining the little mana the team had recovered on their long journey across the ocean. There were petals aplenty – and if they kept the plants secure they would have a lifetime supply.

Light was fading fast, as was the heat of the day. Soon the team were huddled under the Catoblepas pelt for warmth, with their feet to the fire. Before, the nights had been dark and oppressive, the only light being small wyrdlights to guide them to the bushes so that they could relieve themselves. But after travelling so far across the ocean, Fletcher doubted that the orcs would have been able to track them this far. So they slept by the crackle of the fire, casting their little camp in a warm orange glow.

Fletcher woke, realising he had gulped down too much water after their dry flight through the desert. He didn't want to move from his warm cocoon, but his bladder was uncomfortably full and he knew he wouldn't be able to sleep without emptying it. The first glimmerings of dawn were staining the sky, but it wouldn't wait. He sighed and wriggled out from beneath the pelt, careful not to wake his mother and Othello, who were sleeping on either side of him.

Athena hooted softly above as he pushed his way through the barrier of branches on the border of their camp and took a few steps into the darkness. He was wary of going so far from the camp, especially when they hadn't explored any of the surrounding jungle, but it had to be done.

There was a thorny tree among the bushes a hundred feet away that looked promising, so Fletcher made his way towards it, thankful that there was enough residual light from the campfire and the early morning sky to reach the broad trunk without a bright wyrdlight. He stopped and began to unbutton his breeches.

But something felt wrong. It was too quiet. When they had ridden Sheldon, the jungles had been filled with the rustle of small demons, distant hoots and the occasional coughing roar of a night predator. Now, there was barely the stirring of the wind. Something dripped on to his cheek, wet and heavy as a raindrop. He touched his hand to it and it smeared red across his fingers.

Fletcher lifted his hand and produced a wyrdlight. The blue globe spun gently on the end of his finger as he pulsed mana into it, until the ball was as large as his fist. Fletcher's breath caught in his throat as the full horror of what was before him became apparent in the spreading pool of light. Death had visited the jungles.

Dozens of demons were skewered on the thorns of the tree. Directly above was a dead Jackalope, a rabbit-like demon with small, sharpened antlers. Its ribcage was open and empty, and the eyes had been plucked out of its gaping skull. Beside it, the remains of a Mite's carapace had been spiked there, leaving nothing but an empty shell.

Fletcher turned, his heart pounding with horror.

He began to run.

20

The team stood before the tree, inspecting the macabre display as dawn spread across the sky. It was a gruesome sight; though in the new morning glow it looked far less sinister than the ethereal, blue-tinged spectacle that Fletcher had seen a half-hour earlier.

'Well, this is great news,' Sylva mumbled, rubbing the tiredness from her eyes. 'I'm going back to sleep.'

'This? This is great news?' Cress exclaimed, turning to Sylva in confused horror.

'Yep,' Othello mumbled, turning back to their camp, where the crackling campfire beckoned. 'Wake me in half an hour.'

'Am I going mad, or are they?' Cress asked, turning on Fletcher.

But Fletcher already knew what they were talking about, a forgotten fact swimming to the forefront of his mind. It was no surprise he had not immediately recalled it, for it had been taught during a lesson Fletcher had missed, pulled out of class so he could show Dame Fairhaven Baker's journal.

'Do you know how Shrikes got their name?' Fletcher asked, scratching his chin. 'I just remembered.'

'Errr . . . not really,' Cress replied. 'To be honest, I didn't pay much attention in my demonology lessons – I was too focused on winning the Tournament.'

'Well, they're named after a real animal. There's a bird species native to the borders of the Akhad desert, known as a shrike. It has a habit of impaling its prey, usually insects or lizards, on to thorns. It's so it can hold its catch in place while it feeds. Demonic Shrikes have the same feeding habits, so the name stuck.'

'So, it means we haven't lost the Shrikes,' Cress said, understanding dawning on her.

'That's right,' Fletcher said, eyeing the dripping remains and resisting the urge to shudder. 'We just follow the corpses.'

Knowing that they were so close to the Shrikes put the team in a grim mood. They were in danger now, not only from the Shrikes but the predators and carrion eaters that followed in the flock's wake. The deadly Wendigo was perhaps the most feared of these, its penchant for corpses giving it a stench to match its favourite source of nourishment.

From the freshness of the carcasses, Fletcher knew that the Shrikes would be roosting in the trees ahead, so they sent Pria to scout first, then approached carefully on foot, so as not to encounter the deadly creatures.

On its own, a single male Shrike was dangerous, with the wingspan of an albatross, the talons of an eagle and the cruelly hooked beak of a vulture. But when they migrated, the demons would band together in an unstoppable flock, decimating the populations in their path.

Most fearsome of all were the Shrike Matriarchs, the rarer, female leaders of the brood. In a strange reversal, the male Shrike bore an insignificant crest and wattle like that of a hen, while the brood mother's own was fully developed, flaring from her head like a rooster's did. Twice as large as their male counterparts, they were capable of swooping down and plucking a juvenile Canid from the ground.

The team's first sighting of the Shrikes was the next morning, when the flock broke through the canopy only a mile or so in front of them to continue their migration, having stripped the nearby jungle of all living creatures. The team flew after them – but only when the demons were no more than distant dots on the horizon, using Athena's keen sight to keep track.

Day turned to night, turned to day once more. At dusk, the team settled on the trail of the roosting demons, camping as they had done before. They ate their petals and the pitiful remnants of the jerky, supplementing their diet with the edible leftovers that the Shrikes had abandoned. On the next night it rained, and they were soaked but grateful, stretching out the Catoblepas pelt to catch the water and refill their flasks.

So it went, the jungle rolling beneath them in a seemingly endless carpet of green. Fletcher had never imagined such a sight, for it stretched from horizon to horizon on a flat terrain that was devoid of landmarks, rivers or clearings. Only on their far right was any semblance of a break from the trees: a thin red line denoting where the jungle ended and the deadlands began.

On the fourth evening they dined on the haunches of a freshly killed Yale, a demon that looked like a cross between an antelope and a billygoat, with a curved pair of horns that could swivel at will. The beast tasted like aged mutton, tough but flavoursome, and far tastier than the remains of their poorly smoked jerky.

It was that night that they saw the first carnivores that prowled behind the flock, skirting the edges of their makeshift barricade in the darkness, attracted by the light and scent of cooking meat.

The team watched the approaching predators through their scrying crystal, as Athena perched in the trees above. A single zebra-striped Leucrotta trotted by at dusk – a strange mammalian creature with cloven hooves, a lion-like tail and the head of a badger. Later, a pair of mangy Lycans slunk past. The bipedal wolves howled mournfully as they settled down no more than a few dozen yards from their camp. Nobody got much sleep that night.

It was the next morning that they saw their first volcano, the great column of smoke belching into the sky. The sight quickened Fletcher's heart. The land was becoming similar to Hominum's territory, rugged and with a sky darkened by the same clouds of ash he could see now. Only there was no way to be sure. They could fly right over it and never notice.

Worse still, Othello had reminded them of something else – after sitting up in the middle of the night and coming to a terrible realisation. The average time a summoner would hold open a portal into the ether was brief, perhaps a half-hour at the most. The area in which a portal might appear was vast, so that even if they were in the right area, their chances of coming across an open portal as they passed by was even more unlikely.

Their only hope was to somehow spot one as they flew, an

impossibility given the thickness of the canopy. So Fletcher was glad that the Shrikes seemed to be migrating towards the deadlands, where they might better catch a glimpse of a spinning orb. By now they were skirting the red wastelands: a good sign. The Shrikes had been near the deadlands when Valens had been attacked two years ago. Could this be the same place?

They spent hours flying along the edge of the jungle, peering into the red sand bowl, hoping to see the spinning blue orb that would take them home. But there was nothing.

Defeated, they settled down for the fifth night since they had crossed the desert, their eyes bloodshot and red-rimmed from the wind and dust. The others all looked as if they had been crying, and Fletcher supposed they might as well have been. It was hopeless. They were condemned to the ether.

For ever.

21

'Fletcher, wake up!'

Sylva's voice hissed in his ear. He yelped in pain as her nails dug into his shoulders.

'Whuh—' he began, but a hand clamped over his mouth. Above him, first rays of light were already appearing in the sky, casting the world in the faintest tinge of yellow.

He was lifted into a sitting position, and the scrying crystal was laid in his lap. The others were already awake, crowding around him – pale, ashen faces, lit by the glow of a tiny wyrdlight.

'There,' Sylva whispered, pointing at the stone.

For a moment he thought he was looking at the dim reflection of the wyrdlight above. But it wasn't. It was a flicker of indigo, somewhere deep in the deadlands. Too far to see the source.

He tried to sit up, but Othello's arm was like an iron bar across his chest. The image on the crystal panned down, to the jungle's edge.

Shrikes. Hundreds of them, their black forms roosting among the branches as if the trees were laden with rotten fruit.

Othello leaned in and pointed silently upwards. Fletcher lifted his head to see that Pria was hovering just above the tree canopy. The Shrikes were directly over them!

'There's a dust cyclone where they were before,' Sylva whispered, her voice barely more than a breath in his ear. 'They must have moved back here to avoid it while we were sleeping. Athena woke me a few minutes ago.'

Fletcher shuddered and looked for the Gryphowl, and she jumped into his arms. He thanked the stars that she had been on watch. Othello leaned in, so close that his beard tickled Fletcher's cheek.

'If it's a portal, we don't have long,' he murmured. 'It's your call. You got us this far.'

Fletcher's heart was racing uncomfortably in his chest. It was as if he had been drenched in cold water, shocked out of his sleep and filled with sudden terror.

'It could be Will-o'-the-wisps,' Fletcher said softly, looking them each in the eye. 'It could be anything.'

'And it could be our best chance at making it home,' Cress replied, biting her lip. 'If we don't leave now, we'll miss it.'

It was an impossible choice, with the worst possible timing. The Shrikes could begin to wake any minute – dawn was coming soon. If the team left the cover of the trees they might be spotted by an early riser.

'Othello, send Pria to check it out, the rest of you, pack up,' Fletcher ordered, trying to keep his voice low and steady. 'We need to move away from here regardless.'

Pria darted off, making for the deadlands. Already her carapace had turned red, to blend with the dusty plains.

'So we're doing it?' Cress asked, suddenly fearful.

'If we find out it *is* a portal, we'll know that we're in Hominum's territory,' Fletcher whispered. 'That's a blessing in itself – we could have flown by here and never seen it. It might take us a few weeks of searching the area to come across another portal, but it means we'll find one eventually.'

'Weeks?' Othello uttered in a low groan.

'If the Shrikes move on before it closes, we should be ready to go for it,' Fletcher murmured. 'Otherwise, we wait it out. It's not worth dying over.'

There were two minutes of hurried packing, then Lysander and Ignatius were cajoled out of their sleep. The team waited by their prospective mounts, peering at the scrying crystal clutched in Othello's hands.

'Pria's moving slowly,' Othello said, his voice so quiet that Fletcher could barely make out the words. 'Some of the Shrikes are awake, so she's hugging the ground.'

Fletcher looked up and felt the cold rush of fear down his spine, prickling his skin with goosebumps. In the growing light, he could see the bird-demons among the branches far above, their black feathers blending with the murky shadows of the canopy. Already a few of them were awake, their heads untucked from beneath their wings. Fletcher and his team were lucky that they had not been spotted when the birds had come to roost.

'We should move – now,' Fletcher whispered. 'We're not safe here.'

He turned and looked into the scrying crystal. It was still too far to see the source of the blue light, though it was larger in the crystal's screen. At the same time, the blue was less visible, for

145

the growing light of dawn made its glow indistinct.

Silently, Fletcher tugged a few branches from the barricade to make a way out of their camp and motioned the others to mount. He followed suit, gathered Athena, and cajoled Ignatius to move through the gap. The Shrikes might stir any minute.

The Drake tucked his wings against their knees so he would fit through their exit and turned to it, placing each foot with care so as not to snap stray twigs underfoot. Athena wriggled against Fletcher's chest and he realised he was gripping her tightly with unconscious fear. He released her and she pounced on to his shoulder, catching Alice's attention. Fletcher's mother smiled, oblivious to the danger they were in.

Ignatius took one step. Two steps.

Then, the unthinkable. Alice laughed aloud, her voice unbridled as she reached for the Gryphowl. Athena leaped into her arms, hoping to keep her quiet.

But it was too late.

A screech came from above. Then another, cutting through the air like nails on a chalkboard. Slowly, ever so slowly, Fletcher tilted his head back.

A dozen eyes stared at him, black and beady in the dawn light. It was as if time stood still, freezing the world in one horrific moment. Then a dark form dropped from the canopy above to the branches below, landing among its brethren in a rattle of leaves. A second came after it, enormous wings beating the air. It cawed softly, the sound raucous and raw in Fletcher's ears, filling him with terror.

More followed, one after another, seeking the source of the noise beneath them. Pairs turned to dozens, turned to scores, so many that the branches creaked under the weight of the enormous birds. One settled so close that Fletcher could see the red wattle shaking as it snapped its beak in anticipation.

'Three,' Sylva breathed, just loud enough for Fletcher to hear.

He didn't understand, his mind reeling with fear.

'Two.'

Fletcher stared as the first Shrike dropped to the ground, no more than a few yards from Lysander's feet. Sylva and Othello were already mounted.

'One.'

Ignatius was lowering into a crouch.

Oh.

Fletcher lunged for the Drake's neck.

'Now!'

They launched into the air, shooting directly up so that Fletcher was flattened against his mother, feeling her arms tighten around his midriff as the momentum pressed them against Ignatius's back.

A mad cacophony of screeching tore at his eardrums as the two demons hurtled by, then they were twisting through the canopy and into the open air.

The dawn sky was stained the yellow of an old bruise, and the red land in front of them glowed with its light. The world tilted once more as Ignatius jinked into the deadlands, then they were whipping through the air in a flurry of beating wings. Lysander was just ahead, his lighter load and experience giving him the edge over the Drake.

Screeching, ragged with fury, the Shrikes followed in their wake. Fletcher glanced back and his breath caught in his throat.

The Shrikes were in hot pursuit, so many that the jungle was almost blocked from view by the mass of black forms that tore after them.

'The light, where's the light?' Sylva yelled, twisting her head to look over her shoulder.

The sky was bright now, so much so that the portal no longer glowed like a beacon to point their way. They flew on into the deadlands, hoping to catch a glimpse of the blue speck.

'Faster,' Fletcher yelled.

The Shrikes were gaining, and the Matriarchs were leading the flock. Their wings were as large as a cutter's sails, beating the air in long, ponderous sweeps that somehow thrust them through the air at breakneck speeds. It was all Ignatius could do to stay ahead of their outstretched claws, the talons ready to hook into his burgundy flesh.

A flash of pain. Fletcher turned to see Ignatius's tail had been stabbed by a Matriarch's beak, but even as he did so, the Drake's tailspike slashed upwards, stabbing into the demon's plumage and hurling it aside.

Another dropped from above, its wings folded, talons aimed for Cress. Fletcher drew Gale and fired twice without thinking. The Matriarch was snatched away in a double burst of feathers and blood.

Wind tore their hair as they hurtled over the red plains, the rock-strewn terrain rushing beneath them. The land stretched onward, the Abyss on their right, the jungle on their left, with nothing to guide them but the rough direction that Pria had disappeared into.

'There!' Othello bellowed, even as he blasted buckshot from

his blunderbuss into the mass of Shrikes behind. Three jerked and tumbled limply away, but the dwarf's action barely made a dent in the screeching tumult of wings and beaks.

Fletcher saw nothing but the Shrikes behind; he only felt the tilt of Ignatius's path as he followed Lysander in a new direction. His mother's face was at the corner of his vision, calm as she stroked the Gryphowl in her arms.

A crackle of lightning spurted from behind her, Cress's battle gauntlet outstretched and swinging to spread the spell. The nearest birds jerked and spasmed in the air, twisting and dropping like stones, only to recover and join the pursuit once more.

Fletcher tried a shield, but the white light spooled away in the wind, tangling in a nearby Matriarch's claws but doing little else. A fireball followed from his next finger, blasting it beak over claws into another, knocking both from the air.

A small Shrike swooped in from the side, and Cress cried out in pain as its talons tore at her. Her returning kinetic blast sent it flying, accompanied by a crossbow bolt that took its neighbour through the wing. Then the Shrikes were above, below and among them, the flock overtaking to surround them from all sides.

'The portal,' Sylva screamed, and Fletcher turned to see the spinning orb in the distance, a blue mote floating on the horizon. A pair of Shrikes dropped from the sky above Lysander, and Ignatius blasted a torrent of flame, leaving their charred, smoking remains to whip over Fletcher's shoulder.

In response, the Griffin screeched and dropped down, taking a Shrike by the wings and tearing it apart, even as another slammed into his side and scrabbled at his feathered fur.

Fletcher fired Blaze, hitting the attacker in the thigh, enough to send it spinning away. A talon slashed his arm, feathers blinding him as a Matriarch swooped. He snarled with pain and holstered the pistol before it fell from his nerveless fingers, the wound on his arm spreading crimson through his blue jacket.

'Almost. There,' Othello yelled, punctuating each word with a kinetic blast, hurling swooping Shrikes and Matriarchs back with the force. Cress was following his example, the deep *whump* of each spell accompanied by a blast of wind and tumbling plumage. Fletcher drew his khopesh left-handed, clasping his injured right arm to his chest. He extended a finger from the hilt and fired a streak of lightning, the electric-blue bolts searing through the air, punching a hole of falling Shrikes through the mêlée that surrounded them. His mana was near drained.

Shadows streaked past as Shrikes dived and feinted, wary of the ferocious defence of their prey. Another burst of pain crossed his calf, the demon speeding away before he could riposte with his khopesh.

The world spun, the edges of his vision darkening. He could feel the hot trickle of blood down his leg, the deep wound voiding blood fast. Too fast. He tried to etch the healing spell but it sputtered and died in the air, his elbow jarring from the judder of Ignatius's wings.

He heard a cry of warning from Sylva, felt the thud of a Shrike hitting his shoulder. Ignatius dropped into a stomach-churning swoop.

A blue glow rushed towards him.

* * *

The world was suddenly cold and dark. Fletcher felt the jar of Ignatius hitting the ground, then he was sailing through the air, turning once, twice. He slammed against the ground, tumbling over and over until he lay in a crumpled pile of pain. He could feel the stickiness of leather against his face, smell the harsh tang of its scent through his nostrils.

His half-cracked eyes saw the blur of the spinning portal, part blocked by black figures. The glow darkened as a demon emerged, then the blue sphere winked out of existence, leaving the place in utter darkness.

He heard the pounding of feet, sensed Ignatius's presence beside him. There was the warm lap of the demon's tongue across his calf, then a moment later it bathed his arm in saliva. He felt the rush of the last of his mana leaving him, the healing spell imbued in the Salamander's tongue working its way into his flesh, knitting muscle and skin together.

Fletcher was suddenly aware of voices around him, shouts of surprise, of fear. The room, for that was where he was, flared with flickering light as torches sputtered into life. His vision widened.

A man's voice cut through the noise, barking orders. Then he saw him, striding purposefully towards him, eyes flashing with concern.

Arcturus.

22

They had flown into a summoning lesson. The first of the academic year, in fact. Arcturus had returned to teaching after the rescue mission, taking Rook's place.

When Fletcher and his team had spotted the portal, Arcturus had been demonstrating the dangers of the Shrikes' migration to his students, observing the flock from the safe distance of the deadlands. Fortunately, a keen-eyed student had spotted their desperate escape in the Oculus, Vocans's giant scrying stone, before the lesson had ended. Sacharissa had waited behind the portal so Arcturus could watch their progress, and jumped through when they had reached safety.

Now, they sat in the library, revelling in the soft cushions of the armchairs and the warmth of the hearth that crackled nearby. Fletcher had carried his mother up in his arms and laid her out on a sofa by the fire.

The rest of them were seated around a large oak table, piled high with books and surrounded by the tall shelves that divided the room into a maze of book-lined corridors. It was almost midnight; the lesson had been a late one.

'Who are we waiting for?' Othello groaned, fidgeting in his seat nervously. They had not been given the opportunity to wash, or even change their clothes. Instead, Arcturus had told them to infuse their demons and rushed them away from the first year students, who had stared after them with amazement.

'I'll let them explain,' Arcturus said, pacing nervously by the door.

'Who?' Sylva asked, her patience wearing as thin as the line of her pursed lips.

'Look, I don't even know who's coming,' Arcturus replied, running his hands through his hair. 'I sent word to King Harold and Elai– Captain Lovett, but they might bring or send others. A lot has changed while you were out there . . .'

'Well, tell us that part at least,' Fletcher said, sick of the mystery. He had thought they would receive a hero's welcome, not be hidden away like common criminals. It was the shock of that reception that had kept him silent about his mother's rescue. Arcturus had barely given her a second look, and likely still believed her to be Lady Cavendish, Rufus's mother. It could wait.

'Captain Lovett, she heard everything,' Arcturus said, still pacing. 'At least, until Lysander went through the portal and their connection was severed. Jeffrey's confession, how you escaped, all of it. But she had no proof, so she kept it silent. Nobody even believed that you had gone into the ether.'

'We didn't realise she knew,' Sylva murmured. 'We thought Lysander was unconscious.'

'What else?' Othello asked.

Arcturus paused, chewing his lip.

'All of Hominum saw Rufus die,' he finally said. 'They saw one of Cress's blue crossbow bolts hit him, then they saw Jeffrey run over and pull it out, trying to save him. As far as they were concerned, Cress killed Rufus. They didn't know it was Jeffrey that shot him.'

The news hit Fletcher like a shaft of lightning. He had been exhausted, ready to sleep in the warm comfort of the library, but now he felt icy shock running down his spine.

Rufus had been dead when they entered the chamber beneath the pyramid. They had never seen what had killed him, only a deep wound in the boy's stomach. Jeffrey must have thrown the crossbow bolt out of sight.

'But Jeffrey thought he had failed,' Cress gasped, clapping her hand to her mouth.

'It was seen out of the corner of Lysander's eye, just after he was paralysed,' Arcturus explained, his face drawn and grim. 'His eyes closed a few seconds later. Jeffrey probably didn't realise all of Hominum was watching – the only reason he was pretending to help Rufus was to trick the three of you when you came out of the tunnel. The bugger got lucky.'

'So everyone hates the dwarves again,' Othello whispered. 'They think we sent an assassin to kill one of their own.'

Arcturus sighed and rubbed his eyes.

'Old King Alfric has already ordered the Pinkertons to surround the Dwarven Quarter. It's a powder keg, waiting to explode. But that's not the worst of our problems.'

'It's not?' Fletcher asked, horrified.

Arcturus shook his head.

'After years of training, the newly qualified dwarven recruits have been sent to the front lines. They will pass through Corcillum on their march down from the elven border in two days' time. When they get here and find their homes under siege, there will be conflict, one way or another. There is nothing we can do to prevent that.'

Arcturus stopped and looked at them, as if for the first time.

'I don't know what's going to happen when they find out you're alive,' he said, half to himself. 'But you can bet that Cress will be arrested – if not the whole lot of you – as accomplices, given Fletcher and Othello's history with treason charges. Sylva, just your association with these three alone . . .'

'We need to leave, now,' Sylva said, jumping to her feet. Arcturus waved her back to her chair, shaking his head.

'The students downstairs who saw you come through the portal were all commoners, since the nobles didn't bother attending. So, we've got until tomorrow before the word gets out. I've ordered them straight to bed and asked Dame Fairhaven to keep an eye on them, making sure they don't leave their rooms. You're safe for tonight at least.'

Fletcher couldn't believe what he was hearing. From fugitives to fugitives. How could this be possible? They would have been safer living out their lives in the ether.

'Fletcher, what about the—' Sylva began.

But she never finished her sentence, because King Harold burst through the library doors, his eyes wide and unbelieving, sweat-slicked curls of gold plastered across his forehead. Lovett followed behind, wheeling herself through in a high-backed wooden wheelchair.

155

'So it's true,' he panted.

'I told you,' Lovett said drily. She broke into a grin and shook her head in mock disbelief. 'I bet they have quite a story to tell. Sixteen of the ether's days – that's almost a week in our time!'

But the King was not listening, or even looking at the four students seated at the large table in front of him. He was staring at Fletcher's mother. As if he were a sleepwalker, he staggered to the armchair where she sat, her face cast in shadow by the flickering flames.

'Alice,' he croaked, kneeling in front of her. 'Is it you?'

He looked at Fletcher with a questioning gaze, and received a solemn nod back. There were tears in the King's eyes, and he took Alice's limp hand in his own.

'It can't be . . . Fletcher, do you . . .' Arcturus trailed off, his fingers straying to the long scar that marred his face. The same scar he had received while seeking revenge on the orcs that had attacked the Raleighs on that fateful night.

Fletcher could see Arcturus's obvious joy at finding his old friend, the look of astonishment plain on his face, followed by a grin as wide as Fletcher had ever seen on the scarred man's lips.

Arcturus lay a hand on the King's shoulder, gazing into Alice's blank stare. Then, as the two looked at her, Alice's eyes flickered for a moment, and the barest hint of a smile played across her lips. Then it was gone, so swiftly that Fletcher couldn't even be sure that he had seen it.

'Alice, it's me,' Arcturus said, squeezing her other hand.

But the moment had passed. Her eyes stared unblinkingly into the flames.

'Is she . . . always like this?' Harold asked, a slow tear rolling down his face.

'Yes,' Fletcher answered. There was nothing else to say.

23

There was little time to rejoice at Alice's return, bittersweet though it had been. The morning was fast approaching and Fletcher's team would need to be long gone by then.

Their urgency was further stoked when Lovett reminded them that a student was capable of sending a note by flying demon, and it was likely the Forsyths would have spies among even the commoners at Vocans. After all, they had gained the loyalty of two already: Atlas and Jeffrey. An impressionable first-year commoner, stunned by the proffered friendship of a wealthy noble family, could be easily bought.

Lovett had already told the King and Arcturus what had happened during the mission. So, Fletcher stumbled through their journey across the ether, with interruptions from the others when he left out important details. The revelations from his conversation with Khan about Alice's treatment at the orcs' hands elicited growls of anger from the others, and a tirade of furious swearing from Lovett.

By the end, Fletcher's throat was dry and hoarse, leaving the rest of the table brooding over their predicament in the dim glow of the dying hearth fire. Sylva ended the tale with a summary of the contents of Jeffrey's journal and now it was passed around the table as they digested the new information.

Cress was the first to speak in the grim silence.

'Isn't it obvious?' she asked, taking the slim volume from Arcturus's hands and holding it aloft. 'This is it. Proof. Proof that Jeffrey was a traitor, proof that he was behind every explosion, every death – hell, for everything that humanity has laid the blame at dwarven feet over the past year.'

Silence.

'They'll know that I didn't kill Rufus, and that the Anvil attacks were nothing to do with the dwarves,' she continued, brandishing the journal. 'This is enough to have Zacharias Forsyth and Inquisitor Rook thrown in jail.'

Still nothing. She turned to Harold, exasperated.

'What are you going to do about this?' she asked, taking the letter from between the journal's pages and dangling it in front of the King's face. Fletcher couldn't help but grin. King or no king, Cress wasn't one to stand on ceremony.

'It's not that simple,' Harold said, his brows furrowing at her impertinence. 'Who am I supposed to take this to? The Pinkertons? The Inquisition themselves? They're under my father's thumb. Even most of the Judges are under his sway.'

'But – you're King . . .' Cress said, her brows furrowed with confusion.

Fletcher understood her bewilderment. He had told the others that Harold wanted to help the dwarves, and was estranged from his father because of it. But he had never told them that it was Alfric who held the power in Hominum; that his son Harold was King in name alone. Even Lovett and Arcturus looked perplexed. This was news to them as well.

The King sighed and rubbed his temples.

'My father rules in the shadows,' Harold said. 'I am no more than a figurehead, someone to take the fall if things go wrong. He wants to exterminate the dwarves, and has been looking for an excuse to do it for years. His aims align with the Triumvirate's.'

'What about the council?' Cress demanded. 'And the laws you passed to allow dwarves to fight, to remove the child quotas? Was that Alfric too?'

Harold sighed.

'It's true that I have a majority in the council which has some powers over the rule of law, allowing me to pass minor measures. But for something like this . . . no.'

'Could we go to the generals of the army, my King?' Arcturus said, bowing his head in sudden reverence. His intent was clear – to leave Harold in no doubt of where his loyalties lay.

'Yes,' Lovett said, tapping her lips with a finger. 'Could you not take the evidence to them?'

'And throw this country into civil war?' Harold asked, his words spitting like acid. 'Many of the generals are on the Triumvirate's side, and it's the same with the nobles. Let me paint you a picture.'

He stood, and leaned his knuckles against the table.

'I would convene a meeting of the generals and nobility to show them the letter and the journal. Some would believe it and call for the arrest of perpetrators; others, like my father and his friends, would say you had fabricated it and call for yours. Lines

160

would be drawn, sides would be taken. And in the middle of all this, the dwarven recruits arrive. A rebellion in the midst of a civil war. Can you imagine the chaos?'

'That's not all,' Sylva said, her voice low and worried. 'You would not just have the dwarves to contend with. If an arrest warrant is issued against me, a chieftain's daughter, the elven council would go to war with all of Hominum over it too. Our army is mustering as we speak, to help in your war. Only now it would be used against you.'

Harold turned to her, shock stamped across his features.

'I had not considered that,' he said bitterly, his face draining of colour. 'The elven army is only just mobilising, but they will be marching into Hominum when they are ready.'

'And all the soldiers on the northern borders have left,' Arcturus whispered, horrified.

'As soon as they discover you four are alive, there *will* be a warrant for your arrest,' Harold said. 'Maybe I can convince them to leave Sylva out of it, but by then it might be too late . . .'

He sighed and knuckled his brow.

'So, war with the elves if I don't get you to safety . . . and a war with the dwarves regardless.'

'Aye, after seeing Rufus die, all of Hominum believes that Cress is an assassin,' Arcturus said. 'And now they are even more convinced that the Anvil attacks were orchestrated by the dwarves. It will reach a boiling point, soon enough.'

'When the dwarven recruits arrive, my father will send the Pinkertons in to take over the Dwarven Quarter,' Harold said. 'He has told me as much, and will not change his mind, no matter what I say. The fighting will start that very night . . .'

Lovett finished his thought.

'Then, as we fall upon each other, the front lines left unguarded, Khan will strike and wipe us all out.'

The room went silent at her words, the horror of it weighing heavy in the air.

'So what are we supposed to do?' Fletcher finally asked. He was angry now. Angry at how the greed and hatred of a few power-hungry humans would lead to the slaughter of thousands of innocents. Angry that he and his friends were somehow at the centre of it all once again. His pulse was roaring in his ears.

'We get you to the elves in the Great Forest,' Harold said. 'You'll be safest there, if—'

'No,' Othello interrupted, holding up his hand. 'I won't run. If there's to be a war I'll be here, protecting my family, not hiding like some common criminal.'

'Aye, I'll stay too,' Cress said, crossing her arms defiantly.

'Don't you understand? You'll only make things worse,' the King growled. 'Even if you aren't captured, the Pinkertons will start searching for you, breaking down dwarven doors, tearing apart their homes. The dwarven rebellion would start tomorrow. If it's known that you have escaped, that the elves gave you asylum . . . that won't happen. It will buy me more time.'

Othello leaned back and closed his eyes. It looked for all the world as if he was taking a nap, were it not for the tight, whitened knuckles of his fists.

'If war breaks out, then the damage is done,' Harold said, his voice grim and terrible. 'You can return then. In the meantime, you *will* go to the elves, while I try to stave off this disaster. In all honesty, your arrival has made things worse.

Just do as you're told. I have more pressing concerns than your safety at this moment.'

'What concerns could they possibly be?' Cress snapped, her lip curling with anger. 'If the Pinkertons arrest us, you'll have another public trial on your hands, followed by a swift execution. Remember how close you came to war last time that happened, when Othello was on trial for treason? That's right: I, and every dwarf in the ghetto knew what might happen if Othello had been executed.'

Harold turned to Cress with an icy glare.

'In light of Cress's crimes and the Anvil attacks, my father will make an announcement to all of Hominum when the dwarven recruits arrive, rescinding the rights I have managed to give the dwarves over the last decade. The child-quota laws will come back, the dwarven soldiers will be stripped of their uniforms. Worse still, he will enact crippling taxes on dwarven businesses, and decree curfews so that dwarves cannot walk the streets after nightfall.'

'Why?' Fletcher uttered, the word leaving his mouth unbidden.

'Because he wants the dwarven recruits angry when they get here,' Harold growled. 'Imagine a few hundred armed dwarves being told they are no longer citizens or soldiers, after a year of training and misery on the elven borders. Then they are ordered to go home before nightfall under threat of arrest, and when they get there, the Pinkertons move in, patrolling their streets and terrifying their families.'

'They would riot,' Othello said quietly. 'And Alfric would call it a rebellion.'

'That's right,' Harold said. He turned back to Cress. 'Do you see? I need to prevent that from happening. It will buy me a few more days to manoeuvre.'

Fletcher could not believe his ears: that Alfric could be so obvious, so callous. He needed to be stopped.

'So what's your plan?' Fletcher asked.

'Captain – if you would.' Harold leaned back in his chair, covering his eyes with one hand and gesturing to Lovett with the other, as if too exhausted to explain.

'The scrying stones,' she said, leaning across the table. 'The Triumvirate gathered all of them back after your mission, connected them to a single wild Mite and then redistributed them around Hominum. Alfric plans on making his announcement through the crystals. If Harold can kill or capture the Mite, it will delay the announcement long enough for the dwarven recruits to arrive. Of course, they might rebel when they arrive anyway, but it's a start.'

'That's it?' Othello asked, cupping his chin in his hands.

'That's the long and short of it,' Lovett said. 'And there's something else. Alfric will be able to transmit his voice through the crystals as well.'

This was news to Fletcher. 'I thought that was impossible?' he asked, his brows furrowed with confusion.

'It was, but Electra has been busy in her laboratory while you were away,' Lovett explained. 'I've been helping her alchemy experiments.'

She reached into her pocket and tossed a scrying crystal on the table. The surface of it was tinged with black, then the image shifted to the ceiling of the library as Valens emerged from the pocket of Lovett's uniform. He buzzed on to her shoulder, and for a moment, Fletcher heard the faintest humming from the stone. Lovett turned her head and lowered her mouth close to the Mite. Fletcher saw her lips move, heard her say: 'Can you hear me?'

But the words did not just come from her mouth. They also came from the stone, and loudly. The sound was tinny and rough, but unmistakeable. Lovett grinned.

'The stone vibrates to the same frequency as my voice, creating sound using the reverberations. It's like a string on a violin. All it requires is the use of the amplify spell on the corundum crystals, and that they are charged with a small amount of mana. Of course, the charge will run out some time, but the vibrations use up very little of it.'

'I don't know why you're smiling,' Harold snapped. 'I wish you'd never publicised your discovery. It's the perfect propaganda machine for my father. He's been making speeches every day about how the dwarves are behind the Anvil attacks, how they assassinated poor, innocent Rufus as a warning to us. It makes me sick.'

'I only wish we'd had that ability before,' Fletcher groaned. 'Everyone would have heard Jeffrey's confession.'

Sylva stood. She had been sitting in silence for the last few minutes, but now her mouth was half open, and her eyes were bright in the dim firelight.

'There is a way,' she breathed. 'It could solve everything.'

Fletcher stared at her, unable to believe what he was hearing. What idea could she possibly have had?

'You don't need the generals,' Sylva continued, turning her

gaze on to Harold. 'Or the nobility. You need the people.'

'What do you mean?' Harold said. 'What people?'

'Why do you think Alfric needs to make these speeches?' Sylva asked. 'Why did he and the Triumvirate send Jeffrey to frame Cress? Why did they set those bombs? Because he needs the people of Hominum on his side. The soldiers, the farmers, the blacksmiths, the miners, the factory workers. They are the sinews of war. Do you think that he could license the wholesale slaughter of the dwarves without their support? Without this lie he has fabricated?'

Harold stared at Sylva, his face expressionless; the only sign of emotion the gentle flexing of his jaw as he gritted his teeth.

'It's true,' he said finally. 'Of course it's true. If the people thought the dwarves were innocent, that they had been duped, they would never allow this behaviour to continue, or the perpetrators to go unpunished.'

He stopped, as if surprised by his own words.

'But what do you expect me to do?' He sighed. 'Make my own announcement, show them the journal? My father has his spies watch me at all times, and tomorrow night I am to officially confirm Seraph and Didric's noble houses at a ball. There's no way I could slip away and get to the Mite undetected.'

'But couldn't y—' Cress began, but Harold interrupted her sharply.

'And even if I did manage to get to it, what then? My father would know I have turned against him. It would be civil war, with the nobility and generals taking sides once more. No, it would never work.'

'Not you,' Othello said, lifting his head from his hands.

166

He turned his eyes to Fletcher and nodded slowly. It was madness . . . but it was their only choice.

'So who then?' Harold growled.

'Us,' Fletcher said.

24

Fletcher remembered little of the rickety carriage ride to Corcillum, or Arcturus ushering them up the stairs and into the dusty beds of the Anvil Tavern. It was a hazy mix of sleeping and waking, of furtive whispers and stolen glances in the darkness.

He had slept through the night and, it seemed, most of the day also – for the view from his room's window when he was woken by the scent of cooking was the dim blue of winter afternoon. Othello's bed was empty, so he stumbled down the wooden steps to find the source of the delicious smell, tripping over an abandoned boot he had wrenched off on his way up the night before.

He was ravenously hungry, his stomach cramping like a clenched fist with every mouth-watering sniff of the food downstairs. Leaping the last steps, Fletcher came upon a group of tables in front of the bar, haphazardly pushed together and piled high with platters of steaming food. There were fried eggs with fat, golden yolks, and still-sizzling sausages as thick as his wrist. Crisp, thick-cut potato slices sat in bowls, browned to perfection, topped with a garnish of steamed spinach and tossed with fried garlic cloves and sprigs of tarragon. Glass jugs of pulpy orange juice completed the picture, along with pitchers of crystal-clear water.

It was a feast that could feed a small army, but there were only five seated around the table, already halfway through their meal. His teammates did little more than grunt at him, still devouring the food as if it might disappear at any moment. But there was someone else at the head of the table. A figure clad in green robes, who was as short as Othello and Cress.

'Well, look who's up!' said a familiar voice.

It was Briss, Othello's mother. Fletcher grinned and bent down to give her a big hug, which she returned fondly.

'Hurry up and get some food inside you,' she said, waving him over to a seat beside the others. 'Othello showed me a piece of that jerky you've been eating over the past few days. Horrendous!'

Fletcher didn't need to be told twice, pausing only to grab a knife and fork before stuffing his mouth. The next few glorious minutes were spent chewing and swallowing in silence, until his chin was stained with yellow yolk and his belly felt fuller than it had ever been in his life.

'Your mother has already eaten, poor dear,' Briss chattered, filling the void with conversation. 'Thaissa is upstairs looking after her – she'll be bathed by now and tucked up in bed. The King says he'll get her the best care in all of Hominum, so don't you worry about her.'

By the end, the food had somehow miraculously been reduced to a few tattered scraps.

Othello unleashed an exaggerated groan and rubbed his bulging midriff.

'You've murdered us,' he said, shaking his head. 'Death by food.'

'How are you supposed to fit into your costumes now?' Briss teased, prodding his belly. 'I'll have to adjust them at this rate.'

'Costumes?' Fletcher asked.

Briss sighed from beneath her green veil and stood. It was only then that Fletcher noticed the folded clothing on a table behind her, along with a pair of what looked like shoeboxes.

'For the ball,' Cress sighed, her voice glum. 'When we sneak in.'

'Well, don't sound too excited,' Fletcher said, even though the reminder of their new mission filled him with trepidation, too.

'You'll see,' Othello grumbled. 'You got off easy. Anyway, I don't see why you're complaining, Cress. I've got the worst outfit of all.'

Cress broke into a broad grin, her morose expression fading at his words.

'All right, settle down,' Briss chuckled, waving her hand for silence. She picked up a red bundle of cloth and frills, then handed it to Sylva, who took it with an apprehensive look.

'From what Othello has told me, this might not be to your taste, but you have to look the part,' Briss said sheepishly. 'I've made a few of these before, and they're very popular with the young ladies of the nobility. There's a hot bath ready upstairs for you and all the necessaries. Go try it on up there, then Thaissa will help you with your hair.'

'I'm sure I'll love it,' Sylva mumbled, trying to hide her misgivings. She trudged slowly up the stairs, holding the dress as if it were a poisonous snake.

'Right, now – let's see if this fits,' Briss said brightly, once Sylva had gone. She took a pink garment from the table and shook it out. It was a flowing robe, complete with embroidered flowers around the hems of the sleeves and a delicate veil secured with a silver chain along the bottom. It was very pretty and Fletcher could imagine Cress cutting a fine figure in this traditional dwarven garb. But . . .

'The veil,' Fletcher said. 'No wonder you're so grumpy, Cress. Still, it's just for one night.'

Othello shuffled his feet, his face flushing the same colour as the robes.

'Well, yeah, but . . . that's not mine,' Cress chortled, turning on the reddening dwarf. 'Othello, I think pink is your colour – it goes very well with your complexion.'

'Oh, bloody hell,' Othello groaned.

Fletcher couldn't help but burst out laughing as the morose dwarf shuffled forward and allowed his mother to tug the robe over his head.

'Just don't tell Atilla,' Othello begged, as Cress cackled and arranged the veil over his face, tucking in a stray wisp of red beard.

'He should come and have a look, see what he'd look like in a dress,' Fletcher chuckled. 'He is your twin, after all.'

'Trust me, I wish Atilla was in your shoes,' Cress said, wiping a tear from her eye. 'Or should I say, your gown!'

She doubled over into hysterics again, and Othello slumped back into his chair in defeat.

'I don't understand,' Fletcher said, getting his laughter under control. 'Why is he wearing a gown?'

'Arcturus, Lovett and I have been up all night, working out a plan on how to get you through the palace undetected. Obviously there won't be any dwarves invited to the ball, but there will be plenty of dwarven servers, all female, all wearing this uniform. So, Othello's going to be playing dress-up today. It wouldn't be the first time – remember when you were five years old, Othello, and . . .'

'All right, enough now,' Othello said loudly, tossing a half-eaten sausage at his mother. She ducked it and took another, identical robe from the table, then handed it to Cress.

'You know, somehow this doesn't seem so bad any more,' Cress said cheerfully, letting the garment unravel and holding it against her body. 'I haven't worn a robe in ages.'

She shrugged on her own, leaving the veil on the table. Then she twirled, the loose muslin floating in the air, her eyes sparkling as she tossed her red hair.

'It looks wonderful,' Briss said, covering her mouth to hide her smile of pleasure.

'It really does,' Othello agreed, then cleared his throat awkwardly.

Fletcher could not see Othello's face, but he imagined the dwarf's mouth was hanging open beneath the thin pink veil.

'Now you, Fletcher,' Briss said, after giving both he and Othello a knowing look. 'You're too tall to be a dwarf, so you and Sylva will be attending as Seraph's guests – luckily he's staying in a hotel in Corcillum tonight and we were able to bring him up to speed.'

Fletcher grinned at the thought of seeing Seraph again. The noble-to-be was like Fletcher in many ways, a commoner turned noble who had a close relationship with the dwarves. It would be good to see him.

'We'll dress you as two members of his entourage,' Briss announced. 'You'll be wearing this.'

She pointed at the table, where Fletcher could see a clean-cut suit of royal blue satin, edged with gold lace and tasselled epaulettes on the shoulders. A pair of shiny black-leather loafers with brass buckles sat beside them, as well as some elegant white gloves, there to cover the tattoos on his hand.

'Off you go to try it on,' Briss ordered, shooing Fletcher away.

Fletcher took the clothes into his arms and hurried up the stairs.

'Mind you have a bath too,' Briss called after him. 'I won't have you stinking it up. Sylva should be done by now, and Thaissa will have drawn you another.'

Fletcher grinned and turned right at the top of the stairs. He knocked on the girls' room door.

'Next door, Fletcher,' Thaissa's voice came from behind the door. 'Don't come in! Hurry up before it gets cold, we're almost out of wood – Cress and Othello hogged most of it this morning.'

Wood? He moved on to the next room, to find a suite with a small window, a mirror, a stool and a large metal bathtub full of steaming water. The floors and walls were tiled, and there was a large drain beneath the tub and a crackling fireplace with a cauldron hung above it in the wall. There was a fluffy yellow towel on the stool, along with fresh socks, underwear, a razor, pumice stone and scissors. They had thought of everything.

Within a few minutes Fletcher was enjoying the deep heat soaking into his bones, rubbing his body and hair with a bar of lavender-scented soap until suds seeped over the edges. Then, as the water began to cool and the bubbles receded, he attacked the callouses on his hands and feet and scrubbed the rest of his body until his skin was raw-pink, but cleaner than it had ever been.

Next, he shaved away the wisps of hair that had gathered on his upper lip and chin, to leave himself baby-faced, more for Berdon's sake than anything else – and the thought of the gentle giant sent a pang of pain to his heart. He had no idea where he and the villagers of Pelt might be, only that they would still be somewhere to the north, journeying downwards.

Finally, he bundled his locks into a rough ponytail and snipped off the split ends, leaving himself with a handful of hair that he surreptitiously tossed down the drain. That would have to do.

He got out of the water, now tepid and dirty, to dry himself off with the towel in the dim light of the dying fire. Realising he had taken far longer than Sylva had, he tugged on the clothes and returned back down the stairs, barely looking at himself in the mirror.

'Well, well,' Cress laughed, as he arrived in the front room of the tavern. 'Look at you, all fancy.'

Briss clapped her hands with excitement and rushed over, tugging his jacket here, smoothing there, until she stood back and admired her handiwork.

'You cut a fine figure,' Briss said. 'You've lost a bit of weight since I measured you last, but I anticipated that. It fits you like a glove. Why don't you put your shoes on? Let's see if I got those right too.'

Fletcher slipped his feet into the loafers and grinned.

'I could get used to these,' he said. 'Comfy; but I could run a mile in them too.'

'Well, you might need to tonight,' Cress reminded him, and he grimaced at the thought of the purpose of their attire.

'Have a look in there,' Briss said, pointing to a shoebox. Fletcher turned to the table, mystified. He picked it up, and the container felt oddly heavy. Curious, he lifted the lid.

Only to see a pale visage staring back at him.

'What the—' he gasped, dropping the box on the table.

'Ah, you've found your new face,' Briss said, picking the box up and holding it out to him. 'Well go on, try it on, see if it fits.'

Fletcher looked inside once more. It was a mask, made from porcelain so pale that it might have been bleached bone. In fact, with the empty eyeholes it could almost have been a skull, were it not for the soft curves of the cheeks, and the pouting white lips.

A fine filigree of gold traced around the oval edge, curling inwards at intervals with delicate whorls that curved around the eyes to draw attention there. It was terrible and beautiful at the same time, like a bird of prey.

Fletcher lifted it to his face and felt Briss's hands tying the mask in place with ribbons, tight against the back of his head.

'It's a masquerade ball, if you hadn't guessed,' Briss said. 'I took up pottery to sell pots, believe it or not, but we get more requests for these than anything else. The nobles have several

175

masques each year, and they insist on having a new mask for each.'

'Thank you,' Fletcher said, searching for the right words. 'It's . . . it's hauntingly beautiful.'

He turned to Othello, who had lifted his veil to get a closer look.

'You know what, I'd rather wear the veil,' the dwarf said, shaking his head.

'It gives me the creeps,' Cress agreed.

Briss sighed.

'Well, that's what they like to wear, these nobles, and I made it as subtle as possible. You should see Sylva's though, it has feathers.'

'What has feathers?' came a voice from behind them.

Fletcher turned, and his mouth dropped open.

Sylva was coming down the stairs, transformed. Gone was the pale, almost silvery hair, replaced with flowing locks which had been dyed and curled to fall about her shoulders in a wave of sable, and the change was so startling that Fletcher was left speechless. Her shoulders were bare, with the red velvet of the dress hugging her slim curves and waist. Her hips held up a sweeping skirt, edged with delicate folds and layers that gave the impression of a budding rose.

She had never looked more beautiful.

'Nobody laugh,' Sylva growled, stomping past them. 'Let's get this over with.'

25

The streets of Hominum flashed by the carriage window, shadowed in the dying light of the winter evening. Few people were walking, and those who were hurried with their heads bowed in the growing darkness. There was a sense of foreboding in the air, weighing heavy and thick like the smoke of an oil lamp.

Cress and Othello had left for the palace on foot, with Seraph's carriage arriving for Fletcher and Sylva soon after. Their reunion had been a happy affair, but their joy had swiftly deteriorated as they came closer to their destination. Now the three of them sat in silence, contemplating the night's task.

'I should be doing this alone,' Seraph said, shaking his head. 'Or Arcturus should. You're taking a huge risk.'

'He's a known enemy of the Triumvirate, as are you,' Fletcher replied. 'You'll be the centre of attention tonight too, being a guest of honour and all. Far better for Sylva and I to be your anonymous guests, and then sneak off at the first opportunity.'

Seraph grunted with reluctant agreement.

'Let's go over the plan again,' Sylva said, her voice forcefully cheerful.

'Right,' Fletcher agreed. 'You start.'

Seraph leaned in to listen, his eyes wide with curiosity.

'The Mite Alfric uses is being kept in the throne room, directly above the banquet hall,' Sylva said, her eyes shut as she recited from memory. 'The demon itself has had its legs amputated and is fixed on the end of a blackthorn staff, somewhere in the chamber. It should have a cloth covering it.'

Fletcher shuddered, remembering when Arcturus had told them of that horrifying detail. The Mite was wild, unconnected to any summoner, so it had to be kept in place during Alfric's addresses to the people of Hominum.

'To reach it, we must leave through one of the side doors in the hall and make our way up the stairs,' Sylva continued. 'There, we will use the picklock spell to break in. I will remove the journal strapped to my leg and begin reading it aloud, while showing each page to the Mite.'

Fletcher took over as she paused for breath.

'Cress and Othello will be serving food and drink to the guests,' he said. 'They will create a distraction, while we sneak into the throne room. If all goes well, we should be done in a few minutes and the guests will be none the wiser.'

Seraph's eyebrows furrowed.

'What happens if Cress and Othello's distraction doesn't work, and word gets out that you're in there, making a speech?'

'Then we'll just need to hold them off until the story is told,' Fletcher said grimly. 'King Harold will order Rook and Lord Forsyth's arrest. Then we wait. See if Alfric goes along with it.'

'That's the plan?' Seraph asked, his eyes widening with surprise. 'What if Alfric defends them?'

'He's in this up to his neck,' Sylva replied, her voice fierce. 'And all of Hominum will be furious. If he wants to prevent his involvement from coming out and a crowd with pitchforks and torches marching on the palace, he'll take Harold's side and condemn the two as traitors. Hominum's people may dislike the dwarves now, but when they find out who's really behind the bombings, they'll be out for blood. Alfric will sacrifice them to save his own skin.'

There was a knock on the ceiling of the carriage, where the driver was sitting.

'Well, I guess there's no turning back now,' Seraph said. 'We're here.'

They took their masks from their laps and put them on, the dusty scent of fresh-made porcelain thick in their nostrils. It was not a moment too soon, for the door swung open, and Fletcher found himself being invited out of the carriage by a footman in black and white livery and an exaggerated white wig.

Gravel crunched underfoot, and then the full sight of the palace hit his view. He had seen it from a distance before, for the building was out of the way, towards the north of Corcillum. But up close, the true size and majesty of the palace became apparent.

The mansion was built of white marble, but tonight it was tinged gold by the burning flares ensconced in embrasures in its lower walls. It was five storeys high, with a central dome and two broad wings emerging from each side. The facade was held up by scores of pillars, as thick as oak trees and encircled by carvings of twisting vines. All around, carefully trimmed hedges loomed over sloping lawns, with elegant fountains trickling beside the gravelled paths.

Alfric had nearly bankrupted Hominum building this palace – it was why he had abdicated the throne to his son, Harold. The people of Hominum had been close to uprising at the time, and the change of ruler had calmed things down. Or, at least, the impression of a change of ruler.

'Right this way, if you please,' the footman said, bowing and scraping as he led them over the gravel towards the well-lit entrance. There were milling crowds of people waiting to be announced upon entry, their gaudy clothing lit by the flickering flames in a kaleidoscope of colours.

Fletcher turned to Sylva, checking to see if her mask was hiding her ears. The mask itself was similar in design to his, but used silver tracing instead of gold. It was edged with the green-blue of peacock feathers, arching back to cover her elven ears, which had also been folded and tied in place to keep them hidden beneath her new locks.

Turning from Fletcher, Sylva took Seraph by the arm and walked on ahead. After all, she was his guest. Feeling an irrational pang of jealousy, Fletcher scratched at his collar and followed.

The people waiting in the palace courtyard reminded Fletcher of a host of tropical birds, preening and calling to one another in an exaggerated display. He had thought he and Sylva's costumes alarmingly bright and conspicuous, but now he realised that theirs were simple in comparison.

Officers paraded with gaudy medals sparkling on their chests, their military regalia on full show. Many of their masks only covered the upper half of their faces: grotesque affairs of hooked noses and horns, a parody of the chiselled, handsome jaws beneath. Women with painted white faces accompanied them, their hair piled high in fanciful styles, with fake beauty spots stuck strategically about their cheeks. Their skirts were layered with flourishes of silk, so wide and heavy that Fletcher was sure they had to be held up by metal framework. Most wore but a simple eye mask, so as to show off the beauty of their made-up complexions.

Nobles were no less extravagant, marked out only by the symbols of wealth that adorned their bodies. Jewels sparkled on the noblewomen's chests, while the noblemen's fingers were weighed down by heavy rings of gold and silver.

Even in the cool winter air, Fletcher began to sweat as they entered the torch-pooled lights on a red carpet outside, joining the queue behind a gaggle of young women. Ahead, the names of the guests were being announced as they entered between the cloistered pillars and through the enormous double doors to the entrance hall.

A sudden thought hit Fletcher, and fresh sweat broke out on his forehead, slick against the porcelain mask.

'Name,' Fletcher hissed, stepping forward and pulling Seraph aside.

'What?' Seraph asked.

'My name, what is it?' Fletcher hissed. The queue edged closer, and a pair of unaccompanied junior officers joined behind them.

'I don't know. Make something up,' Seraph replied, tugging

his arm away and rejoining Sylva. Seraph's own mask only covered his eyes, and Fletcher could see the tan skin of the noble-to-be's jaw tightening with anxiety.

The girls ahead had reached the front of the queue, pausing to cackle uproariously as one of their group stumbled, her foot caught in her dress.

Fletcher's mind was blank. James Baker. Mason. Why couldn't he think of anything else? He gritted his teeth as the announcer took the invitations from the women ahead, announcing their names in quick succession.

'Priscilla Hawthorne!'

The name swirled around his head.

'Vivien Findlay!'

Was his name supposed to sound common? Or eastern, like Baybars or Pasha?

'Rosamund Bambridge!'

Something simple. Anything.

'Helena Bambridge!'

And then Seraph was showing his invitation, motioning for Fletcher to come forward.

'Name, sir?' the announcer asked.

'James Rotherham,' Fletcher stuttered, the words out of his mouth before he could take them back.

'James Rotherham!' the announcer bellowed. Then he was through, stumbling into the golden glow of the entrance hall. He was blinded by the bright chandelier, heard the jabbering of a thousand conversations.

The entryway was packed with people, standing in circles and reaching out to snatch proffered carafes of sparkling wine and salmon-cream crowned canapés.

A broad marble stairway dominated the room, with a red felt carpet up the centre leading up to an elegant double doorway above. The chamber itself was as wide as the Atrium at Vocans, though not as tall. As he looked up, Fletcher was enthralled to see the ceiling was painted with a colourful mural of an ancient, white-haired king, a golden crown resting on his head and his hands outstretched to spill dozens of demons across the vaulting in a vortex of pale light.

Realising he was gawping, Fletcher lowered his eyes, to see servant girls in pink dwarven garb weaving through the waiting crowds, drinks and food held aloft on platters. One hurried closer, her veiled head turned towards him.

'A drink, sir?' she asked.

Fletcher nodded wordlessly, accepting a fluted glass of fizzy wine and bringing it to his lips.

'Don't actually drink it,' the dwarf whispered, shuffling closer. 'You need a clear head tonight. Seriously, don't drink anything but water, just in case we . . .'

She tailed off as a noble wandered by and took a drink from her platter. Fletcher couldn't help but grin, his anxiety dropping a few notches. He lowered the glass and Cress scurried off, dodging through the crowds with her empty platter held aloft. She paused beside another dwarf, one whose overly broad shoulders left Fletcher in little doubt that it was Othello. It was only now that he recognised the red espadrille shoes the two wore, the prearranged identifier to set them apart from the other dwarven servants, whose shoes were plain beige.

'When does it start?' Sylva said from behind him, making

183

him jump. He spilled a splash of wine on the marble floor, and he hastily covered it up with his loafer.

'Relax,' Seraph said, squeezing Fletcher's shoulder. 'They're just waiting for Didric to arrive. It should be any minute now. You two should get away from me, I'm the guest of honour remem—'

Seraph froze, the word dying on his lips. Then Fletcher saw them, walking purposefully into the entrance hall. Tarquin and Isadora.

And they were heading right for them.

26

The two nobles were dressed in black military regalia, complete with matching masks that were no more than a simple white visor across their eyes. Indeed, Isadora was not the only woman to be wearing military dress – in the corner of his eye Fletcher saw that several other recent arrivals had foregone ballgowns for the more clean-cut look: noblewomen who bore high-ranking positions in the military, or their own private armies.

Fletcher's breathing quickened at the sight of the twins, sweat bursting across his palms. They stalked through the room like a pair of golden-haired lions, completely at ease in the ostentatious gathering of Hominum's elite.

Ignoring the calls of greeting from the other guests, the pair walked directly towards Seraph. Fletcher felt Sylva snatching at his sleeve, but the shock of seeing the pair had rooted him to the spot. By the time he came to his senses, it was too late, and Tarquin and Isadora stood before them, masked eyes flicking between the three of them.

'Congratulations, Seraph,' Tarquin said, his voice flat and

unenthusiastic. 'A noble at last. You have come up in the world.'

'Thank you,' Seraph replied stiffly.

Tarquin barely registered the response. His eyes were boring into Fletcher's own, narrowing beneath his mask. Fletcher remained silent, but inclined his head slightly, as if in greeting.

'Well, don't be rude, Seraph darling,' Isadora said, flicking her mane of hair. 'Won't you introduce us to your guests?'

Seraph cleared his throat, buying himself time.

'James Rotherham,' Seraph finally said, his voice an octave higher than usual. 'He's from Swazulu. Come to oversee our sulphur mines.'

'James Rotherham,' Tarquin asked, his brows furrowing. 'That's a northern name. And you're a little pale to be from Swazulu, aren't you, James?'

'Uh, he doesn't speak our language very well,' Seraph said hastily. 'His forefathers are originally from Hominum, hence the name and appearance, but he's as foreign as they come.'

Fletcher bowed his head lower, and clasped his hands together in a gesture of respect. Tarquin grunted, the suspicion plain on his face – even with the eye mask. Still, his main interest was in Sylva, his eyes lingering on her slim frame a touch longer than Fletcher would have liked.

'Tell me, Seraph, why have you brought an elf to the ball?' Isadora said, then laughed at Seraph's sharp intake of breath.

'Well, don't act so surprised,' she giggled, slapping Seraph playfully on the shoulder. 'Her eyes, they're far too colourful. Even Mummy's eyes aren't *that* blue. Honestly Seraph, don't you have any friends from your own nation?'

She pretended to pause and think, then covered her mouth

with a gasp of mock mortification. 'Oh wait, they all died, didn't they? I'm so sorry.'

Seraph stuttered with anger, and Fletcher had to resist balling his hands into fists. Fortunately, Sylva stepped smoothly forward and curtsied deeply before Seraph could reply.

'Good evening.'

An elven accent, pure and lilting, lay thick over her words. It was an impressive performance, and Fletcher grinned beneath his mask.

'I am a representative of the clans, here to negotiate a weapons deal with Lord Pasha.' She nodded at Seraph. 'Our troops will be arriving on the front lines soon, and they need arms. We thought it best that I do not make my presence at the ball known, given the current . . . climate.'

Tarquin set his jaw, and the furrow in his brow deepened.

'Did you not consider the Triumvirate for your weapons?' Isadora asked, her voice sickly sweet. 'Our factories are far closer to your borders than the Pashas' are.'

'We choose who we do business with very carefully,' Sylva stated, crossing her arms. 'It is a matter of . . . taste.'

The two stiffened at her words, and Fletcher saw twin spots of red appear on Tarquin's cheeks.

'Come on, Isadora,' Tarquin snapped, taking his sister's arm. 'We must pay our respects to Lady Faversham.'

The duo swept off, disappearing into the crowd without a second glance.

'Swazulu?' Fletcher hissed. 'Is that the best you could come up with?'

'Hey, don't blame me,' Seraph muttered under his breath,

stepping closer so Fletcher could hear him. 'You're the one who didn't have a story ready, or even a bloody name. You know I only got told about this harebrained scheme of yours a few hours ago, right? I had to leave my two real guests twiddling their thumbs in my hotel room, and you're lucky their invitations didn't have names on them. Don't forget, if this goes wrong, my life is on the line. Aiding and abetting traitors makes me one too.'

Fletcher sighed and took a sip of his wine. It was bitter in his mouth, and he swallowed it with a grimace. He instantly regretted it, feeling the acid liquid trickle down and sit in the pit of his stomach.

'I'm sorry,' he said. 'But we seem to have got away with it, so no harm done.'

'Well, Sylva did no better. Did you have to antagonise them?' Seraph moaned.

'I couldn't help myself,' Sylva said, with a hint of regret in her voice.

'Just move away from me, before someone else we know comes to say hello.'

As if on cue, the announcer called Didric's name, reducing the hubbub of noise to hushed whispering. Fletcher caught a glimpse of his nemesis, dressed in the bee-striped dress uniform of his private army: an elegantly tailored two-piece with the chevrons of a captain emblazoned across the shoulders. He wore a silver, crescent-shaped mask that perfectly covered the burned half of his face. Instantly, he was surrounded by fawning lesser nobles, desperate to become acquainted with the new lord.

But there was no need to hurry away, for the announcer called out to the guests. 'Ladies and gentlemen, please proceed to the banquet hall.'

Fletcher needed no further coaxing, and Sylva hooked her arm through his and joined the chattering crowds up the stairs. She struggled somewhat with every step, for the dress was long and caught under her heels. Fletcher realised that these dainty, high-heeled slippers were a poor choice of footwear for their night's work, and pointless because they could barely be seen beneath the trailing skirts.

By the time they reached the doors, Fletcher was sweating under the heat from the bright torches that lit the way, leaving the black curls of his hair soaked with perspiration. They stumbled through into the new light of the banquet hall, only to gape in wonder.

Three long tables stood side by side, in a room lit with so many chandeliers that it was as if the very ceiling was ablaze. The floor was the warm umber of polished mahogany, and marble busts that depicted generations of the royal family lined the walls, glowering at the assembled guests as if disapproving of the extravagant display.

Foppish footmen bowed and scraped as they walked in, before leading the guests to their places. Fletcher found himself sitting with Seraph and Sylva, opposite a heavyset nobleman, whose face was already red from drink. The man was seated between two young women who were clearly his guests, for they fawned over his every word. Both were heavily made-up, with their hair piled high and matching golden masks across their eyes.

'Of course, it's a damned shame,' the man was saying as Sylva and Seraph sat down on either side of Fletcher. 'I mean, King Harold's a good sort, heart in the right place and all that, but he's gone too far this time.'

'You're *so* right, Bertie dearest, far too far,' one of the women gushed, leaning closer so that Fletcher could see a large black beauty spot on her left cheek.

'Far too far,' the other repeated, nodding along. She had an unusually long neck, her head bobbing like that of a stork.

'Give them an inch and they'll take a mile, that's what I always say,' Bertie continued, his jowls wobbling as he rapped the table with his knuckle for emphasis. 'Dwarves need to know their place. Now look what's happened. A few hundred of the buggers marching down here, armed to the teeth, and all the while their bombs going off left and right.'

'It's positively ghastly,' Beauty Spot said. 'We aren't safe in our beds at night.'

'Now old King Alfric, he's got the right idea,' Bertie mumbled. He held up a finger, then lifted a fluted glass of sparkling wine and quaffed it in a single gulp, spilling half of the pale liquid down his lacy white shirt.

Then he leaned in and beckoned Fletcher, Seraph and Sylva closer. Reluctantly the three bent their necks, if only not to appear rude and attract attention.

'I have it on good authority that the old king has ordered the Pinkertons to seize the dwarven workshops tomorrow night,' he whispered, looking over his shoulder in case a dwarven servant girl was nearby. 'Because, of course, that's where the bombs are being made. I'm old chums with Alfric and, of course, he confided in me.'

'You're so *in the know*,' Long Neck said, covering her mouth with a hand.

'Of course, Alfric comes to me for advice all the time,' Bertie continued bombastically. 'Can't make a decision without me.'

'That's very interesting,' Seraph said, humouring the loud-mouthed man. 'He must trust your opinion a great deal.'

Fletcher very much doubted that the cold, calculating Alfric would be friendly with the drunken braggart before him. Most likely the man had heard it through the rumour mill, and was simply boasting to the impressionable young ladies.

But the news was troubling. The dwarven foundries were located in the basements of the dwarven homes, built into the bedrock and secured by metal doors. Alfric would be hard-pressed to break into them, which meant that the Pinkertons would have to invade the dwarven homes themselves. On top of it all they would be trying to enter the most secret sanctums of the dwarves. If this was true, there would be riots that night, one way or another. All part of Alfric's grand plan to instigate a revolt.

'The best part of it all is that we'll finally get a look at how they're making their damned guns,' Bertie continued. 'I told him, I said, "Alfric, you've got to see about the guns." Once we have that, we'll have no need for the sneaky little buggers. We can arrest the lot of them and throw away the key.'

The noble tossed the dregs at the bottom of his glass into his mouth, then smacked his lips and sighed contentedly.

'Well, that seems jolly harsh, Bertie,' Beauty Spot said, fanning herself. 'Couldn't we just . . . send them on their way? Maybe put them on a ship or something?'

'Far too dangerous,' Bertie said, glancing around the room for a servant girl to refill his glass. 'They started it, after all. The bombing was all their doing, and then one of them killed that brave boy on that mission, right in front of our eyes. That proves it – they'd come back and wipe us off the face of the earth if they could. No, Gertrude, it's them or us.'

'But why?'

It took Fletcher a moment to realise it was he who had spoken.

'I'm sorry?' Bertie said, the sweaty forehead above his mask wrinkling into a frown.

'Why did she kill Rufus Cavendish?' Fletcher faltered, unsure if he should continue.

'Who knows why these creatures do such things?' Bertie said, waving away the question as if it were an annoying fly. 'Probably to send a message to all of Hominum, tell us all exactly how dwarven bread is buttered, so to speak. The point is, she did it.'

The wrinkles of the nobleman's frown deepened and his eyes narrowed behind his mask. Clearly the man was not used to being questioned in this manner.

'I say, who the devil are you, anyway?' he said. 'I don't recognise your uniform.'

'My guest,' Seraph said smoothly, while laying a calming hand on Fletcher's thigh. 'And I am Lord Pasha.'

Even beneath the mask, Fletcher saw Bertie blanch. After all, Seraph's affiliation with the dwarves was no secret.

'I . . . that is . . .' The man's Adam's apple bobbed as he swallowed. 'I know you have a certain . . . sympathy for the dwarves. I didn't mean to cause offence.'

'None taken,' Seraph said, tightening his grip on Fletcher's knee, as if to warn him not to take it further. He needn't have bothered – Fletcher was already regretting his outburst.

Further awkwardness was avoided by the gentle dingle of bells, announcing that food was ready. Soon servants were sweeping between the tables, balancing enormous platters, complete with gleaming covers to keep the food warm. Within minutes the centre of the table was filled with the steaming silverware, and the waiting stewards removed the covers with a simultaneous flourish.

Fletcher's stomach clenched with hunger at the sight of it. The delicious scent that wafted beneath his nose filled his mouth with saliva.

The largest offering was the quarter of a stag, its rump slow-roasted overnight to leave the flesh succulent and soft. A swan stuffed with mushrooms and oysters sat beside it, the crispy skin basted in a pulped sauce of figs and saffron, glistening beneath the flickering flames of the chandeliers above. Further down the table was a whole roast boar, a crisp red apple held in its mouth.

Even with these enormous dishes, yet more meat lined the tables; skillets of hare with tangerine jelly, fritters of river pike, poached sturgeon with a garnish of its own caviar and even a gooducken, the extravagant portmanteau of a chicken stuffed within a duck, stuffed within a goose.

Surrounding the meats were more delicacies: garlicky winter greens, plums stewed in rose water, candied chestnuts and bowls of red berries in clotted cream. Fletcher could only see the food on his own table, but he found even this too much to take in. He tried to resist reaching out a hand to taste the nearest dish.

Instead, he worked at unclipping the lower segment of his mask, so as to allow himself to eat.

'Cress says to stick with water,' Seraph whispered, as a pink-clad dwarf swept away from him.

Then the announcer's voice cut through the gasps of wonder and clinking cutlery.

'Lords, ladies and honourable gentlemen. Let the banquet commence!'

27

Fletcher didn't even have time to reach for the food before Sylva's long leg slid under Seraph's seat to kick his ankle. He stifled a groan of disappointment and saw her stand and curtsy.

'I am feeling a little weak from the smell of all this rich food,' Sylva said, lifting a hand dramatically to her brow. 'Mr Rotherham, would you be so kind as to escort me to get some fresh air?'

Fletcher took a moment to realise she was speaking to him, then reluctantly got to his feet and took her arm. The two needn't have bothered with the theatrics – the nobles surrounding them barely gave the pair a second glance, already devouring the food with as much decorum as they could muster.

To Fletcher, the only silver lining was that he would not need to work out which cutlery to use, for the tablecloth had been festooned with a variety of knives, spoons, forks and other implements he could not recognise. Still, it was the best time to leave, while the rest of the room were distracted.

'Come on,' Sylva hissed, tugging him away from his seat and

down the long table. They knew where they had to go – a pair of heavy double doors in the side of the room. Fletcher felt a shudder run down his spine as eyes turned to them, for they were the only guests standing. He distracted himself by examining the other foods on the table. To his surprise and horror, the roasted carcass of an entire porpoise was being carved by a mincing footman at the head of the principal table.

Then he saw the people surrounding the poor animal and a new sense of revulsion took hold. Almost all of his enemies were seated there: Old King Alfric, Lord and Lady Faversham, the Forsyth twins, even Didric himself. King Harold sat among them, laughing at a joke his father had told.

Fletcher almost found himself faltering in his pace, but Sylva drew him inexorably onwards, her grip firm on his arm. He couldn't help but look over his shoulder as they passed. It was fascinating, to see them socialising. Somehow he always pictured them plotting in dark rooms, not enjoying meals together.

Moments later and they were through the double doors, opened by confused servants who weren't sure where the two guests were going, but were too anxious to stop what could be important nobles.

They were in a long, dark corridor with red velvet carpet. Only a few flickering candles revealed a staircase halfway down the passage. They tugged off their masks, and Fletcher breathed in deep relief.

'Walk, don't run,' Sylva said, taking command of the situation and tugging him behind her. 'We don't want to look suspicious, and guests aren't supposed to go exploring.'

Fletcher panted with shallow breaths, and his palms sweated beneath his white gloves.

'It must be hard for Harold to keep up his act, day in and day out,' Fletcher said, talking to steady his nerves.

But he never heard Sylva's response, because the double doors slammed open behind them. Fletcher caught a glimpse of a guardsman, a candelabra clutched in one hand, a sword in the other. Then he felt himself pulled against Sylva, her hands around his neck, lips seeking his. She kissed him with a fierce abandon, and Fletcher returned it with the same passion. He sank into it, feeling the softness of her body against his. For a moment, nothing else mattered.

'Just two lovebirds,' the guard grunted. 'Nothing to worry about.'

The doors shut with a gentle thud.

Instantly, Sylva pulled away, sweeping back towards the stairs as quickly as possible.

'Come on,' she said, looking at him over her shoulder. 'They'll expect us to go back soon. Othello and Cress will have to catch up.'

Fletcher followed, a pang of sadness running through him. It had been a ploy – nothing more.

They mounted the stairs two at a time, Sylva going barefoot with her heels in her hands, Fletcher avoiding the train of her dress. It was ridiculous how much material she had to drag behind her.

The corridor they emerged into was darker still, lit only by the glow from the stairs behind them and a single candle in an alcove nearby. They had reached their destination – a set of enormous doors directly opposite the stairway. The throne room's entrance loomed, dark and ominous.

'Let's hope Othello and Cress have begun their distraction,' Fletcher whispered.

'Let me,' Sylva said. Her finger glowed blue and she etched the shape of a keyhole in the air. Slowly, she lowered it over the deep lock on the door and streamed a jet of silvery light into it. There was a loud snap, and then the door swung open with a groan of creaking hinges.

Beyond, an enormous chamber came into view, lit by a beam of moonlight from a skylight. The room was bisected by a line of thick, red carpet, with marble flooring on either side. Pillars of stone lined the walls, cast in deep shadow. But one thing dominated above all else. A throne, made of gold, silver and precious gems, inlaid with mother-of-pearl and skirted with polished wood, was set on a dais at the end of the long, red mantle at the back of the room. Every element on the throne was designed in a mosaic of interwoven demons, the gems forming their eyes, the metals delineating the lines of their bodies. It was magnificent, sparkling even in the dim light. Fletcher could hardly take his eyes from it – he had never seen so much wealth in one place.

Then they saw it, embedded in the floor directly in front of the throne. A black staff, covered by a laced cloth. Their target.

'Hurry,' Sylva hissed, oblivious to the splendour of the royal seat. Fletcher followed, the dull thud of their footsteps echoing.

But they were barely halfway across the room when the screech of hinges cut through the air behind them, followed by the slam of the doors.

Fletcher turned, his hand reaching for a sword that was not there.

'Well, well,' Rook said, stepping out of the shadows. 'Look what we have here, Zacharias. A she-elf and a traitor, out for a stroll.'

28

The hulking figure of Lord Forsyth emerged from behind the Inquisitor, shaking his leonine mane of hair to reveal the missing ear. Neither wore their masks, but both were dressed in their pompous dress uniforms: Rook's a silver-laced cassock of dark cloth and Zacharias's a tassled black uniform, sewn with epaulettes and golden buttons.

'It was foolish of you to come here,' Zacharias Forsyth said, his voice booming and deep. 'When my children told me there was an elf at the ball . . . well. We kept an eye on you. It didn't take us long to work out who you were, or see what you were up to.'

He took a step closer, into the light, and the scarred remnants of his ear gave his head a lopsided appearance.

'You've got courage, I'll give you that,' he said, smiling at them. 'Here for the staff, I assume.'

He nodded towards the staff behind them.

'Stealing it won't do you any good. The seed is sown, and you shall reap the consequences. Preventing a few more speeches won't make a damned bit of difference. Not that you'll be around to see it.'

Fletcher let his hands drift behind his back and slowly eased the gloves from his hands. The two men before him were master battlemages, and Zacharias was a tried and tested veteran of a brutal war. The odds were stacked against him.

There was a ripping sound, and Fletcher saw Sylva out of the corner of his eye, tearing the excess fabric away from her dress, then slitting the side with a stiletto blade to free up her movement – and revealing the journal strapped to her thigh.

'What's that?' Rook demanded, as Sylva took it and backed away, the thin booklet swiftly stowed behind her.

Fletcher whipped his hand up, billowing out a wall of shield energy. It was broad enough to protect both himself and Sylva, but the two men simply smirked and watched them through the opaque barrier.

They didn't understand that he and Sylva weren't trying to steal the staff, but get a message out to the people of Hominum. They both thought they had all the time in the world.

'The question is, do we kill them here, or do we have them arrested and wait for the trial and summary execution?' Rook mused. 'A trial might be more public, sow more dissent.'

His voice was low – they were close to the staff now, and his words might be heard across all of Hominum if they were any louder.

'We kill them,' Zacharias replied, crouching slightly and sweeping his hands apart, ready for a potential attack. 'If we arrest the she-elf, that fool Harold will step in and protect her, to prevent a war with the elves. As you know, trials are . . . unpredictable.'

Fletcher heard a flutter of cloth as Sylva removed the staff's cover. There was a glow of blue as she etched in the air, then a beam of pale light from a ball of white wyrdlight, a spell rarely used because it drained so much mana. The bright rays cast a long shadow in front of Fletcher, his black outline stretched between him and his two enemies.

'Yes, that's right,' Zacharias laughed. 'Turn the staff this way, let the world get a clear view. When the elves see us kill their precious princess, we'll have another war – a real one this time. The dwarves tomorrow and the elves next.'

'And you'll line your pockets with blood money,' Fletcher snarled.

'If it's elven or dwarven blood, it will make it all the sweeter,' Rook said, a cruel smile playing across his sallow face.

Sylva began to speak. Her voice was low, for she was muttering right above the frozen Mite's head. Fletcher allowed himself a glance behind, and saw her brandishing Zacharias's letter in front of the immobilised demon's eyes, her finger pointing to the Forsyth seal at the bottom.

'Stop that,' Rook snapped, taking a step forward. 'What are you saying?'

Then Zacharias's eyes lit up in recognition, seeing the scrap of paper through the opaque shield.

'Stop her!' he bellowed, and suddenly his fingers were scoring the air and a blast of lightning crackled across the room. It slammed into the shield, cleaving and rending the wall of white, the surface snapping and fracturing like broken ice on a lake.

Rook added a vortex of fire a moment later, the billowing flame flattening against the shield and dissolving the surface, layer by layer.

'Hurry, Sylva,' Fletcher yelled, as the shield disintegrated before his eyes. 'Show them the journal!'

He needed to summon Ignatius, but all he could do was pulse more and more mana into the shield, reinforcing it in ribbons of white light where it was weakest. His right hand etched the fire symbol desperately in the air, but even as he fixed the spell to his finger, Rook and Zacharias formed their own oval shields using their free hands.

Now Sylva was shouting, the words lost before they reached Fletcher's ears against the roar of the spells battering against his shield.

Fletcher hurled a ball of fire into the air, arcing it over to burst on Zacharias's shield, cascading around the edges in a waterfall of flame to singe the noble's clothing. Still the spells battered at Fletcher's barrier.

He could feel his mana draining, and the consciousnesses of Ignatius and Athena, desperate to be unleashed. He forced through a last burst of mana into the shield and then let it hang without his reinforcement, shaking and shivering beneath the onslaught of blue lightning and orange flame. His mind twisted as he forced Ignatius through his hand and into existence.

It was harder now, for Ignatius was much larger and the pentacle on his hand was small, but within moments the Drake was roaring beside him.

The two men's spells ceased at the sight of the Drake. A piece fell from the shield and dissolved on the smouldering red carpet beneath. All was silent, but for the gentle sizzle of burning fibres and Sylva's muttering as she read another page from Jeffrey's journal.

Rook and Zacharias must have known they were in trouble. They had no summoning leathers, and Fletcher's demons could easily tear through their shields.

Fletcher used the time to bolster his faltering barrier, draining the last dribble of mana within him to add a reparative layer across the fractured surface. He had been low on mana to begin with, for his reserves had not recovered from his time in the ether. But Rook and Zacharias didn't know that.

Now all he needed to do was wait for Sylva to finish. Whatever Cress and Othello had done, it had worked – no guards had arrived yet.

'Why don't you come face me, man on man?' Zacharias called out from behind his shield. 'No demons, no Rook. Just me and you.'

'Sylva, how much longer?' Fletcher asked over his shoulder, ignoring the offer.

'A few more minutes,' Sylva called out. 'I need to tell them what happened to Rufus.'

Fletcher smiled grimly and turned back to his opponents. He stared at them with what he hoped was cool confidence.

'Are you scared, Fletcher?' Rook said. 'The great Fletcher Raleigh has a chance to duel with his worst enemy on equal footing and he refuses. I always knew you were a coward.'

Fletcher knew they were goading him, hoping he would lower his shield and attack Zacharias head on, losing the defensive advantage.

'A coward *and* a fool, trusting dwarves and elves over his own race,' Zacharias spat, striding forward until he stood directly in front of Fletcher's shield, the pale oval of his own still fixed to his wrist. 'You're so much like your father. Edmund was a race traitor too. Always visiting the elves, trying to broker trade between our nations.'

He paused, as if contemplating his next words.

'But that's not the only reason I betrayed him,' he continued, his voice lower, so only Fletcher could hear.

'What did you say?' Fletcher said. A chill ran across the back of his neck.

'My weapons business was stagnating. Too much peace, you see.' Zacharias's eyes bore into Fletcher's own, willing him to see the truth there. 'I needed a catalyst. So I sent the orcs a message. Told them about Raleighshire's secret passage, when and where to attack, all of it. You would not believe how perfectly it came together – your family's lands, inherited by your mother's sister, my wife. A war with the orcs, to fuel my weapons business. And another race traitor dead, just icing on the cake. Tonight I'll have to finish the job. Never send an orc to do a man's work.'

Fletcher looked into the man's cold, serpentine eyes and knew it was true. Perhaps he had always known, ever since Sir Caulder had spoken of a 'betrayer' at his trial. But he had cast it from his mind. He hadn't wanted to contemplate it – that a man could truly be that evil. He hadn't wanted to give in to hatred.

But now that hatred bubbled inside his chest, caustic and hot. Zacharias needed to die. If this worked, the man would soon be locked away, out of Fletcher's reach for ever. There would never be a chance like this again.

The shield. He could resorb it into himself, replenish his mana. Enough for one, powerful attack.

Now.

Fletcher roared, draining the white wall in a vortex of swirling light. Even as he did so, he was already firing all three spells in a twisting beam from his fingers. It corkscrewed into Zacharias's shield in a blaze of spitting energy. The oval split like an egg, exploding in a blast of spinning shards that hurled the noble into a pillar with a sickening thud. He crumpled to the floor, limp as a corpse.

'Fletcher!' Sylva screamed, and Fletcher's shout of triumph died on his lips. Because Rook's shield was gone, and a wave of fire was roaring across the hall.

Ignatius dived to take the brunt, his wings outstretched. Missed.

The blaze hit Fletcher like a flood, tumbling him from his feet and into the dark recesses of the throne room. He skidded across the floor as the flames billowed over him, blinding bright in his eyes. He could hear the roaring of the inferno, feel his clothing blacken and peel away into nothingness. The heat blew scalding hot against his skin.

But no pain. No agony of his flesh being scorched to ash, nor the stench of burning hair. Instead, he rolled and rolled, until the worst of the flames had left the tattered remains of his clothing. He staggered to his feet, beating at the smouldering cloth, blinking the smoke from his eyes.

Rook stood there, his chest heaving in and out with exertion. By the size of the conflagration that had blown Fletcher across the hall, the Inquisitor must have put everything into that attack

– every last drop of mana he had. But somehow, Fletcher had come away practically unscathed.

A translucent ball of kinetic energy hit Rook in the chest, flinging him against the floor and pinning him there. Sylva strode across the room, a cold fury in her eyes.

'We should kill them both,' she said. Her finger was raised, a bolt of lightning crackling from the symbol fixed to its tip. Ignatius barked in agreement, his large chest turning the sound into more the roar of a lion than the baying of a dog. A jolt of anger from Athena's consciousness confirmed her opinion on the matter. The two demons were shocked at how close their master had come to death.

Fletcher turned to the scrying staff, suddenly fearful that her words could be heard across Hominum, but it had been covered with the heavy cloth once again. It was then that he realised they had succeeded. Hominum had heard their story. Now all they could do was wait.

Rook was emitting a keening sound, wheezing from the blow to his chest. He had had the wind knocked out of him, and could barely move as Sylva leaned over him, the sizzling lightning poised over his face.

Fletcher stumbled towards them, and somehow the hatred that had bubbled inside him seemed diminished at the sight of the men's prone bodies. Instead, his mind drifted to why he was alive at all. The fire should have killed him. How had he survived?

'No,' Fletcher coughed, his throat raw from the smoke. 'If we kill them, Hominum will have no one left to blame, and Harold nobody to imprison. We need the world to see them condemned.'

And for a moment he wondered if that was truly the reason.

Or was it because he didn't want to commit the cold-blooded murder of two helpless men? He wished he could say he was surprised that Sylva seemed capable of such an act – but the look in her eyes left Fletcher in no doubt.

Sylva used the ripped cloth from her dress to bind Zacharias and Rook's hands and feet, with Ignatius keeping a watchful eye beside her. Rook's mouth was stuffed and tied too, for he began to spit obscenities at the two as soon as he recovered his breath. Once they were trussed up like chickens for a roast, Fletcher and Sylvia lifted the two on to Ignatius's back and walked out through the main doors.

Fletcher took the liberty of purloining the unconscious Zacharias's trousers, for his own had been reduced to a bunch of charred threads. He took grim satisfaction in how ridiculous the bear of a man looked in his underwear, his pale legs contrasting with the golden tan across his face and forearms.

'Come on,' Sylva said, once Fletcher had rolled up the bottoms of the trousers. 'Let's see what's waiting for us outside.'

The corridors were deserted. Likewise, the stairs showed no sign of disturbance. It was as if their speech had never happened, and for a moment Fletcher's heart began to pound with the worry that it had somehow not worked, that Sylva had done it wrong. But when they kicked open the doors to the banquet hall, the reason for the absence of pursuit became apparent.

The stench hit them in a wave, and the gorge rose in Fletcher's throat. It was the acrid scent of vomit, so heavy he could taste it. Nobles, generals, guests and even a few servants lay splayed around the hall, groaning in discomfort. The occasional gurgle and splash of lumpy liquid told Fletcher exactly which form of distraction Othello and Cress had gone for.

There had been several plans: blocking the fireplaces so that the smoke would fill the rooms, breaking pipes to flood the floors with water, using spellcraft to make loud noises, even setting fire to the hedges outside. But this plan . . . it had been ruled out as too risky. Obviously Othello and Cress had changed their minds.

The pair had sabotaged the drinks, sneaking into the kitchens and tainting as much of it as possible with ground ayahuasca – a plant traditionally associated with orc shamans, who would drink it to induce vomiting and wild hallucinations. Signs of the latter were already visible, with some nobles reaching up at the bright candles above, stupid grins plastered across their vomit-stained faces. Fletcher took a perverse pleasure in seeing Bertie wandering the room in nothing but his underwear, giggling to himself.

Even Sylva could not help but laugh when they saw the Forsyth twins laid low, pawing deliriously at the bright chandeliers above, drool dribbling down their cheeks as they cooed and smiled inanely. Tarquin giggled and waved as their father was carried past them.

'Serves them right,' Sylva said, stepping delicately over Isadora's outstretched arm. 'What I wouldn't give to see their faces in the morning. This has been a long time coming.'

'You and me both.' Fletcher grinned.

There was no sign of any dwarves – the serving girls had obviously run away for fear of repercussions, and Othello and Cress with them.

Scanning the room, Fletcher noticed that many of the more

important nobles were no longer there, including Alfric and Harold. They had obviously been rushed to safety by the guards. In fact, even with Ignatius and their captives in tow, they were able to walk the full length of the hall and down the stairs with barely more than a second glance. Even the servants were too busy tending to the sick.

The whole situation seemed unbelievable to Fletcher as they walked out into the fresh air, gravel crunching beneath their feet, the moonlight streaming down upon them. They looked a complete state – Fletcher in his half-burned clothing and rolled-up trousers, Sylva with her ripped dress, not to mention the bare-legged Zacharias on the back of their hitherto unnoticed Drake.

Yet somehow, they were outside, with no pursuers, nor even a raised alarm.

'We made it,' he breathed.

'That we did,' Sylva said quietly. 'But what happens now?'

Fletcher did not know. Only Harold had thought this far ahead – once again they were pawns in a far greater game. But he knew where they needed to go.

'Ignatius, do you reckon you could carry all four of us into the Dwarven Quarter?' Fletcher asked, pressing his head against the Drake's own. 'It's not far.'

The demon purred and nudged him in assent. Fletcher and Sylva pulled themselves on to his shoulders, sitting astride the backs of their captives, grinning as Rook growled through his gag.

Ignatius roared in triumph, rearing up and throwing himself into the air.

And then they were gone, into the night.

29

They landed beside Othello's home under cover of darkness, waiting for a cloud to obscure the moon before making their descent. They had seen the watchfires from the Pinkertons around the edges of the Dwarven Quarter, and knew that their presence would set off too many alarms if noticed.

Once inside the enormous tent, they were reunited with Cress, Othello and his mother Briss, who greeted them with applause. Then they were told that Athol, Atilla, Thaissa and Uhtred were away in the caves beneath the Dwarven Quarter, preparing for the worst.

The group's celebration of a successful mission was short-lived, however – the three dwarves immediately began fretting at the presence of the two nobles in their home. The kidnapping had never been part of the plan. Now all they could do was send word to Harold via a Mite the King had left in Briss's care, in the hopes that he would know what to do. So they waited in nervous silence, with Ignatius's claws resting on their prisoners' throats, in case of any sudden movements.

Harold and his men came for them within the hour, marching through the Dwarven Quarter and into Othello's home like an invading army. These were not Pinkertons or Inquisitors, but royal guardsmen, wearing the traditional garb of breastplates, feathered helms and pikes. It was only Harold's presence that prevented weapons from being drawn as the ten men burst in.

'What is the meaning of this?' Othello snapped, as the armoured soldiers crowded into their tent, scattering cushions beneath their feet.

'These are my bodyguards,' Harold said, holding up his hands and smiling disarmingly. 'Don't worry, I trust them with my life.'

'I don't care if you trust them – why are they here?' Othello demanded.

'They're only here because most dwarves do not know I am their ally. Given the current tensions, I couldn't just go for a stroll through the ghetto without adequate protection. I am technically King of Hominum, after all.'

'All right, but let's make this quick.' Othello stepped back, smoothing his beard.

At the sight of Harold, Zacharias began yelling incoherently from behind his gag. Rook remained silent, glowering with black eyes.

Harold stared at the pair for a moment, then strolled over and hunkered down beside them. He lowered his face until it was mere inches from Zacharias's own, as close as a lover.

'That's right,' he whispered. 'After all these years, your treachery will be justly rewarded.'

Zacharias's face reddened, and his muffled grunts were

212

accompanied by spittle as he struggled against his bonds. Harold stood and etched a webbed symbol in the air. Moments later, glowing threads, not unlike that of an Arach, whipped around the pair's hands and feet, even wrapping their fingers in a tight ball to prevent their use of spellcraft.

'I think it's best you let us take these two criminals off your hands before their imprisonment here is discovered and misinterpreted as dwarven aggression.'

'Thank goodness,' Briss said, flapping at her veiled face with her hands.

Harold nodded at his men, and the soldiers marched over and threaded pikes between the nobles' arms and legs. They lifted them like hunters carrying deer on a pole, leaving the pair helplessly swinging in the air.

'Here, use this to cover them,' Thaissa said, pointing at one of the large rugs in the corner of the tent. 'They won't be recognisable with that draped over them.'

'Do it, then take them outside,' Harold ordered. The men rushed to obey.

Moments later, they were alone in the tent, and the tension dropped several notches.

'What happened to you?' Harold asked Fletcher, his brow furrowing at the charred remains of Fletcher's clothing.

'Rook hit me with a fire spell,' Fletcher replied, finding his words hard to believe even as he said them. 'It was bad. But . . . it didn't hurt me.'

Harold raised his eyebrows, then a slow grin spread across his face.

'Immune to Manticore venom *and* fire,' he laughed. 'You're a veritable trove of surprises, Fletcher Raleigh. That Drake of yours must have given you some protection.'

'That's why?' Sylva asked. 'I thought Fletcher had healed himself.'

'Of course not,' Harold said, shaking his head in astonishment. 'He'd never be able to heal himself fast enough. Think about it – a summoner with an Arach or Mite becomes immune to their own individual demon's venom. Fletcher's immunity to fire must be an extension of this phenomenon. You're a lucky young man, Fletcher Raleigh.'

Fletcher turned to Ignatius and smiled to see that the lazy demon had fallen asleep beside the hot, metal chimney that extended through the spiral staircase in the centre of the room and into the roof of the tent. He was lucky indeed.

'So what happens now?' Cress asked, disinterested in Fletcher's immunity. 'Did it work? Did the people hear us?'

The future of her race was at stake, and she wanted answers.

'Most of the guests have recovered from your . . . how shall I put it . . . *flavouring* of the drinks,' Harold said. 'Fortunately, the more important nobles were spirited away by their bodyguards before they could suffer too much embarrassment. I must admit, I still feel a little queasy. You could have warned me!'

He winked at Cress and Othello to show there were no hard feelings.

'News of your proclamations has already spread throughout the land: even the guests at the banquet now know every word of Sylva's speech. We won't know if you're believed or not until tomorrow.'

214

'So it might all have been for nothing?' Cress asked.

'All I know is that Fletcher and Sylva have forced my hand by capturing those two traitors,' Harold said, motioning over his shoulder. 'I told my father I sent the orders for their arrest myself – hence their disappearance. He wasn't too happy with that, but the evidence was so damning that he accepted it readily enough. Anything to prevent himself being implicated in this sordid state of affairs.'

'Well, that's good, right?' Cress persisted. 'We've won?'

'Not quite.' Harold sighed, running his hand over his face. 'Look. Alfric has ordered half the army into the city. Originally it was in preparation for the announcement where he rescinds all dwarven rights, so they could crush the dwarven recruits and the rest of your people as soon as they began to riot. But now he can't make that announcement – it's too much of a risk for him. Instead, he's declared a national holiday and organised a last-minute military parade, to celebrate the success of your mission and the rescue of Lady Raleigh.'

'Great – so what's the problem?' Fletcher asked.

'If the people of Hominum believe what Sylva said, they will welcome the dwarven recruits with open arms. "All is forgiven, we were wrong," so to speak. Alfric knows that if he makes his planned announcement then, the whole thing will backfire – the people will be even more sympathetic to the dwarves. Even if the dwarves riot, the soldiers certainly won't view it as a revolution and start slaughtering them.'

'Exactly, that was the plan all along,' Fletcher agreed.

But Harold wasn't finished.

'On the other hand, if the dwarven recruits arrive and the

people and soldiers give them a cold welcome, my father will know that their hatred runs so deep that they'll ignore the truth. If that happens, he'll make the announcement there and then. The Pinkertons invade dwarven homes, the dwarves riot and the soldiers are told to march into the Dwarven Quarter and put down the "rebellion". Violently.'

'So even after everything we've done, the future of my species rests on how welcoming everyone is tomorrow?' Othello asked, his face dark with anger.

'I'm afraid so,' Harold said.

30

It was strange to see a sky so bright and cheerful in the midst of such tension. Spring had come early, and the day was unnaturally hot. They were in the Anvil Tavern, sitting on the balcony and watching the people mill below. Othello and Cress were long past caring if they were seen, and Fletcher and Sylva had joined them there after some cajoling from the two dwarves.

In truth, few people looked up at them as the human soldiers marched by in all their finery, bayonets glinting in the sunlight, red coats fluttering in the warm breeze. All along the pavements, the citizens of Corcillum cheered, waving flags and pennants and joining in as the men sang ribald marching songs. The beat was rattled out by the drummer boys, young lads of no more than thirteen who marched proudly in uniform beside the soldiers.

Even Othello found himself humming along to the jaunty tunes, and had to catch himself. The mood was gay and joyful, which boded well for the dwarven recruits' arrival. Yet at the same time, there was none of the anger that Fletcher had

217

expected, given the revelation that one of Hominum's nobles had been bombing their own people. Either way, there would be no guarantees that day.

'They're all so young, aren't they?' Cress said, leaning out to get a better view of the soldiers.

'That's because they're all from the recruitment camps on the elven border,' Sylva said. 'They arrived a few days ahead of the dwarves, so they're pretty raw. I doubt any of them have seen action yet.'

'Does that make them more, or less likely to welcome the dwarves?' Fletcher asked, half to himself.

Othello considered it for a moment. 'Well, they've been training beside the dwarven recruits for more than a year now, but since the Anvil attacks tensions between them have been high: a few heated discussions here and there, even a brawl or two. Alfric probably couldn't risk bringing the veterans up from the front lines, so he's marched this lot down. It's good news, I think. These men have never killed before – I doubt they'd have the stomach to slaughter women and children. He probably reckons they're more likely to take orders though, being green and all. We'll see.'

But Fletcher was barely listening. There was a commotion down the road, and for a moment he thought it was the dwarves. But then the new arrivals came into view, and Fletcher couldn't help but grin and lean out for a better look.

Dragoons. The battlemage cavalry, dozens of blue-clad men and women riding powerful demons. Fast-moving and deadly, their reputation was legendary. And a familiar, dark-haired figure was leading them, with Sacharissa padding by his side.

Arcturus was riding a Hippalectryon, and the beast was one of the most beautiful demons Fletcher had ever seen. Its front half was that of a horse, but its muzzle ended in a sharp yellow beak and a red wattle replaced the mane along the back of its neck. Its hind legs were clawed like a rooster's, with razor-sharp spurs that flexed with every pace. A flare of brightly coloured tail feathers extended in a vibrant mix of reds and greens that matched the fur and plumage along the demon's body. It had the sleek lines of a horse combined with the harsh beauty of a bird of prey – both graceful and deadly in equal measures.

'What happened to Bucephalus?' Cress wondered aloud.

'He's Captain Lovett's demon now,' Sylva said, a hint of guilt in her voice. 'After she lost Lysander, he gave Buck to her so she could fly in the Celestial Corps again, and he could join the Dragoons. She told me when I offered to return Lysander to her, back when we were at Vocans.'

'She didn't take you up on that?' Othello asked, surprised. 'Lovett adored that Griffin.'

'I know. I am indebted to her,' Sylva said, the guilt in her voice deepening.

The parade of Dragoons neared and Fletcher began to see the other demons that the battlemages rode. It became obvious that Hippalectryons were the most popular demons among the elite troops.

He could see Sleipnirs, muscle-bound horses with eight powerful legs that made them one of the fastest land demons in existence. And Musimon, like enormous, bearded billy goats with two pairs of horns, the lower curled and thick, the other long and sharp like a bull's.

There was even a rare Kirin, horse-like in appearance but with a reptilian snout, a single antler on its forehead, shimmering green scales armouring its body and plumes of red hair that erupted from its mane, tail and legs.

It was clear to Fletcher that all of the demons were designed for speed and sudden violence, ideal for the crack troops of the empire.

Each battlemage wore an armoured breastplate and a plumed helmet, and was armed with a cavalry sabre: a long, curved blade that could chop down with brutal efficiency. Accompanying the deadly weapons were shortened carbines, pairs holstered on either side of their hips. Fletcher watched them enviously: the guns were longer and more accurate than pistols but shorter and lighter than muskets. They were awesome weapons, but an impractical middle ground for a foot soldier like Fletcher.

'How could we lose with them on our side?' Fletcher said, watching as the fearsome cavalcade passed below them.

'Will the dwarves come through this way?' Sylva asked.

'No, they'll march through the northern end of Corcillum, down towards Corwin Plaza,' Othello replied, the excitement of the passing Dragoons instantly wiped from his face at the reminder. 'That's where the parade ends. There will be some ceremony there, an oath of fealty to the King from all the new recruits, dwarves included.'

'Will they do it?' Fletcher asked.

Othello chewed his lip.

'They have to,' was his only response.

'Can't your father talk to them, tell them what might happen if they don't?' Fletcher asked.

'If my father and the elders had that control over our men, then Alfric's speech wouldn't matter either,' Othello said, shaking his head dejectedly. 'He's gone out there and spoken with them, but they're keeping tight-lipped about the whole thing. You don't know what it's like, Fletcher. Hundreds of years of subjugation. Pinkertons killing us with impunity, our lives ruled by the laws of our oppressors.'

'I'm sorry,' Fletcher murmured. 'I didn't think . . .'

'These young dwarven men put all of that aside for a chance to become free and equal citizens,' Othello explained. 'They endured the misery of the elven front, endless drills, marching and barked orders from their officers. And now, when it's finally at an end, to be told it was all for nothing? That the old laws are back in place? Then ordered to stand aside, and watch our homes invaded by the Pinkertons.'

There was a knock on the door behind them, and Briss emerged on to the balcony.

'Athol just sent word. The dwarves have arrived,' she said. 'They're a mile out.'

Cress sighed and got to her feet.

'Come on,' she said. 'We should go to the square before it fills up.'

So they went, hurrying out of the tavern and pushing through the crowded streets. They kept their heads down and wore hoods despite the warm day, to prevent themselves being recognised.

As they fought their way through the crowded streets, Fletcher was amazed at the number of vendors, hawking their wares to the crowds. Men and women walked around with platters of food: the intermingled smells of their pickled whelks, jellied eels, meat pies and fried fish permeated the air. Others sold ginger ale and honeyed beer in paper cups, the remains of which already littered the streets, crumpled balls of white that were trampled underfoot.

Fortunately for Fletcher and the others, the crowds were gathered along the parade through the main roads, allowing them to cut through the side streets unmolested. Fletcher was amazed by how easily Othello navigated the warren of alleys, cutting left and right to avoid the thoroughfares, even scampering along the low roof of an abandoned building to get them to the square.

'Almost there,' Othello panted as they squeezed through a particularly narrow street. The space between the buildings was so tight that Fletcher could stretch out his arms and put his hands through the windows on either side. Already they could hear the roar of the masses just beyond, singing the national anthem of Hominum in raucous unison.

They reached what appeared to be a bricked-up dead end, but Othello grinned at his friends' confused faces and shifted aside a wooden slat leaning against the wall. Behind, a hole just large enough to squeeze through had been knocked into the brickwork.

'Get chased by enough Pinkertons, you'll end up knowing all the short cuts.' Othello winked. 'Come on, before someone notices.'

And with that, they emerged into Corwin Plaza.

31

The noise hit Fletcher like a solid wall. The plaza was enormous, and thousands of people had gathered, surrounding a red-roped cordon where the soldiers were gathering in neat ranks. When he craned his neck, Fletcher could see that three of the roads into the square were filled with crowds, leaving a single way in, through which battalions of soldiers continued to march.

'Come on, let's find a good spot,' Sylva yelled, her voice barely audible over the singing of the assembled masses.

She grasped Fletcher's hand and dragged him through a gap in the crowds. He had just enough time to snatch Cress's sleeve before they were pushing their way to the front. Soon Fletcher's world was full of elbows, squashed toes and angry cursing as they fought past the heaving bodies.

Then somehow they were through, their stomachs pressed against the rope as the spectators surged back and forth. Now that their view was clear, Fletcher saw that a platform covered with an ornate canvas roof had been raised within the centre of the plaza, with a thin line of royal guards surrounding the base.

Upon it were two familiar figures, seated on extravagant thrones.

Alfric stared icily at the uniform rows beneath him, while on the larger throne beside him was King Harold, a benevolent smile on his face. He looked far too calm for Fletcher's liking. Had he forgotten what a dwarven rebellion could mean for Hominum? Was he not thinking of the thousands of lives that would be lost on both sides, or the vulnerability of the empire while the army was divided, fighting a war on two fronts?

'He's a good actor, isn't he?' Sylva half-yelled into Fletcher's ear, as if she could read his mind.

Fletcher hoped that was the case. He had met the King on no more than three brief occasions, and now the future of the dwarves' race seemed to rest in this man's ability to manage his despot father. Fletcher only hoped that his trust was not unfounded. Who knew what game Harold might be playing?

Only some of the troops before them were the fresh-faced boys they had seen from the balcony earlier. The others' appearance was more slovenly, most with untucked shirts and scraggly beards. While the boys stood to attention, these men slumped and spat on the ground, some even swigging from hip flasks.

Fletcher thought they might be veterans from the front lines, but their uniforms were brand new. He suspected these were the conscripted convicts from Didric's prisons – muggers, burglars, conmen and all the rest of the undesirables who had been offered freedom in exchange for their enlistment.

A fresh cheer drew his attention back to the entrance, and for a moment he felt a flash of hope that it was the dwarves. But no, it was the Dragoons, riding straight-backed into the plaza, their right hands touching their foreheads in a salute to their King.

Once they reached their places, even the demons themselves kneeled, one foreleg bent, the other extended in a gesture of subservience. The effect of their disciplined lines was only slightly marred by the lesser demons that accompanied their masters at random alongside their neat rows; mostly a smattering of Canids, Felids and Vulpids. Sacharissa was among them, her great pink tongue lolling out as she panted beneath the warmth of the bright, cloudless sky above. There was only space in the plaza for one more regiment.

Then, as if they had received some signal, the crowd fell into silence. Because beyond the Dragoons, shimmering in the heat haze, the dwarves were marching.

Even in the distance, Fletcher could see that their uniforms and weaponry were different. The glint of metal shone from rounded helms and the heads of back-slung battleaxes. They carried muskets too, though theirs were somewhat shorter to match their height and lacked the fixed bayonets of the human soldiers'. Strangest of all was their hodgepodge of clothing – only the red jackets they wore over their shirts were the same, the rest was traditional dwarves' garb of heavy leathers and canvas cloth.

The silence drew on as the marching dwarves neared. The spectators on either side did nothing but watch, occasionally leaning in to whisper in each other's ears. Now Fletcher could see the sweat on the dwarven brows, the exhaustion on their faces. These men had marched from one end of Hominum to the other, for King and country. Would they kneel, after all that had happened? They had joined before the Anvil attacks had happened, before the hatred had become commonplace. It was a neat trick of Alfric's, to force them to kneel.

Fletcher looked at the faces around him. Many were expressionless, others, solemn. A man squinted. Was that anger in his eyes . . . or just the sun?

Still they came. Now he could hear the tramp of their feet, the jingle of metal. Othello's breath came thick and fast beside him. The quiet was deafening. Was the crowd's apathy enough for Alfric to make his speech?

Fletcher looked up – the old king had the staff with him, the black carapace of the Mite stark on the tip. It was uncovered, facing the approaching dwarves. The whole of Hominum would be watching through its eyes.

The dwarves reached the square. Still, no reaction from the watching crowds, except for the gentle susurration of whispers that Fletcher could not make out. Then they were there, standing in place before the platform, eyes staring straight ahead. Harold stood.

'People of Corcillum,' he began. His voice was loud, unnaturally so. The amplify spell was being used. 'We are gathered here to pay our respects to the men and women who protect our empire from the savage hordes gathering just beyond the horizon.'

His words echoed around the square, the noise broken only by the flutter of tarpaulin above him and the gentle soughing of the breeze.

'In honour of their sacrifice, we will sing the national anthem. Bandsmen, if you please!'

At his command, the drummer boys began a slow, deliberate beat that signalled the introduction to the age-old song. Sergeants brandished their bugles, usually used to signal orders to their men in the heat of battle. In unison, they added their brassy fanfare to the melody.

It was a tune as old as Hominum itself, sang by Hominum's first ruler, King Corwin and his men as they marched into battle and drove the orcs back into the jungles. It was more of a short chant than anything else, but every girl and boy in Hominum knew it by heart.

A chill ran through Fletcher as he looked at the stage. Alfric was grinning, glee plastered across his face. It was a song full of history, tainted with the reminder of when the dwarves lost their homeland to the human invaders.

Alfric didn't think the dwarves would sing. Didn't think they would even know the words. This was all part of his plan, and Harold had been forced to go along with it.

But Alfric was wrong.

Hear us all ye foes, o'er land or sea,
Our lads'll march to hell an' back,
To take the fight to thee.

The dwarves sang in a deep baritone, their bass voices raised above the scattered recitation of the crowd.

Ye'll ne'er see us falter, nor spurn duty's call,
Not one of ye can break our lines,
Nor watch our banners fall.

Even the sound of thousands of people chanting was lost in the depth of the dwarven choir, so much so that many of the voices from the crowd were beginning to fade, put to shame by their lack of fervour.

Bring all yer soldiers, o'er sea or land,
Our folk'll fight till our last breath,
Under our King's command.

The dwarves powered into their final stanza, heads thrown back, voices soaring with the rising tide of trumpets and drums. Not even the gruff soldiers could match the rich timbre of their song.

Hominum, Hominum, Hom-in-uuuum!

Silence. It hung heavy in the air. The dwarves were grim-faced, their eyes almost defiant as they stared out into the surrounding crowds. It was a gesture that told the people of Corcillum that nobody could question their patriotism.

Then there was a single cheer. A young boy, sitting on his father's shoulders a few feet from Fletcher, clapping and laughing at the performance. Then another, and another.

'Bravo,' shouted a woman in the crowd. The smattering of applause turned into a tumult, accompanied by whoops and yells from the spectators. Soon the entire square was cheering, no longer afraid of being the first to react.

Then the dwarves did something Fletcher never thought they would do. One after the other, they kneeled, facing the crowd. On bended knee, they placed their fists against their hearts and lowered their heads to the surrounding masses. It was an oath of loyalty . . . to them. The people.

Fletcher knew what to do then. He fell to his knees, dragging Othello and Sylva down with him.

'What are you doing?' Cress hissed, crouching beside them.

'Just trust me,' Fletcher said, praying he was right.

It was an old lady who joined them first. She smiled apologetically as she leaned on Fletcher's shoulder to get herself down, kneeling beside him on dusty cobbles. A ruddy-faced man followed next, perhaps wishing more to be off his feet than to show respect to the dwarves. But more followed, most sitting, but many kneeling as the dwarves did. It was like a wave, as row after row of people settled on the ground.

It took all of thirty seconds – not one person beyond the cordon remained standing. The soldiers within stood with nervous expressions, unsure of whether they ought to follow suit.

Harold's voice echoed through the square.

'Kneel,' he barked.

The men responded with alacrity, metal clanging as their weapons hit the ground. Harold took a deep breath.

'Do you swear to fight for King and country? Say aye.'

'Aye!' Every man, woman and child in the square yelled out in unison, caught up in the patriotic fervour, but none so loudly as the dwarves.

'Do you swear to defend these lands with every fibre of your being and kill any that threaten its safety?'

'Aye!'

Harold's smile beamed out across the crowd, but it was nothing compared to the glowering look of black hatred coming from old King Alfric.

King Harold spread his arms wide.

'Rise, soldiers of Hominum!'

32

There were celebrations that night. The Anvil Tavern had opened once again, the boards that had covered the windows piled up and burned in the fireplace, and rickety tables brought from the basement and covered with food and beer.

Most of the guests were the dwarven recruits, having sneaked away from their camp outside of Corcillum. It was hard to tell how many had crammed themselves into the building, and Fletcher found himself huddled beside a low table of swarthy dwarven men, resisting the temptation to sample the jugs of beer they generously offered him every few minutes.

They all knew who he was, knew what he and his friends had done for the dwarves. He had more tankards of beer in front of him than he knew what to do with. Uhtred had spent most of the past few days in deep conversation with the recruits. It was he who was responsible for their performance that day – though it had been touch and go for a while.

Dwarven songs were being sung simultaneously on different sides of the room, with each group trying to drown out the others in a cacophony of deep voices. Sylva and Cress had been adopted by an opposite table, and their sweet voices trilled above it all, much to the encouragement of the men around them. A strange instrument that looked like a mix of a bagpipe and a trumpet was playing a tune that somehow managed to be the only tune that nobody was singing to.

The entire Thorsager family were busy behind the bar, the happy reunion between Othello and the male members of his family swiftly superseded by the need to cater for their scores of hungry guests. Traditional dwarven food was being rushed out of the small kitchenette in the back at an impressive rate, and disappearing down throats just as quickly.

Fletcher gave the hungry soldiers a run for their money though, revelling in the variety of the food and mouthwatering flavours. Soft, honeyed bread studded with nuts and fruit was hand-torn away in hunks, an appetiser to the piles of steaming dumplings stuffed with garlic and pork. Baskets of crispy root vegetables seemed the most popular – parsnips, yams and cassava that had been thin-sliced and seasoned with rock salt, all of it golden fried and still sizzling.

It was only just beginning to dawn on Fletcher that his immediate troubles were over, and for the first time in a long while he found his mind wandering to Pelt, his old home. But Pelt was gone. Berdon – that was what home meant to him.

But he had no way of knowing where his surrogate father and fellow villagers were. The journey from Pelt down to Raleighshire was a dangerous one, patrolled by brigands and con men.

He was already planning to fly out in the morning, scan the main roads for their passage. His own route had been in the back of a sheep cart, which as far as he knew could have taken many detours along its way down. That journey had taken two weeks, but theirs . . . well, they could arrive any time between that very minute and another month.

It was these thoughts that were swimming in his mind when the Anvil doors slammed open and the armoured men marched in, their pikes crossed in a solid wall of wood and steel. Fletcher's heart leaped, but he soon relaxed when he saw Harold following behind them, his hands held up and an apologetic smile on his face.

The mood dropped faster than a cannonball at his appearance, and he shuffled his feet awkwardly at the myriad of bearded faces that looked his way. The low buzz of murmuring began.

'Lads, I'm sorry to interrupt,' Harold said, his face becoming grim now that he had their attention. 'But I must ask you to leave at once.'

The murmuring turned to silence. Then: 'Ah, come off it,' one of the more inebriated dwarves groaned. 'Come join us for a wee drinkie.'

Harold gave the dwarf a forced smile, but very few of the other dwarves chuckled. Dwarves knew Harold was a friend to their people, but his intrusion on their night was unwelcome. Fletcher could tell he had misjudged the situation. In the back of his mind, he wondered if they would obey at all if he ordered them. Had they meant that oath they had sworn but a few hours ago?

'Uhtred,' Harold called, 'Fletcher, Othello. Might I have a word? Carry on for now, lads.'

The three of them shouldered their way through the dwarves

and ducked beneath the pikes. The spell was already broken – the music had stopped, and disgruntled muttering had begun to pervade the room.

'It's the Pinkertons,' Harold muttered under his breath. 'They're still outside the Dwarven Quarter. My father hasn't ordered them away.'

'Why?' Othello asked, his brows furrowing. 'They should be gone by now.'

'After what he saw today, he . . . he's furious. When we arrived back at the palace, he said he might risk it anyway. Even without the people on his side, or the soldiers, he thinks sending the Pinkertons in to invade your homes might be enough to make your dwarves riot, especially if they *rough up your women a bit*. His words.'

'But if he ordered that now, he'd look like a monster,' Uhtred growled, looking over his shoulder to make sure the other dwarves couldn't hear. 'That's why he didn't make the speech today: the people would turn against him and he'd lose all his power.'

'Well, if the dwarves don't resist and start fighting the Pinkertons then of course that's true, but if they *do* then he has a rebellion on his hands, one that he can put down with all the violence he can muster. I've convinced him it just won't happen, so for now we're holding back. But if he finds out that there're a hundred drunken dwarves in a tavern down the road, he'll roll the dice. We need to get them out of here. Now.'

Uhtred closed his eyes and clenched his fists.

'No matter what we do, there's always something else, some new threat,' Uhtred said, his voice tight with emotion. 'What happens if we're unlucky next time? What then?'

'We'll discuss that in a minute. Right now I need you to get these men out of here before something bad happens.'

Uhtred turned and ducked under the crossed pikes of the royal guards.

He stood on a table and addressed the crowd:

'Tavern's closed. Everybody out. Take as much food as you like, leave the tankards. Athol, Atilla, Cress, Thaissa – make sure they go straight back to the barracks. No exceptions.'

33

There were six of them left in the tavern, seated around a table beside the flickering embers of the dying fire: Fletcher, Sylva and Harold sitting opposite Othello and his parents. Even the royal guards had been sent outside, forming a perimeter around the entrance.

'I have news for you,' Harold said, 'and I'm sorry to say it's bad.'

'Well, spit it out then,' Uhtred snapped, his big hands clenching on the table. He was clearly still angry about the Pinkertons. About how close they had come, even after everything.

'It's Lord Forsyth and Inquisitor Rook. Their prison. It's in Pelt.'

Uhtred let out a deep sigh and closed his eyes.

'I don't understand,' Fletcher said. 'Pelt's become a hellhole – I should know.'

'Not for them,' Uhtred growled. 'Right, Harold?'

Harold nodded in reluctant agreement.

'My father arranged it with Didric earlier today. They're

sitting pretty in that new castle of his, with penthouse rooms and servants at their beck and call. We've hurt them, taken away their freedom, but there won't be a public trial or an execution. He'll probably let them out in a year or two, once the anger has died down.'

Fletcher's heart sank at the news. Even when caught red-handed, the pair had escaped punishment. Was there no justice for the rich and powerful?

'Don't you have any say at all?' Briss demanded.

'Not nearly enough to go against my father,' Harold said, running a hand through his curls. 'He still thinks we're friends, and doesn't realise I know about his involvement in the bombings. Fortunately, he understands I'm angry with Forsyth and Rook, as are the commoners, so he didn't push for me to pardon them. But he'd never let his two closest allies rot in a jail cell.'

Now it was Briss's turn to sigh.

'Well at least that's something.'

There was silence for a moment, broken only by the crackle of flames in the hearth. Then Uhtred spoke.

'We cannot live on a knife's edge, always one step away from extinction. Those two will be plotting in the shadows, waiting for their next chance. And as for your father . . .'

He hesitated.

'Have you ever considered . . . removing him?'

Harold gave a bitter laugh.

'You mean kill him? Much as it pains me to say it, the thought has crossed my mind. Unfortunately, my father has taken precautions against sudden attack. Are you familiar with the barrier spell?'

'Aye, you use it during the tournaments at Vocans, right?' Uhtred replied.

'That's right.' Harold nodded. 'Well, that very spell is my father's constant companion, an invisible barrier that protects him at all times.'

He motioned outside, where Fletcher could see the outlines of Harold's men's pikes through the windows.

'While my own bodyguards are just well-trained men, Father's are all battlemages of the Inquisition that keep the spell going night and day. Of course, a powerful enough attack might break through it and a demon is able to penetrate it with relative ease, just like a shield spell, but that alone would make it difficult for anyone but a summoner to kill him. No bullet or sword could come close.'

'But *we* could,' Fletcher said, the words slipping unbidden from his mouth. He felt a sudden twinge of guilt. They were discussing a coldblooded assassination – of Harold's father, no less. It was the sort of thing their enemies would do.

'I'm sorry to say it, but I don't believe that's true,' Harold said, shaking his head. 'Four young battlemages against ten trained Inquisitors and the most powerful summoner in all of Hominum? It would never work.'

'Forgive me, but why don't *you* do it?' Sylva asked. 'You both have similarly high summoning levels, if the rumours are true.'

'Can you imagine the turmoil the empire would be thrown into if the people discovered I had committed patricide for no apparent reason?' Harold snapped, as if he were stating the obvious. 'With the Inquisitors protecting him night and day . . . it would not be a quiet battle, even if I could win. I suspect the palace would be a smouldering ruin by the end of it.'

Then he took a breath and his eyes fell to his lap.

'And, in truth, I do not think I could bring myself to do it.'

Silence fell once again, and Fletcher felt a sense of relief wash over him. Alfric was a monster, but somehow plotting his murder had made his skin crawl.

'This can't go on,' Sylva broke the silence. 'The dwarven people are not safe in Corcillum. All we have done is bought them a respite, until the next scheme.'

'If there was ever a time to make a bold move, it is now,' Thaissa said.

Harold nodded grimly. He stood suddenly, and walked closer to the fire. For a moment he gazed into the flames, his brow furrowed with concentration.

'Yes . . .' he said to himself. 'It could work.'

He turned and looked at Fletcher, the edges of his eyes crinkling with what Fletcher thought might be amusement.

'I believe I have an idea,' Harold said, striding back to the table and sitting down with speed borne of excitement. 'One that has never been possible before. But with Fletcher here . . . It is not perfect, nor does it solve all of our problems. But it's the only one I can think of.'

'What is it?' Fletcher asked, confused.

Harold leaned forward and steepled his fingers.

'Raleighshire. The dwarves can resettle there.'

Understanding dawned on Fletcher then. Of course. No noble would have allowed dwarves to live on their land, and Seraph's patch of desert was made up of hot, shifting sands, near impossible to build liveable dwarven homes on.

But Raleighshire belonged to him, gifted to him by the King as his inheritance from his parents, and his to do with as he pleased. He was already resettling the people of Pelt there . . . why not the dwarves?

Even as he opened his mouth to agree, Uhtred shook his head and interrupted.

'Our businesses are here. Our workshops, our friends, our homes. Everything. You want us to leave it all behind to go and live in the wilderness?'

'No offence, Fletcher,' Briss said quickly, giving her husband's arm a remonstrative squeeze.

Fletcher held up his hands and forced a smile.

'None taken.'

A sudden fear, about trying to relocate the citizens of Pelt to this unknown place, bubbled at Uhtred's words, but Fletcher forced it away. This discussion was too important.

'I don't mean every dwarf,' Harold said. 'But a colony. The young men and women, those who are yet to put down roots.'

'What good would that do?' Othello asked.

'Your entire species would no longer be confined to one place,' Harold explained. 'It would spread the risk. Get some of them away from the Pinkertons and the army.'

'You say it like it's a mathematic equation,' Uhtred said. 'These are real people, Harold. Mothers, fathers, children.'

'There's another reason,' Harold said, ignoring Uhtred's protest. 'If anything like this ever happened again, you would have somewhere to go at the first sign of trouble. You could disappear through the tunnels without Alfric even knowing, and follow the paths to Raleighshire. It's only a day or so's journey on foot, even faster with your boars and carts. You could be there before anyone even noticed you had gone.'

Uhtred stroked his beard, leaning back and closing his eyes as he did so.

'Would Fletcher even be open to such a suggestion?' Briss asked, her veiled face turning towards Fletcher. 'He might not want us there at all – it's his land. And the people of Pelt would not relish the idea of sharing their new home with a bunch of dwarves. Corcillum's folk have accepted us, but humans from a rural village like Pelt may be more . . . stuck in their ways.'

'If they're anything like Fletcher,' Othello said, smiling, 'we shouldn't have a problem.'

'And if they're like Didric, Calista or Jakov?' Fletcher said, his heart sinking. The thought of conflict between the dwarves and the people of Pelt had not occurred to him until that moment. Dealing with the small group of refugees would be hard enough, without adding dwarves to the mix.

'Fletcher, you will need more than the impoverished remnants of Pelt's population to bring Raleighshire back from the dead,' Harold said, waving away Briss's concerns.

'Nobody has agreed to anything yet,' Uhtred said, his eyes still closed. Harold threw his hands up in frustration and stood once again, walking to the fireside to curb his impatience.

Finally, Uhtred sighed and leaned forward, before spreading his big hands on the table.

'If we do this, I won't force anyone. Volunteers only,' he said, looking into Fletcher's eyes. 'And we do this fairly. Fletcher gets compensated for allowing us to move on to his land.'

'That's between you and him,' Harold said, holding his hands up. Uhtred's demeanour had changed. He was sitting up straight, and his voice took on a businesslike tone.

'You're going to need supplies to rebuild Raleighshire,' he said. 'Money, manpower, materials. Right now, you have little of all three. Knowing this, we can provide you with the latter – food, tools, livestock, transport, everything you could need to start a new life. But in exchange, we need more than the simple leasing of your land.'

'Father . . .' Othello began.

Uhtred held up a hand, silencing his son.

'Seraph was the first to suggest it, back when you were in prison, Fletcher. Bringing in a third partner to our business. One with land, real land, not the barren dunes his father owns. Where there are resources that we dwarves and the Pashas don't have access to – things like wood, iron, wool. At the moment we pay exorbitant prices for these raw materials. It's killing our business.'

'But nobody would risk going against the Triumvirate,' Briss interjected. 'Even Captain Lovett's family refused us.'

'So what are you suggesting?' Fletcher asked, his mind reeling. Where had this come from? One moment they had been celebrating their success, the next he was negotiating a business deal.

'An equal partnership between the dwarves, the Pashas and you,' Uhtred said. 'Our own Triumvirate, so to speak.'

Fletcher felt sweat break out on his forehead. This was not how he had thought the night would go.

'How would it work?' Fletcher asked. 'How would it be equal if we are all putting in different things?'

241

'The details can be hammered out later,' Uhtred said. 'But we will make sure that nobody is providing more than their fair share. You can trust us.'

It was all so abstract. Exploiting a land he had never seen, in a business he barely understood. But he needed all the help he could get. He pictured the hovels that the people of Pelt had been living in before. Would their settlement in Raleighshire be any better, without the dwarven help?

Fletcher turned to Othello.

'What do you think?' he asked. If anyone knew the ins and outs of what Uhtred was asking for, it was Othello.

But Othello looked panicked, caught between family and friendship.

'I think . . . it's up to you,' he said carefully. 'It's a big decision. I can only promise you that we will be true to our word.'

Fletcher was scared. Somehow, the pressure of this decision was far greater than when he had risked his life in the ether. He wished Berdon was there, to advise him. But this was a burden he must bear alone.

'Fifty dwarves at the most,' Fletcher said, after a moment's thought. 'At least to begin with. So that they do not outnumber my own people.'

'Agreed,' Uhtred said.

'My people will need accommodation for when they arrive in Corcillum, before we make the journey to Raleighshire and you prepare the supplies for them. Can you arrange it?'

'Yes,' Uhtred said, waving at the stairs behind him. 'This tavern has fifteen rooms, and the rest of them can use this bar area and the basement. I'll have Athol arrange the extra bedding.'

'And they arrive tomorrow,' Harold said, turning away from the fire. 'Sir Caulder sent word ahead. I took the liberty of telling them to meet us outside the tavern, since this is where you have been staying.'

Fletcher couldn't help but smile at the news. The short time he and Berdon had spent together after his release had been fleeting. He hadn't realised how much he had missed the gruff blacksmith until that moment. For a second Fletcher felt a lump in his throat, tears stinging the corners of his eyes. He forced them back and stood up.

'OK then,' he said, holding out his hand. 'Equal partners.'

Uhtred's bearded face broke into a grin. He ignored Fletcher's hand and wrapped him in a bear hug. Fletcher patted him frantically on the back, the breath whooshing from him.

'You're family now,' Thaissa smiled, as Uhtred released him.

'As if he wasn't already,' Othello laughed. He took Fletcher's hand, and this time Fletcher winced in pain at the dwarf's powerful grip.

'Congratulations,' Sylva said, grinning. She kissed him lightly on the cheek.

'Well, that's settled then,' Thaissa said. 'Harold, do you have any more bad news, or can we relax now?'

'I have good news actually,' Harold said, the hint of a smile suddenly playing on his lips. 'For three of you, at least, and Cress, when she returns. Believe it or not, I have brought a gift.'

The King had a leather satchel with him, left by one of the bodyguards before he had gone outside. Now Harold lifted it with a wince – the bag was heavier than it looked. It jingled as he placed it on the table.

'Your winnings from the mission. One thousand, five hundred gold sovereigns, for destroying the goblin eggs and rescuing Lady Cav— or should I say, Lady Raleigh.'

'I had forgotten about that,' Sylva said, looking at the bag in awe. The top was open, and heavy golden coins sparkled within.

'Enough for each of you to hire a small army,' Harold said with a smile. 'Speaking of which, that is another thing I have come here to discuss.'

He turned to Fletcher, the smile on his face fading somewhat.

'Fletcher, you are now a noble, with your own land. Legally, you have a responsibility to protect that land. Up until recently, Lord Forsyth owned Raleighshire and defended its borders from the orcs with his own men, a band of warriors camped at the old mountain pass. Soon, you will have to replace them.'

'How soon?' Fletcher asked, the weight of responsibility suddenly descending upon his shoulders again.

'I do not know,' Harold said. 'But it will be a few months at the most, before Lord Forsyth sends for them. You have the means now, at least. I sent word this morning to Corcillum's central barracks that you will be needing men. There should be some volunteers there tomorrow. It is up to you to hire, train and outfit them.'

Fletcher tried not to think about the many tasks that faced him now. He didn't even know where to begin.

Harold patted Fletcher on the shoulder and gave him an apologetic smile. Fletcher forced one in return. The King had a way of turning his life upside down whenever he showed up.

'Now, you should all get some rest,' Harold said, clapping his hands together. 'Tomorrow is a new day.'

34

They looked like beggars. Their clothes were little more than rags, their belongings pushed on rickety handcarts and makeshift sleds that rattled along Corcillum's cobbled streets. Fletcher barely recognised the men and women who slumped in exhaustion beside the tavern.

Then he saw him. Berdon. The man stood head and shoulders above the rest, his long red hair and beard tangled and unkempt. He was carrying two children on his back and dragged the largest cart behind him, but still he walked tall and proud.

He barely had enough time to let the children down before Fletcher's arms were around him, face buried in Berdon's shoulder. Beneath the shirt, Fletcher could feel his father's ribs. The journey had not been easy on his adoptive parent.

'Easy there, son,' Berdon said, cupping Fletcher's face in his big hands and smiling down at him. 'It's good to see you.'

'I thought *I'd* been through the wars,' Fletcher said, smiling through tears. 'But you look like you've had it worse.'

'Oh I don't know about that,' Berdon said, wiping at his own eyes. 'We watched every minute of that mission of yours. Those orcs and goblins made the highway robbers look like milksops.'

'Robbers?' Fletcher asked, looking at the band and suddenly noticing their numbers were far lower than he remembered. 'Was anyone hurt?'

'Not with Sir Caulder around.' Berdon winked, motioning over his shoulder with his bushy eyebrows.

Fletcher looked up to see the cantankerous old man striding towards them, still skinny as a rake but no worse for wear. The children were imitating his lopsided gait, and he feigned a swipe at them with his hook, sending them squealing to their parents. He grinned and patted Fletcher on the back with his good hand.

'All right, lad – nice to see you made it out in one piece. More than you could say I did when I fought them last, eh, boy?' He knocked his peg leg with his hook.

'I'm sure there are a couple of orcs out there who are missing a limb or two thanks to you,' Fletcher replied with a grin.

The people of Pelt were already being welcomed into the tavern, where the Thorsager family were waiting with warm food and fresh clothing. Fletcher caught a glimpse of Janet, the leatherworker who had been the spokesperson for Pelt, back when they had been evicted by Didric's men. She ignored a greeting from Thaissa and stomped into the tavern without giving her a second glance. He grimaced at her behaviour and put it down to tiredness from their long journey.

'Right, so where are these recruits Harold informed me of?' Sir Caulder growled, squinting around. 'His message said there would be plenty of them for me to whip into shape. They should be out here, helping us get this baggage sorted!'

'We haven't gone to collect them yet,' Fletcher replied. 'They're in the barracks, a few streets from here. Although, in all honesty, I'm not sure if any will show up.'

'No time like the present,' Sir Caulder barked. 'We could use some likely lads to help sort this mess out. Well, come on, don't dawdle.'

Berdon chuckled at Fletcher's expression of incredulity and gave him a gentle nudge.

'You go on, son. I've been to this tavern before – I'll make sure everyone gets squared away.'

Fletcher stared at Berdon.

'What, you didn't know?' Berdon laughed. 'When you were in prison, the Thorsagers and I were busy petitioning the King for your trial, remember? Uhtred and I spent many a night in there, sharing our sorrows over a beer. Of course, that was before the Anvil attacks started and it closed down.'

Fletcher felt a twinge of shame. He knew so little of Berdon's life now.

'All right,' Fletcher said, shaking his head in mild disbelief. 'But you tell Uhtred I will need the transports and our dwarven volunteers ready to set out, first thing tomorrow morning.'

'Volunteers?' Berdon asked.

'Uhtred will explain,' Fletcher mumbled, unwilling to go further. No matter how he cut it, the people of Pelt would be unlikely to relish sharing their new home with strangers, especially ones who until recently had been reviled as anarchists and assassins. He would put off telling them as long as he could.

'All right,' Berdon said, his brows furrowed. 'You'd better get on, before Janet accosts you. She's been doubting their decision since we left the damned mountains.'

Fletcher gave Berdon another quick hug and then hurried off, Sir Caulder in tow.

The barracks were a five-minute walk from the Anvil Tavern. On the way, Sir Caulder regaled Fletcher with tales from their journey down from Pelt; of hungry mountain wolves prowling in their wake and marauding brigands who had underestimated the preparedness of the intrepid band.

Their numbers had dwindled from roughly eighty to sixty, mostly families with young children peeling off to seek work in the towns they had passed by. But Berdon's confidence in his son had kept most of their group together. On hearing each story, Fletcher's heart sank deeper and deeper. He could only hope that their trust wasn't misplaced.

The barracks was a compound that took up an entire street, with a palisade surrounding it. Blockhouses with firing slots could be seen above the wooden stakes, and sentries kept a lookout from towers on each corner. It was a fortress inside a city, and Fletcher felt out of place as they walked past marching squads of soldiers and through the open gates.

They found themselves at the edge of a courtyard, with more blockhouses hemming in on each side. There was a single occupant in the centre – an aged man with a long, bent nose, upon which rested a pair of golden spectacles. He sat at a wide desk that was covered in ledgers, and he was busily scribbling away with a quill.

'Come!' he barked, without looking up from his books.

Startled, Fletcher obeyed, standing before the man's desk like a naughty schoolboy. Sir Caulder stomped in his wake, a bemused look upon his face.

'Lord Raleigh, I presume,' the man said in a reedy voice, his quill still scratching.

'Yes, that's right,' Fletcher answered. Was he expected? Perhaps Harold had sent word ahead.

The man sighed.

'Squeems!' he yelled, making Fletcher jump.

A door opened in the building behind them and a young lad wearing a red uniform and a peaked cap hurried out.

'Get the volunteers for our young lord here, sharpish now,' the bespectacled man ordered.

'Right away, Staff Clerk Murray,' Squeems said, doffing his cap to Fletcher before scurrying back the way he had come.

'Clerks,' Sir Caulder muttered derisively.

Murray paused and looked up from his writing.

'The administration of the military is often disdained by the feeble-minded,' he snapped at Sir Caulder. 'Any fool can load and fire a musket.'

'And any coward can hide behind the walls with his books, while the real soldiers do the fighting,' Sir Caulder replied.

Murray did not respond, only smiled as Squeems emerged from the door behind him. A troop of boys no older than Fletcher followed in a ragged line. No sooner had the boys entered the courtyard, Squeems disappeared back into the blockhouse.

'One of the best parts of being a clerk is deciding which volunteers to send off for training, and which to keep back for skivvy work and outside hires,' Murray said, his smile widening.

'I've saved you some of the best. Fresh delinquents from jail these ones, volunteering to escape a trip up to Pelt prison.'

Fletcher tried not to let his disappointment show as he took a closer look at his new soldiers. There were fifteen in all, wearing homespun canvas shirts and trousers – most likely the clothing they were given in jail. They were a rough-looking bunch, with greasy, unkempt hair and unshaved faces. Those who weren't staring at their feet gave him surly glances, resentful of their predicament.

'You'll want to watch them,' Murray said in a loud, exaggerated whisper. 'There's already been a few escape attempts.'

'Is this all?' Sir Caulder asked, his tone apparently unconcerned at the pedigree of their new recruits. 'Fifteen lads to defend an entire county?'

'These are just the jailbirds,' Murray said nastily. 'There's a few freemen mad enough to volunteer for you. They say they know our young lord here.'

'Know me?' Fletcher asked aloud. Who could they possibly be?

Already Squeems was leading out some more young men, all of them strangers in Fletcher's eyes. They were on the skinny side, and there were only six of them, fewer than Fletcher had hoped for, but otherwise they did not look unusual.

'Still not nearly enough,' Sir Caulder said.

'Squeems, get the guests who arrived last week,' Murray ordered. 'I think I've found the ideal place for them.'

'You mean . . .' Squeems began.

'Now, boy,' Murray ordered.

Squeems shot off, a look of apprehension on his face.

'Lord Raleigh,' a dark-skinned boy from the new arrivals stepped forward. 'We came as soon as we heard you were hiring.'

'I'm sorry, I . . .' Fletcher began. Then he knew. It seemed so long ago, but he had seen this young lad only two weeks before, chained to a wall and surrounded by a horde of sleeping goblins. These boys were some of the slaves he had freed back in the pyramid.

'. . . almost didn't recognise you,' Fletcher said, shaking the young man's hand. 'What's your name?'

'Kobe, my lord,' the boy replied.

'I'd have thought, after your ordeal, you'd want to get as far from the orcs as possible,' Fletcher said to the escaped slaves.

Kobe smiled, his teeth shining bright against his dark skin.

'We've a few scores to settle first.'

But Fletcher barely heard the young man's response, because Squeems had appeared with the next group of arrivals.

Elves.

35

Wood elves, to be exact. There were ten of them, both males and females, all dressed in the traditional robes of their people. Fletcher could tell their caste by the amber of their eyes and the colouring of their hair – a mix of russets, brunettes and auburns, rather than the pale gold of their high-elf brethren.

'You look surprised,' Murray said, his reedy voice filled with amusement. 'The elves sent a few volunteers down, to learn the way of the musket. Arrived last week. We've been keeping them busy with sweeping the grounds. A bit of discipline, you know how it is. Lucky for us, you've arrived to take them off our hands.'

He cackled as if he had just scored a victory over Fletcher, but soon stopped when he saw Fletcher's expression of satisfaction. The wood elves were experienced trackers by trade, and would make a fine addition to his little band of soldiers.

His only qualm was the attitude of the waiting elves, who stood with their faces scowling and arms crossed at the sight of him. One she-elf in particular seemed downright hostile, glaring at Fletcher beneath furrowed brows.

'We'll have to take them,' Sir Caulder said, less excited than Fletcher was about the prospect of training a group of elves.

'Aye, that you will,' Murray said, irritated by Fletcher's lack of disappointment. 'Now, be on your way, they're your responsibility now.'

Fletcher hesitated, looking at the thirty odd faces that stared back expectantly at him. Sir Caulder caught Fletcher's expression and stepped forward with a bemused shrug.

'All right you layabouts, step lively, you're in the army now! Form up, form up! Three files, sharpish now.'

His voice cracked like a whip across the courtyard, forcing the recruits to hurry into a makeshift parade line.

'Come on, we haven't got all day. You there, straighten up – you're a soldier, not an elbow.' Fletcher couldn't help but smile as the old veteran hounded them into what might pass for a parade line.

'Now, left foot first, eyes front. Quick march!'

Their column was a shambles, out of step and too close together, but it got the recruits out into the street in short order. But before they could begin the task of turning the men in the direction of the tavern, Athol appeared, jogging towards them, his face puffy and red.

For a moment Fletcher's heart skipped a beat at the sight of the flustered dwarf, his mind flashing to some terrible emergency, but Athol smiled apologetically as he bent over and caught his breath.

'I'm glad you're still here,' he panted, pointing further down the street. 'Don't go to the tavern. We've got to get your men set up.'

He caught sight of the elves. 'Er, and ladies.'

'Hold it,' Sir Caulder barked, bringing the recruits to a standstill. Athol took a few more breaths, then straightened and pointed at a shop front further down the street. Fletcher could see the sword and shield banner hanging above it, and the glint of weapons in the window.

'Follow me,' Athol said, leading the way.

'Left turn . . . march!' Sir Caulder barked, kicking one of the men into position when he turned the other way.

Outside the shop, the recruits were ordered to stand to attention, and Sir Caulder instructed Kobe and the other escaped slaves to keep an eye on the convicts, in case of desertion, while they went inside.

'We'll have no trouble when we're in Raleighshire, miles from the nearest town, but we'd best be careful of 'em for now,' Sir Caulder muttered as they followed Athol into the shop.

The blacksmith in Fletcher was amazed at the array of weapons arranged on the shelves. Each of them was displayed in a velvet case, with the light from high windows at the front of the shop artfully arranged to fall upon the glittering metal.

Above and on the left, there was every type of sword imaginable, from wide-bladed falchions to dual-wielded claymores that were long as a man was tall. Beneath were the axes, kept lower down for dwarven patrons, whose preference for the weapons was well known.

On the right side, firearms were kept in glass cabinets, for their value was many times that of a bladed weapon. Engraved pistols with inlaid gold and silver were the most popular, designed for wealthy officers who were allowed to carry side arms.

'You won't be wanting any of these,' Athol said, catching Fletcher's expression. 'Far too pretty for your lot – they'd probably sell one of these at the first opportunity, from the looks of them. Come on, follow me down to surplus.'

Athol led them through a door behind the counter at the end of the shop and into another room. This one was far less glamorous, but the number of weapons was astounding – hundreds of blades, guns and armour stacked like kindling on shelves and in racks along the walls. Strangely, there were bales of cloth alongside them, and mannequins interspersed among the weaponry. Athol lit an oil lamp and lifted it high, casting flickering shadows about the room.

'We share our storage with a tailor,' Athol explained, as Fletcher examined one of the wooden models. 'Speaking of which, Briss has already sorted out your uniforms – poor dear spent half the night getting your prototype ready. But for now, let's get started on arming your men, eh?'

'I can choose anything?' Fletcher asked, resisting the urge to ask more about Briss's new uniforms.

'Aye.' Athol grinned. 'We'll be wanting to keep the new colony protected. It's in our interest.'

Fletcher resisted the temptation to hug the swarthy dwarf and instead turned to Sir Caulder.

'What do you think?' Fletcher asked.

Sir Caulder paused and considered the question.

'The common soldier is supplied with a standard musket and bayonet to stick on the end of it,' he mused, picking up a sword and hefting it for balance. 'Personally, I always hated bayonets. It's just a stabbing blade: no versatility, no finesse. Cheap and easy enough to sharpen, that's why they're used.'

'He's got a point there,' Athol agreed, pointing to a barrelful of the simple weapons. 'If you'll pardon the pun. They're a last resort, and the musket gets damaged half the time, especially when you're using them to parry a war club.'

Athol paused, scanning the multitude of blades.

'I guess the question is, what kind of fighters do you want your company of soldiers to be?' he asked.

'More than just people who can load a gun and pull a trigger,' Fletcher said. 'I want soldiers who can counter cassowary riders, and cut a charging orc's knees from under him. Soldiers who can hold their own in close combat, be it against macana, spear or club, wielded by orc or goblin.'

Athol took a deep breath and grinned.

'Is that all?' he asked.

'We'll want muskets too,' Fletcher said. 'Nothing fancy, just solid, reliable weapons that won't rust at the first drop of rain.'

'Well, that's more like it,' Athol said, walking a few steps to a gun rack and lifting one of the guns from its slot. It looked much like any other musket in Fletcher's eyes, with a long, single barrel, a carved wooden stock, a trigger and a flintlock.

'These are lighter than your average musket – we've used maplewood rather than walnut – just as sturdy but more weatherproof and less dense. Both the steel and the wood itself has been treated with linseed oil to keep it from rust and rot.'

'We'll take them.' Fletcher grinned, wresting the gun from Athol's hands and feeling the weight of it. It was barely heavier than his own sword.

'Now for your close-combat problem,' Athol said, replacing

the musket and browsing through the weapons. 'If you need to block a cavalry charge – or a cassowary charge, as the case may be – you'll need a pole-arm, wouldn't you say, Sir Caulder?'

'That's right,' Sir Caulder said. 'Something you can brace against the ground and let them run into. Plus, the extra length will help with orcs – they've twice the reach a man has.'

They followed Athol to where a mix of spears, pole-arms and other staff weapons were stacked vertically on a long wooden rack, from tallest to shortest.

'You'll be wanting a spear tip for stabbing and slicing,' Athol said, 'and an axe head for chopping when they get in too close and you shift your hands up the staff. So I reckon the best weapon for you is a poleaxe.'

Athol took a new pole-arm from the rack and held it up to the dim light of the oil lamp. It was a fearsome weapon, and Fletcher could hardly believe a combination of so many implements could exist. A sharp spear point extended from the tip, and beneath it a broad, curved axe blade. On the other side of the axe, he saw the square cube of a hammer, with a strange hooked spike emerging from its centre.

Fletcher recognised the spike as a blade known as a crow's beak, designed for both piercing as well as hooking riders from their mounts or fighters from their feet. The hammer acted as added weight to give the axe momentum in its swing, and allowed the crow's beak enough force to penetrate armour, or a thick orc skull.

Athol pointed to a metal bracing along the top third of the pole, covering the wood in a shaft of metal.

'You'll not find a more versatile weapon,' he said. 'See here, we've put a steel lancet along the haft, so that you can block with the handle without shattering the wood.'

Fletcher smiled and ran his fingers along the axe blade, then winced as he felt its razor sharpness.

'There's even a spike on the other end to help ground the poleaxe in the soil, or back-stab as the case may be,' Athol said, pointing to a short metal spike at the butt of the handle. 'And there's a rondel guard to stop a blade sliding down and taking off your fingers.'

He tapped a small disc of metal near the top of the pole, just beneath the lancet, which looked similar to a hilt.

'All right, don't over-egg the pudding,' Sir Caulder said, clapping Athol on the back. 'Fletcher, I think it's a fine weapon. If you want 'em, I'll train the lads up to use 'em properly. I'm as good with the quarterstaff as I am with a sword.'

'We'll take those too,' Fletcher said, amazed that they had found such an ideal weapon so quickly.

'Great!' Athol said, with a hint of relief in his voice. 'I thought we'd be here all day otherwise. Now, for the big reveal. It's a shame Briss couldn't be here to show you it, but she's too busy looking after all your guests.'

He began walking deeper into the room.

Fletcher could hardly resist jogging ahead of Athol, but he didn't have to wait long; Athol stopped only a dozen paces away. He held the oil lamp up to reveal a mannequin, positioned as if it was standing to attention. It was clad in a brand-new uniform.

'It's beautiful,' Fletcher breathed.

The uniform was made from dark-green cloth, with black buttons and calf-length boots of dark leather. The jacket was double-breasted and extended down to just above the knee, beneath which straight trousers were tucked into laced boot tops.

Athol's handiwork had provided the most beautiful parts to the ensemble. The mannequin wore two armoured bracers along the outer forearms, to deflect blows that would otherwise shatter or dismember, while around the neck there was a steel gorget, which protected the shoulders, upper chest and throat without constricting movement.

'We didn't want to weigh them down with too much armour,' Athol said, shuffling his feet self-consciously. 'So we had to compromise. It's made of the same oil-rubbed wool that Briss used for your uniform in the mission, so it's warm, but breathable and waterproof.'

'Bloody hell,' Sir Caulder said, stroking the fabric. 'You've struck gold here, lad.'

'Yes.' Fletcher grinned. 'That I have.'

36

From the height of the sun, it was already late in the morning when Fletcher woke. It was time to face the music.

Fletcher put on his new uniform – for he had little else in the way of clothing – then strapped on his pistols, sword, bow and quiver. His satchel from the mission went on his back, and then Fletcher realised that that was it. All his worldly possessions were with him now.

For a moment he had the mad desire to avoid the responsibilities of nobility. To sneak out of the window, catch a boat to Swazulu and never come back. He shook the temptation from his thoughts with a rueful grin and headed for the door.

Downstairs, the bar area was packed to the rafters with scores of men and women sitting on the right side, dwarves on the left. The room, once abuzz with conversation, fell silent as their faces turned towards him. Berdon was the only human seated among the dwarves, and he gave Fletcher an encouraging nod.

Fletcher cleared his throat.

'It is good to see you all,' he said. 'To see so many familiar faces.'

Silence.

'Our new friends, the dwarves,' he said, motioning to his left, 'have kindly organised our accommodation for the night, as well as transport to our destination. They have also provided tools, food, clothing and building materials. Everything we need to begin our new lives. I am sure I am not alone in saying that we are grateful for everything they have done for us.'

His words elicited a smattering of applause from the right side of the room, and a twinge of relief ran through him. But only for a moment.

'And I am sure I'm not alone in asking, at what cost?' demanded a voice.

The speaker stood, and Fletcher saw that it was Janet, the spokesperson for Pelt.

'What's the catch?' she asked. 'And why are they all gathered here? There's something you're not telling us, and I think I know what it is.'

'I am about to tell you,' Fletcher said, lacing his voice with what he hoped was authority. 'If you'd be so kind as to sit down and listen.'

Janet sat down, but her crossed arms and glare told him he had done little to mollify her.

'In exchange for their help, I have agreed that fifty dwarves can join our colony. These are the people you see sitting here with you.' He waved to the dwarves, who looked nervously for a reaction from the humans.

Janet's brow furrowed.

'So . . . we don't owe them anything?' she asked. 'They're not here to collect payment?'

'No. Of course not,' Fletcher said, confused. 'Is that what you thought?'

'Have you seen what's out there?' Janet said, pointing at the tavern entrance. 'There's a score of wagons full of bales of cloth and canvas, fishing gear, axes, picks and spades, wax candles, cooking utensils, hunting muskets, goddamn seeds of every crop under the sun.'

She took a breath.

'I saw chests full of soaps and medicines, inks and papers, linens and bloody pillows – hell, they've got half a dozen goats at the back somewhere. You're saying we can just have it? No debt, no nothing?'

'It's for all of us,' Fletcher said, motioning to the entire room. 'Dwarf, man, whoever. We are in this together now.'

Janet broke into a smile.

'Well, I think that's bloody marvellous!'

Already some of the villagers were grinning, some even raising their glasses to the dwarves from across the room. But Fletcher could see not all of the villagers were happy with the situation – a few were glowering into their mugs, some even muttering under their breath. He held up a hand for their attention.

'We will be leaving soon, so I want you all to gather your belongings and join the dwarves on the wagons immediately. But first, I want to make something clear. If any of you are unhappy with the living arrangements, you can leave right now. There are a thousand opportunities in this city, especially for skilled workers such as yourselves. So if you don't think you can stomach living with dwarves, there's the door.'

Fletcher allowed his eyes to linger on each of the most unhappy-looking villagers. He knew them all by name, knew their personalities. Pelt was a small village.

'I'm out,' someone announced, standing up and heading for the door. He was a big bruiser of a man, formally of the town guard. His name was Clint, and he had been a rival of Didric's, long ago. Fletcher suspected that was why he had not been offered a position in Pelt's new prison guard.

'I'll take my chances with my fellow man,' he continued, ignoring the dark glances from his fellow villagers. 'I hear the Pinkertons are hiring.'

More villagers followed him, some shamefaced, others standing proudly and slapping Clint on the back.

'Tell Sergeants Murphy and Turner I said hello,' Fletcher called after Clint as he and the others strolled out.

The door slammed shut behind them, but with their departure a weight seemed to lift from the room. All in all, a dozen men and women had departed, leaving roughly a hundred dwarves and humans in the tavern.

'Right,' Fletcher said, clapping his hands together. 'Let's get moving.'

37

The goodbyes were all too swift. Othello, Cress and Atilla had received their marching orders from the King that very morning, commissioning all three as officers in the dwarven battalion. Cress had sniffled as she bade Fletcher farewell, and both Fletcher and Othello had to surreptitiously wipe at their eyes after a gruff hug. The three dwarves departed before the convoy had even left, eager to take command of their men. He had not envied them – while he only had to manage thirty-two soldiers, theirs would number in the hundreds.

Sylva flew to meet the elven army on their way down from the north, and her soft, parting kiss on Fletcher's cheek lingered long after she and Lysander disappeared into the sky. Fletcher caught her backward glance as she took off. It was a bittersweet reminder of what he knew could never be.

In the rush to prepare for the expedition, he had almost forgotten that he would be parting ways with his dearest friends, and he felt their loss even before they were out of sight. Worst of all would be his mother, whom he had not had time to visit. It was only thanks to the knowledge that he could fly back on Ignatius and visit her that he could bring himself to leave at all. Until then, Harold had promised she would receive the best care that the doctors of Corcillum could provide.

One happy surprise came with the discovery that Thaissa would be joining the colonists. She shyly introduced her husband before embarking on their wagon, a young dwarven blacksmith named Millo who had apprenticed beneath Uhtred before opening his own workshop.

There was a brief scramble as Uhtred held up the morning traffic of carriages so their convoy could leave, and then they were off in a rumble of wheels and clopping trotters on the cobbled streets. Dwarves waved handkerchiefs as they passed, others running up and handing them last-minute gifts of food as the wagons rolled by. Within the hour they were outside of the city and trundling along the dusty road south, surrounded by the rolling hills of crops and minor hamlets.

At first, Fletcher rode at the front with Sir Caulder and Berdon, but soon the pair's eyes grew heavy, for the two were exhausted from their long journey down south. So as they slept, he climbed out on to the roof plate, sitting beside the dwarven wagon master and discussing the route ahead. But the old dwarf seemed fearful, constantly looking over his shoulder. Fletcher asked what he was afraid of.

'Bandits,' the wagon master replied curtly, staring out across the empty landscape.

It was only then that Fletcher realised how valuable their convoy actually was. Leaving aside his share of the prize money, stashed in his satchel, the contents of the wagons could be sold for a great deal on the black market. They were a prime target for any one of the roving bands of highwaymen that ranged across Hominum, and his little band of soldiers were far from prepared to defend it.

Someone needed to scout the surrounding area. So he jumped from the wagon and walked into a nearby cornfield. He watched as the convoy rolled past, and was pleased to see that Sir Caulder had placed his soldiers on three wagons in the front, middle and back, preparing the convoy for attack from any direction. There were twenty vehicles in all, and each was hitched to a pair of boars, enormous animals as large as donkeys and twice as wide. He watched the strange beasts as he waited for them to pass by, fascinated by the marmalade colouring of their bristly fur and the short tusks that curved from their lower jaws.

Then, when the wagons were out of sight, he summoned Ignatius and Athena, and took off. It was as exhilarating as it had been the first time, to shoot into the sky and watch the road turn into a thin brown line along the patchwork yellow-green quilt of the surrounding fields. But this time it was better – there were no demons to fear, no orcs to escape. The sky was all but empty, filled only with wisps of cloud and, far in the distance, a skein of geese flying in formation.

Athena's wing was still on the mend, though well on its way to being usable again, so she perched on Ignatius's rump and peered out over the landscape. To the east, Fletcher could see the distant shape of Vocans, half obscured by a haze of morning mist. For a moment he was tempted to fly by it, perhaps even catch a glimpse of students through the domed skylight on its roof. Only the safety of the convoy held him back.

At first Fletcher had wished for Pria's heat vision, but he needn't have worried – Athena's sharp eyes missed nothing. So the rest of the day was spent gliding on the breeze, searching the plains surrounding the convoy for suspicious movements. But if there were any bandits, they did not show themselves. Only the occasional goatherd and his flock broke the stillness of the plains – that and the thin streams of chimney smoke from the rare sleepy hamlet that dotted the landscape.

As they journeyed on, the land became less and less populated. Fields of crops became rocky hills, and the remains of scattered homesteads long abandoned appeared as overgrown mounds of rubble and tile. Fletcher knew that the front lines lay just beyond the horizon, and the ground below them had been ravaged by endless conflict between orc and man: from the orc raids in the centuries before the war began, to the bloody battles since. The entire area was devoid of human life, a buffer between civilisation and savagery.

The road beneath branched, one path heading towards the southern front, the other curving west, towards the Vesanian Sea. The convoy took the west road, and now the going became slower. Fletcher swooped for a closer look, and saw that the route was poorly maintained. Weeds and wayward roots had invaded the dirt road, requiring Sir Caulder to occasionally call a halt and order the recruits to hack apart the scrub. At other times muddy puddles blocked the way, and the passengers were forced to get off and walk around so that the heavy wagons weren't bogged down as the wheels churned through the mires.

And so it went on. Afternoon turned to dusk, until the setting sun hung fat and yellow on the skyline. Still the road stretched into the horizon, and Fletcher was forced to send wyrdlights down to illuminate their way, great balls of raw mana that ate at his reserves but hung above the convoy like miniature blue moons.

It was around midnight when they reached the river. In the dark of night the water looked black, rushing silent beneath a wide stone bridge that looked as if it had stood there since the beginning of time. It was the marker for where Raleighshire began, the land behind them owned by the King, the land beyond . . . his.

As the convoy crossed over, he listened to the fearful snorts of the boars, skittish at the sound of the roiling water beneath them. His mind wandered to the history of this place. A great battle had been fought here once, named after the bridge itself – Watford Bridge.

They were in savannah country now – what had once been a sea of undulating green took on a yellow tinge, flat and interspersed with copses of trees and shrubs. The road was barely existent, overgrown with tall grasses and strewn with stray rocks and nascent plants. Faced with the wild growth of almost two decades, Fletcher's recruits were forced to use their poleaxes to hack a path, working from the early morning hours to the first hint of dawn. The dwarves and villagers lent a hand, carrying the detritus aside as the soldiers cut it away.

And then, as the first rays of the sun spread across the sky, he saw it.

Raleightown.

38

It was early dawn when the convoy arrived. The wyrdlights were snuffed out, having shrunk into nothingness overnight as the mana depleted. So, the town was cast with a dim glow of orange as the wagons rolled to a halt and Ignatius landed with a bone-juddering thud beside the lead wagon.

Nothing stirred. They had made it to the centre of the ruined town, the wheels rattling on the still-cobbled streets, overgrown though they were with the grasses that squeezed through the cracks in between. They were in a small square, a simple space that could just fit the wagons in if they crowded together.

The remains of decaying buildings shadowed them on all sides, their stone walls still standing after almost two decades of abandonment. The roofs had long fallen in with neglect, and the window spaces were nothing more than empty hollows. Everything was covered in a layer of green, from a coat of furry moss on the dew-damp stones, to tangled vines that flowed down the dwellings and along the streets like an iridescent waterfall. All was cast in the golden blush of sunrise, warming the night-cold air.

Fletcher dismounted, taking in the sounds of his new home. There was a constant chirr of insects, broken by the warbles and trills of birdsong, welcoming in the morning. These were the noises of the wild lands that they had come to conquer. The music of his homeland.

Sir Caulder stomped down the sides of the wagons, cajoling the exhausted soldiers out of them and into ranks. Fletcher pitied the poor recruits, many of them swaying on their feet, their heads nodding as the warmth of the morning took hold. The passengers emerged behind them, yawning and stretching in the dawn light.

'Listen up for Lord Raleigh's orders now,' Sir Caulder barked.

The old knight raised his eyebrows at Fletcher and signalled with his eyes. It was time for Fletcher to take control. Only – he hadn't planned on giving any orders.

'I know it's been a long night.' Fletcher cursed the quaver in his voice as he began to speak. 'You've done me proud, getting our people here. Now we've one last task before we can rest and settle in to our new home.'

The recruits stood silently, sullen-faced. Only the elven woman, the one who had glowered at Fletcher so vehemently back at the barracks, showed any sign of vigour. She managed a surly kick at a pebble, but said nothing.

Her face was angular and fierce, with light brown hair braided tightly on the sides, and a thick plume arching up along the centre and down her back. Most striking of all were her eyes, a deep amber that reminded Fletcher of a wildcat's.

A polite cough from Sir Caulder brought Fletcher back to the task at hand; his first order. There were a thousand things to do.

But if he knew anything about survival in the wilderness, it was that shelter was their first priority. At least, as long as the water barrels in the wagons lasted.

'These homes have been abandoned for nearly two decades. The wooden floors will be rotten, if there are any at all. All manner of animals could have made their homes in the buildings – snakes, hyena, warthogs. I need two groups to scout and clear each building and find a suitable place that's safe for us to camp in.'

He paused, contemplating who to choose. It would help if he knew more than one name.

'Kobe, take fifteen recruits with you and search the east side of the town,' Fletcher ordered, dividing the group into two with a motion of his arm. 'If you find a likely spot, leave your men there to clear it out and return to make your report.'

Kobe grinned, clearly taking the responsibility as a compliment.

'As for the rest of you . . . What's your name?' he asked, pointing at the surly elf.

'Dalia,' she replied, lifting her chin.

'Dalia, take the remainder west,' Fletcher said, pointing down the dilapidated street. 'I want both team leaders back in twenty minutes.'

Dalia and Kobe stood uncertainly for a moment, unsure of the protocol.

'Well, you heard him. Move out!' Sir Caulder ordered.

The teams jumped to obey, but their faces still showed their discontentment as they stumbled down the overgrown streets. Fletcher wondered what they had expected when they signed up at the barracks. All he knew was that they would never have imagined they would be out here, starting a colony deep in the wilderness. Were they disappointed? Relieved? He didn't know what to think, and suspected neither did they.

'Good work, lad,' Sir Caulder said, stomping up to him. 'Now the colonists. You lead them too, you know.'

Fletcher turned to the gathering of villagers and dwarves. Many were wandering aimlessly, others standing with bewildered looks. Even Berdon had sidled up to one of the buildings and was peering through the rotten remains of a door. They needed direction, and as their lord, it was up to Fletcher to give it to them.

It was strange, looking around, to know that all of this was his, ruined though it was. And the land, as far as the eye could see, and further still. All his. It felt wrong to have so much.

'I need everyone to stay by the convoy,' Fletcher called. 'Berdon, Thaissa, Janet, Millo, might I have a word?'

As the four hurried up to him, Fletcher tried to wrap his mind around the fact that it was not just the soldiers, but everyone in the convoy that answered to him now. Even his own father.

'I've thirty-two soldiers, if we include Sir Caulder. Add fifty dwarves makes eighty-two. Janet, how many villagers?' Fletcher asked.

'Fifty-two,' she said, after a moment's thought.

'So that's one hundred and thirty-five souls all told,' Fletcher said, amazed at the numbers of his colony. It was almost as large as Pelt's population had been, before Didric had turned it into a prison.

'So what's the plan?' Thaissa asked, smoothing her veil anxiously.

'Let's set up camp somewhere to rest, and get to work tomorrow,' Fletcher said, watching a nearby villager yawn and resisting the urge to do the same. 'But I'll need a complete manifest of our rations, tools and supplies before the day is out. Thaissa, Millo – you'll have a better understanding of what was packed, so I'll leave you in charge of that. Janet, Berdon – I'd like you to assess the skills of our colonists. We know we have at least two blacksmiths but we'll need carpenters, masons, farmers, lumberjacks, potters, to name but a few. Can you do that for me?'

'Aye, we can do that,' Berdon answered for them, smiling proudly at his son. The four set off to their tasks, waving over nearby colonists to help.

'What about us?' Sir Caulder asked.

'Let's explore a little,' Fletcher said, beginning to enjoy himself. 'You can show me where everything once was.'

The pair strolled along the street, towards the south of the town. Sir Caulder stared at the ruins he had once called home, and Fletcher wondered how it would feel to be back after all these years. To see the ruins of another life.

'Blacksmith's there,' Sir Caulder said, pointing to a low building with a wide entrance, the double doors long rotted away. Within, Fletcher could see the block of an anvil, and rusty tools strewn about the floor. A pile of metal ingots was neatly stacked in the corner.

'We'll be able to clean off the rust on some of those, make 'em usable,' Sir Caulder said, continuing on.

They walked deeper into the town, and Fletcher began to get a sense of its size. It was smaller than he had first thought – many of the buildings were two or three storeys high, making for a dense population in a space that could easily fit within the circle of Vocans' moat. He could walk around the edge of the town in less than ten minutes.

'Stables and kennels there,' Sir Caulder said, pointing at another low structure, separated into stalls. 'Carpenters, apothecary, bakery, town hall . . .'

He stopped suddenly in front of the town hall: a large, round-walled building with a gaping hole in its rotted roof. His eyes fell on a depression in the ground, in the centre of an empty space opposite the front entrance. Rubble surrounded it.

'This is where they came from,' he said, his eyes flinty as he crouched beside the hole and trailed his fingers through the dirt and loose stones within its centre.

'The orcs?' Fletcher asked.

'Aye,' Sir Caulder said, hurling a pebble down the overgrown street. 'Used to be a statue of your grandfather here. The tunnel to the other side of the mountains was beneath. Look.'

They were almost at the border of the town, and the savannah could be seen between the buildings. And beyond were the mountains, reaching into the sky.

'That range stretches from the river to the sea,' Sir Caulder said, sweeping a finger across the plains. 'It blocks off Raleighshire from the orc jungles, except for the pass, just a forty-minute walk away.'

But Fletcher was no longer looking at the mountains. He had just seen a structure a hundred feet beyond the town's edge. The remains of a mansion that he recognised, even after seventeen years of neglect.

His family home.

39

The ruins of the old mansion were more broken than the rest of the town. Building stones from the explosion during his parents' last battle were strewn across what was once the lawn, now wild with shrubs and tangled weeds. Half of the front of the mansion was missing, revealing the stone flooring of the second storey.

'I saw this place once,' Fletcher said as they picked their way to the gaping hole. 'An infusion dream from Athena's memory.'

Sir Caulder said nothing, instead sitting heavily on the ragged edge of the entrance. He stared blankly at the wreckage around them, his eyes seeming to settle on the remains of a staircase that wound halfway to the second floor.

'How did you survive it?' Fletcher asked, sitting beside him. 'They say all the bodies were taken by the orcs and . . .' He trailed off, remembering the fate that had awaited his father's body.

'An orc saved me,' Sir Caulder said, then caught Fletcher's expression and shook his head. 'Its body, anyway. He was a big bugger, covered me completely. When the Celestial Corps arrived a few hours later, they found me there, flew me out before the orcs came back. Too late for my arm and leg, but they saved my life.'

Sir Caulder sighed and stared into the distance.

'I wish I'd had a chance to see your mother, Fletcher,' Sir Caulder murmured, so quiet Fletcher had to strain to hear. 'I need to apologise to her. I didn't stop them. Didn't save Edmund.'

Fletcher shook his head and patted the old man on the shoulder.

'There's nothing to apologise for. They were betrayed, and there was nothing anyone could do to stop it.'

At the mention of his father, Fletcher tried to picture the dark-haired man he had seen so briefly in that dream. Then he realised he didn't have to remember. There was a painting, still hanging above an ancient fireplace on the left side of the room.

He hurried over to it, amazed at its condition. There was his father, Edmund, stubble-chinned and tousle-haired, his swarthy arms wrapped around Alice. She was smiling with joy, clutching a newborn baby in her arms. Himself.

'My god. How is this still here?' Sir Caulder breathed. 'They commissioned it on the day of your birth.'

Fletcher reached out to touch the baby's forehead. The faintest hint of a slippery barrier met his finger before it touched the canvas. Then he noticed. Corundum crystals, embedded around the edge of the painting. All these years, they had powered a weak barrier spell that had kept it safe from the ravages of time, wind, heat and rain. The expense would have been immense. This must have been his parents' most prized possession.

It hit him then. The loss of it all. To have grown up without the love of his parents. Without the knowledge of this beautiful, wild land. What would life have been like if Lord Forysth had not betrayed them? His thoughts turned to his mother, an empty shell of the woman she once was. She looked so happy in the painting.

He felt his eyes water, and fought the tears.

'It looks just like you,' came a voice from behind them. Berdon.

Berdon was staring at the painting, his face filled with sadness.

'Exactly like you. I remember when I held you for the first time . . . how happy I was,' he said. 'To think . . . that you had just lost your family. I'm so sorry, son.'

'I lost a family,' Fletcher said, smiling through his tears and hugging the bluff blacksmith close. 'But I gained a new one, thanks to you. You have nothing to apologise for. I wouldn't be the man I am today without you.'

For a moment they held each other, and Sir Caulder wandered off, wiping at his eyes when he thought they weren't looking.

Finally, Berdon released him.

'The soldiers are back,' he said gruffly. 'We've found somewhere to camp.'

It was a church. The stained-glass windows were gone, but the ceiling and roofs were made from arched stone, standing the test of time to leave a stable covering over their heads. The benches had remained dry and out of the brunt of the wind, so they remained serviceable. Other than some wayward weeds and the detritus of dead leaves that had blown in through the windows, it was as good a shelter as any for the colonists to make camp in.

Sir Caulder had showed them an old well as they walked back, which would be useable once it was cleared of the animal remains and rotting vegetation that had made their way in over the years.

Their main concern was food – what had seemed like plenty to Fletcher was barely enough to last them a few more meals at most, for one hundred and thirty-five people easily consumed the two barrels of salt pork and venison that the dwarves had brought with them.

For now, though, Fletcher's main priority was setting up the shelter and solving more pressing concerns. He ordered spare sheets of canvas to be placed over the window holes. The dust was removed with old brooms found in nearby houses, and pillows and bedding were laid out for the sleepy colonists.

The boars and goats were tied up in the stables, for the surrounding countryside would be too full of predators to allow them to roam free – hyenas, jackals and big cats had been spotted nearby. Villagers were sent to cut fodder from the long grasses around the camp, while nuts and roots were gathered and tugged from the ground for the hungry boars. The chickens were left in their cages and fed with the sparse handfuls of seeds that could be gathered from local wheatgrass.

A meal had to be cooked, with three cauldrons boiling a simple broth of salt meat and chopped tubers to stave off the hunger. Sentries were organised to watch for predators, and poleaxes were cleaned and oiled after the night's work. Sleeping spaces were divided, introductions hastily made and forgotten just as quickly.

Endless questions were asked, nearly all of which Fletcher had no answer for. Only the stern support of Sir Caulder and Berdon's calming presence kept him from losing his patience.

It was late afternoon by the time the wagons had been emptied and organised, and all the crucial tasks were completed.

And then, as the sun began its slow descent towards the horizon, the colonists finally slept.

40

The main problem was wood. Weeds could be pulled, vegetation cut, debris cleared away. But many roofs were gone or rotten to the brink of collapse and the wooden floors between the storeys were worse.

Then there was food. Many houses had the remains of vegetable gardens, now overgrown and interspersed with brambles and vines. They salvaged what they could to supplement their supplies, but the meat was half gone after breakfast. Unless they wanted to subsist on handfuls of roots, vegetables, fruit and berries, they would need to hunt, and soon.

There were three carpenters from Pelt – a husband, wife and their son who had made furniture and boarding from the local pinewood in the mountains. Four dwarves, two male and two female, also had some woodworking skills, though theirs was limited to carving gunstocks and bows. Still, it was more than enough to begin restoring the houses nearby, and teach unskilled colonists the rudiments. They just needed the raw materials.

When midday approached, Fletcher finally finished dividing

the tasks, having separated the colonists into groups that would focus on minding the animals, sanitising the well, replanting the gardens and the hard work of removing the weeds and debris from the town. Berdon and Millo were sent to salvage what tools they could from the carpenters and blacksmiths, scrubbing them free of rust with the help of juice from wild limes and steel wool from their supplies.

Fletcher gathered his army the next day, now well fed and rested, and led them into the green-yellow savannah of tall grasses, shrubs and tree copses. This far south the weather was warm, even in early spring, so the sun was high and hot as they waded through the grasses and on to the Raleighshire plains. They walked fully armed, with bandoliers of musket cartridges strung across their chests and their muskets and poleaxes slung crosswise on their backs.

'I want your muskets at the ready,' Fletcher ordered. 'Keep your eyes peeled for anything for our cooking pot tonight.'

Sir Caulder sidled up to him.

'Their muskets aren't loaded yet,' he whispered. 'They don't know how.'

'So teach them,' Fletcher said.

'I'm an old warrior,' Sir Caulder replied, looking over his shoulder at the waiting soldiers. 'The guns came after my time.'

'Kobe,' Fletcher called. The boy jogged over, wiping his brow.

'What can I do for you, Lord Raleigh?' Kobe asked.

'You used to be a private, right? Can you load a musket?'

'It's been a few years, but . . . more or less.'

'Show them how it's done,' Fletcher ordered.

'Aye, sir.'

Fletcher watched as Kobe returned to the others and unslung his musket. The boy was hesitant, but the motions he went through looked right to Fletcher, if loading a musket was anything like loading a pistol.

'We need to teach them the proper techniques,' Fletcher said, squinting in the midday sun. 'Firing lines, formations, fast loading, aiming. In the army they go through basic training, but this lot . . .'

'Didn't they teach you that in Vocans?' Sir Caulder asked.

'No. I missed my second year,' Fletcher said, remembering the books on strategy and tactics that had been sitting on the library shelves while he studied demonology and spellcraft. 'Kobe probably knows more about musketry than I do.'

'I can't help you there. But give me a few weeks with them and they'll be better with those poleaxes than any warrior.'

'Let's hope.'

Fletcher sighed and looked out over the savannah. There was a large copse of trees nearby, the trunks tall and straight, the tops capped with a wide umbrella of branches. Shade.

'We'll be needing timber soon enough,' Fletcher said, motioning at the trees with his chin. 'You know much about trees?'

'Only what your grandfather told me,' Sir Caulder said, looking at the copse with a rueful smile. 'He planted those when he was your age – wanted a forest for his descendants to play in. Makes me feel my age – I remember when they were nought but saplings.'

The beginnings of an idea began to form in Fletcher's mind. He turned.

'Men, follow me,' Fletcher said loudly.

A startled elf fired his half-loaded musket, his finger tightening involuntarily on the trigger. There was a bang, the stench of brimstone, and a ramrod spun through the air to land in the grassland a dozen feet away. Fletcher shook his head in disappointment.

'Let's find some shade,' he said, turning his back on them and making his way to the trees.

They filed in behind him, sweaty and frustrated. Without waiting to be dismissed, most of the soldiers collapsed on to the ground to relax in the cool. Fletcher didn't have the heart to reprimand them. Or was it fear that made him hesitate?

There were a hundred trees or so in the copse, all as tall as three men standing on each other's shoulders. Many had termite nests growing around the base, though the trees looked unharmed by the insects' ministrations.

Round fruit littered the ground, having fallen from the tree branches above. They looked like limes, with a yellow-green rind on the outside. Sir Caulder picked one up from the ground and split it open on the edge of his sword.

'Jackalberries,' he said, as the tart citrus smell filled Fletcher's nostrils. 'Try it. They're not quite ripe yet, but you'll rarely manage to find one that's purpled – the animals get to them first. Jackals in particular, hence the name.'

Fletcher bit into it, the juices bursting in his mouth like sweetened lemon juice. It was delicious, and reminded him of persimmon.

'Well, they'll add to our meagre supplies, even if we don't catch anything to eat tonight,' Fletcher said, his mouth half full.

He peered into the grasslands. There were antelope herds in

the distance, but the shimmer of a heat haze made it difficult to gauge the distance.

'You can make flour from them once they're dried and ground – not to mention a pretty decent brandy,' Sir Caulder said wistfully, biting into one himself. 'And don't spit out the seeds, you can eat them too.'

Surprised, Fletcher crunched down on the seeds he had been holding between his teeth and found them to have a pleasant, nutty taste, not unlike almonds.

'What about the wood itself?' Fletcher asked, skewering a jackalberry on his khopesh and tossing it to one of the soldiers. The man pulled it apart, then groaned with delight as he bit into it, setting off a chain reaction as the recruits picked their own fruit from the ground.

'Well, that's the best part,' Sir Caulder said, grinning. 'Your grandfather picked these because of their fruit, but there's something else that's special about them. They're termite proof.'

He pointed to the red humps of the insect mounds growing around the tree bases.

'They've got a special relationship, termites and these trees. Their roots protect their homes, so the termites leave them alone in exchange. Even when you cut them down, the termites won't touch the wood.'

Fletcher smiled and ran his hand along the rough-grooved bark of the nearest tree. He had found a source of timber.

'So that's what they're called then, jackalberry trees?' Fletcher asked. 'I can't say I've heard of them.'

'No, they've another name,' Sir Caulder said, a smile playing across his lips. 'Most people call them ebony trees.'

41

There was no hunting that day. The men were put to work, using their poleaxes to cut down the first trees for the rebuilding of Raleightown. The wagons were refitted and wheeled out over the flat ground of the savannah to take the first branches, cut away from the main trunks for the carpenters to turn into the smaller necessities, like wooden bowls and furniture struts.

Despite their numbers, Fletcher weighed in with the men, stripping down to his shirtsleeves and chopping at the base of his own tree with one of the few felling axes that had come with the convoy.

Every hour, the shout of *Timber!* would precede the crackle of falling branches, and the ground-shaking thud of the trunk hitting the ground. Then the men would swarm over it like the termites that crawled beneath, hacking away the branches to leave long, straight trunks to be turned into planks, beams and lumber.

When the sun began to set, the soldiers were finally given a brief reprieve. Their arms were near-dead, but within half an hour Fletcher called for ropes and colonists to be brought up from the town, even as he staggered with exhaustion from their labours.

The logs were too heavy for them to lift on to the wagons. So the trunks were tied with ropes around their stumps and dragged inch by backbreaking inch to the carpenters, where the tools had been prepared for the night's work. If the boars had not been on hand to help, they might not have managed it at all.

Then it was the carpenters' turn to begin their labours, with the aid of a score of helpers. The exhausted soldiers were billeted in the church, where they were served hot goat's milk and dwarven fried root-vegetables to sate their hunger. But Fletcher did not join them, for the first trunks were being hewn into what would return their settlement to its former glory.

As he walked from the church to the carpenters' workshop, he was amazed at the difference just a day had made. The detritus of the village was all but gone. Brambles had been shorn, vines torn away and moss peeled from the lower stoneworks.

The carpenters were ecstatic when Fletcher arrived, for there were over a dozen logs for them to work upon. He was shown how the cross section of each trunk was made up of a thin ring of lighter brown bark surrounding a heartwood so dark that it verged on black. It was ebony of the highest quality, or so the carpenters told him – fine-grained and dense.

They were not alone in their work. Berdon and Millo were melting down the rusted iron that could not be saved, then beating the molten metal into the tools they would need to rebuild the settlement – nails, hammers, awls and the steel bracings that would be required for the wood beams.

Thaissa provided Fletcher with the measurements for the windows around the town, as well as the name of a dwarven glassmaker who would give them a fair price. Janet helped Fletcher work out what other equipment and necessities they lacked: needles, spices, salt and dry foods. Then there were the extras that Fletcher wanted. They needed steel ingots to supplement those left over in the old forge. There were too few goats and chickens, no sheep for wool, nor were there mules to help with the carrying and construction.

With all these in mind, Fletcher made a detailed list of orders and chose ten colonists to take a wagon convoy back to Corcillum to resupply. For the first time, he dug into his bag of gold to pay for it all, sacrificing a portion of the heavy coins. It was an investment.

The trade caravan left in the late afternoon, in the hope that they would reach Corcillum by morning and return at nightfall the next day – the trip would be faster with fewer wagons, not to mention the lighter load and the cleared passage from their previous journey. Fletcher gave them their spare hunting muskets for defence, and hoped that they would not have to use them. Then, at a mental prod from Ignatius, he summoned the Drake to watch over them on their journey, and for the next few hours his consciousness was filled with the demon's elation at being free to roam the night skies.

Still there was more to do. Under the light of sputtering torches, the carpenters toiled into the night, carving the first dark-wooded planks that looked as smooth and hard as onyx stone beneath the star-filled sky. The water barrels had to be refilled from the well, the meat needed to be rationed out and cooked over their fire. Wild berries had made two colonists sick, and they had to be attended to. So it went, late into the night, until finally, as the first rays of dawn broke over the plains, Fletcher collapsed into a deep, dreamless sleep.

'Wake up, sleepyhead.'

Berdon's face swam into view and Fletcher sat up, rubbing the back of his neck.

'Here, eat something,' Berdon said, handing him a slice of cold pork.

Fletcher tore off a mouthful and gulped it down, savouring the gamey taste. He was ravenously hungry, and realised he hadn't eaten anything the previous night. There had just been too much to do.

'What time is it?' Fletcher asked. He and Berdon were alone in the church, and the sun was glowing strongly through the canvas on the windows.

'It's almost evening.'

Fletcher groaned and moved to get up, but Berdon laid a hand on his shoulder.

'Slow down. Sir Caulder's started training your soldiers this morning, and the other colonists are keeping busy. You don't need to do everything yourself, you know.'

'We need more timber,' Fletcher said, easing himself into sitting position.

'There're some colonists working on it as we speak,' Berdon replied, handing him a cup of water. 'There are more logs already on their way. Probably enough to work with over the next few days.'

'What about the food?' Fletcher asked, after a long gulp.

'Well, that's why I woke you. The convoy's back, and they've brought enough for another day. But that's not all they've brought with them.'

'What do you mean?' Fletcher said.

'Let's just say we have some new guests, and a couple of old friends we haven't seen in quite some time. They're in the square.'

Fletcher stood and uttered a low moan. His body ached all over from their work the day before.

'Might as well go see then,' he said, making for the door. A twitch from Ignatius's consciousness told him the demon was asleep somewhere. No clues there.

As they walked down the street towards the square, Fletcher saw that the repairs on the first houses were already underway. Arched beams were being manhandled through doorways, and rope ladders dangled alongside houses where colonists were beginning to work on the rooftops. Even the bakery was being used to fire roof tiles for waterproofing, using a cartful of red clay from a local watering hole.

Fletcher was so enamoured with the sight of their progress that he didn't notice the newcomers until he had almost walked into them. That and the fact that they were dressed in the same uniform as his soldiers.

Dwarves. There were seven in all, shuffling their feet nervously as he stared disbelievingly at them. Then a familiar voice called out from behind a wagon.

'I hope you're not angry,' Athol said, his hands raised in surrender. 'Othello and Cress heard you only had thirty-odd soldiers. These brave young lads volunteered recently, but they're not too raw to fit in with recruits who have had a year's training. So our friends thought you might make use of them.'

Fletcher smiled, happy to see his old friend.

'Why would I be angry?' Fletcher asked, slapping the swarthy dwarf on the back. 'They're most welcome here.'

He turned to the dwarves.

'Welcome to Raleightown, lads. It's a bit rough and ready at the moment but we're glad to have you.'

The dwarves smiled, and it felt strange to see the shaggy-bearded young men so worried about his opinion of them.

'Berdon, where are the rest of the soldiers?' Fletcher asked.

'Near the old mansion,' Berdon replied, pointing the way for the dwarven recruits.

'Please send your thanks to Othello, Cress and Atilla.'

'Well, Uhtred thought you might take it as us trying to sneak a few more dwarves to the colony,' Athol said, his face tinging red with embarrassment.

'Now we've got rid of the troublemakers, I don't think it will be a problem if we take on a few more dwarven colonists,' Fletcher said, rubbing the back of his neck. 'But to be honest, with our food intake, we might not be wanting too many more just yet.'

Even as he spoke, Fletcher felt his stomach twist with hunger. He would send Ignatius out to hunt – at least until they found a more sustainable way of finding food. But it worried him how little they had been able to forage so far. Then again, there had been no hunting parties sent out, so their success was yet to be seen.

'Well, I might have just the thing for you. Something new we've been working on. Have a look at these.'

He motioned Fletcher over to a nearby wagon. Within, nine guns lay on a cloth blanket.

'We call them rifles, thanks to the rifling inside the barrel. Remember your pistol, Blaze, how it has those grooves to make the bullets spin? Well, these are just like it.'

Fletcher picked one up. It was longer and heavier than the other muskets, and even had a carved cheek-rest on the stock of the gun for easier aiming.

'These prototypes have twice the range and accuracy of a musket,' Athol explained. 'The bullets come prewrapped inside the cartridge with a scrap of leather to grip the rifling as the shot spins out of the chamber. Trouble is, those grooves make it hard to ram down the shot and powder with your ramrod, so it takes twice as long to reload as a smoothbore musket. Not much good for massed volleys, but I'm sure they'll come in handy when hunting for game. Just be sure to use the ammunition sparingly – there's only a hundred rounds or so.'

'We'll be sure to make use of them,' Fletcher said, laying down the weapon. 'It sure is nice to see you. Did you want a tour of the place before you head on back?'

'Not exactly,' Athol said, hesitantly. He paused, embarrassed.

'We've heard about your ebony,' he went on.

'Yes, it's been a blessing.' Fletcher said. 'We'd never be able to rebuild without it.'

He pointed at one of the nearby houses, where the wooden structure of the roof was already visible above the stone shell.

'Well, we were hoping we could take some back with us,'

291

Athol said. 'The wood is resistant to mould and termites, and is beautifully black and dense. It would be perfect for making gunstocks, hilts and hafts, especially for rich officers and nobles.'

So that was it.

'How much would you need?' Fletcher asked.

'One log would be enough to begin with. We'd give you a fair share of the profits from each sale, as agreed.'

Fletcher did not have to consider it for long. It was the first trade in what he hoped would be a long and fruitful relationship.

'Head over to the carpenters down the road and pick up one from there,' Fletcher said, shaking Athol's hand. 'Take some of the branches too.'

'Aye, that I will,' Athol said, smiling with relief. 'Thank you, Fletcher. I'll be seeing you soon. We'll let you know how it goes.'

Fletcher couldn't help but feel elated as he watched the dwarf nod respectfully to Berdon and stomp off down the road. Every village needed to produce something. Pelt had been known for its furs and leather working. Perhaps Raleighshire would be known for its ebony. Although he also had plans for the sheep that had arrived, waiting in the stables nearby.

'You know, you didn't need to be so mysterious – talking about seeing old friends again,' Fletcher said, turning to Berdon. 'I only saw Athol a few days ago.'

'Actually, I wasn't talking about him,' Berdon said, clapping a hand on Fletcher's shoulder and propelling him towards the southern exit of the square. 'They must be with the soldiers.'

'Just tell me who it is,' Fletcher groaned, tired of the mystery. Then he saw them, standing where the town ended and the savannah began. They were looking out over the plains, where the soldiers could be seen exercising – so he couldn't see their faces. But he would recognise that shock of blond hair and the red curls beside them anywhere.

Rory and Genevieve had come to Raleighshire!

He broke into a run, amazed at the sight of them. Sir Caulder was standing between the pair, surveying the soldiers exercising in front of him.

'Hey!' Fletcher shouted.

They turned at the sound of his voice. It was then that Fletcher realised it wasn't Sir Caulder. It was a face he hadn't seen in over two years. A man who had come and gone like a strong wind, and turned his life upside down in the process.

Rotherham.

42

Fletcher stopped dead in his tracks and stared at the old warrior.

'Well, well,' Rotherham said, hands on his hips. 'Would you look who it is?'

'Hello, Fletcher,' Rory said, running a nervous hand through his hair.

'What are you guys doing here?' Fletcher asked incredulously.

'Well, a little bird told me you were hiring men,' Rotherham said, the hint of a smile playing across his grizzled face. 'That little bird being our King, of course.'

'The King?' Fletcher asked.

'Oh yeah, we're thick as thieves, us two,' Rotherham said, scratching at his salt and pepper stubble. 'Why do you reckon I wasn't there during your murder trial? That King of ours is a sneaky bugger – as soon as the Triumvirate's men started looking for me, he had me disappear, quiet like. Knew I wouldn't help your chances if I took the stand, me being such a colourful sort and a so-called deserter to boot. I've been bleedin' coolin' my heels on a farmstead ever since.'

'You're a sight for sore eyes,' Fletcher said, smiling at the hoary old veteran. 'We could use your experience, that's for sure.'

'Aye, sir. Or lord. Bleeding heck, how things change, eh? Best and worst decision I ever made, giving you that book. From what I saw in those scrying crystals, we'd be up to our eyeballs in goblin dung by now if it weren't for you and your little demon.'

'Well, he's not so little any more,' Fletcher said, clapping Rotherham on the back. 'You'll see.'

He turned to Rory and Genevieve, who had been standing silently in awkward embarrassment.

'And you two?'

'Well . . . we'd heard you needed soldiers, same as Rotter here,' Genevieve said. 'And, so . . . the army . . . well.'

'What Genevieve is trying to say is we didn't like the army,' Rory said, rubbing the back of his neck. 'They didn't want us for our leadership, didn't even want us to fight.'

'What do you mean?' Fletcher asked. 'We need every battlemage we can get on the front lines.'

'They wanted us for their charging stones,' Genevieve explained.

Understanding dawned on Fletcher, and his mind flashed back to his lessons with Rook in their first year. Charging stones were a grouping of smaller corundum crystals of the same colour, and were used to store mana for later use. He had only seen them used as an aide for novice summoners when first trying to open portals into the ether. But he knew they were essential on the front lines, the excess mana used to keep battlemages' shields up over the trenches when orc shamans rained fireballs down upon them at night.

'Mites have low mana, but they recover it quicker than most demons. So every day we were ordered to drain our mana into them, then we were dismissed. We weren't seen as important, because our summoning levels are so low,' Rory said, scuffing the ground with his boot.

'So, we petitioned the King for a transfer, and he granted it, on the condition that you accept us,' Genevieve said. She looked at him with pleading in her eyes.

Inwardly, Fletcher was rejoicing. Low-level though they were, having the pair on hand would be a huge advantage in battle. Not to mention the fact that they would both have had training in military strategy and command.

'You'll be second lieutenants,' Fletcher said, trying to keep the excitement from his voice. 'But you'll be given command of a squad each. If you'd be willing to accept those terms, I'll be honoured to have you.'

'We would!' Genevieve laughed, and then Fletcher found himself with a mouthful of red hair as the young battlemage gave him a tight hug.

'Thank you,' Rory said, holding out his hand.

Fletcher extricated an arm from Genevieve's hug and shook the proffered hand warmly. For the first time, he felt as if Rory and Genevieve had truly forgiven him for almost killing Malachi in the Tournament. He hadn't realised how heavily that guilt had weighed on his conscience until that very moment.

'If I may be so bold,' Rotherham said, as Genevieve released Fletcher and wiped a tear from her eye, 'you'll be needing a sergeant or two to whip these troops into shape. Show them the ropes, as it were. I'm an old hand, been fighting since I was a nipper. Would it be presumptuous of me to recommend myself to the position?'

The grizzled veteran seemed to squirm under his gaze as Fletcher considered him. He owed him, certainly, and he needed a sergeant to relay Rory and Genevieve's orders. And he was an experienced fighter. He'd know every trick and short cut the troops would take. Why not . . .

'All right then, sergeant it is,' Fletcher said, clapping Rotherham on the shoulder and walking out into the savannah. 'Just know that Sir Caulder will be our Sergeant Major, and you'll be taking orders from him. That goes for you too, Rory and Genevieve: Sir Caulder outranks the both of you.'

Fletcher resisted the urge to turn and catch the look on Rotherham's face. The old man must have been passed over for promotion a thousand times in the military. Only a choke of surprise gave him a clue to the man's reaction.

'Now let's have a look at our troops,' Fletcher called, striding through the tall grasses to where the soldiers were training.

They had been spread into a circle, and Sir Caulder had paired two off to fence against each other. The fighters battled not with their poleaxes but instead with weighted quarterstaffs, simple wooden poles that had a heavy lump of wood affixed to the end, to imitate the poleaxes' weight, length and balance.

'Good lad, Kobe,' Sir Caulder was shouting, for the young soldier had just swept his opponent's feet from under him with the pole and now held the wooden block to his throat. 'Use every part of the weapon. The haft and butt are as useful as the tip.'

Kobe smiled a brilliant smile, his teeth bright against his dark skin, and held out a hand to help his opponent up. Fletcher recognised the downed fighter as one of the convicts: a skinny, bucktoothed lad with acne scars on both cheeks. The boy ignored the proffered hand and scrambled to his feet. He spat at Kobe's feet and stalked off.

Kobe shrugged and saluted Sir Caulder instead, before joining the circle.

'At ease, lads,' Sir Caulder called, spotting Fletcher approaching. 'Take a breather.'

The troops gratefully collapsed to the ground, many gulping at water flasks. Their faces were coated with sweat from the day's exertions, and Fletcher suspected Sir Caulder had been training them since early morning.

'Bless my soul and damn my eyes, is that Rotter?' Sir Caulder cried, limping over to the foursome.

'Wait, you know each other?' Fletcher asked. Then he realised. The gasp of breath from Rotherham had been at recognising Sir Caulder's name, not his promotion.

'Too right I bleeding know him,' Rotherham said, laughing with delight. 'We've been thick as thieves since we were nought but little lads. Served in the same regiment for a time too, before the old git got airs and graces and became Lord Raleigh's bodyguard.'

'Less of the old git,' Sir Caulder said, prodding Rotherham with his hooked hand. 'I'm only a few years older than you.'

'What are the chances!' Genevieve laughed.

'You know what they say,' Rotherham said, embracing his long-lost friend. 'There's old soldiers and bold soldiers, but no old bold soldiers. I reckon we're the two exceptions.'

'Hah, maybe one of us is,' Sir Caulder said. He turned to the two new officers and winked at them.

'Rory, Genevieve – nice of you to join us. I hope you've not forgotten my training.'

'No, sir,' Rory said, tapping a rapier at his belt. 'We're ready to get in the thick of it.'

'Well, you won't be just yet – we've a few weeks to go before we take our position in that mountain pass up there.' Sir Caulder pointed at the sierra of peaks beyond the ruins of the Raleigh mansion.

Fletcher peered at the mountains, trying to spy where the pass might be. There seemed to be a point where the peaks curved inwards on each side in the shape of a U, with a dip in the very bottom. Now that he looked at them, the mountains seemed very near. He shuddered at the thought of how close they were to the orc jungles. He needed his men to be ready sooner rather than later.

Who knew when Lord Forsyth's troops would abandon their posts?

43

'All right men, pay attention now!' Rotherham snapped.

It was dusk, and Sir Caulder had finally finished his lesson with the recruits, allowing them a moment to wolf down venison sandwiches before returning to what had become their training field – the old lawn of the Raleigh mansion.

'I will demonstrate the proper way to load and fire a musket,' Rotherham continued. 'An elite soldier can fire four shots in a single minute. It can be done, and I shall prove it. I shall fire five.'

Rotherham unslung his musket, a weapon identical to the soldiers' in every way. He lifted it to his eye and swung the weapon until he found a target – a mushroom-covered tree stump.

'A musket will be able to hit a five-inch target at fifty yards, around the distance of that log over there,' Rotherham said, squinting down the barrel. 'When shooting at a group of enemies, we will open fire at more than twice that, but I'll be damned if you won't be able to pick your targets once they get in range. Sir Caulder, start the minute when I fire.'

Sir Caulder nodded, holding up a pocket watch.

Rotherham shouted, 'Now count with me. One!'

He fired in a belch of white smoke, and the log shivered as a bullet splintered its centre. Fletcher's eyes widened as Rotherham's hand flashed, tugged a paper cartridge from a pouch at his side, and then tore the end open with his teeth. He tilted a dash of the black powder within into the firing pan of the musket, then down the end of the barrel it went. The ramrod rattled out of its slot beneath the muzzle, rammed it down once, twice. Then it was back in its place and the gun was wedged into Rotherham's shoulder, his hand tugging back the hammer of the gun. One heartbeat. Boom.

'Two!'

The stump jumped as another musket ball hammered home, and the whole process was repeated again. Fletcher grinned at the wily old veteran, his hands practising the motions that had been drilled into him for the better part of a decade. The air was filled with the smell of brimstone, the smoke drifting across the recruits who watched Rotherham in awe. Now they joined in the counting with gusto, their voices echoing across the plains, a chorus to the bang of musket fire.

'Three!'

Another shot whipped into the wood, glancing off and throwing up a cloud of dirt. Rotherham never faltered, spitting the paper from his mouth and loading once again. His movements were almost mechanical, his fingers nimble and fast as he worked the gun like a musical instrument.

'Four!'

His target was in tatters, raw wood hanging ragged in a mess of splinters and sawdust. Surely a minute had passed by now. But no, Sir Caulder was still staring at his pocket watch. Rotherham was sweating, but his hands moved unerringly. The ramrod rattled down the barrel and then, just a split second after Rotherham had fired his fifth and final shot, Sir Caulder shouted, 'Time!'

The soldiers whooped and clapped, some coughing at the smoke that still billowed in a haze around them. It had been a feat of pure skill, one that Fletcher would remember in the days to come. To have an army who could shoot as well as that – they would be a force to be reckoned with.

'I gave him an extra second,' Sir Caulder whispered, sidling up to Fletcher. 'But it sure inspired the men, eh lad?'

'That it did,' Fletcher said, watching as his soldiers got to their tired feet and congratulated their sergeant. 'Don't tell him, he'd be disappointed.'

'Wouldn't dream of it,' Sir Caulder said, grinning as the old veteran grudgingly accepted the recruits' praise. 'He and I fought side by side in many a battle, and he's pulled my bacon out of the fire more times than I can count. He'll make an excellent sergeant.'

Dusk was approaching once again, casting a warm, orange glow across the land. The men were lined up and given targets at a distance of fifty feet – moss-laden flagstones long discarded from the explosion all those years ago. Rotherham had them go through the motions of loading without real ammunition at first so as not to waste it, but after an hour of correcting their technique he felt they were ready to begin firing with real cartridges. Now Fletcher, Rory and Genevieve stood to the side, watching the proceedings.

'Make ready,' Rotherham shouted. There was the click of thirty-eight hammers being pulled back.

'Present.' Thirty-eight muskets were raised and seated in thirty-eight shoulders. Fletcher looked down the line. Seven guns appeared lower due to the dwarves' height difference.

'Fire!'

A wall of noise hit Fletcher's ears, smoke blasting out in great gouts of white. Musket balls peppered the flagstones, but Fletcher counted no more than a dozen puffs of dust from the targets. The remainder scattered off into the tall grasses beyond, or smacked into the earth a few feet away.

'Load!' Rotherham barked.

There was the clatter of weapons and frantic movements as the men reached for cartridges and tore at them with their teeth.

Fletcher counted under his breath. Fifteen seconds ticked by before Rotherham shouted,

'Make ready!'

It was a shambles. Most of the men were still ramming their shot down the barrels, and even the fastest were still prodding at their ramrod slots, trying to slide the rods into place.

'Present,' Rotherham yelled.

No more than a handful of muskets were raised.

'Fire!'

A pitiful three shots scattered into the long grass, followed by a pinwheeling ramrod from a shooter who had forgotten to remove it from the barrel. Not one bullet hit its target.

Rotherham sighed, running a worn hand across his face.

'Shocking,' he growled. 'Marksmanship, pitiful. Loading, dreadful. You will meet me here every day at sunset, for practice. And we will continue to do so until you can fire at least four shots in a single minute. You will be the best, gentlemen.'

'It's only our first time,' the pockmarked convict complained.

'If you did this on a battlefield, the orcs would have you for breakfast,' Rotherham snapped, rounding on him. 'Your very survival depends on how quickly and accurately you can fire that musket.'

The recruits looked at their feet, ashamed.

'But don't you worry,' Rotherham said, his voice suddenly cheerful. 'We'll have you turning tree stumps into sawdust in no time. Dismissed!'

The soldiers groaned with relief and stomped back towards the church, leaving Fletcher alone with Rory, Genevieve, Sir Caulder and Rotherham. They waited until they were alone.

'We're going to need more ammunition for our training,' Rotherham said apologetically. 'It's the best way to learn.'

'You'll have it,' Fletcher said. 'But I'll need you to give me the names of your eight best shooters. They don't need to be fast, just accurate.'

'For the rifles?' Rotherham asked.

'That's right.'

'Athol showed me on the ride over,' Rotherham said, scratching his chin. 'I already have a few in mind. Sharpshooters are always useful – they can pick off the frontrunners in a charge and take out enemy scouts or sentries, as the case may be.'

'Good,' Fletcher said. 'Sir Caulder, you may have the afternoon for training.'

'Fine with me,' Sir Caulder replied. 'I'll have them trained up soon enough. I'll have 'em learn how to counter spears, clubs, macanas, cavalry – you name it. Just give me a few weeks with 'em.'

'We have until those men protecting the mountain pass leave,' Fletcher said, looking out at the sierra. 'Then we'll just have to hope the orcs don't make a run at us.'

A chill ran down Fletcher's spine. He had told Khan he was a Raleigh. The albino orc knew that these were his ancestral lands. If he was seeking revenge, this was the first place he would attack.

'Get them ready,' Fletcher said, shuddering despite the warmth. 'We might be fighting sooner than we think.'

44

The days seemed to blur together as the training began in earnest. Fletcher, Rory and Genevieve would take the soldiers out on to the plains early each morning to train them in manoeuvres – marching, turning, forming and reforming into varying ranks in quick succession.

Then there were the more complex formations – making a schiltron to protect from mounted attack, where the men would fall into a circle, the front ranks bristling with poleaxes to skewer the charging beasts, while the back ranks fired indiscriminately into approaching cavalry.

Another tactic was an ordered retreat, when firing teams would provide cover for each other as they fell back in groups of five. In skirmishing, the men would scatter into a loose formation to make themselves harder targets for falling javelins. They also practised disciplined charging, designed so that a wall of men would crash into their opponents in a single wave.

Under Fletcher, Rory and Genevieve were given a team of fifteen soldiers each to train, with an equal split of dwarves, elves and humans. The remaining eight were selected by Rotherham to become riflemen, and he trained them separately every other morning, until they could shoot a jackalberry out of a tree at a hundred yards, and could hit a trunk three times out of five at four hundred. Their marksmanship was practised on moving targets, and every night the colony would dine on the fruits of their endeavours – sizzling steaks of agile gazelles, long-horned oryx, and on one night even a single, heavyset buffalo that fed the entire population of Raleightown on its own.

In the afternoons, Sir Caulder trained the recruits in combat until they were coated in sweat, honing their skills until Fletcher barely recognised the sun-bronzed soldiers as they battled each other in the heat of the afternoon. The men soon learned to fear Sir Caulder; those who faced him walked away limping with red welts across their arms and faces. Even so, the soldiers were becoming a formidable force, their practice weapons blurring with the speed and ferocity that they attacked one another. There were more than a few bruises by the end of each training session, and Fletcher amazed the soldiers by healing each wound as if he were wiping away a stain.

As for the evenings, the colonists began to know the hours of the day by the intensity of gunfire, and knew the sun was setting when silence fell across the plains once more. Fletcher made sure that he, Rory and Genevieve were as practised as their own soldiers in the art of musketry, and though they slept each night with aching shoulders and skinned knuckles, all of them could fire four shots every minute, like clockwork, by the end of the first month.

It was a relief when Rotherham declared the men ready,

but then came the firing strategies.

They were to fire by rank: the first rank firing and kneeling as they reloaded, the second standing and firing next to provide a blast of musket balls into the enemy every seven seconds. Platoon fire, where five men would fire at a time down the line of infantry, provided a constant buzz of bullets whipping into the enemy.

By the end of that first month, the soldiers were well-accustomed to military manoeuvres, so Fletcher and his two lieutenants took them on expeditions across the savannah, hunting for game or scouting for ebony. Soon they had more meat than they knew what to do with, even after Ignatius had gorged himself on the surplus.

So Fletcher sent trade convoys to sell the game in Corcillum's markets, packing the meat in barrels of salt. As for the timber, Fletcher had the men cut, trim and part the trees far out in the savannah, and drag the wood back on makeshift sleds. He joined in every task, making sure that he worked harder than any of them, earning their grudging respect. Before the second month was out, the soldiers had shed all of their puppy fat, and their bodies were as lean and hard as hunting dogs. Even Kobe and his skinny compatriots became layered in cords of muscle, and Fletcher had never felt stronger in his life.

Now that the soldiers were weighing in, Raleightown soon had enough timber to complete all its own repairs and building projects, and fresh logs of ebony eventually found their way on to the trade convoys. Under Berdon and Thaissa's guidance, houses were completed swiftly, and the colonists moved in. Soon the church became their dining hall and meeting place, with new glass in the windows and great long tables of black wood filling it from wall to wall.

Fletcher began to look forward to each night, where the happy buzz of conversation flooded the room and he could lose himself in their contentment. He and Berdon had converted the old blacksmith's into their own home and they would spend every night reminiscing over old times and making plans for the future.

With every trade convoy's return, gold and supplies came with them, and Fletcher divided the proceeds fairly between the workers and himself. Noticing the profits, soon new products began to emerge from enterprising colonists. Exotic fruit were plucked by the bushel from the wild trees and sold beside their meats. The first bales of wool from their small herd of sheep soon joined them, though attacks from lions and jackals had reduced their fledgling flock by three already.

But it was not all good news. Fletcher was unable to visit his mother. He had received word from the King's doctors, who said she was making progress, but feared she would regress to her former, animalistic state at the sight of him at such a fragile juncture in her recovery. It killed him to be unable to see her, for she had been whisked away without even a proper goodbye on the night they had returned to their dimension.

Still, being able to fly again kept his spirits up, even at his most despondent. At daybreak each morning, he would mount Ignatius and soar into the cloudless skies. Athena's wing had finally mended, and her joy compounded his own as they glided above the wild landscape, learning every fold and turn in the land that they had come to call home. It was glorious to fly, and Fletcher could not believe that some people could go their entire lives without experiencing it. But no matter how much he cajoled Berdon, the bluff blacksmith refused to even mount Ignatius, let alone allow the Drake to take him a few feet off the ground.

Although he and the colonists were contented, there were divisions within Fletcher's army. This was nowhere more apparent than at dinner. The dwarves preferred to sit at their own tables, led by a dour-faced dwarf named Gallo, whose beard was so long that he had to tuck it into his belt. Fletcher knew from Thaissa that he and the other dwarven recruits spoke dwarfish between themselves even when the humans were present, earning them the ire of many of their fellow soldiers.

Kobe and his ex-slaves had bonded with the convicts, who were loud and brash but good-natured enough. Unfortunately, the most popular among them was the pockmarked boy who went by the name of Logan, a born troublemaker. He and his allies could often be seen sniggering away, usually at a joke made at dwarven or elven expense.

Then there were the stand-offish elves, with Dalia as their ringleader. She had warmed to Fletcher in the past months, and her manner was civil, if a little terse. However, Fletcher could not be sure if he had truly earned her respect, or whether it was the arrival of an unlikely mascot for his army that had prompted her improved mood: a fennec fox, as small as a puppy, with gold-white fur and the overly large, bat-like ears that were synonymous with their species.

It had taken to following them on their forays into the savannah, begging for scraps of meat and revelling in the belly rubs that the soldiers would give him. Dalia had immediately adopted the little creature, and the fox had become her constant companion, trotting at her heels during the day and sleeping beside her at night. Though the fox was ostensibly hers, the entire company of soldiers considered the fox a good omen, and had named him Rabbit on account of his ears. He was spoiled rotten by each and every one of them, and did a good job of bringing the occasional smile to Dalia's usually stern face.

They were two months into their training when the trouble began, on an evening much like any other. Almost all of the colonists had left for bed already, as training had run late and most had already eaten by the time the soldiers arrived in the church. Hunting had been sparse that day – their meal consisted of a stew made from the leftovers of the day before, and the mood was more sombre because of it.

Fletcher was sitting at the head table with Rory, Genevieve, Sir Caulder and Rotherham when he noticed it. Logan had taken a half-loaf of bread and held it up to his chin as if it were a beard, waggling his tongue at the dwarves. Perhaps it had been meant as a joke, but the dwarves were not smiling; much the opposite in fact, and the way they glowered at Logan made Fletcher think it was not the first time that he had teased them in that way.

'If I got to my knees, ye couldn't tell the difference,' Logan announced, earning himself an appreciative chuckle from the boys sitting around him. 'Then again, the dwarves have been doin' a lot of kneelin' lately too, ain't that right, boys?'

The jibe prompted one dwarf to get to his feet, but he was pulled down by Gallo, who whispered furtively in his ear.

Disappointed by the lack of reaction, Logan turned his attention to the elves. He tore the bread in two and held a piece to each side of his face, imitating their ears.

'What do you reckon, ladies?' he called to the female elves. 'Close enough for ye? They all look the same in the dark anyway, eh lads?'

Dalia closed the distance between them in one agile leap, and gripped Logan by the scruff of his neck. A stiletto blade flashed up as if from nowhere, and she hissed.

'You want to look like an elf? Let me sharpen your ears for you.'

Suddenly knives that had been used for eating were grasped and stowed under tables. Convicts jumped to their feet, and Logan bellowed, in a combination of fear and outrage.

'Stop, right now!' Fletcher yelled. His heart hammered in his chest, shocked at the speed at which his soldiers had gone from companions to enemies. But before he could say another word, the stiletto disappeared, and Dalia was backing away with a predatory smile.

'What's the problem, Logan?' she asked, cocking her head to one side. 'Can't take a joke?'

He spluttered in response. The room held its breath – then Logan overturned his bowl with a snarl and stalked off, ducking through the door to disappear into the night air. The tension eased by a few notches. Knives were replaced on tables, and a low buzz of conversation returned to the room.

Fletcher sunk into his seat, breathing out in a slow sigh. It was over for now, but even as the first hint of relief slowed his heart, his mind turned to the rest of the night.

'I want all four of you sleeping in the barracks tonight,' Fletcher said to Rory, Genevieve, Sir Caulder and Rotherham, thinking of the confined space that the soldiers were lodged in. 'Make sure this doesn't turn into something ugly.'

'You've got a point, lad,' Sir Caulder sighed, 'but this won't go away overnight. It's been brewing for some time now.'

'I know,' Fletcher said, watching as the dwarves exited the room, their eyes fixed on the convicts with open aggression. Then Gallo turned and drew a finger across his neck, the meaning as subtle as a brick through a window.

Fletcher hissed a tight breath through his teeth, frustration seething inside him. He had allowed it to grow and fester, choosing to turn a blind eye with every day that the divide deepened. Now the damage had been done.

And it was up to him to fix it.

45

The drumming of falling raindrops accompanied the tramp of soldiers' feet as they lined up in Raleightown Square. It was warm rain, fat and heavy, that drenched Fletcher's hair and ran into his eyes as he surveyed the army before him. The morning training had been cancelled, and now they would face the music.

Somewhere in the distance, the soft rumble of thunder echoed through the loud patter of the droplets. In his mind, Fletcher sensed that Ignatius and Athena were above the storm, enjoying the rushing winds that allowed them to glide high without a single flap of their wings. Fletcher had sent them to fly out without him, not wishing to punish them for his own failure.

The soldiers stood there, sullen and brooding. Not one of them would meet his gaze as he waited, arms crossed, eyes narrowed. He watched them, waiting for the green of their uniforms to darken in the wet, and their hair to plaster against their heads. The message was clear. This was punishment.

'I am ashamed,' he shouted, tempering the frustration in his voice, turning it into controlled fury. 'You were supposed to be the best, an army to be proud of. Now look at you. Squabbling like spoiled children.'

He stopped, examining their faces. Was that shame there? Or just frustration at being kept out in the rain?

'I blame myself,' Fletcher snarled. 'I let it go on for far too long. So I'm going to let you have your chance. Get it all over and done with.'

Now they looked at him.

'Logan, Dalia, Gallo, get up here,' he ordered.

The three reluctantly stepped out of line and made their way to the front. He signalled to Rory and Genevieve with a subtle twist of his hand, and the two officers stepped out from the shelter of the barracks and joined him in the rain. Sir Caulder and Rotherham looked on.

Then Fletcher raised his hand. Transparent strands of kinetic energy bloomed from the tip of his tattooed finger, twisting around Logan's feet and hands. The boy gasped as they tightened around him, and rain spattered from the invisible cord that now connected him to Fletcher's glowing finger.

Beside him, Gallo and Dalia also struggled against their bonds, as Rory and Genevieve followed the instructions he had given them that morning.

'What are you doing?' Logan yelled.

'Like I said,' Fletcher replied grimly, 'everyone gets their chance.'

He turned to the soldiers, who were watching with shock on their faces.

'Dwarves, elves, I want a single file of you in front of Logan. The rest of you, in front of Gallo and Dalia.'

They stared back at him, eyes darting from him to their bound companions.

'You heard him, move it!' Sir Caulder barked, sending the soldiers scurrying to their places.

'Logan made hateful comments to both your races last night,' Fletcher announced. 'Gallo drew a finger across his neck, and Dalia held a knife to his throat. None of them are innocent.'

He took a deep breath, hoping his plan would work.

'You there, Tallon,' Fletcher said, pointing at a dwarf in the front. He was the one who had stood up in anger at Logan's comments.

Tallon looked at him, fear plastered across his face.

'Hit him.'

Tallon hesitated.

'I . . .'

'Last night I saw you stand, ready to fight him,' Fletcher shouted through the downpour, striding up to Tallon. 'Is this how you treat your comrades-in-arms?'

He rounded on the troops behind him.

'Most of you had knives in your hands. Don't deny it!'

Now he could see shame. Downturned gazes, faces turned away from him.

'So here's your chance,' Fletcher growled.

Tallon stared at the boy in front of him. Logan met his gaze and lifted his chin defiantly.

'Go on,' Fletcher snapped, shoving Tallon forward. The dwarf stumbled on the cobbles, catching his balance a few inches from Logan. He stared at his rival, squinting through the rain that flooded down. Then Tallon gave him a half-hearted shove on the shoulder.

'This is foolish,' Tallon said, looking for supporters among the crowd. But they remained silent, only staring back with fear in their eyes.

'You call that a punch?' Fletcher asked. 'I thought you hated him.'

'It's wrong,' Tallon said.

'You were ready to take a knife to him last night,' Fletcher said, stabbing a finger at Logan. 'This is nothing compared to that.'

'I will nae do it,' Tallon replied.

'Then get back in line,' Fletcher growled, shoving him away.

He turned back to the troops, stalking across the three files. His eyes settled on Cooper, one of Logan's cronies.

'How about you, Cooper?' Fletcher asked. 'You hate Gallo enough to take him to task?'

The boy glared at Gallo, whose face whitened as the boy stepped forward.

'Let 'im go,' Cooper said. 'We'll settle it like men. One on one.'

'What's the matter?' Fletcher asked. 'There's your enemy, right there. All you need to do is reach out and hit him.'

'He's helpless,' Cooper said, shaking his head.

'Would you not kill an orc, if it'd lost its weapon in battle?' Fletcher asked. 'It would be helpless, would it not?'

'That's different,' Cooper argued.

'You hate both as enemies, right?' Fletcher said. 'He's nothing to you. Do it.'

317

Cooper stepped forward, cracking his neck. He looked into Gallo's eyes, the muscles flexing in his jaw as he gritted his teeth. But something held him back.

'No,' Cooper said, shaking his head. 'I won't do it.'

Fletcher shoved the boy down the line.

'Anyone else?' Fletcher asked. 'Someone here must have some anger to take out on these three individuals. Now's your chance.'

He looked to the boy in front of Dalia, an ex-slave named Arif, who had been swift to pick up a knife in Logan's defence.

Arif held up his hands and backed away, retreating to the end of the line.

'So suddenly nobody wants to hurt each other any more,' Fletcher said, forcing a bitter laugh. 'What's changed?'

His only answer was the splash of rain, and the distant rumble of thunder.

'Here's the thing,' Fletcher said, running a hand through his sodden hair. 'If you hated each other, this little dog-and-pony show would have gone a very different way. But hate isn't your problem. It's pride.'

He shook his head at them in disgust.

'Too proud to bear insult. Too proud to lose face. Too proud to forgive.'

The soldiers stood silent, miserable under the vent of his anger.

'Do you see that?' Fletcher asked, pointing over their shoulders at the ruin of his ancestral home. 'My family were slaughtered by the orcs. Every person in this town was impaled on spikes and left to rot on the borders of the jungle beyond those mountains. That is hatred. That is the enemy.'

He released Logan from the kinetic spell, letting the boy crumple to his knees on the cobbles. At his nod, Genevieve and Rory followed suite, Gallo and Dalia falling to the ground.

'The Forsyths organised it,' Fletcher said, and he saw surprise flash across their faces. 'Told the orcs how to get in, where to go. It's true.'

He lifted Logan to his feet.

'And as you well know, their family have sown disunity among our peoples, to further their interests. And you're playing right into their hands. They feed on your pride. On your fear of the unfamiliar. Don't. Let. Them.'

Fletcher leaned in and whispered in Logan's ear.

'Make comments like that again and you'll be cut from my army,' he whispered. 'That was your one and only chance.'

Logan scurried back to the men, helped along by a shove from Fletcher's hand. His message to Logan had been loud and clear, even if the words themselves had not been heard by the rest of the troops. Gallo gave Fletcher a nod of respect as he rejoined the ranks, even as Dalia stalked away without giving him a second glance.

Fletcher sighed inwardly. She was as hard to read as Sylva. Still, he knew that, for the moment, the troop's anger had been abated. He could only hope that it would stay that way.

'My lord,' a voice called. Fletcher turned to see a young boy emerge from the street behind him, his eyes wide with fear. 'There's soldiers comin'.'

Fletcher spun to look out at the mountains, where the Forsyth guards would come from. But there was nothing. The boy tugged at his sleeve and pointed down the street the way he had come.

'No, milord, down that way.'

'There's no reas—'

Fletcher's words died in his mouth. There were men marching from the north, coming into view as they turned up Raleightown's main road.

Even from all the way down the street, Fletcher recognised the black-and-yellow of their uniforms.

These were Didric's soldiers.

46

There were scores of them – at least sixty, by Fletcher's estimation – marching smartly down the road despite the rain. At their head, Fletcher could see the familiar, gorilla-like shape of Jakov lumbering along, and beside him stalked Didric. To Fletcher's surprise, the young noble still wore the half-mask from the ball. Clearly he liked the way it had made him look.

Berdon ducked through the forge's double doors and walked over to Fletcher, squinting through the downpour at the approaching men.

'What do you think they're doing here?' he asked. 'Those are Didric's wardens, if I'm not mistaken.'

'I don't know,' Fletcher replied. 'But I know it can't be good.'

He could see a smirk on Didric's face, which widened as their eyes met.

'Should we tell the men to level their muskets?' Berdon asked.

'No,' Fletcher replied. 'If they were here to slaughter us they'd have kept the element of surprise. And the muskets wouldn't fire in this rain anyway.'

He contemplated the situation. His men had their poleaxes and muskets, but the rifles were still inside.

'Sergeants, a moment!' he shouted.

Sir Caulder and Rotherham hurried up to him.

'Sergeant Rotherham, take the rifles up to the second-floor window and load them. Be ready to shoot in case of trouble.'

'Aye sir,' Rotherham replied.

'Sir Caulder, put the men in a crescent formation at the entrance. I want them surrounded when they walk in.'

Sir Caulder nodded and began barking orders at the soldiers.

'Genevieve, Rory – take command of your troops. Don't let them start something we can't finish. This is going to get ugly.'

The pair ran to do his bidding and, as if on cue, the rain eased to a thin drizzle.

'Berdon, get inside,' Fletcher said.

'Not this time, son,' Berdon said, standing firmly beside him. He tugged a forging hammer from his belt and let it dangle from his fingers.

In his mind, Fletcher called to Ignatius and Athena to return. But they were miles away, having flown north-west to the farthest reaches of Raleighshire. It would take them a half hour to get back.

Then Didric's soldiers were there, stopping just in front of the thin line of Fletcher's troops. Behind them, Fletcher could see his townspeople had followed, another twenty adult men and women. It put them at almost even numbers.

'So this is where you all ran off to,' Didric announced, spreading his arms wide. Behind him, window shutters shivered open as other, more timid townsfolk watched from behind their curtains.

'Why are you here, Didric?' Fletcher demanded.

'Not much to look at, is it?' Didric continued. 'I reckon you were better off in the hovels back in Pelt.'

Didric's men sniggered at his words.

'Get to the point,' Fletcher snapped. 'Or you'll find yourself on the end of one.'

He loosened his khopesh in the scabbard at his side.

'I see you've joined with some other undesirables,' Didric said, ignoring Fletcher's threat and looking pointedly at the dwarven recruits, then the elves. 'I can't say I'm surprised.'

Dalia spat derisively at his words. As she did so, Didric noticed Rabbit, sitting close by her feet. The little fox gave him a high-pitched snarl as he looked down at it, and Didric lashed out with his boot, sending the fox scampering away with a yelp.

'Don't you touch him,' Dalia hissed, jabbing at him with her poleaxe.

'Nasty little rat,' Didric smirked, watching as the fox disappeared into the brush with his tail between his legs.

'I won't ask you again. What are you doing here, Didric?' Fletcher snapped, his arms crossed.

'Why, we're here to pick up Lord Forsyth's men for him,' Didric replied, throwing a hand out at the mountains beyond the ruin behind Fletcher. 'Unfortunately, this hellhole was on the way.'

'Doing Forsyth's dirty work for him?'

'A favour for a friend,' Didric said. 'He's rather indisposed at the moment, thanks to your little stunt.'

'You call him a friend?' Fletcher replied, pointing to the remains of his parents' old home. 'See that? That's what the treacherous snake does to his friends.'

'You call it treachery; I call it the cost of doing business.' Didric shrugged. 'You must admit, it was a bold move. Your fool father never saw it coming.'

Each word felt like a slap across the face. Fletcher felt the blood rise in his cheeks.

'Say that again,' Fletcher snarled, drawing his blade.

Didric smiled and stepped back, allowing Jakov to speak for him.

'Stand aside,' Jakov said, his hand firmly on the hilt of his sword. 'We've business to attend to.'

'Not on my land, you don't,' Fletcher replied. 'You are trespassing. Turn back and wait for Forsyth's men at Watford Bridge. We will send them on.'

Jakov unsheathed his sword in a scrape of metal. Behind him, Didric's soldiers did the same.

'I said, stand aside!' Jakov bellowed, lifting the blade.

Then a shot rang out. The sword clanged in a shower of sparks, tumbling from Jakov's hands and into the grass.

'You want to fight, leave the blades on the ground,' Rotherham's voice sung out from the barracks. 'The next man to move gets a bullet in his skull. Or maybe I'll start with Didric – I haven't decided yet.'

Jakov spun around, his eyes searching the windows of the houses. He crouched and reached for his sword, his eyes still fixed above. Another shot whipped by, knocking the sword out of reach.

'I can do this all day,' Rotherham called.

'All right!' Didric shouted. He looked around him, seeing his predicament. With weapons, his men would have had the advantage. But with Raleightown's citizens joining in the fistfight . . . not so much.

'Please, let's drop the weapons,' Berdon rumbled from beside Fletcher. 'I've unfinished business with that man over there.'

He cracked his neck and raised his fists. Jakov blanched as the big man took a step forward, standing only an inch shorter than him, but with the same broad shoulders. Jakov and his guards had beaten Berdon unconscious and burned down his home on the night of Fletcher's escape. Unfinished business, indeed.

'Aye, let's have ye,' Gallo shouted from behind Fletcher. 'Ye'll see how undesirable we are when ye've got a dwarven boot up yer arse.'

More soldiers joined in the shouting – elves, humans and dwarves alike.

'Back,' Didric ordered, tugging at Jakov. The black-and-yellow uniformed men retreated, their backs against each other, swords raised in a porcupine of blades.

'Phalanx formation,' Fletcher ordered. His men jumped to obey, ordering themselves into three rows that bristled with poleaxes.

'Advance!'

They followed the retreating soldiers down the street, stepping in time to present an unassailable wall to the enemy. All the while, Didric and Jakov stared fearfully out at the houses around them, terrified of the shot that might pluck them from their feet.

Step after step took them to the edge of the town. Now the

rain had stopped, and the grey stains of cloud were beginning to recede. Didric's men moved into the tall grasses, lifting their feet high to avoid tripping.

'Load!' Fletcher ordered. Immediately, the poleaxes were slung over shoulders, and the rattle of ramrods began.

At the sight of the muskets, Didric's men broke into full retreat, tripping over each other in their desperation to get away. The muskets were unlikely to fire in the rain, but it didn't hurt to give them some incentive.

'No discipline,' Sir Caulder murmured.

The men cheered as the enemy soldiers sprinted. Then, all of a sudden, they fell silent.

Didric and Jakov were out of range, but their figures could still be clearly seen across the grasslands. They had stopped beside a stunted tree.

Jakov was holding something up. Something with golden fur, wriggling in his grasp. He swung it against the trunk. Once, twice. Then they turned back, running into the grasslands.

'No!' Dalia cried, falling to her knees.

They had killed Rabbit.

47

They buried Rabbit under the training ground, laying the broken body six feet beneath the earth and leaving Jakov's sword beside him. No words were spoken, but tears were shed, even by the gruffest dwarves.

The little fox's death had been an act of meaningless cruelty, and it had taken all of Fletcher's reasoning to prevent the soldiers from going after Didric's men. But the enemy had the numbers, and would be waiting for them. That, and the fact that Fletcher could not justify a costly battle for the sake of a single animal's life, beloved pet or not.

Still, the fox's death had united them in grief. Dwarves, humans and elves mourned together, commiserating and telling stories about their lost friend. Ignatius returned with an impala clutched in his claws, and they roasted it over a fire and supped on jackalberry beer. That night, drunk and full of food, the soldiers sang songs of sorrow from their respective lands. All the while, Fletcher watched from the barracks with his officers and sergeants. They could not partake – it wouldn't be right.

'Let them bond,' Rotherham had said. 'They don't need an officer ruining their night.'

So instead, Fletcher began preparations for the next day.

Training was over. Didric's men would be expecting Forsyth's troops; Athena had followed them back to their camp beside Watford Bridge, where they waited behind a hastily constructed barricade.

If Fletcher's trade convoys were to make it to Corcillum, Didric's men would need to leave, and that meant fetching Lord Forsyth's soldiers.

They would need to go to the pass, and soon. But they needed supplies. So Fletcher and his officers secured a wagon from their small fleet. Berdon was tasked with reinforcing the wheels to handle the bumpy terrain, and in the meantime they organised everything they might need.

Barrels of salted antelope meat and water were taken from the stores, along with canvas tents, cooking utensils, oilcloths to keep weapons from rusting and whetstones to keep them sharp. They secured a spare barrel of gunpowder that Seraph had sent them, with cartridge paper, musket-ball moulds and bars of lead from Berdon, all for the production of their own ammunition.

They took two goats for milk, and four of their clutch of chickens were put in makeshift wooden cages to provide a regular supply of eggs. Bushels of fruit were added, and not just jackalberries, but the other fruit that the townsfolk had begun to cultivate; horned cucumbers – spiky yellow on the outside, but inside a sweet dark-green pulp that tasted of lime, papaya and banana all at once; giant breadfruit that grew like hairy, pimpled melons as large as an orc's head. There were even a few baskets of durian fruit that stunk like death but tasted unexpectedly sweet – the fruit had, unsurprisingly, not sold well in Corcillum, so Fletcher took their entire supply.

And there was one other, more secret task that Fletcher gave Thaissa, one she would need to work through the night to complete in time. But it would be worth it.

The next morning, the troops were paraded out on the training ground, and watched by the townsfolk, who had gathered to wish them goodbye. They were packed and ready to go, leather satchels and weapons strapped to their backs, uniforms cleaned and brushed. Each and every one of them looked lean and eager, like hunting dogs straining at the leash.

Rory and Genevieve stood proudly at the heads of their squads, with Rotherham and his small band of riflemen at the back, and Sir Caulder at the front, ready to act as drillmaster. An immense gratitude swelled in Fletcher's chest – to have the honour of leading such men.

He took a deep breath, for the words that he had so carefully prepared over the long night seemed to waver in his head. Last night he had berated them. Now, he would need to unify them.

'I am proud of what we have achieved here,' Fletcher said, standing in front of them with his hands behind his back. 'You are now the elite, soldiers I would be proud to lead into the heart of orcdom itself. For that, I thank you.'

The troops stood silent, their chests puffed, eyes straight ahead. A scatter of applause began from the townsfolk, but Fletcher was not finished.

'Today, we shall head to our new encampment, on the border

between the orc jungles and the place we have come to call home. There, we shall prepare for our long vigil to keep not only Raleighshire safe, but the entirety of Hominum. For we defend the gateway to an empire.'

Fletcher turned and pointed into the distance.

'Out there beyond the horizon, no more than a day's ride away, lies Corcillum. Thousands of innocents, going about their daily lives. You are the thin line that keeps them safe from the savage hordes on our southern border. I can think of none better to fight in that endeavour.'

Smiles now, even the hint of one from Dalia herself. He knew he was being dramatic, but he meant every word of it.

'But what are we to call ourselves?' Fletcher asked, pointing at his uniform. 'We go to collect a contingent of Forsyth Furies. Yesterday we were accosted by the men Didric calls his wardens. So, who are we?'

Even as he spoke, Thaissa was hurrying towards him from up the street. He saw the furrowing of brows from the men, even the hesitant twitch of their lips as they bit back a response to his question.

Thaissa handed him a roll of cloth, attached to a pole. She curtsied and backed away, whispering,

'I did the best with what I had, only we didn't have green left.'

'I'm sure it's great, Thaissa, thank you,' Fletcher whispered back.

With a flourish, he unravelled the cloth with a sweep from the pole, allowing a flag to unfurl and flutter in the breeze.

'People of Raleightown, I give you . . . the Foxes!' Fletcher announced, and was relieved to hear a roar of approval from both soldiers and townsfolk as they saw Thaissa's handiwork.

It was the first time he had seen the flag, and the result astounded him. Stitched on a cloth of rich burgundy, was the golden outline of a fennec fox, a single paw lifted, nose pointing straight as an arrow. It rippled in the wind, glorious in its detail and colour.

'Foxes, are you ready to fight?' Fletcher yelled, cutting short the cheers.

'Sir, yes, sir!' came the reply, shouted in perfect unison.

'Sir Caulder, give the order,' Fletcher said, forcing back a grin.

'About turn,' Sir Caulder barked.

Forty-two pairs of feet spun on their heels. Forty-two more stamped down.

'Forward . . . march!'

And Fletcher's heart sang with excitement.

Because Fletcher's Foxes were on the move.

48

It felt as if they reached the foot of the mountains in no time at all. But then, the pass they were heading for was only forty minutes' walk as the crow flew. Now that Fletcher thought about it, it seemed strange to know that the Forsyth men were so close, yet they had not seen them in over two months.

As he took in the sierra, stretching left and right as far as the eye could see, Fletcher realised that these were no Beartooth Mountains. The sides were as sheer as the walls of Vocans itself, and the colouration was the light brown of sun-dried clay, though he knew from Sir Caulder's stories that the mountains were actually made from a crumbly sandstone. But regardless of their composition, they had come to be known as the Bronzestone Bluffs, an ignoble and inaccurate name for the natural wonder that separated the tropical jungles from the temperate plains of Raleighshire, not to mention the civilised world from the barbarian orc hordes.

'I've not been back here since . . . you know,' Sir Caulder said over the squeak of the wagon wheels. He was sitting on the back axle – walking for too long chafed his stump against the leather holder of his peg leg. 'Wasn't much to look at then, nor will it be now.'

They were going up an incline now, where the steep walls of the mountains funnelled in on either side. Above, the sky was a bright, empty blue, and Fletcher was filled with the temptation to summon Ignatius and fly ahead. But then . . .

'Halt!' Rotherham's voice called out from ahead.

Fletcher hurried past the wagons, shouldering his way through the ordered rows of his troops. Then he stopped, filled with confusion. They were in the right place – but there was nobody there.

'Where are Forsyth's men?' Rotherham growled. 'The buggers should be here.'

Looking around, Fletcher could see they were in a canyon, not dissimilar to the one they had passed through in the ether. There was no grass here, just a dry, desiccated mud beneath their feet, shadowed by the natural bulwarks stretching into the sky around them. The walls of the mountains angled inwards, ending with a gap no wider than a stone's throw across. Through it, Fletcher could see the green of tangled grasses and beyond, the rippling leaves and thickets of the jungle edge.

On the right-hand wall, a natural ledge seemed to have been worn up the side, just broad enough for a man to walk upon. At its highest point, perhaps two storeys up and two score yards from the canyon entrance, the ledge extended outwards into a platform of sorts. There, the remains of some kind of building could be seen, now no more than a ring of foundation stones, with the remaining rubble strewn about the ground far beneath it.

''Tis the old watchtower,' Sir Caulder said, stomping up behind him. 'Fell down long ago, before your father was even born. We used to post sentries on the ledge – you can fit half a dozen men and a campfire up there, and the base keeps most of the wind out. You get a pretty good view of the approach into the canyon too.'

'Handy,' Fletcher said, avoiding the temptation to walk up the ledge and have a look.

Instead, he wandered forward, towards the mouth of the canyon. It amazed him how narrow the gap was – Ignatius could have sat in the centre and scraped the edges if he extended his wings. If an army were to pass here, they would have to march through the bottleneck in a column of no more than ten men abreast.

'We call it the Cleft,' Rotherham said, following behind Fletcher. 'If you saw it from above, it'd look like an hourglass, with this gap as the pinch in the middle.'

'And this is the only way into Raleighshire?' Fletcher asked.

'That's right,' Rotherham said. 'The mountains extend into the Vesanian Sea to the west, and the front lines protect the borders to the east, beyond Watford River. This is it.'

Fletcher took a step closer, then stumbled, his foot hitting something hollow and metal.

'What's this?' he said, half to himself. He kneeled down and scraped away the mud from a round shape, so badly rusted that it blended with the earth.

'Another relic from the past?' he asked.

'Actually, that's a bit newer,' Sir Caulder said, getting down

334

on one knee and laying his hand on the rusted object. 'Believe it or not, this is the first cannon ever made, not a few weeks before you were born. The first gun, in fact, by all accounts.'

He chuckled and shook his head.

'I'm surprised the old girl is still here.'

'Wait . . . didn't Othello's father invent the gun?' Fletcher asked.

'That he did, lad,' Sir Caulder said, brushing aside some dirt to reveal a word embossed on the side.

Thorsager

'What's it doing here?' Fletcher asked, tracing his fingers across the old lettering of Othello's family name.

'Your father, Edmund, commissioned it. Challenged all the blacksmiths in Corcillum to come up with something that would be devastating across a small area, with that gap over there in mind. So, Uhtred showed him this. Of course, it wasn't much more than an iron tube packed with rudimentary gunpowder and old nails, but it did the trick. The early prototypes used bamboo segments, would you believe it!'

Fletcher grinned, picturing Uhtred as a young man, pottering about in his forge with pieces of bamboo. Sir Caulder sighed and patted the rusted frame.

'We never fired the bloody thing, except when Uhtred demonstrated it, of course. Must have sat here since the night your parents died. The Forsyths probably thought it was junk.'

'It's a piece of history,' Fletcher said. 'For both Uhtred and my family. I'll have it taken to Raleightown and mounted.'

It pleased him, to know that his father and Othello's family had some connection. In fact, the invention of the gun was what had begun the dwarven bid for equality. Perhaps if his father had not issued the challenge, the world would be a different place.

'Ah, that's where Forsyth's lads are hiding. There's a campfire,' Rotherham shouted. 'Tents too.'

Fletcher turned, scanning the empty canyon behind him as if he had somehow missed them as they walked in. But no – Rotherham's hand was pointing through the canyon exit, into the knee-high grass beyond. As Fletcher looked more closely, he could make out the shapes of tents in the grasses.

'Those idiots,' Sir Caulder snarled, stomping through the Cleft and into the grasses. 'They're camping on the wrong damned side.'

Fletcher followed. He winced, the glare of the sun hitting him as he stepped out of the canyon's shadow. To the left and right, the mountain curved outwards and away, leaving a few hundred feet of tangled grasses and low bushes before a wall of jungle began. A few stunted trees dotted the area, but otherwise it was devoid of life.

'Anyone here?' Fletcher called, beginning to feel uneasy. There were dozens of tents littering the ground, but if there were occupants, they did not make their presence felt. Many of the sorry structures had collapsed in on themselves, and various barrels and crates lay abandoned beside them.

A hollow breeze rushed past, funnelled through the canyon behind.

'Lazy fools have abandoned their posts,' Sir Caulder concluded, kicking at a ring of stones on the ground with his peg leg, tumbling a rock into a pile of half-burnt bamboo in its centre. 'Probably snuck back to Corcillum as soon as we arrived in Raleightown. We've been undefended all this time!'

But Fletcher was not so sure. He crouched down and buried his finger in the ashes in the fire pit.

'No,' he said, feeling the barest hint of warmth. 'This fire burned itself out only an hour or so ago; plus the ashes would have been blown away by now if this had been here any longer. Maybe Didric got a message to them last night, told them to make their way to Watford Bridge this morning. We might have just missed them.'

'But that doesn't explain why they left everything here,' Sir Caulder said, scratching at his grizzled beard.

The Foxes were pouring through the Cleft now, peering curiously at the remains of the Forsyth camp. Soon the soldiers were wandering aimlessly through the abandoned tents, prodding them with their swords and lifting the lids from the barrels.

It was only then that Fletcher noticed him. A topless man, standing in front of a tree, halfway between the Cleft and the jungle. It was hard to tell – he could just see him through a shimmering heat haze. No . . . not standing. Tied to it.

'Foxes, skirmish formation!' Fletcher shouted. Instantly, the soldiers snapped into action, sprinting into a loose line, spread across the grassy basin.

Fletcher's heart pounded in his chest. The man could be anyone. A deserter perhaps, left by the Forsyth Furies to die. But Fletcher's gut told him different.

'Forward, slowly now,' Fletcher commanded, striding towards the man.

He walked twenty paces ahead of his soldiers, eyes scanning the edge of the jungle. The fronds of the vegetation wavered in the breeze, presenting Fletcher with an ever-shifting wall of green.

At first, he had thought he'd seen rocks, strewn about just in front of the jungle's edge. But then he saw the red stains on the grass around them, the muskets and swords, scattered like discarded branches.

Dead men, in black, Forsyth uniform. Eyes, wide and staring, mouths half open in petrified terror. There was so much blood, more than Fletcher had ever thought possible.

'Halt!' Fletcher shouted.

The men could see the bodies too now, their exclamations of horror loud in his ears. Fletcher's eyes flicked to the semi-naked man. He was . . . moving.

Fletcher ran ahead, his eyes flicking between the tree and the corpses beyond, heart juddering in his chest. Now, he saw the death apples rotting on the ground beneath the foliage. This was a manchineel tree, so poisonous that were one to shelter beneath it, the very raindrops that dribbled through its leaves would sear your skin like acid. And the poor man was strapped bare-skinned to its bark.

A shock of dark brown hair obscured the man's face. Though he was more a boy, truth be told, if his skinny frame and sunken chest were anything to go by.

Fletcher drew his khopesh and struck the vines that tied the boy to the trunk, wincing in horror at the sight of the blistered skin along the lad's back, red and weeping with sores. This was orc handiwork.

Then the boy turned, and Fletcher jerked with recognition. It was Mason – the escaped slave who had guided Malik's team during their mission. Even as Fletcher's eyes widened with surprise, the boy whispered something, barely more than a croak forced through cracked lips.

Fletcher leaned down and lifted the boy into his arms, careful to avoid the raw skin on his back. The body seemed to weigh almost nothing; so little meat existed on his frame.

'What happened?' Fletcher asked, leaning forward.

It was little more than whisper, but the word rang like a death knell in Fletcher's ears.

'Run.'

49

They erupted from the trees in a crash of snapping branches. Cassowaries, too many to count, their black-feathered bodies tearing over the ground, red wattles dangling beneath blue necks and fierce orange eyes. Astride them were grey-skinned goblins, screaming their battle cries, spears and wood-clubs held aloft.

'Close ranks,' Sir Caulder roared from behind Fletcher. 'Schiltron formation!'

There was no time to get back to the men. Fletcher summoned Ignatius in a burst of white light and shoved Mason's body across the Drake's back. He threw himself on top of the boy as a javelin whistled past his head, so close Fletcher felt the flutter of air on his cheek. Another grazed Ignatius's side, leaving a furrow of welling blood between exposed, pink flesh. There were dull thuds of more javelins, striking the tree trunk. Spears buried themselves in the shaded ground around them. Ignatius beat aloft, thrusting into the air with the two boys on his back. More and more enemies burst from the jungle.

Fletcher circled out of javelin range, watching the figures

340

below. Gunshots blasted, as desperate soldiers emptied their muskets into the frontrunners. Already, cassowaries were tumbling into the grass, but still more came from the jungle border. Fifty or so were already on the battlefield, and as many more emerged from the foliage . . . then more again, over a hundred now, a seemingly endless flood of squawking riders.

A soldier went down, a javelin through his thigh before he could reach the small circle of men, half formed in the first few seconds of battle. Rotherham picked him up and threw him over his shoulder, reaching reinforcements in the nick of time.

Then the first wave of cassowaries broke upon the small knot of soldiers, parting around them like a wave, hurling spears and sweeping with their clubs. More Foxes fell, even as goblins were blasted from their seats and cassowaries were skewered on poleaxes, falling in a flurry of kicking talons and floating plumage.

Riders circled and broke, then formed again, charging on to the poleaxes, meeting the bullets with their bodies in suicidal abandon. It was mad, brutal fighting, where sheer force of numbers threatened to engulf the beleaguered circle of soldiers.

A crackle of lightning from Genevieve hurled cassowaries back, earning the men time to drag injured into the centre, where Rory's healing touch waited. Beside him, taller men's muskets cracked and spouted gouts of smoke, whipping death over the long grass with practised accuracy, felling the stragglers who bore down upon them. Dwarves swept poleaxes low as cassowaries lunged, cutting their long legs from under them and finishing the job with swift, precise chops. The Foxes' formation held, but barely; the weight of the cassowaries falling among their tightly packed ranks and leaving vulnerable gaps, even as more riders thundered from the edge of the jungles.

'Down!' Fletcher yelled, sweeping Blaze towards the second wave of riders. He tugged Gale from his holster as they hurtled through the air, Ignatius's baying matching the roar of the wind in Fletcher's ears. He emptied both barrels, seeing the twin spurts of black feathers and blood from the frontrunners, spilling them and their goblins on to the ground.

Then Ignatius was tearing through their lines, claws outstretched, beak snapping. Goblins were slashed from their saddles, cassowaries bowled to the earth. Fletcher fired Blaze into a goblin's chest – the spear it was about to throw falling from nerveless fingers.

Mana roiled within Fletcher's consciousness as Ignatius landed, then spun and poured a flood of flame over the fallen bodies of goblin and cassowary alike. Half the riders were down, the rest wheeling away in disarray.

But the third wave of enemies was bearing down now, and they were forced to take off once again, pain flaring in their consciousness as a thrown spear pierced Ignatius through the delicate membrane of his wing, and another thudded into his haunches.

They limped into the sky, mana draining as Ignatius's wounds healed, far more slowly than Fletcher would have liked. He tugged the spear from the Drake's rump, grimacing at the spurt of blood and hurling it ineffectually at the charging enemies beneath them. Ignatius was flagging now, and Fletcher dared not risk summoning Athena with all the javelins flying, especially with her penchant for disobedience.

Far below, the final wave smashed into the schiltron. This time, the formation dissolved into knots of fighting soldiers, broken by the momentum of the impaled cassowaries. The gunfire slowed, the battle now a bloody mess of flailing poleaxes and the occasional fireball from Rory and Genevieve. At the centre, Sir Caulder and Rotherham stood over a pile of wounded soldiers, killing all comers with deadly efficiency. But they were too few, and the riders many. They needed help.

Fletcher sheathed his pistols and drew his khopesh, pointing it down at the enemy.

'Again!' he shouted, and Ignatius was already swooping down for one final charge. They smashed into the back of the riders, sending a half-dozen goblins flying. Fletcher's vision was filled with struggling soldiers, parrying and hammering; thrashing clubs held by grey limbs above hook-nosed faces; cassowaries kicking with savage abandon.

Then he was leaning out and stabbing over Ignatius's shoulder, spitting a goblin through its mouth. The creature fell back, and Fletcher lost his sword in the mêlée, unable to tug the blade from the skull. A burst of gunfire half deafened him, smoke stinging his eyes as it plumed by his face.

They were losing. The few Foxes still standing staggered from exhaustion, while more and more wounded fell behind the fragile ring of defenders. There were fewer gunshots now – no time to reload as the baying horde of creatures pressed in.

An elf screamed in front of him, a spear buried in her midriff by a snarling goblin. It was Dalia, her face white with shock. Weaponless, Fletcher could only curse and fire a bolt of lightning into the perpetrator's back, killing it in a sizzling screech as Dalia clawed herself over the blood-slick grass into the safety beneath Rotherham and Sir Caulder's swords.

Pain. So bad that Fletcher could hardly believe it. Ignatius collapsed beneath them, sending Mason's body sprawling over Fletcher as they fell into the bloodied grass. A spear was buried deep into Ignatius's neck, held by a triumphant goblin. Ignatius's tail whipped around and near decapitated it with his spike, but the damage was done. The Drake collapsed, the pain too much for him.

'Fletcher!' Genevieve screamed, and he rolled aside in the nick of time as a club thrummed by his head, thudding into the grass. Mason grasped at the offending goblin's leg, using the last of his strength. It gave Fletcher time to snatch Dalia's discarded poleaxe from the ground and stab the goblin through the stomach.

It collapsed on top of him, pinning him in place, and a spear stabbed down as if from nowhere, the point slitting his cheek and missing his eye by a hairsbreadth. Fletcher felt the hot gush of blood on his face, saw a goblin raise his spear again. His hands were pinned beneath him. No time.

Then a brown, furry blur whipped by, and the goblin clutched at its throat, trying to seal the gaping wound that had suddenly appeared there. A warbling cry cut through the sounds of battle – and suddenly there were gremlins everywhere.

They rode their rabbit-like maras, ululating as they sliced their shark-tooth daggers into exposed goblin ankles, parting tendons and opening arteries with deadly efficiency. Poison darts flitted from outriders along the edges, sending cassowaries and goblins tumbling, twitching horribly as the toxins took hold.

'Don't hurt the gremlins!' Fletcher bellowed with the last of his breath, crushed under the weight of Mason and the dead goblin. He heaved them aside and staggered to his feet. Pain spiked his skull, blinding him to the seething battle around him. His hands felt the shaft of the spear in Ignatius's neck, and he tugged it out. For a moment black waves of nausea rolled over him, the Drake's agony like a scream in his mind as he etched the healing spell. Then he was pulsing white, healing light into the wound.

The world cleared, pain receding. Guns were firing again now while, all around him, maras pattered by, leaping high to allow their gremlin riders to slice at goblin necks. The battle had taken a dramatic turn. Dead goblins were sprawled about like beached fish, eyes glazed over in death. A cassowary limped back towards the jungle, dragging a dead rider tangled in its claws. There was no more than a half-dozen goblins left now, and even as the last of Ignatius's wounds were sealed, they were shot ragged by the Foxes still standing.

Then it was over, and all that could be heard were the groans of the dying.

50

Fletcher turned his healing spell on his own cheek, then staggered through the corpses to the injured, ignoring the gremlins as they dismounted nearby. He kneeled beside Dalia, white light pulsing through his finger to heal her wound, wiping away the jagged puncture as if pouring clear water over a stain of red paint.

Rotherham reformed the surviving soldiers in a circle, wary of more enemies. Only Rory and Genevieve were spared, collapsing to the ground beside him so they could help with the healing.

'I've barely any mana left,' Genevieve said, her hands shaking with nerves.

'Just do what you can,' Fletcher croaked, his throat suddenly hoarse with thirst.

It was tough work, and his own mana reserve was draining far faster than he would have liked. The worst injured were healed first, though Fletcher's heart twisted as he passed over a dwarf who had died before they could get to him, his green uniform red with blood from the two spears that had passed through his chest.

Others had broken arms and fractured skulls, which Fletcher could not heal for fear of fusing the bone and causing permanent disfigurement. When Genevieve and Rory ran out of mana, they did what they could to splint broken limbs with strips of cloth and broken spear hafts, but the wounded soldiers would not be fighting any time soon.

'What's the butcher's bill?' Fletcher called, as he healed the last man of a deep gash in his thigh. Sir Caulder stomped from the ring of soldiers surrounding the three battlemages and kneeled.

'Four dead,' he said. 'A dwarf, two men and an elf. Then there's a young lad with a dented head and two more with broken limbs.'

Fletcher closed his eyes. How had this happened?

'Easy there, lad,' Sir Caulder said, his voice low in Fletcher's ear. 'We did well. There were almost two hundred of the blighters. It could've been a lot worse. Trust me, I've seen it.'

Fletcher nodded, but could not help but let a tear trickle down his cheek, mixing with the blood that still caked his face. They had done well, but good men and women had died. Was it his fault, for taking them so close to the jungle's edge? And who knew how many more would have been lost if it weren't for the sudden appearance of the gremlins? He ran a hand over his eyelids, unwilling to get to his feet just yet. A sudden exhaustion had taken hold of him.

'About our rescuers – looks like one of 'em wants to talk to you.' Sir Caulder jerked a thumb over his shoulder.

Fletcher sighed and struggled to his feet, making his way out of the ring of soldiers. As he did so, he pushed down the muskets that the men held pointed at the gremlins, and forced an encouraging smile. After so many years of regarding gremlins as enemies, he could hardly blame them for their apprehension, especially given the similarities in appearance between their race and the goblin species. He had felt the same way not so long ago.

There were as many as forty gremlins wandering the field, stabbing the hundreds of enemy corpses to make sure they were dead. It was brutal to look at, but the occasional squeal revealed that at least a few goblins had been faking, though driven more by animal instinct than cunning – Fletcher knew from experience that goblins were barely smarter than a jungle chimp, incapable of complex language or intelligent thought.

One gremlin stood ahead of all the others, its hands on its hips, legs spread akimbo. Fletcher recognised it instantly, from the tattered stump of an ear on the side of its head. It was Half-ear, one of the gremlin leaders he had met at the Warren during their mission.

'What are you doing here?' Fletcher asked, hunkering down so that he was more level with the short-statured gremlin.

Half-ear crossed his arms and spat derisively. Clearly, the choice to aid them had not been his. Instead, the gremlin pointed over his shoulder, towards the edge of the jungle. Fletcher gaped at what he saw there.

There were hundreds of gremlins, blinking in the sunlight as they emerged from the undergrowth. Females, elders, children, most carrying bundles of food, tools and weapons on their backs. Beside them, a multitude of animals walked, and not just maras. Tiny jerboa could be seen, held on leashes of grass twine, appearing like mice with over-large ears and long, skinny hind legs that made them hop like a kangaroo. Bandicoots dragged infant-laden sleds, sniffing the ground ahead of them with their shrew-like noses. There were even lumbering, pot-bellied wombats being used as beasts of burden, carrying baskets of fruit and dried fish on their backs and looking for all the world like miniature bears.

But despite the procession of beasts and gremlins, Fletcher's eyes were fixed on the figure at their head, one that he recognised even from all the way across the field. Blue.

The gremlin was riding a fossa, a creature that might have been the love child of a cat and a ferret, padding sinuously over the grass with feline grace.

Seeing Fletcher, Blue dug his heels back, sending the animal racing towards him. He halted just in front of Fletcher, a wide grin spread across his frog-like face, the large, bulbous eyes filled with joy.

'We is meeting again, Fletcher,' Blue said, jumping down from his mount to stand beside Half-ear. 'You is lucky, I think.'

'Lucky is an understatement,' Fletcher said forcing a smile, in spite of the dead bodies of his troops so close by.

'I is hoping you is well?' Blue asked, shuffling his feet nervously. Behind him, the masses of gremlins had slowed, yet still more were emerging from the jungle. Now there were at least a thousand, and the muskets behind Fletcher were slowly rising again. It was not the time for small talk.

'Blue, let's dispense with the niceties, eh?' Fletcher said, lowering his voice so the men couldn't hear. 'What are you doing here? Where's Mother?'

At the sound of the orc matriarch's name, Blue's ears flattened, and his large eyes filled with tears.

'Dead. The orcs is killing her,' Blue said, his whispery voice quavering, as if on the verge of a sob. Even Half-ear looked away, his usually hate-filled face a picture of misery.

'They is on the move,' Blue said, pointing into the jungle. 'They is attacking all our Warrens at once, filling them with smoke and sending down hyenas. They is hunting us to extinction.'

'Even the slaves?' Fletcher asked, horrified.

'They is killing them. Some escape,' Blue fluted, twisting his webbed fingers as he spoke. 'Not many.'

'Why?' Fletcher asked, hardly able to believe the madness of it all. 'Orcs have been keeping gremlins as slaves for thousands of years.'

'Because Khan is saying that they will have human slaves soon. No more need for gremlins.'

Blue was speaking more quickly now, spurred on by the approach of the band of refugees behind him.

'There is an invasion happening, now,' Blue said, his voice low and urgent. 'Thousands and thousands of orcs is attacking the front lines. All of their tribes is fighting together. It is the battle to end all battles.'

He pointed east, past the mountains, where the southern border of Hominum lay. Was that the distant booming of cannons he heard? Or just the echo of the wind?

'Heaven help them,' Fletcher murmured. 'I have to warn—'

'It is being too late,' Blue interrupted, shaking his head sadly. 'It has already begun.'

Fletcher chewed his lip, considering the news. He could

be at the battle within the hour if he flew.

Even as the thought crossed his mind, he looked at Ignatius, who had dragged himself a short way from the battlefield and curled up in a patch of thick grass. The Drake was half asleep, but the horror of their near deaths was still simmering in the demon's mind. Could he fly Ignatius into danger once again, so soon after they had barely escaped with their lives?

'So the cassowary riders – they were hunting you down?' Fletcher asked, as the first, timid refugees slunk past him, parting like a branching river around the small band of Foxes.

'No,' Blue said, looking over his shoulder once again. For the first time, Fletcher realised he was not looking at the other gremlins, but at the jungle behind them.

'The orcs is attacking in two armies. Orcs to the east. Goblins to the west . . . here.' Blue opened his arms, then crooked them towards each other. 'It is . . . how you say? Pincer movement.'

'So that was it, right?' Fletcher asked, feeling a cold lump of apprehension hit the pit of his stomach. 'We just killed them.'

Blue shook his head, his ears flattening once again.

'That was the vanguard, the scouts. There is more coming on foot. Maybe an hour behind,' Blue explained.

'How many?' Fletcher asked, looking back at his exhausted, bloodstained soldiers.

Blue said nothing, instead mounting his Fossa again and stroking the silky fur of its head.

'I asked how many?' Fletcher snapped again, the apprehension morphing into abject fear. Blue closed his eyes, and answered with one, brutal word.

'Thousands.'

51

Fletcher convened an urgent war council with his officers and sergeants, away from the soldiers. Already the mass exodus of refugees had made their way through the Cleft, heading to the uncertain safety of Hominum's countryside. Fletcher had sent his injured men with them, along with a message to Berdon, warning him of the approaching army and instructing him to evacuate to Corcillum.

'We cannot hold the pass alone,' Sir Caulder said, the first to speak after Fletcher told them the dire news.

'We aren't alone,' Fletcher said. 'Blue has promised us forty-two gremlin warriors to help us.'

'So few?' Genevieve asked.

'I'm told most of the gremlin warriors died in the escape,' Fletcher answered. 'They had to fight a running battle all the way here, using most of their darts, I might add. We're lucky he's sparing them at all. That's most of the adult males left in their entire species.'

'Fat lot of good they'll be to us,' Rotherham grumbled. 'They took the goblins by surprise and in the rear, on open ground. They'd not survive the battle we're about to fight.'

'We'll work out how to use them later,' Fletcher said. 'But what's important is that we don't need to win, we just need to hold the goblins off until help arrives.'

'What help?' Rory asked. 'You think the townsfolk would help? They don't even know how to load a musket.'

His eyes were wide with fear, with Malachi flitting nervously around his head.

'No,' Fletcher said. 'They're colonists, not soldiers. I wouldn't ask that of them.'

'So who then?' Genevieve asked.

Fletcher took a deep breath.

'Didric,' he said.

'You what?' Rory said. 'Are you bleeding mad?'

'There's sixty trained soldiers no more than a few hours' march away,' Fletcher replied. 'If it means holding Raleighshire, I'll take them.'

'And what if they're not enough?' Rory replied angrily. 'Your gremlin mate said thousands. What's that? Two thousand? Ten thousand? There's a big difference!'

'It's not like he stopped to count,' Fletcher snapped. 'The fact is, if we don't hold the pass, the goblins will march right through Raleighshire and attack the front lines from behind before the night is out. We can't let that happen.'

'Less than a hundred soldiers – who hate each other, I might add – and a few mangy gremlins, against all the goblins in existence. Makes you wonder how many had hatched before you destroyed the rest,' Sir Caulder grumbled to himself.

'We're not running,' Fletcher said. 'But you're right. Even with Didric's men it might not be enough. We'll send word to the King and the men on the western front. Mounted reinforcements could arrive in half a day, with a bit of luck.'

He turned to Rory and Genevieve.

'I need you both to run back to the wagon and write letters on my behalf, explaining the threat to Hominum. Genevieve, write to Didric imploring him to return. Rory, I need messages for King Harold, Arcturus, Othello, Lovett – anyone who might be out there on the front lines. Then send every one of your Mites out with the notes strapped to their backs.'

'We're out of mana,' Rory said. 'Without our demons we'll be . . .'

'Just like any other of these soldiers, that's right,' Fletcher said, looking them each in the eye. 'But I'll need your leadership, your courage. You're more than battlemages. You're officers, and damned fine ones at that.'

They nodded grimly.

'Now go, there's not much time,' Fletcher ordered, sending them scurrying away.

Fletcher's mind raced, trying to work out how to turn the battle to his advantage. He scanned the landscape ahead of him, his eyes flicking back and forth. The first inklings began to emerge. Half conceived, with no way of knowing if they would work. But he had to try.

He turned and walked over to his soldiers, his hands clasped behind his back.

'All right, lads,' Fletcher announced, so suddenly that he saw Kobe jump in surprise. 'Listen up. We've another fight ahead of us.'

He saw the fear in their eyes then; some even glancing at the Cleft behind them, as if searching for an avenue of escape.

'You've done me proud today. We were ambushed by ten score of their riders and won, on open ground, no less. Now, we're ready for them. Let's show them what we can really do.'

Some nodded in fierce agreement but, still, there were a few who muttered among themselves – Logan and a couple of his cronies.

'I am asking you to trust me,' Fletcher said, striding in front of Logan and forcing the boy to meet his gaze. 'You know who I am. I have fought the goblin hordes in the heart of orcdom itself, and lived. I have battled the shamans and their Wyverns alone in an alien Abyss, yet here I stand. It can be done.'

He swept his eyes across his troops, letting them see his conviction.

'I am friend to both dwarf and elf. I am a summoner and a trained battlemage. A noble-born with the upbringing of a commoner and the record of a criminal.'

His words echoed across the pass, accompanied by the soft rustle of the grass in the wind.

'I am all these things, yet none of them compare to what *we* will become tonight. This is where we make our name. This is where we take the fight to the enemy.'

Fletcher paused, allowing his words to sink in.

'I want you to know that, across the mountains, a battle the like of which has never been seen is raging. Thousands are dying as we speak, and the outcome is yet to be determined. But if we don't stop the enemy right here, they will march through Raleighshire and destroy everything we hold dear. There's nobody else but us. We *will* hold the line, until help arrives.'

The soldiers stared back at him now and he saw their resolve shift, jaws setting, eyes hardening. It was enough. It had to be.

'Rotherham, take ten men and have them salvage what ammunition, swords and muskets they can from the corpses,' Fletcher ordered, motioning at the forlorn forms of the dead Forsyth soldiers. 'Kobe, Gallo, cut the Manchineel tree into pieces and bring it to me. Careful of the sap, and don't touch it with your bare hands.'

'The tree, sir?' Kobe asked, hesitantly.

'We have less than an hour until the enemy arrives. Just do it!' Fletcher's voice cracked like a whip.

The men rushed to do his bidding.

'I want the riflemen up in the watchtower, ready and loaded. The rest of you, head to the jungle and cut an armful of bamboo, then meet me at the Cleft. Hurry now.'

There was no delay, and soon Fletcher was left alone with the dead bodies of his soldiers. He stared at them ashamedly, burning the image into his memory. There was no time to bury them, nor the bodies of Forsyth's men. A poor fate, for brave men and women.

Then someone cleared their throat behind him.

Mason. Fletcher had almost forgotten the young lad, for he had looked almost like a corpse himself, lying spread-eagled among the bodies. The boy was gulping down water from a borrowed flask.

'Thanks for fixin' me wounds, milord,' Mason said, touching his forelock. 'I was 'alfway dead.'

'Tell me what happened,' Fletcher asked, cutting to the chase.

'The Forsyths promoted me, after bein' such an 'elp in the mission an' all. Sent me 'ere, told me it would be a cushy job.'

'I'm guessing they were wrong,' Fletcher said.

'Only problem, our captain was a right pillock, if you'll pardon my language,' Mason said, shaking his head in disgust. 'Camped on the wrong side, cos 'e wanted a tan, the bleedin' eejit. We was caught with our pants down, so to speak.'

'And the tree? Why you?'

'Well, I killed a fair few of 'em, so it was revenge, I reckon. They wanted me to die slow-like. So they left me as bait for any newcomers. Although, another hour an' I would've been a goner anyway.'

'Well, I wouldn't speak so soon,' Fletcher said, lifting a musket from the ground and placing it in Mason's hands. 'We'll need every man we can get to hold the line. That means you too.'

'I'll fight for ye,' Mason said, giving him a level look. 'I'll be fetchin' me falchion then, and some bamboo, was it? What d'ye need that for?'

'Never you mind,' Fletcher said mysteriously. 'Now hop to it. There isn't a moment to lose.'

52

They crouched behind the low stone wall, watching the swaying trees through the Cleft. The past hour had been frantic, but they were as ready as they could be. The dead soldiers had been moved into the mountain pass, and covered with tents out of respect.

The wall was a fragile thing, constructed from the loose boulders left over from the watchtower and a clay mortar mixture of drinking water and the powdery earth beneath their feet. It curved in a U-shape, so that the enemy would receive fire from all sides as they came into the space beyond the Cleft. Fletcher's soldiers were spread around it in a single row, their muskets loaded and aimed at the jungles. There were thirty extra muskets gathered from the Forsyths – not all of them had carried guns but it allowed most of the men a spare to fire before they had to reload.

Blue and his fellow gremlins stood nearby, unable to see over the top, but ready with ramrods to load the spare muskets once they had been fired. Half-ear scowled, still angry that their mounts had been sent on with the refugees: they would be little use in the tight confines of the mountain pass.

'Do you see anything?' Sir Caulder asked, his knees creaking as he peered over the parapet.

'Nothing yet,' Fletcher replied.

He was wearing his scrying crystal, strapped like an eyepatch across his face. Far above, Athena had found a crevice to shelter in and was watching the jungles with a keen eye. But despite the clarity of the image, the foliage obscured the contents of the forest. The army could be waiting just a few feet beyond the tree line and Fletcher wouldn't know.

As for Ignatius, Fletcher had learned his lesson after their battle. The Drake had no armour like a Wyvern, but was still a large target that would be vulnerable to javelins and spears in prolonged combat. So, Ignatius had instead been sent into the sky above, to intercept any scouting demons that might be flying ahead of the goblin army and then serve as their reinforcements should the tide of battle turn. Occasionally his shadow flitted over them as the Drake wheeled and swooped, eager for the fight.

'How are we coming with the ammunition?' Fletcher called over his shoulder.

'We've a few hundred extra rounds,' came the reply from Gallo, holding up a misshapen cartridge. 'They're not pretty though.'

Gallo and three other soldiers had been tasked with melting the lead ingots over a small campfire and casting them into musket balls, while two more wrapped them in paper with what remained of their gunpowder. With the numbers of goblins that would be storming the breach, Fletcher knew they needed to meet them with a hail of bullets, and their current levels of ammunition would run out swiftly.

The wall also served a different purpose: it would not only protect them from the hail of javelins and stabbing spears, but it would also shelter them from Fletcher's other plans – if it all went wrong, that is. He had a surprise waiting for the first goblins to pass through the Cleft.

'We're out of lead,' Gallo called, holding up the last heavy sack of newly minted cartridges. 'That's all of it. Scraping the bottom of the barrel for gunpowder too.'

'All right, well done. Hand the new cartridges out to the men,' Fletcher ordered, pointing at the other sacks at Gallo's feet. 'And send a few up to the watchtower too. Once they're out of rifle rounds, they'll be able to fire these at close range.'

Gallo blanched at the narrow path up to the platform high on their right, where rifle barrels could be seen, balanced on the low ring of rocks that had once been the base of the watchtower. Rotherham was up there with them, guiding his small squad of snipers.

'I'll do it,' Logan volunteered, seeing Gallo's expression. He jogged over and took the sack from the pale-faced dwarf, earning himself a respectful nod.

Fletcher smiled, despite his nervousness. That was one silver lining – whatever grievances the soldiers had before were now firmly in the past. If they survived this, the Foxes would be as close as any band of brothers in Hominum's army.

He felt a twinge of excitement from Ignatius, just as Sir Caulder growled under his breath,

'Where the hell are the—'

A corpse thudded beside them in a burst of black and white

feathers, and Sir Caulder unleashed a tirade of curses as he was spattered in blood. It was the broken body of a Shrike, with a gaping slash across its midriff. Above, Ignatius roared in challenge. A second, smaller Shrike, crashed on to the wall, its corpse knocking a stone free in a puff of dust. The Drake was in his element, and Fletcher could see him swooping and diving as small black dots made a bee-line towards him. It could only mean one thing.

'It's starting,' Fletcher said, drawing Blaze from his holster and resting it on the wall's parapet.

But his words were drowned out, for a horrendous noise had begun. It was like hundreds of voices, screaming in agony, accompanied by an unearthly rattling. It echoed eerily through the canyon and into their ravine, setting Fletcher's teeth on edge.

And then, at the forest edge, the first goblins could be seen marching out of the trees in a wave of grey. Hundreds of them.

'Hold your fire,' Fletcher called, watching as the man next to him tightened his grip on his gun, so much so that his knuckles turned white.

His eyes focused on the pink overlay of the scrying crystal. There were too many goblins to count, marching over the grass in a great unordered mass that poured out of the jungle. Just like their cassowary-riding counterparts, these goblins wore nothing more than a loincloth to protect their dubious modesty. But as well as the usual variety of spears, stone-studded clubs and javelins, they carried rawhide shields on their left forearms, and they clattered their weapons against them as they marched into the canyon, providing some answers for the terrible din. But not the screaming.

'Where's that noise coming from?' Logan shouted, returning from his precarious journey up to the watchtower.

'Death whistles,' Mason answered. He was crouched to Fletcher's left, still shirtless, but now armed with his cleaver-like falchion. 'You'll see some orcs blowin' 'em. Bloody 'orrible things, made to scare the enemy. Ignore 'em, lads.'

And indeed, orcs were emerging from the foliage behind the first wave, carrying great macana club-swords strapped to their backs. They held baying hyenas on rope leashes and lashed rawhide whips across the backs of the goblins nearby, driving them like cattle before them. As Athena's gaze focused on them, Fletcher could see skull-shaped clay pipes clutched between their tusks, the source of the terrifying noise.

'Well, it's bloody working,' Logan shuddered, taking his place at the wall.

Even from his vantage behind the wall, Fletcher knew the goblins were just out of rifle range. Rotherham had embedded two lines of stakes along the grasslands, so the men knew when to fire; one for the riflemen, another for the musketeers. Now the enemy army waited, just beyond the first scattered palisade, called to a halt by guttural barks from the orc commanders.

'Come on, let's be havin' ye,' Fletcher heard Rotherham growl from his perch above.

But the goblins walked no further, and the noise began to die down. Soon silence reigned across the grassy canyon. They had seen what Fletcher had left for them, just beyond their lines.

The corpses of the goblin riders had been strewn across the grass, their bodies arranged in a macabre display of splayed limbs and open wounds. The cassowaries lay beside them in forlorn humps of black feathers. Fletcher knew that the stench of rotting flesh would be thick and cloying in their nostrils, but not, in fact, because of their allies' corpses – they were too fresh for that.

No, Fletcher had devised a use for the barrels of durian fruit from their wagon of supplies – slicing each open and strategically concealing them beneath the corpses, giving off their telltale stench of death. The enemy had tried to use fear on him. He would return the favour tenfold.

Their vanguard was dead to the last fighter, with no sign of their killers. There could be a thousand men on the other side of the Cleft as far as they knew.

'Rotherham, give them a rifle volley,' Fletcher called, his voice echoing unnaturally loud in the ravine. 'Aim for the orcs. Take out their leaders.'

'Aye,' Rotherham replied. 'All right lads, make these shots count.'

'They're out of range, sir,' came a nervous reply.

'Well, then you'd better aim at their chests,' Rotherham said cheerily. 'Easy now. Pick your targets. Slow squeeze of the trigger as you breathe out. On my mark . . . *Fire!*'

The crackle of rifles hit Fletcher's ears, and a half-second later the volley whipped into the massed ranks. A missed shot threw a goblin to the ground, and another splintered one of Rotherham's stakes, but the remaining shots struck home. One orc's head snapped back, the others jerked as if stung; two falling to their knees, another clutching its arm. Not a single bullet struck the same target, a testament to Rotherham's training.

Screeches began, spreading through the massed goblins as they retreated a dozen feet, scrambling over each other in their sudden fear. To them, the gunfire had come from the heavens themselves.

'Stop your gawping and reload,' Rotherham's voice echoed above. 'This is war, not target practice.'

The rattle of ramrods followed soon after, but the noise was drowned out by a sudden roar from the scores of remaining orcs, primal and deep with rage. A baying hyena took a retreating goblin by the neck in a sudden leap, shaking it back and forth like a rag doll. Whips cracked overhead, and the tide was turned more swiftly than it had begun, the goblins falling over themselves as they returned to their positions, some even stumbling beyond, over the corpses of their rider comrades.

'Like bleedin' sheep herdin',' Mason whispered.

'But those ain't no sheep dogs,' Logan replied. 'More like wolves.'

'Silence in the ranks,' Sir Caulder barked, quieting the pair.

But Fletcher's attention was elsewhere, his eyes focused on a movement in his scrying crystal. A disturbance within the jungle, so great that the trees shook in a slow moving beeline that headed straight for them. A *thud*, *thud* of steps, that seemed to shake the very ground, reverberated through the canyon, quelling the panicked screeches of the goblins.

Then a grey-skinned giant burst from the forest, scattering goblins left and right as it stampeded into the light. Its great ears flapped in the wind, the enormous bulk of its body clearly visible as it lumbered through the clearing.

'What the bleedin' hell is that?' Logan moaned.

It was a Phantaur. The rarest of all orc demons, a bipedal elephant that towered above the orcs as a mother did a child. It had a leathery hide so thick that bullets couldn't penetrate it, and its great fists were as formidable as the long, sweeping trunk and serrated tusks that swung back and forth above the ground.

The demon halted as its shaman emerged from the jungle edge. In his crystal, Fletcher saw it was a decrepit, hunched specimen with a toothless mouth and a tattered cloak of woven fibres. A gnarled staff was clutched in its hands, and the old orc leaned on it with every faltering step. For a moment Fletcher felt a flash of pity for it.

Then it raised a long, hoary finger, and even without Athena's overlay, Fletcher could see the orange glow of a fireball at the jungle edge, larger than any he had seen before.

'Take cover,' Fletcher yelled.

He and the men hurled themselves to the ground, hugging the earth for dear life. Suddenly their stone wall felt as solid as a paper sheet.

In the scrying stone, Fletcher saw the fireball swell and swell again, so enormous that it blotted out the shaman behind it. Then it was aloft, blazing through the air in a great, curving arc, trailing smoke and shimmering air. No shield of Fletcher's could hope to withstand such an attack – not with the scant mana left in his reserves. Still it rose, so bright and blinding that it was as if Athena were staring into the sun.

As the ball began its slow descent, the Phantaur unleashed a trumpeting squeal that put Fletcher's teeth on edge. Two heartbeats of stunned silence passed.

And then, like an unstoppable wave, the goblins charged across the grass, screeching with bloodlust.

The battle for Raleighshire had begun.

53

'Ignatius, hurry!' Fletcher yelled.

Far above, the Drake was already plummeting towards the fireball, his wings pinned back in a raptor's dive. He tore through it like an arrow through an apple, the burst of light blinding in Athena's vision.

Fletcher sensed no pain from Ignatius, the fire passing harmlessly over the demon's skin as the fireball split into scores of smaller spells, spraying across the mountainside in a shower of glowing streaks.

Half a dozen made it through the Cleft, alighting in pools of fire on the wall and ground ahead of them. Rocks exploded from their makeshift barricade, sending soldiers tumbling. A single dwarf screamed frantically as his sleeve caught fire, beating at it with his jacket. It was extinguished by a gust of air as Ignatius swooped through the pass, returning to the heavens to battle the orcish demons above once again.

'Make ready,' Sir Caulder yelled, emptying his canteen over the smouldering clothing on the dwarf's arm.

The rumble of hundreds of goblin feet could be heard as the Foxes scrambled up, levelling their muskets over the barricade. Pools of molten rock bubbled in front of the walls, already fusing into crystals as they cooled. Fletcher lifted Blaze, and thanked the heavens that the fire had missed the surprise his men had prepared.

Between the gap, he could see a shifting maelstrom of grey bodies charging towards them. Already the rifles were firing, orcs jerking and stumbling from the spiralling bullets, even as their berserk rage carried their injured bodies onwards. The first goblins trampled through the second line of stakes.

'Fire!' Sir Caulder barked.

A single clap of noise and billowing smoke tore at Fletcher's senses, then he pulled the trigger. Goblins were thrown back as a hail of musket balls tore through the first ranks, tripping those behind with their corpses. Forsyth muskets were snatched up and pointed with trembling hands.

'Fire!' Fletcher yelled.

A second volley whipped into the masses, more ragged than the first but no less deadly. Blood misted the air as more goblins fell, but still the baying crowd surged on, driven by the whips of their orc masters. Rifles cracked above, and another orc's head snapped back. But it was not enough. Only one thing could stop this now.

'Load,' Sir Caulder ordered, his voice loud but calm as he stomped behind the men. 'Steady now, lads, easy does it.'

A Vesp thumped to the ground, near severed in two by Ignatius's beak, far above. Ramrods rattled in their barrels, and a man cursed as he dropped his to the ground. Fifty paces. Forty.

'Fire at will, boys!' Sir Caulder growled. 'Give 'em hell.'

Musket balls whipped sporadically over the wall, the closer shots bowling goblins head over heels, their bodies disappearing into the masses as they were trampled underfoot.

'Take out their frontrunners,' Fletcher yelled, tugging Gale from his holster and aiming it at the smattering of goblins that had outpaced the horde.

He fired, and felt the kick up his arm as the ball took the closest goblin through the neck, plucking it from its feet a dozen yards from the gap. His second shot went wide, disappearing into the mob in a spurt of smoke and blood, but a slug from Mason left his target crumpled over the body of the first.

The space ahead of the wall was filled with smoke, a brimstone haze that blended with the grey of goblins as the first of them hurtled through the Cleft, spears raised, shields held aloft. A smattering of gunfire took these eager runners out. In Fletcher's mind, he could feel Athena's fear, and fragments of pain from Ignatius as he battled the dozens of lesser demons in the sky.

The main body was twenty paces from the Cleft. Just a little closer . . .

Ten paces. *Now.*

Fletcher leaped the wall.

'Hold your fire,' Sir Caulder bellowed. 'Load your spares.'

'Rifles, cover him,' Rotherham shouted.

And then Fletcher was running, a twist of flame flaring on the end of his finger. Still the goblins came, a dozen of them breaching the gap in a mad dash towards him. He could smell the unwashed stench of their bodies as he sprinted forward, his blood pounding in his ears, feet drumming on the ground. Rifle shots snatched the closest goblins away, and a javelin fluttered past, splintering on the wall behind him.

A hundred of the enemy were through the Cleft now, slowing as they saw the lone man running towards them, but pushed inexorably on by the momentum of the screaming masses behind.

Fletcher skidded in a slide-tackle along the ground, a stone's throw away from them. The fire spun from his finger in a strand of orange, heading for Fletcher's target. Their surprise.

It was a row of a hundred, half-buried bamboo segments, each with a rudimentary fuse of gunpowder-coated cordage shoved in its back end. And in the centre of them all, sat the squat, rust-covered hulk of the Thorsager cannon, propped up by a hillock of shovelled earth. All were filled to the brim with gunpowder and a charge of pebbles.

A spear buried itself beside him, slicing the edge of his jacket. The fuses sparked, Fletcher's spell threading along the line. They burned down to their explosive charges with sizzling speed. Too fast.

'Run!' Rory yelled, seeing what was about to happen.

Fletcher ran.

It was a mad dash, and Fletcher beamed a shield over his shoulder in the nick of time, feeling the crackle of impacts as javelins and spears whistled overhead. A rattle of rifle-fire echoed above, and then Genevieve screamed: 'Get down!'

Fletcher dived – and the world flipped sideways.

Dust and smoke howled over him as the explosion roared through the ravine. In his crystal, Fletcher saw blood mist the air as a thousand projectiles ripped through the mass of goblins, hurling them back as if a giant invisible fist had punched through their ranks. The centre received the brunt of the damage, the cannon concentrating the blast in a tight cone of spraying death that extended beyond the Cleft and into the crowds that still pressed in behind. For a moment, all that could be heard was the whistling of the wind, and the groans of the dying.

'Fire!' Fletcher yelled.

A pause, and then a flurry of musket balls whipped through the gap and into the stunned survivors.

'Again,' Sir Caulder barked, snatching a proffered musket from Blue's hands.

The second volley smacked into the ranks, downing goblins left and right. The rifles fired a moment later, and this time the closest of the few dozen orcs that remained were killed – unmissable at such close range.

Far above, Ignatius roared in triumph, and an Ahool plummeted out of the sky, its leathery-winged body thudding among the goblin corpses.

And then, as one, the goblins turned and fled.

54

The tide had turned, the grey forms of the goblins rushing back to the jungle's edge, leaving hundreds of dead in their wake. The remaining orcs bellowed orders, but even they had moved to a safe distance, and could not prevent the goblins from hurrying back into the safety of the rainforest. Far above, Ignatius roared again, the enemy demons beating a hasty retreat. Clearly the Ahool had been the most powerful among them.

Despite it all, what horrified Fletcher most was that yet more goblins seemed to be appearing, shouldering their way past their fleeing companions as they left the trees and rallying around the immovable form of the Phantaur. Who knew how many more lurked within the foliage, just out of sight?

As he sat up, Fletcher realised his shield had protected him from the backdraft of the explosion, though thankfully most of the bamboo tubes had held together, directing their contents out of their open ends. But some of the wooden tubes had shattered from the explosion, flinging projectiles in every direction, including at him. This damage, combined with that of the javelins and spears, meant the shredded shield was barely worth resorbing when he eased his battered body from the ground. He did so anyway – his reserves were nearly empty.

By the time he made it back to the Foxes, Blue and his gremlins had vaulted over the walls and were already hunting through the goblins for survivors, their shark-tooth daggers rising and falling. Fletcher tried to ignore the grisly gurgling noises and swung himself over the barricade, knocking a chunk away in his haste to return to safety.

He was shaking, though whether it was from adrenaline or fear he could not be sure.

'Craven bastards,' Logan shouted, his pockmarked face split wide in a grin. Through his crystal, Fletcher saw the orcs whipping the retreating goblins mercilessly, their hyenas unleashed to roam along the jungle edges, snapping at those who ran by. It would not be long before the masters took control of them once again, or led a new assault with the fresh troops emerging from the jungles.

Even so, they would be more wary now. A good third of the orcs had been killed, and it was unlikely their leaders would venture into range again. But at some point, the goblins would make another charge for the Cleft, and there was no more gunpowder for another blast. He only had one more trick up his sleeve.

'Fletcher, a word,' Rory called.

He beckoned Fletcher away from the line of celebrating men. Fletcher saw the young boy's cheek was stained with soot from firing his musket, and his blond hair was stained red from a cut at his hairline.

'We've got a problem,' Rory muttered, as soon as Fletcher was out of the Foxes' earshot. 'I haven't told anyone, not that there was time when the goblins appeared. But . . . it's Didric. He's not coming.'

If Fletcher had felt even a shred of relief earlier, it was now washed away by a cold rush of fear.

'He has to come,' Fletcher hissed, struggling to keep himself from shouting. 'The future of the empire depends on it! Are you sure your note explained it all?'

Rory shook his head in disgust.

'It explained everything. He's hightailing it to the north as we speak, back to his castle. His exact words were, "Why throw good men after bad?", if you can believe that. He thinks the war is lost already.'

'The coward,' Fletcher spat.

'There's something else,' Rory said, avoiding Fletcher's eyes. 'It's the townsfolk. When Malachi left his message, they started arguing about whether they should leave. Berdon's doing his best, but Malachi didn't see any sign of them while waiting for Didric's decision on the bridge. I don't think they've left yet.'

'The fools,' Fletcher snapped, looking back down the canyon, into the grasslands. In the distance, he could see the shapes of the town's buildings. So close. Could they not hear the gunfire, the explosions?

'We can't worry about that now. What about the rest of your messages?' Fletcher asked, trying to keep the panic from his voice.

'Still flying,' he said. 'And I sent Malachi on to help with the search for the King, a general, anyone who might help us. Most should get to the front lines within the hour, Genevieve's included. But . . . my Mites can hear booming, see smoke and bright flashes over the horizon. Whatever battle we're fighting, it's nothing compared to what's going on out there. Finding someone important to give a message to might be difficult.'

Fletcher gripped Rory by the shoulders.

'If we don't get help soon, we'll all be dead and thousands of goblins will attack the Hominum army from behind. That is, if they don't sack Corcillum on their way first.'

Rory's eyes widened with fear, and Fletcher released him with a sigh.

'Tell Genevieve, but no one else. You must get your message through. I'd send Ignatius, but he's needed above. You're our only hope now.'

The young officer scurried away, and Fletcher saw Genevieve's face fall as he gave her the news. She caught Fletcher's eye and gave him a determined nod.

'Right lads, that's enough cheering,' Sir Caulder's voice cut through the jubilant shouting of the Foxes. 'Dalia, Gallo, bring the water barrels from the wagon – fighting's thirsty work. The rest of you, clean out the powder from your fouled barrels. Use the water, or piss down 'em if you have to.'

Spurred on by Sir Caulder's orders, Fletcher's mind turned to the battle ahead. With no rescue coming any time soon, they would be likely to run out of ammunition before long. The poleaxes would be essential, one way or another.

'Logan, Kobe – go with them,' Fletcher ordered, returning to the wall and peering into the milling crowds. 'I want the whetstone wheel brought back here and every poleaxe sharpened to a fine edge.'

The two lads groaned but went to do his bidding, leaving him alone with Mason. The boy had not joined in the celebrations with the others, though it was not surprising since he knew so few of them.

'You've done a brave thing, staying here,' Fletcher said.

'I've been fightin' 'em me whole life,' Mason said. 'Plus, me mam and sisters live in Corcillum. Wouldn't be right, leavin'.'

'You got any advice for me?' Fletcher said, motioning at the gathering goblins with his chin.

'They're cowards at heart, goblins,' Mason said. 'You hurt 'em enough, they'll turn and run. Problem is, they've been kicked about by orcs their entire short lives, so they're more afraid of 'em than anythin' else.'

Fletcher's eyes turned to the pile of chopped manchineel wood, oozing white sap from where the poleaxes had bitten it.

'We'll see about that,' he said.

55

The poleaxes were whetted, with Kobe sitting behind a spinning wheel of rough stone that he pedalled with his feet and soldiers kneeling beside him to sharpen their blades against it in a screeching shower of sparks. Even Fletcher managed a turn with his khopesh, once he had finished reloading Gale and Blaze.

Guns were cleaned, inspected and cleaned again, while the wall was repaired and reinforced with a combination of mud and scavenged shields and spears. The gremlins had brought back grisly trophies from the battlefield, and Half-ear proudly paraded around, wearing a necklace of goblin ears threaded through a dirty string. Fletcher did not discourage them, even requesting that the gremlins display their trophies beside the bodies within the Cleft – a warning to any goblins that chose to venture through once again.

All the while, orcs barked and bellowed guttural commands, shoving goblins into position, just beyond rifle range. The hyenas had been unleashed into the forests, presumably to hunt down the goblins that had fled earlier and herd them back to the killing fields. What Fletcher knew for sure was that there would be a massive attack coming, and not much time to prepare for it.

The wagon had come with shovels, which they had used to churn the earth to make the mud-mortar for their walls. But Fletcher came up with another use for them. The ground just before the Cleft had been torn up by the explosions of the bamboo bombs, and Fletcher sent a contingent of men to extend it into a trench, as deep as their waists. When this was done, they embedded the stone points of the goblin spears at the bottom, covered it with the canvas of the Forsyth tents and camouflaged it with a thin layer of earth.

It was too narrow to prevent goblins from leaping over it, nor could they conceal their actions from the watching enemy, but Fletcher was sure that in the chaos of battle, at least a few goblins would fall in and cripple themselves on the spikes below.

As for the manchineel tree timber, Fletcher ordered it moved into the space beyond the wall, and had spare tent covers, spears and the bamboo that had been left over from the bomb-making added to the pile. It was still a far smaller heap than Fletcher would have liked, but it would have to do.

'Rory, any news?' Fletcher asked, sidling up to the young officer. He and Genevieve were sitting apart from the others, their eyes closed, brows furrowed in concentration. They had small fragments of scrying crystal in their hands, and Fletcher could see the rushing images of a war-torn landscape within them.

'We can only hear and see from Malachi and Azura,' Genevieve answered, before Rory could speak, 'since they're the ones connected to our scrying crystals.'

'Of course,' Fletcher said, biting his lip. Rory spoke, his eyes still closed.

'The others just have instructions, but we won't hear who they've reached. We'll only know that the message has been delivered and we'll sense the emotions our Mites feel. If they're happy, we can assume rescue is on its way.'

'Not rescue, reinforcements,' Genevieve rebuked him gently. It was only then that Fletcher saw the pair were holding hands. He smiled. It was about time.

'One message has been delivered,' Rory said suddenly, a smile breaking across his pale face. 'Hang on . . . I think—'

'My lord, movement!' shouted Kobe. Rory's eyes snapped open, and the pair scrambled back to their squads on either side of the wall, his words forgotten.

Fletcher refocused on his scrying crystal, and his heart filled with cold horror. It was the Phantaur. The enormous beast was advancing with its great flapping ears and arms extended wide. Behind it, a column of what could have been a hundred goblins followed, their rawhide shields raised as they took cover behind the demon's bulk.

Already it was past the first row of stakes, and was nearly in musket range. With every stomp, the chorus of death whistles and rattling slowly increased in volume, accompanied by the squalling of the many hundreds of goblins behind them.

Sir Caulder took a breath to order a volley, but Fletcher knew better.

'Hold your fire!' Fletcher yelled to the Foxes. 'Its skin is too thick.'

'So what are we supposed to do?' Dalia snapped, sighting

down her musket regardless. 'Let them come in and finish us off? As soon as we're in close combat the rest of them will charge.'

'No,' Fletcher said. His mind raced and then he turned to the riflemen in the stone ring of the old watchtower.

'Can you hit its eyes?' Fletcher asked.

'We're low on ammunition, but it's worth a shot, if you'll pardon the pun, milord,' Rotherham's voice called back.

'Do it then,' Fletcher ordered.

The Phantaur was in musket range now, and Fletcher could see the goblins behind it through the gaps in its great, tree-trunk legs. Should he order his musketeers to fire?

But even the riflemen were failing. The first shot glanced off the demon's cheek, then as more gunfire whipped down, the great beast did nothing more than flap its ears inwards over its face, slowing its pace as it stomped ever closer to the Cleft. It extended its arms, walking blindly.

Fletcher looked to Sir Caulder, hoping for a solution, but the old man simply stared at the approaching beast, his knuckles tightening white against the pommel of his sword.

He needed to solve this himself.

Fletcher's mind flashed back to his lessons at Vocans. He'd read dusty journals from battlemages long dead that spoke of the Phantaur's trunk-tips as being like a thumb and forefinger, with equal sensitivity and dexterity. He had learned that their skin was so thick that only a speeding lance might penetrate it, and that Phantaurs used the clusters of nerves in their footpads to sense tremors of potential mates from as far as a mile away.

And that was when Fletcher knew what he had to do. It would take a bit of luck, and a big roll of the dice. But he would be damned if he was going to go down without a fight.

'Rory, I need your squad,' Fletcher said, jumping over the wall once again. 'Poleaxes only.'

Rory's mouth flapped open. For a moment Fletcher thought he would ask something, but then he nodded grimly and gave the order. Fletcher looked to the platform above.

'Rotherham, I want a rolling fire on those ears, keep him blinded.'

'Aye, sir,' Rotherham said, punctuating his answer with a shot from his rifle.

By now Rory and his fifteen soldiers had leaped the wall, with a brief moment of awkward confusion as the three dwarves in the group struggled over the top. Gallo and Dalia were among his squad and, to Fletcher's surprise, Half-ear, Blue and a handful of gremlins had clambered over the wall to join them.

'We come too,' Half-ear sneered, licking a wicked looking dagger malevolently.

Fletcher grinned and waved the soldiers on. If all went to plan, there would only be a few moments of fighting. If it didn't . . . well . . . a few more warriors wouldn't hurt.

'There's a hundred goblins and a Phantaur about to come through there,' Mason said, less concerned with propriety than the men. 'I hope you know what you're doing.'

'Just cover us,' Fletcher replied, his voice loud for the benefit of Genevieve's squad.

Then, without looking back, he drew his sword and ran towards the Cleft.

56

The clamour from the goblins was near deafening as they approached the Cleft entrance, where Fletcher and his soldiers waited. They had crouched beside the pile of wood and bamboo, to protect them from the occasional projectile that the goblins hurled from behind the Phantaur. Luckily, the demon's bulk was as good a barrier to the javelins as it was for the Foxes' musket balls, and most went wide.

'We should charge them at the Cleft, where the gap's narrow,' Rory whispered, hunkering down beside Fletcher. 'Leap the trench, go for the Phantaur's legs. Numbers won't matter so much then.'

'No, we wait,' Fletcher said, watching as the great beast continued its ponderous journey. It was almost at the Cleft now, its enormous body shrouded by the mountain's shadow.

'Fletcher, if we don't move now, it'll be too late!' Rory hissed.

'I said no, Rory,' Fletcher replied, willing the Phantaur on. It lifted an ear for a brief second, then let it drop as a shot glanced off a serrated tusk. Fletcher could see the pockmarks where the bullets had struck, gouging the skin, some even drawing blood. But none going deep enough to cause any real damage.

'Come on,' Fletcher whispered.

The Phantaur was through the Cleft now, and the ground shook with each stomp from its round-bottomed feet. The goblins crowded in behind it, gathering the nerve to charge.

One foot lifted, and thudded down on the other side of the trench. Damn. Then the next one began to swing . . . too far.

Fletcher drew and fired Gale in one fluid motion, emptying both barrels. One shot glanced off the Phantaur's belly in a puff of dust – but the other struck its sensitive trunk-tip. It squealed in pain and stepped back. Right into the trench.

'Now, Foxes!' Fletcher yelled, charging towards the enemy.

The air was filled with their battle cries, but they were instantly drowned out by the scream of agony from the Phantaur as its sensitive footpad was impaled by the spear-tips. It wheeled its arms and fell, crushing a dozen goblins behind it in a crackle of breaking bones and squeals of terror.

There was a roar from Ignatius as he swooped from far above, called by Fletcher's consciousness. And then they were in among the goblins, swinging their weapons. A scar-faced specimen stabbed at Fletcher's belly, but he parried it with the crook of his blade and head-butted it with a satisfying crunch. Then it was on to the enemy behind as Rory skewered the reeling goblin with his rapier, and Fletcher slashed the next one's shoulder to the bone. He kicked it off the blade and it collapsed to the ground, where Half-ear was waiting with his dagger.

'Drive them back!' Fletcher bellowed, ducking as the

Phantaur's trunk swung down, grasping for enemies. 'Protect Ignatius!'

The rifles were firing in earnest now, and the bullets ricocheted dangerously from the giant demon's unprotected face and into the milling goblins behind. The ears flapped back into place, and the rifles switched their aim to the goblins themselves, the shots whizzing uncomfortably close to Fletcher's ears. Even a few muskets were firing, their shots aimed at the enemies who charged around the small band of Foxes' flanks.

'The rest of them are coming,' Fletcher heard Rotherham holler, and his gaze flicked to his crystal eyeglass; the gathered crowds of the enemy army were rushing towards the Cleft, hundreds upon hundreds of screaming, mindless savages. He had less than a minute.

With a rush of wind, Ignatius landed on the Phantaur's chest, digging his claws deep into the demon's skin for purchase. The beast's tusks swung left and right, but the canny Drake had his head between them, and his beak clamped on the demon's trunk.

'Hurry,' Fletcher called, stabbing wildly at a snarling goblin. He pulsed urgency through his consciousness, even as the uproar from the charging army washed over them. Rory leaped past him, slashing madly to send the nearest goblins reeling, their faces cut to ribbons. On the other side of the Phantaur, Dalia sang an elven battle song, her pure, lilting voice carrying above the uproar of battle.

Fletcher turned to help Ignatius, but the Drake had already clamped his claws on either side of the Phantaur's elephantine mouth, levering it open with brute force. Fletcher felt the mana roil in the demon's consciousness, and then Ignatius's beak released from the trunk and dipped into the cavernous opening. Flames burst out with explosive force, the heat palpable in the narrow Cleft as the Drake poured gouts of fire into the Phantaur's throat.

The beast managed one last squeal, smoke erupting from the end of its flailing trunk. Then it was silenced, charred from within. Dead.

'Back,' Fletcher yelled, tugging Rory away from the goblins. The boy was staggering, but followed him out of the Cleft, the ground so thick with goblin corpses that they stumbled over splayed limbs and staring faces. None of the survivors of the Phantaur regiment pursued them, stunned by the ferocity of the counter-attack.

The rest of the men did not need telling twice, leaping the trench and sprinting back towards the wall. Fletcher stopped at the wood pile, even as Rory reeled past him. Ignatius had used almost all of their mana in that attack, but there was still a small amount of it left. Enough for one, last spell.

Fletcher closed his eyes and drew the mana from his reserves, allowing the last dribble of energy to surge through his veins. There was a thud as Ignatius landed in front of him, and a flash of pain as a javelin took the Drake in his haunches. The demon was shielding him with his body.

With a primal yell of fury, Fletcher hurled a wave of flame into the wood, flaring it into a bonfire that crackled with intense heat.

'They're almost at the Cleft!' Genevieve screamed from behind the walls. Ignatius's tail encircled Fletcher's waist and hurled him back, even as more javelins buried themselves in the ground around them. Fletcher caught a spinning glimpse of a pyre of smoke, billowing into the sky.

And then Ignatius flared his wings and began to beat them in a long, slow pulse that gusted the black smog into the bottleneck between the mountains. That was when the screaming began.

Fletcher staggered to his feet and held his khopesh aloft.

'Charge,' he yelled breathlessly, running towards the Cleft once again. The Foxes roared as they followed their leader into battle, a few dozen brave souls against an endless legion of savages.

They took positions on either side of the trench, their muskets raised at the deep cloud of smoke, hair fluttering with each flap of Ignatius's wings. Fletcher could make out the vague shape of the Phantaur, blocking the cleft with its bulk. Still the woodpile crackled, and Fletcher could see the smoke staining the walls of the Cleft with a tar-like substance, so thick and cloying was the ash within.

Then the first score of goblins staggered forth from the haze, clutching at their eyes and coughing, spears and shields forgotten. The toxic smoke from the manchineel tree blinded and choked them, as Fletcher had known it would.

'Fire!' Sir Caulder barked, and gunfire rippled down the line, plucking goblins from their feet. The gremlins handed up their spare muskets, and the order was barked again.

'Fire!'

Death whipped over the ground, thinning rows of goblins as they screeched and clutched at their throats. A pair tumbled into the trench, their hoarse cries of pain snuffed out as they were impaled on the spear tips below. Then the gremlins vaulted the ditch and were in among the rest, slicing at ankle and knee tendons with sickening abandon, tumbling more into the pit behind them. The men loaded frantically, while above, Fletcher heard Rotherham shout.

'That's the last of it. Switch to musket ammunition, lads.'

It hardly mattered: at this distance Rotherham's riflemen couldn't miss. Seven more shots buzzed into the blinded ranks.

The smoke was thinning now, and Fletcher could see masses of goblins clawing at their faces, choking the entrance to the Cleft in their confusion. A few tried to clamber over the Phantaur corpse, but they were plucked away by Rotherham's sharpshooters, leaving two thin channels on either side where the goblins could pass. That was where Fletcher's Foxes concentrated their fire.

Volley after volley tore through the enemy. Even when the Foxes paused to load and a few goblins escaped through the Cleft, the gremlins cut them down, their short stature protecting them from the gunfire that whipped overhead. It was a grisly slaughter. Far from triumphant, Fletcher felt sickened at the sight of the blood-soaked ground, and the piles of the blank-eyed dead.

'Sir, we're almost out of ammunition,' called Gallo. The dwarf's moustache was blackened from biting the cartridges open. Even as he spoke, Fletcher noticed a few Foxes slinging their muskets, while others rummaged desperately through their cartridge bags. A last ragged volley fired through fouled barrels. Then silence.

The white smoke of their final shots blended with the black of the manchineel's, even as it smouldered down to a pile of glowing embers. In his scrying crystal, Fletcher saw the smog drifting through the canyon, as far back as the jungle's edge. There, the goblins hawked phlegm and covered their eyes, cowering beneath their rawhide shields as if they could somehow protect them from the oppressive smoke. The effects were not so strong that far back, but still enough to itch and blur their vision, as well as turn their throats raw with the toxins.

Already many were turning to flee, but a dozen orcs had spread themselves out along the jungle's edge, their whips ready for any that came within reach. It was a milling mass of grey as the goblins teetered on the edge of full retreat. But the muskets were empty, and the smoke had cleared from the Cleft.

'One last push,' Fletcher yelled. 'For Raleighshire. For Hominum!'

They charged, as one.

The battle became a massacre. The goblins could not see, nor could they even hear them over the cracked screams of agony from their compatriots. Poleaxes rose and fell, then rose again, hammering and chopping with both sides of their weapons. The enemy fell like wheat before the reaper.

Goblins clawed their way past each other, those at the front retreating, those at the back pushed on by fear of their masters. Then the first goblins fought back; fresh troops from the valley. They squinted through red-rimmed, streaming eyes and their breathing was choked, but the first of Fletcher's men began to cry out – a spear through an elf's shoulder, a boy's elbow shattered by a club.

Still they fought, the battle becoming a bitter crush of bodies in the narrow confines between the Phantaur's shoulders and the steep walls of the Cleft's bottleneck.

Then, Ignatius landed on the Phantaur, his tail whipping down to impale goblins from above. He opened his mouth and roared, the earth-shattering noise blasting through the Cleft and into the canyon.

And, with that, the goblins turned and ran.

57

The world was filled with the dead and the dying. Fletcher did not look down as he staggered back to the safety of the wall, and tried to ignore the shrieks of the wounded as the Gremlins went about their work, finishing off the survivors. His men followed, dazed by their victory. Some limped, others groaned from their wounds, but none were mortally injured.

In his scrying crystal, Fletcher could see the goblins were in full retreat, running past the orcs despite the cruel whips that beat at them. No more than a handful remained on the field of battle, staring at the corpse-laden gap between the rock walls of the mountain.

And then Fletcher saw him, his eyes refocusing past the crystal. A still figure, sitting with his back pressed against the wall. Rory.

The boy was staring vacantly, a mild smile upon his face. His hands were clutched around his stomach, where blood had spread across the green cloth of his uniform.

'Rory,' Genevieve uttered, dropping her sword and running

to his side. She shook him, tears streaming down her face. 'No, no, no, no.'

She repeated the word, slapping his face, at first gently, then harder as she tried to bring him back to life. Fletcher kneeled beside her and pulled her away, taking her hands in his.

'He's gone,' Fletcher said, hugging her close. He was almost unable to believe his own words.

He had not seen Rory in this last battle. His mind flashed back to the young officer, staggering ahead of him after the battle with the Phantaur.

Rory must have been injured in the fight. If he had known it, he could have healed him. But now it was too late.

Was this his fault?

'He . . . he didn't tell me he was hurt,' Fletcher whispered, unable to look away from Rory's face.

Sir Caulder crouched beside them, and closed the boy's eyes with a gentle hand.

'Come away now,' he said, pulling them both up. 'Let's leave him be.'

But Genevieve wouldn't. She slid down the wall beside him, and took his hand in hers once again.

'He's still warm,' she said, stroking it.

Sir Caulder sniffed, and Fletcher saw a glimmer of a tear in his eye. The Foxes gathered around, their heads bowed.

'He died fighting for his country,' Fletcher said, the words struggling to come past the lump in his throat. 'And he was a braver man than I. Let's make sure that he did not die in vain.'

As Genevieve's sobs began, Fletcher turned away. It was only minutes later, when the troops had left them, that he allowed himself to cry.

Two hours ticked by. Half the orcs remained, along with a hundred goblins, scattered across the canyon. They used their shields to shade themselves from the sun above, waiting for their next orders.

The Foxes used the time to sharpen their blades once again, but other than that all they could do was rest and take turns watching the goblins, halfway up the watchtower's pathway.

Ignatius was infused, as there was no mana left for him to self-heal and the javelin wounds were deep in the Drake's haunches and back. Fletcher thanked him with a kiss upon the demon's beak.

He took on the demon's pain, as Ignatius disappeared within him.

As for Genevieve, she remained by Rory, her eyes blazing with anger as her Mites continued their search across what she told Fletcher was a frantic battle along the front lines, filled with gunfire and the screams of the dying.

So Fletcher waited at the wall, watching the proceedings through his scrying crystal. There was nothing else he could do, but hope.

'Maybe the orcs've run away,' Logan said, spitting over the wall. 'Could've scared 'em off.'

'Not a chance,' Fletcher replied, taking a deep gulp of water from his hip flask. 'The Phantaur saw how few of us there were before it died, which means the shaman knows it too. They won't give up. Let's just hope that Genevieve gets a message through. The Celestial Corps could be here in time, if we're lucky.'

Even as he spoke, a noise echoed through the canyon – a horn, being blown long and hard. It was deep and loud, reverberating the walls that surrounded them. Fletcher felt a burst of fear pulsing through Athena in a frantic warning. He looked in the pink overlay of his scrying crystal.

Hundreds upon hundreds of goblins were emerging from the jungle's edge. Hyenas prowled through their ranks, accompanied by their orc masters. The first wave of goblins had been herded back, and worse still, Fletcher could see red-eyed specimens smattered throughout the masses. The enemies they had just routed were coming back, caught up in the horde that had returned to the battlefield.

'What is it?' Mason called out. The Cleft was so choked with bodies, they could not see the gathering storm that was bearing down on them.

Fletcher would not lie to them. They had no ammunition. No more gunpowder, no more tricks. They could not survive this next onslaught. They would barely slow it down, before the goblins flooded into Raleighshire.

He looked at his brave soldiers, who had fought a force that had outnumbered them a hundred to one. Who had faced down an army designed to bring all of Hominum to their knees, and beaten them back time and again.

And he saw Rory's still face, and the line of tent-covered bodies beyond. He could not ask his men to die, not in a battle they could not win. They had already given him so much.

'They're coming, and we're leaving,' Fletcher said. 'Logan,

Kobe – bring the wagon up here. Throw out the food and put the bodies of our Foxes on there. Leave the Forsyth Furies, there's no room for them now.'

The two soldiers snapped into action, running pell-mell down the canyon. Fletcher walked over to Rory and gently lifted him on to his shoulder. He called after the Foxes as they stumbled over the walls.

'I want the injured and the gremlins on the wagon too, we'll be running for Watford Bridge.'

In the crystal, Fletcher could see the goblins gathering for the attack. The orcs were in no rush, waiting as more and more goblins streamed through the jungles, hyenas snapping at their heels. He counted the seconds, knowing that every moment was another few steps ahead of the oncoming horde. Would they make it? The wagon was a blessing and a curse, able to transport those unable to walk, but likely slower than they could run. It would be a mad, two-hour sprint to Watford Bridge, if they stuck to the roads.

As he considered their predicament their transport arrived, Logan snapping the reins at the two boars at its head. Fletcher allowed Genevieve to take Rory's body to the wagon, unable to refuse her grief-stricken gaze as she held out her arms for it.

'You've done more than anyone could ask,' Sir Caulder said, wrapping his good arm around Fletcher's shoulders. 'Your parents would be proud of the man you've become.'

Fletcher watched as the last of Rotherham's men made their way down from the platform. It was time.

'It won't make a blind bit of difference,' Fletcher said, kicking at the dirt with his feet. 'We'll be lucky if they don't catch up with us. You'd better get on the wagon. With your leg . . .'

'Well, that's the thing,' Sir Caulder said, giving Fletcher a grim smile. 'I'm not going.'

'What do you mean?' Fletcher asked, half listening as he watched the wounded and the gremlins clamber into the back of the wagon.

'I've got a score to settle,' Sir Caulder said, hefting his blade.

'Sir Caul—'

'No,' the old soldier said, cutting him off. 'This is where I belong. I failed Raleighshire once. Never again. I'll hold them off, give my lads a chance to escape.'

'You'll never hold them off alone, you silly bag o' bones,' came Rotherham's voice from behind him. 'There's two ways in past that corpse.'

Sir Caulder growled.

'Listen Rotter, this isn't the time for—'

'So I guess I'd better stay with you,' the grizzled sergeant interrupted, drawing his sword. He looked at it and smiled fondly.

'You sold me this sword, Fletcher. Funny that, eh? How things change.'

'Listen, there's no time for this madness,' Fletcher snapped.

'Then you'd better get goin' then,' Rotherham said, 'because we won't be changin' our minds. Go on, or it'll all be for nought.'

Fletcher opened his mouth to yell at them, but then he saw the stubborn look in the old men's eyes. It was useless arguing with them.

'I . . . don't know what to say,' he managed.

Sir Caulder stepped forward and wrapped him in a hug. His

body felt so frail beneath the cloth of his uniform.

'Look after the place when I'm gone, eh lad?' he said, rubbing a knuckle against Fletcher's cheek. 'You're your father's son. It's been an honour.'

Then he stomped away, his sword thrumming the air.

'See you on the other side, kid,' Rotherham said. 'One last battle for me and that grumpy bugger. We'll make it one for the books.'

'I won't let anyone forget it,' Fletcher said, smiling through his tears.

'See that you don't,' Rotherham growled, giving him an encouraging wink.

Then he too was gone, whistling a jaunty tune.

Fletcher watched the pair for a moment, striding resolutely towards their final stand. Then he turned away.

'Right, Foxes,' Fletcher said, wiping his face dry. 'Let's get out of here!'

58

They ran. They ran until their chests burned with the dry air of the savannah, stumbling over the uneven ground towards Raleightown, the rattle of the wagon's wheels ringing in their ears.

Fletcher had left Athena in the rocks above the Cleft, to let them know just how far the goblins were behind. He did his best not to look at the two forlorn figures waiting with their swords drawn below. Yet still the orcs waited, allowing their ranks to swell with the reinforcements that continued to emerge from the jungles. Soon there were so many that they had expanded beyond the first row of stakes in the ground, and were well on their way to the second. As many as three thousand goblins could be gathered there – an army that could raze Corcillum to the ground if given the chance.

Half an hour had passed when Fletcher and his soldiers stumbled through the empty, cobbled streets of Raleightown and on to the dirt path on the other side. But just as Fletcher felt a surge of relief that the settlement had been deserted, it happened. The goblins began their attack.

They had learned their lesson. The orcs sent a scouting party first, twenty odd goblins that walked with fearful steps into the corpse-laden Cleft.

'Come on, you ugly runts!' Athena heard Rotherham yell faintly, and Fletcher smiled bitterly.

He could not watch, but heard the goblins shriek as they discovered the two lone swordsmen waiting for them.

'Got the blighter,' Sir Caulder barked, as a hard fight began in the narrow confines of the Cleft.

Fletcher let his eyes stray from the crystal. The sun was ending its long journey down towards the horizon. Had that much time really gone by? Perhaps the battle had been lost, and thousands of orcs were streaming across Hominum. And where were Berdon and the rest of his colonists? Had they made it safely back to Corcillum – or had they left too late, and were only a few miles ahead of them?

Even as the cries of the goblins reverberated in his head, Fletcher's heart dropped. Just behind a copse of trees, a great convoy of wagons could be seen. And it wasn't moving.

'What the hell are you still doing here!' Fletcher yelled hoarsely, running ahead of his soldiers.

He could see Berdon there, his red hair flaming in the dusk light. The big man was crouched behind the back of the rearmost wagon, surrounded by a dozen colonists.

Fletcher's father's eyes widened as he took in Fletcher's bloodied, soot-stained clothes. Then Fletcher was wrapped in a great bear hug, so tight that his ribs felt they would crack under the strain. He patted Berdon's back frantically, until the affectionate bear of a man allowed his feet to return to the ground once more.

'You're alive,' Berdon said, wiping a tear from his eye.

'Not for long, if we don't get a move on,' Fletcher said, resisting the urge to cry himself. 'You should be in Corcillum by now.'

The colonists around them muttered darkly under their breaths.

'It's the wagons,' Berdon said, kicking the nearby carriage with a grunt of frustration. 'Somebody came by last night and sawed most of the way through the axles. We were lucky to get this far at all before they started breaking. Yours is the only one unharmed, because we were loading it up that evening.'

'Didric,' Fletcher breathed. 'He sabotaged us, to cripple our trade.'

'Aye,' Berdon said, leaning closer to Fletcher. 'The spiteful little git. And now these fools won't leave. Not without their belongings.'

Fletcher turned to the colonists. More had gathered round at the sight of the exhausted soldiers. Fletcher saw the children, and the elderly among them. Too many to fit on his wagon.

'Listen to me,' Fletcher said, his eyes boring into theirs as he swept his gaze through the gathered men and women. 'In less than an hour, thousands of goblins will be spreading across the land. Sir Caulder and Rotherham have stayed behind to hold them off. Their sacrifice will give us mere minutes. I will not let them die while we waste their last gift to us arguing over your possessions. We are *leaving*. Anyone who wants to stay can do so. Hell, you'd be doing us a favour – killing you would slow them down.'

He knew his words were harsh, but the truth rang loud with every syllable.

'Those that cannot keep up will join the wounded in our wagon – elders, children. The rest of you, leave everything but the clothes on your backs. Now come on!'

The soldiers had caught up by now, and the wagon barely stopped as the elderly and youngest children were loaded on, through the back. With the added weight, the boars strained at their traces, and the vehicle moved slowly along the ground, more slowly than Fletcher would have liked.

Already the gremlins were leaping out to lighten the load, scampering alongside easily enough, even with their short legs.

'Swap out our boars with a fresh pair,' he ordered Gallo as the wagon trundled on to the grass, the dirt road blocked by the crippled convoy. 'And bring along as many as you can, and let the slowest ride them. We'll need to swap them out with the wagon regularly if we want to reach Corcillum.'

The noise of battle was thick in his mind, and then Athena was swooping dizzily from the rocks above. Ten goblins were limping away from the channel, while Sir Caulder, bloodied but triumphant, held his sword aloft in salute to the Gryphowl. Rotherham leaned heavily on the Phantaur's side, clutching a wound in his thigh, but grinning as he yelled over the demon's bulk.

The horn sounded again, so loud that Fletcher winced as the noise reverberated around his skull. And then the hordes charged across the canyon, trampling over the retreating band of scouts they had sent before.

'No,' Fletcher breathed, as Athena circled above.

He concentrated on putting one foot in front of the other, but could not tear his eyes away from the scene unfolding in the crystal at his eye.

Twice more the goblins charged, and again and again the enemy were hurled back by the veterans' skill and courage. An invading army, stoppered in the bottleneck to an empire by two brave old men. Fletcher's heart swelled with pride, even as tendrils of despair began to take hold. It couldn't last.

Goblins were climbing over the Phantaur's corpse, hurling javelins and spears, forcing the embattled men to retreat. The two men fought back to back, their swords flashing and jabbing, sending goblin after goblin to their deaths as the squealing masses pressed in. An orc shouldered his way through and lashed his whip at their feet, tugging Rotherham to his knees.

Sir Caulder hurled his sword, skewering the orc in its throat. Then he stiffened, a spear going deep into his back.

'It's time to leave, Athena,' Fletcher whispered, ordering the Gryphowl away.

He caught one last glimpse of the two men, surrounded by the baying hordes. Sir Caulder on his knees, Rotherham beside him, his sword raised in defiance. A howl of victory from the goblins as they crowded in.

Then they were out of sight.

Fletcher felt the bitter tears stream down his face, even as Berdon silently put his arm around his shoulders.

'They're gone,' Fletcher said.

His two friends had died fighting – and Raleighshire had fallen.

59

Athena could not linger, for the demons that had battled Ignatius in the skies had finally returned. Fletcher hugged her to his chest when she landed beside him, absorbing the love and comfort that was there. He missed his friends.

The going was slow, the wagon overloaded with the wounded and the old. Even when the children got off to piggyback with their parents, the pace felt to Fletcher like that of a funeral procession. Here and there, he could see signs of where the gremlins had gone before them – a smattering of fruit rinds here, the droppings of a small mammal there. Blue and Half-ear chittered happily at the sight, even sniffing dung and kneading it to determine their distance ahead.

As the minutes ticked by, Fletcher distracted himself with his responsibilities, making sure the boars were swapped out every half-hour as they hauled their heavy load across the poor dirt road, and sending Athena to keep an eye on the land behind them.

It took no more than an hour before she saw the dust cloud of the goblin pursuit, staining the horizon like a bruise. The goblins were travelling at a furious pace, of that he was certain.

And all the while his heart sank, twisting in his chest. Because as the enemy edged nearer, he knew they would not make it. Not to Corcillum.

They would be lucky if they even reached the bridge in time. But still, he pushed on. Watford Bridge was a place to do battle, where his soldiers could stand ten abreast and fight the goblins to the last man. Perhaps the rest of them would have a chance then, hiding among the rough, uneven landscape as the goblins turned their eyes on Corcillum.

'Genevieve, anything?' Fletcher called. The young officer was stumbling like a sleepwalker, her eyes fixed on the scrying crystal in her hands. She shook her head dumbly.

So they trekked on through the savannah, watched by curious antelopes and a lazy pride of lions. Fletcher kept back, hurrying along the stragglers and watching the ever-growing haze of dust that followed in their wake.

Soon Athena could see the grey forms of the goblins that followed, ranging in a great horde that spread out over the plains. The front runners were no more than a few minutes behind now.

Fletcher heard calls ahead of him. There was an incline there, part of a broad hill, up which the dirt road continued before the bridge. The boars were struggling to pull their heavy load up the path, exhausted after their full-tilt pace across the savannah. Worse still, the track had become rutted after all the trade convoys that had passed that way in the recent months, and now the wheels spun weakly in the deep channels.

Berdon and the others added their weight to the back

of the carriage, hoping to shift it upwards, but it was no use – the boars refused to pull, one of them collapsing to its front knees in fatigue.

'Lord Raleigh,' Mason yelled.

Fletcher turned, only to see the first goblins advancing through the long grass towards them. They had less than a minute until they were upon them. Behind them, the hulking forms of the orcs could be seen in the shimmering heat, their warpaint stark against their grey skin.

'Foxes, to me!' Fletcher called. 'Berdon, get everyone off the wagon and over the bridge. We'll fight our way back to you.'

But as Fletcher's soldiers gathered wearily around him, Berdon was with them, accompanied by a dozen of their strongest colonists. A few carried felling axes with them, while others had pickaxes and kitchen knives.

'Thaissa and Millo are taking care of it,' Berdon growled, brandishing a hammer from his forge. 'We won't leave you to fight alone.'

'Berdon . . .' Fletcher began.

'No!' Berdon shouted, seizing Fletcher by the shoulders. 'I won't lose you again. We stay together, no matter what.'

Fletcher stared up at his father's face, and saw the defiance there. There was no stopping him.

'Get behind us then,' Fletcher said, giving Berdon a grim smile.

The men formed up beside the carriage, and Fletcher cut the boars from their traces. The beasts collapsed to the ground, too tired to move. Behind them, the colonists carried the wounded up the hill, some already disappearing over the top. Fletcher only hoped he could hold the goblins long enough for them to hide.

Fletcher looked for Rotherham to give the order, or Sir Caulder, or even Rory. His heart twisted at the realisation that they were not there. Genevieve's eyes were dull and lifeless as she stumbled back to the wagon. She was still in shock.

It was up to him.

'Face the enemy and move back in crescent formation,' Fletcher ordered. 'Watch your flanks!'

They moved back in a rough half circle, their poleaxes drooping in their tired arms. It was all so hopeless. On open ground, they wouldn't last more than a few minutes.

The goblins were but a hundred paces away from them now, gathering their courage for a charge at the small band of survivors. But even as Fletcher began to hope that they might make it over the hill and to the narrow bridge beyond it, a horn sounded. And with a scream of hatred, the grey wave surged forward.

'This is it, Foxes,' Fletcher heard Kobe call out. 'Let's take a few of 'em with us.'

The soldiers gave a cheer, their thin voices briefly cutting through the blare of the bugle. Now Fletcher could feel a rumbling beneath his feet as the hundreds of goblins broke into a run, their shields raised, baying for blood.

But the noise that echoed out over the plains was not coming from the enemy. No. It was behind them. Fletcher turned to look at the hilltop, squinting in the sun that hung above its zenith.

The ground was shaking now, and Fletcher's heart froze as a row of shadows appeared at the hill's summit. The goblins had them surrounded.

'Form a schiltron,' Fletcher called desperately. 'Berdon, Blue – get your people to the centre!'

But there was no time – the figures on the hill were on the move, and Fletcher could hear the drum of hooves, see the glint of metal.

But these were no goblins.

They were dwarves, beards streaming in the wind as they rode their bristling boars in a thundering charge. They parted like a branching river around Fletcher's small knot of fighters and tore into the scattered goblin runners, their battleaxes swinging, helmets burnished in the dawn light. And there was Othello at their head, wielding a great warhammer with long sweeps of his powerful arms.

'Run, Fletcher,' Othello bellowed.

'They came,' Fletcher breathed, hope flaring in his chest. And yet, even as their rescuers clashed with the enemy, he knew this would be no easy fight.

There were only a hundred riders, and behind the scattered frontrunners the hordes were waiting with a massed wall of spears. A half-dozen dwarves were already down, their boars dead or dying from spear thrusts. The remainder baulked at the row of points, turning and sweeping out alongside the lines. Fletcher knew what he had to do. The dwarves needed a gap in the wall of spears. He would not abandon Othello, not now.

'Charge,' he yelled. 'For Hominum!'

They hurled themselves at the enemy, sprinting pell-mell down the incline, poleaxes stretched out in front of them. Screaming, they crashed into the half-formed lines of goblins, hammering aside the spears and stabbing at the shocked creatures with frenzied abandon. Othello bellowed an order.

'Fire!'

Blunderbusses unloaded sprays of buckshot into the gathered hordes, blowing ragged holes in their rough formation. Fletcher snarled, stabbing a goblin through its throat, Berdon's hammer clearing the way by his side. Gremlins screeched underfoot, slashing their daggers to cripple the enemy, before the poleaxes dispatched them with swift, brutal chops of their axe blades.

And then the boars were ploughing into the goblins beside them, ripping through their broken lines like reapers in the fields. The air shook with a rumbling roar as the craggy figure of Solomon crashed through the survivors behind in an indomitable charge, sending goblins flying high in the air with great sweeps from his fists.

Pain flashed as a spear sliced through Fletcher's forearm, and Berdon roared to smash the culprit into bloody oblivion. Lightning crackled on their right, sending a score of goblins convulsing to their deaths. Fletcher saw Cress running over them, screaming her battle cry as she led the dwarves who had lost their boars in a charge, Tosk bounding at her feet. The reinforcements shored up Fletcher's flanks as, together, their warriors pushed on through the savage masses, carving a path for the boar riders to exploit. He could hear the snorting of the porcine beasts behind him, see goblins reeling as they were gored by long, yellow tusks.

Now they had penetrated deep into the horde, a circle of struggling men and dwarves, enemies closing behind them. But the goblins were turning back, frantic with fear as they tried to escape the mad, suicidal onslaught of the courageous allies.

Fletcher suddenly found his blade slashing empty air, the goblins scrambling away from his small band of soldiers. He saw the blue glow of a spell, but before he could turn to it, a wall of noise rushed towards him. The shockwave threw him head over heels, the world flipping and spinning as he tumbled through the air. He landed in the grass, his sword still clutched in his hands.

There was blood on his lips as he staggered to his feet.

Then his mind reeled as he saw the devastation before him. A kinetic blast had blown a hundred goblins into oblivion in the centre of the enemy army. Someone had used all of their mana in a single, brutal attack.

At the edges of the detonation, goblins stumbled dizzily, their weapons lost. There were at least a thousand still standing, with half as many again getting to their feet. Their screeches had been suddenly silenced by the explosion.

Now, they stared at the dwarves, still slaughtering those that had escaped the blast near the front lines of the battle; at the corpses of their brethren, thick on the ground.

And, as one, they turned and ran.

It was a great exodus of grey, the orcs leading the pack in a mad bid to escape any pursuers. Weapons were discarded, and the slow were trampled underfoot as the wave of enemies pulled away.

Soon only the injured remained, limping as fast as they could while the dwarves finished off the remains of their front lines.

They had won. Fletcher collapsed to his knees, his hands shaking as they released the khopesh. He felt Berdon's arms wrap around him, and he buried his face in his father's chest, gasping with relief.

'Onwards!' a dwarf bellowed. 'Chase them back to the jungles.'

The ground shook nearby as the boars galloped in pursuit.

'Infantry, with me,' he heard Cress order. 'Kill the survivors.'

Fletcher pulled away, and Berdon lifted him to his feet. They stood there, too exhausted to join the slaughter of the goblins, many of whom lay wounded and dying among the messy row of carcasses that stretched along their line of battle. Fletcher could see the corpse-laden swathe they had cut behind him, a path of grey bodies and bloodstained grass. And there were green uniforms among them. He looked away; not wanting to see their faces. He couldn't bear it. Not yet.

The gremlins and dwarves did not share his qualms, and Fletcher had to avert his eyes as they went about their bloody business. He was sick of all the death, all the killing. Already the vultures were circling above, waiting to feast. There was no glory here.

Then he heard a scream of anguish from Cress. Something was wrong. She was kneeling among the bodies, her head bowed. And there was a limp, bearded figure clutched in her arms.

A face he recognised.

'Othello,' Fletcher sobbed, staggering through the broken bodies. 'No. No, no, no.'

He repeated the words over and over as he reached Cress, falling to his knees beside the dwarf.

'He's gone,' Cress wept, brushing a curl of red hair from the young dwarf's bloodstained forehead. 'I couldn't heal him.'

60

Fletcher took the dwarf's hands in his, unable to believe it. He felt sick, the world spinning around him.

'It's going to be OK,' he whispered. 'He's not dead. He's not.'

In the distance, Fletcher saw Solomon's craggy figure lumbering in pursuit of the goblins, oblivious to it all.

No, it couldn't be. The Golem would know.

Then a bird screeched above. A Caladrius, flying high as it cried out in misery. And that was when Fletcher realised – the knowledge like a cold stone in the pit of his stomach. It wasn't Othello. It was Atilla.

His twin.

It was over. Humans, dwarves and elves alike wandered through the battlefield, dumbstruck by their victory. There were so many bodies. More even than at the Cleft.

'You saved us,' Fletcher said to Cress, wiping his eyes. 'We didn't think you were coming.'

They sat beside Atilla's body, unable to leave him alone

among the corpses. There were no more tears to be shed.

'It was Atilla who saved all of us,' Cress sniffed. 'He ran right into their midst with our last mana vial, and detonated the spell right there. These wounds . . . he knew he wasn't coming back.'

Fletcher looked at his friend, who had given so much so that others could live. The dwarf looked almost peaceful, his face upturned to the still-warm skies.

'How did you find us?' Fletcher asked, trying to quell the tremor of emotion in his voice.

'It was Malachi,' Cress replied, staring out over the landscape, her knees hugged to her chest. 'He found us. But the generals wouldn't let us leave.'

She clenched her hands at the memory.

'Heaven knows we wanted to, but the front lines were being overrun. Thousands of orcs, charging out of the jungles. No warning, no preparation. The first hour was a slaughter.'

Cress looked at him, her eyes filled with sadness.

'And the demons. Hundreds upon hundreds of them. The orcs were sending them to die, only to summon new ones with scrolls that they've been saving. They've been planning this for years.'

'What happened?' Fletcher asked, looking to the east, as if he could somehow see the battlefield, all those miles away.

'We fell back again and again. So many died. Tens of thousands. We're losing ground, but it's not over. At least, it wasn't when I left.'

Silence. Fletcher could hardly believe it. They were losing.

'The King is hoping the elves will arrive in time to aid us,' Cress muttered. 'He says their army left their lands a few days ago. They're our last hope.'

'So, why did you come here?' Fletcher asked, horrified. 'Hominum could fall, if it hasn't already. You're needed.'

'The King ordered it,' she said, meeting his gaze. 'Malachi got to him too. Though, I'm surprised the little Mite managed it – he was acting strangely when he left us. Like all the fight had gone out of him.'

Fletcher's heart twisted at her words. The brave Mite had continued its mission, even when its master had died. He didn't have the strength to tell her what had happened to Rory.

'But it wasn't to stop the goblins,' Cress continued, oblivious to the pain in Fletcher's eyes. 'Nor was it to save Raleighshire. It was to save you, Fletcher.'

'Me?' Fletcher asked dumbly.

'There's a reason we're losing,' Cress said, speaking quickly now, as if she had remembered why she was there. 'It's Khan. His demon . . . it's . . . it's like a giant version of Ignatius. Only it's armoured, like a Wyvern.'

'A Dragon,' Fletcher breathed, his mind flashing back to the volcano, all those months ago.

'Our Celestial Corps tried to kill it . . . but . . . the fire. It's killing everything. Every time we think we have the upper hand, it swoops in and turns everything to ash. Nobody can even get close. Except . . .'

She tailed off.

'Except me,' Fletcher said, the realisation leaving him numb.

He was immune to fire, and so was Ignatius.

His fight was not over . . . it was just beginning.

* * *

411

Fletcher wanted to wait for Othello to return from routing the goblins. To be there for him when he saw his fallen brother. But there was no time.

He bade a last farewell from his friends and soldiers, most unable to stand from injury or exhaustion.

'You come back, you hear?' Berdon choked, as Fletcher hugged him goodbye.

'Depend on it,' Fletcher whispered.

A final embrace from Cress, all too brief as she took command of the scattered dwarves.

Then he was on Ignatius and limping into the sky.

The poor Drake was still suffering from the wounds he had sustained in the battle with the Phantaur, so their flight was erratic and slow. Fletcher could see the jagged holes in Ignatius's wings, and blood had caked around his haunches where a spear had penetrated deeply. They were nearly crippled, but had no choice. Nothing else stood a chance against the Dragon.

Cress had barely been able to treat Ignatius's wounds, using her last trickle of mana to heal a scratch on the Drake's forearm. Now they circled the battlefield, orienting themselves. In the distance, Fletcher could see Othello and his dwarves chasing the goblin army, leaving a trail of dead stragglers in their wake. He sent them a silent thanks, and angled Ignatius away.

As they turned, Athena gliding alongside them, Fletcher heard a high-pitched cry from above him. The Caladrius was spiralling down out of the clouds, appearing for all the world like a dove descending from heaven. It landed gently on Ignatius's back, and Fletcher saw a strange aura around the demon, a blurry haze along its edges.

412

The Caladrius was fading back into the ether, its master gone, the call of the wild taking hold of it. Fletcher wondered at the demon, its blue eyes boring into his as it spread its long, delicate wings across Ignatius's own. He could see pain there.

A glow of white light suffused Ignatius's body. Fletcher felt his demon's pain receding, and before his eyes, the wounds began to fade, shrinking and healing over as if time were in reverse. Then the wound on his own arm was wiped away.

All the while, the demon watched him. The white light dimmed, and the Caladrius stroked his cheek with the edge of its beak. Then it was gone, gliding away to mourn its loss among the clouds above.

Fletcher had once heard that part of a summoner's soul lived on through their demons – that their consciousnesses merged upon death. It was an old wives' tale, one that Major Goodwin had scoffed at when Seraph had asked about it in one of their lessons. He had replied that the character of their masters might rub off on their demons over the years, but that was all.

Yet now, as they flew east, Fletcher was not so sure. His gaze wandered to Athena, who had loved him unconditionally from the moment they had met. Did his father live on, within her? Had the Caladrius's healing been a parting gift from Atilla?

He took solace in that sentiment as Athena led the way, using her hearing to guide them towards the booms of cannon fire that echoed over the rugged lands beneath them. With every minute the sun continued its slow descent towards the horizon, its rays turning the world sepia.

It was only now that the enormity of his task began to settle on his shoulders – and the fate of an empire weighed heavy.

Could they do this? Did they even have a chance? Doubts plagued his mind.

Before long, Fletcher could hear the distant echoes of battle, carried by the warm evening breeze. Worried about finding himself behind enemy lines, Fletcher angled Ignatius's flight north.

They flew on, blindly now, hoping to see Corcillum somewhere in the distance to orient themselves. But instead, he saw something else.

A great herd of deer, spread out over the green fields below him. On their backs, armed with bows and long-handled swords, were the elves.

They were divided into clans, each one delineated by the colour of their armour. Leading the way, Fletcher could see the red of Sylva's family, a moose-riding elf at their head – a tall, straight-backed figure that could only be her father. Behind him, powerful elk tossed their branching antlers, eager for battle.

Even as he watched, the cavalcade broke into a gallop, bounding along the ground. Fletcher could see their target, a nearby cloud of smoke, beneath which were flashes of light and the crackle of gunfire.

Then his eyes widened. In the centre of it all, he could see the outline of an ancient castle, stark against the horizon. It was Vocans. Somehow, the orcs had forced Hominum's army deep into the empire. Corcillum, with all its innocent inhabitants, was no more than a few hours' march away. The very future of their world now lay on a knife's edge.

A flash of warning from Athena pulsed through Fletcher's mind. Below, a creature was flying up towards them. A Griffin.

His heart leaped.

Sylva.

Within moments she was beside him, the long, curved blade of her falx sword held aloft. She wore the red lamellar armour of her clan, and her hair was braided into a bun at the nape of her neck.

'Fletcher,' she shouted, guiding Lysander closer. 'You're alive. I thought . . . I'm glad you're OK.'

He could see the relief in her face, lips half parted, eyes wide with emotion.

Despite the fear that gripped him, Fletcher could not help but smile at the sight of her. With her by his side, perhaps he had a chance.

She looked fiercer than he had ever seen her, with a rouge of warpaint highlighting her cheeks. He wanted to reach out and hold her, tell her how he felt, politics be damned.

But there was no time.

'We thought you were Khan on his Dragon,' Sylva said, her voice raised to cut through the rush of wind between them. 'Our scouts are reporting that all is lost, that it's decimating the battlefield.'

'He's out there,' Fletcher replied, pointing at the cloud of smoke that drew ever closer. 'I'm going to fight him.'

'Well, let's go, then,' Sylva said, pushing Lysander on in a burst of speed.

'Sylva, go back to your clan. Only I can do this,' Fletcher yelled. 'I'm immune to the flames.'

Sylva turned back, and yelled over her shoulder,

'Try and stop me!'

And with that, she disappeared into the smoke.

61

They were everywhere. Thousands of orcs, more than Fletcher thought existed, sprawling in a great horde across a smoking landscape, the villages and trees behind burning like funeral pyres.

And a few hundred feet in front of them, spread in a thin red line in front of Vocans' gates, were the remains of Hominum's army. Perhaps a thousand men were left, garbed in red uniforms with a patchwork of a few hundred others, survivors from noble regiments that had been decimated in the fighting. And a single platoon of dwarves, strewn along the centre in twos and threes.

'So few,' Fletcher choked through the smog.

The stench of brimstone was thick in the air – a heady mix of gunpowder and smoke from the burning buildings of the hamlets that had been put to torch a mile away. The entire world was tinged orange by the distant flames, merging with the red glow of the setting sun. It would be night soon.

As the world below them smouldered, Fletcher was aware of

Sylva's every move beside him, and he couldn't help but wish they could remain here, together, far above the fighting. Sylva's hair streamed behind her as Lysander hurtled through the air, his wingtips brushing Ignatius's. She looked glorious in the setting sun, her face drawn with determination, falx sword held ready for battle.

'We can do this,' Sylva said, her eyes meeting his.

Fletcher held her gaze, daring to share in her hope. With renewed resolve, he turned back to the scene below.

Flashes now, streaks of lightning and fire in the no-man's-land between the two armies. There was a battle being fought there. Beasts, tearing into each other in shuddering clashes of claws, scales and fur. Hundreds of demons were waging war below him, the preamble to the final clash of civilisations.

He saw a row of battlemages scattered in front of their men, hurling fireballs and lightning at shamanic counterparts across the smouldering remains of the land. Harold and his father stood at the front of it all, a shield like a glass dome around them as they ordered a fresh pack of Lycans and Anubids into the fray.

Ahead of them, the Dragoons fought in the midst of the battlefield itself, their mounts lashing out at lumbering humanoid Oni and shark-like Nanaues in the centre of the war-torn turf. Arcturus's dark hair streamed behind him as his Hippalectryon reared, leading a counter-charge towards the embattled western front. Pride swelled Fletcher's chest as his mentor struck the enemy lines, holding his own against insurmountable odds. Even from a distance, Fletcher could see Hominum's demons were outnumbered.

417

Above, a roar.

Ignatius was moving before Fletcher could think, shooting upwards into the haze of fumes and mist. It was dark, the smoke-tinged mantle of vapour blocking the red rays of the setting sun below. All was silent now.

No. Wingbeats. Like the slow pulse of a beating heart, somewhere to the south. In his scrying crystal, Athena hovered beneath the cloud bank, searching for clues of the Dragon's whereabouts. Nothing.

And then it was there. Swooping out of the clouds, a dark mass on leathery wings. Talons stretched out and gouged the earth itself, ripping through a pack of Hominum's Canids and snapping one up in its beak. Gliding the length of the battlefield, it swallowed its quarry in a single gulp, and began a long, looping turn for a second pass.

As it swung around, Fletcher saw it was a Drake in all but size and skin, its body covered in armoured scales. It might have been as large as three Phantaurs combined, with a wingspan that eclipsed the sun as it wheeled across the horizon.

'Fletcher!' Sylva's voice called.

Lysander emerged from the cloud bank with a screech of frustration, his wings rotating in the air.

'The Celestial Corps are all dead or hiding,' Sylva spat derisively. 'They took out the Wyverns, but only Captain Lovett and Ophelia Faversham are still fighting. They've been trying to blindside Khan in the clouds, but the Dragon flames at them whenever they get close.'

Behind Sylva, Fletcher could see the shadows of the pair, floating just behind the clouds.

But before he could greet them, there was a flash of light, and Fletcher turned to see.

The great demon was swooping again, a vast tidal wave of fire scouring the earth along the front of Hominum's lines. Dragoons scattered out of its way, Arcturus just escaping the scorched trail of destruction with a flying leap from his mount. Behind, the less fortunate screamed, until only charred skeletons remained.

A roar of triumph erupted from the Dragon's jaws. On its back, Fletcher could see the pale figure of Khan, riding astride its neck. The orc waved his long macana club. Once. Twice.

It was a signal. In a great rolling surge, the orc ranks crashed forward, running through the flame-burnt earth with an ululating chorus of war cries that chilled Fletcher to the bone. Sweeping around the edges, rhino riders charged in, horns lowered in preparation for impact. An unstoppable wave of barbarians.

Gunfire rippled down the line of men. Orcs spun, jerked and fell, but still they came, never faltering, never slowing. Fifty feet. Forty. Lightning and fire blazed from the battlemages and demons as they fell back to the lines, tearing holes in the hordes. It wasn't enough. Not even close.

But there was something else. A rumbling could be heard. A thundering of hooves, and . . . singing. Voices, raised in harmony, sending elven words swirling across the landscape.

And then, galloping gracefully around the thin line of desperate men, came the elks, curling in like a ram's horns, meeting the flanks of the orc attack.

Antlers swung down and tossed orcs aside, while bows thrummed arrows into oncoming ranks, whistling into skulls and necks with deadly accuracy. Falx swords swept left and right, cleaving tusked heads from their shoulders.

Rhinos and deer clashed in bone-shattering impacts, riders from both sides flying from their seats in the mêlée. And down the centre, Hominum's muskets swung inwards to concentrate their fire where the elven pincer had not met. Twenty feet.

Orcs were thrown back by the ferocity of the gunfire, the closest hurled back like puppets jerked on strings. They staggered and fell, ragged with a dozen wounds. The charge was faltering.

To Fletcher's east, the Dragon roared, circling in a long arc for an attack. And he could see what was about to happen. The flames, crashing over the thin line of men. The mass of elves drowning in a sea of fire. This was what Khan had been waiting for. He had been toying with them before. Waiting for the allied armies to meet.

Yet, as Fletcher watched the slow wheeling of the great beast, he knew what he had to do.

One last throw of the dice.

'Get Lovett and Ophelia and hide in the clouds above it,' Fletcher yelled to Sylva, digging his heels into Ignatius's side. 'Wait for my signal.'

Ignatius dived, and Fletcher heard Sylva's response before it was snatched away.

'What are you doing?'

But he was committed. No time to respond.

'Thank you, my friend,' Fletcher breathed, hugging the demon's neck close. He felt a pulse of love from the brave demon as they hurtled towards the Dragon, the wind tearing at his hair and watering his eyes. They would either win, or die together. There was no other outcome.

On they flew, over the screams of battle and the crackle of gunfire. He could see the Dragon complete its turn ahead and begin its pass towards the massed allies. A cry from Athena warned him of the danger.

It was now or never. He etched the amplify spell on his neck, squeezing the last trace of mana that he had left.

'Khan!' Fletcher bellowed, his voice booming out over the plains.

Even through the turmoil of battle, the albino orc heard his words. The Dragon looked up as Fletcher plummeted through the sky towards them, his khopesh outstretched.

Khan shook his head, ignoring him. The target beneath was too tempting. Thousands of his enemies, packed in a long strip along the battlefield.

'Face me, coward!' Fletcher taunted, attacking the orc leader's pride.

Now Khan looked up, his lips drawn back over his tusks with a snarl. He raised a hand, and Ignatius jerked aside just in time. A lightning bolt sizzled by. Still they plunged towards their enemy.

'Where are your Wyverns, Great Khan?' Fletcher shouted. 'Did you lose the rest of them on your way back from the ether?'

Now the Dragon was angling upwards, its enormous wings throwing dust along the battlefield below. It was working. Khan spoke, his words drifting up.

'I am the Redeemer.' His voice tinged with religious fervour. 'I am the Chosen.'

'Prove it,' Fletcher bellowed back. 'Fight me! Or is "the

Chosen" scared of a single boy?'

A roar, so loud that Fletcher felt it in his chest. And then the Dragon was flying towards them, its maw gaping wide. Within, Fletcher saw the roil of flame.

'Do it,' Fletcher whispered.

Ignatius pulled out of the dive with a howl, the speed creating a gale-force wind that nearly tore Fletcher from his seat. Then they were beating for the clouds above, Ignatius lunging with every flap of his wings. Too slow.

Khan was laughing madly now, swinging his club-sword in anticipation. Seconds raced by as the Dragon gained on them, the draft of its wingbeats pulling them down. Almost there. He could feel the moisture of the clouds in the air, see the grey-white bank a stone's throw away.

Beneath, the demon's mouth stretched open like a snake's. Fire pooled within, casting Ignatius in an orange glow.

'Now, Sylva!' Fletcher screamed.

Three figures burst from above, hurtling towards them. He caught a glimpse of Lovett's Alicorn. The antlers of a Peryton. Lysander, screeching an eagle's cry.

Light flashed over them as the flames tore through the air.

'Now,' Fletcher breathed.

Ignatius unfurled his wings, holding them dead still in the sky. Fire rushed up to meet them. Flames beat at Fletcher's body, smashing him into Ignatius's back. He breathed in the inferno, felt the dry heat in his chest. His shirt and jacket were torn away.

He cracked open his eyes, saw the blaze part around them and twist into the sky, blocked by Ignatius's outstretched wings.

422

A vortex of flame – with three demons flying down the empty tunnel in its centre.

The fire stopped, the Dragon's attack petering out. He heard the sizzle of heat on his skin. And a scream of hatred as Lovett, Sylva and Ophelia whipped by them. Then they too were falling, Ignatius's wings pinned back as they joined in the attack.

Already, Ophelia was gone, the Peryton limp in the Dragon's beak, the battlemage's body twisting as it plummeted to the ground below.

Lovett's lance shattering on the Dragon's cheek as she was nearly thrown from her saddle, tumbling away in a jumble of wings and hooves. And then Sylva, leaping, her falx outstretched. The Griffin snarled in the beast's wing, tearing at the delicate membrane. A roar of pain as Sylva's blade buried itself in the demon's eye, and she hung on for dear life.

Time seemed to slow.

Ignatius crashed into the Dragon's head, his claws tearing at the armoured scales for purchase. Fletcher was hurled from the Drake's back by the impact. He spun through the air, hitting Khan in a tangle of limbs.

They were falling. Spinning. He could see Vocans, rushing up to meet them. The dome of glass at its centre. Shattering.

Darkness.

62

The atrium swam in front of Fletcher's eyes. There was so much pain, crushing his skull like a vice. Ignatius. He had to find Ignatius.

The leathery surface beneath him had tempered his fall: a broken wing, splayed across the length of the cavernous hall. He staggered to his feet, stumbling along the uneven ridges of the shattered appendage.

The Dragon was dead.

Its neck was twisted back on itself at a grotesque right angle, its beak half open, tongue lolling. And near the base of its shoulders, Fletcher saw a limp, burgundy shape.

'Ignatius,' Fletcher cried, stumbling towards him. Above, the soft echoes of the battle outside drifted down.

The Drake lifted his head as Fletcher approached. He mewled, and tried to get up. Then he collapsed, the pain too much for him. The agony in Fletcher's mind redoubled its intensity, and Fletcher fell to his knees. Shards of glass had embedded themselves in the Drake's neck and sides, each one as wide and deep as any sword. Curled up against the demon's chest, Fletcher saw the unconscious form of Sylva. The brave creature had protected her with his body as they fell through the dome above.

'You're going to be OK,' Fletcher whispered, laying a hand on the demon's side. 'Sylva will wake up and heal you.'

He shook the elf, but she remained still and lifeless; the only sign of vitality was the slow rise and fall of her chest. He could see a bruise, spreading along her forehead. And Ignatius's blood, dripping on the marble floor. The demon had no mana to heal himself. He was dying.

'I was wrong.' A voice spoke.

Fletcher's heart filled with horror.

Slowly, a pale figure emerged out of the darkness.

Khan.

He strode into the light of the broken dome above, his long, white hair shining like silver in the dim glow of the evening sky. He was clad in nothing more than a simple loincloth, its colouring as pale as its wearer's skin.

The orc raised his macana sword, and pointed it at Fletcher.

'My Salamander was not the one prophesied. It was yours.'

Fletcher's eyes darted back and forth, searching for a weapon. His khopesh was nowhere to be found, lost somewhere in the depths of the atrium. Then he saw a gleam behind the enormous orc. It was Sylva's falx, buried deep in the Dragon's eye. He had to get to it.

'You've lost, Khan,' Fletcher said, trying to edge around his opponent. 'The prophecy was a lie.'

The orc smiled through his tusks and cut him off with a

languid step to the side. Fletcher could hardly believe how big the orc truly was. He towered above him at eight feet, and his sword was almost as tall as Fletcher himself.

'The prophecy is true,' Khan said, shaking his head. 'He who holds the Salamander will win the war.'

Fletcher was distracted. Athena. He could sense her, hiding among the rafters that held up the great room's ceiling. He forced himself to keep his eyes focused on Khan, ignoring her gliding form as she descended to the floor above them, hiding behind the metal railings.

'If that's true, then I've already won,' Fletcher said.

'No,' the orc snarled. 'Not if I take it from you.'

Fletcher raised his tattooed hand, and Khan flinched at the sight of it.

'Your Dragon is dead,' Fletcher bluffed. 'You have no mana. I could kill you in a second.'

As the orc's eyes focused on his fingers, Fletcher edged around again, managing to put himself a few feet closer to the sword.

'Show me,' Khan said suddenly.

'Don't make me laugh,' Fletcher countered, uncurling the finger with the lightning tattoo. He took a few steps closer to the sword.

'I said, show me!' Khan bellowed, lunging towards Fletcher.

Fletcher dived forward, and felt the macana graze past his head as the orc slashed down at him. Then he was rolling across the stone floor, and the falx sword was in his grasp.

He jerked it from the Dragon's eye with a sickening squelch, and held it in front of him.

Khan laughed.

'So, the puppy wants to play,' he mocked, twirling the macana in his hand. 'I like that.'

The long-handled blade was heavy and unfamiliar in Fletcher's hands. He had never held a falx before.

'Come, let us begin,' Khan said, swiping the macana at Fletcher.

Their swords met, and Fletcher's arms shuddered at the power behind the orc's blow, nearly jarring the weapon from his hands. He leaped back, slipping on the smooth marble.

'That was but a touch,' Khan sneered.

The blow had shaven away a chip of obsidian from the long, black-edged club, which skittered along the ground and into the shadows. Fletcher knew the volcanic glass was brittle, but still sharper than the most fine-edged scalpel, and could quarter flesh with far more ease. He could not meet the orc head on. It would be suicide.

Khan sliced the macana again, his blow whistling over Fletcher's head as he ducked. A back-slash followed blazingly fast, and Fletcher had to roll to avoid the crushing blow. If he had tried to parry, the macana would have blown right through his guard.

'Dance, little boy,' Khan laughed.

Rotherham had taught him to go for the knees.

Fletcher lashed out with his blade as he got to his feet, an awkward thrust that Khan slapped down with the flat of the wooden club. A foot swung forward and took Fletcher in the ribs, knocking him spinning across the atrium. The sword nearly flew from his grip, the blade clanging on the stone floor. Agony flared along his side.

'Enough games,' Khan snarled, as Fletcher lurched to his feet. 'I have an empire to burn.'

'You've . . . already . . . lost,' Fletcher gasped.

He could barely lift the falx – something was broken inside. It hurt to breathe.

Athena could sense his pain. She crouched above Khan, her eyes boring into the white orc's exposed back. It was now or never. *Now.*

Fletcher sprinted towards the orc with a primal yell, fighting against the pain that tore through him. Athena dived, her claws outstretched. Khan swung his blade as the Gryphowl struck, clawing deep into his eyes. Blinded, his blow missed Fletcher's face by a hairsbreadth, slicing his ear instead.

Fletcher cut with all the force he could muster. Felt the sword bite into Khan's leg, jarring against bone. Heard the clatter of the macana falling to the ground.

But his attack had lacked force, his broken ribs hampering his swing. Athena screeched as a huge hand swatted her away. Fletcher felt fingers encircle his neck, and lift him off the ground.

Khan roared into his face, bringing him as close as a lover.

'Die!' the orc snarled through his tusks.

Fletcher kicked out at his stomach. It was like hitting rock. The grip tightened as Khan brought him closer still.

'Look me in the eyes,' the orc hissed, the red orbs of his own narrowing as he squeezed. 'I want to see the light go out of you.'

The world swam in and out of focus. Darkness pressed in at the edges of his vision. He could see Athena dragging herself along the ground, felt the pain of her broken bones mirror his own. Ignatius. He could barely feel Ignatius.

He was dying. Fletcher closed his eyes, and waited for the end.

And then the pressure released. He fell to the ground, gasping for air. Blood puddled on the floor beside him, trickling down the white trunks of the orc's legs.

He looked up, and saw the blade of his khopesh buried in Khan's side. Saw the giant spin, slamming his attacker to the ground with an outstretched fist.

Sylva.

'Elf-filth,' Khan snarled, kicking her body over the floor and pressing a foot against her neck. She lay there, struggling weakly as he leaned forward. Her hands clutched at her throat.

'No,' Fletcher gasped. Her mana. She had to use her mana.

But she was oblivious, her hands clawing at the foot on her neck.

A wave of nausea overtook him as he grasped for the falx. His hand met a handle. The macana.

He could hear Sylva's gurgles, and the throaty laughter of the albino orc as he choked the life from her.

Then he felt it. A slim, trickle of mana, coming from the twin consciousness within him. Athena and Ignatius. They were giving him everything they had, even when they needed it most. Enough for one last, desperate bid.

He raised a hand, pain tearing through his side. Lifted a finger, pointed it at the inside of Khan's knee. And pulsed out the last of his mana in a kinetic blast.

The orc's leg jerked forward, and Khan fell to his knee, bellowing with anger. And, with the final vestiges of his strength, Fletcher reared up, swinging and yelling with all his might.

Time seemed to slow as the great club slewed through the air. A moment of doubt, as the obsidian blade met pale flesh. Then it was through the orc's neck, sending the great head tumbling to the ground. Khan's body keeled over, slapping the ground like a haunch of meat.

But there was no time for relief, even in victory. He had to heal Ignatius.

Sylva turned her head, gasping like a beached fish.

'I came as soon as I could,' she whispered.

Her eyes were unfocused, and the bruise on her head had spread in an ugly stain across her temple.

Fletcher felt a wave of dizziness grip him as he struggled to his feet. With every breath, his strength was returning. Enough to stumble to Sylva and drag her along the marble floor, even as the pain of his ribs flared like red-hot pokers, skewering his chest. He heaved and slipped on Khan's blood, cursing his weakness.

The Drake's eyes were closed; blood pooled around him in a halo of red. Fletcher searched his consciousness. There was still the faintest glimmer of life. Fading fast.

Sylva's head lolled, her eyes flickering on the edge of unconsciousness.

'Wake up,' Fletcher yelled, shaking Sylva. 'You need to heal Ignatius.'

She opened her eyes, and stretched out a limp hand. A finger swirled in the air, the heart symbol sketched in blue thread. White light pulsed out, flowing over the shards of glass.

Slowly, the wounds sealed – long crystal fragments pushing out and tinkling on the floor. The spark of consciousness burned again, at first a small light in Fletcher's mind, then flared fierce as the demon stood, and gasped in a deep breath.

Fletcher sobbed and threw himself around the demon's neck. Relief flooded through him like a drug, softening the pain in his side.

He felt a downy body slip beneath his arm, nuzzling his injury – Athena had returned to him. She was battered and bruised, but alive as well. He broke from his embrace and clutched the Gryphowl to his chest.

'Thank you,' he whispered, kissing the demon on her forehead.

And then he noticed. The silence. No gunfire. No screams, nor clash of weapons.

'Did we win?' Sylva whispered. She held out her arm, and Fletcher lifted the elf to her feet. They leaned against each other like drunken sailors.

Despite the silence, Fletcher felt no fear. It was out of his hands now. He had done all he could.

'Let's go and find out,' Fletcher murmured.

Ignatius lowered himself to the ground, and Fletcher winced as they eased on to his back. Sylva sat in front of him so he could hold her in place if she fell unconscious again. She rested her head on Fletcher's shoulder.

'You sure you're strong enough for this, buddy?' Fletcher asked, stroking Ignatius's side. 'You lost a lot of blood.'

The demon barked, and with a slow leap they were flying through the air, spiralling upwards to the broken dome. Fletcher shuddered as they passed through the jagged hole, emerging into the empty skies and gliding on the wind.

He gripped Sylva tightly as they saw the result of the battle below, obscured by gunsmoke, blood and mud. The screaming of the injured drifted on the wind, and he felt Athena's body shudder against his chest.

Death and devastation had turned the battlefield into a mess of scorched earth and corpses. Men moved like sleepwalkers through the fields of dead, putting the orcs that remained out of their misery.

In the distance, elks and their riders rode out over the plains. And, just beyond them, a horde of orcs, retreating into the red-stained horizon.

'We won, Sylva,' Fletcher whispered, hugging Sylva to his chest. Her hands covered his, and they gazed at the horrors beneath them.

There was no triumph in this victory. Only sorrow. Only loss.

'We won.'

Epilogue

Fletcher thought Lovett had never looked more beautiful as Arcturus wheeled her down the ramp of Raleightown's church. The townsfolk cheered as he lifted her from her chair and carried her to the horse-drawn carriage.

White suited her. Marriage . . . suited her.

Arcturus was beaming from ear to ear, his face red from the wine he had drunk at the reception. Fletcher threw another handful of rice over the pair, and Sacharissa sneezed as it fell around her. Her hair had been brushed and curled, and a bow had been tied around her, like a collar. She gazed darkly at the revellers, daring someone to stroke her. Fletcher couldn't help but grin.

'Wait, wait,' Lovett said, stopping Arcturus in his tracks. He turned her around and she grabbed Fletcher's face, planting a wet kiss on his cheek.

'Thank you for organising this,' she said, her face glowing with joy.

'Think nothing of it – I owe the both of you a thousand times over,' Fletcher said, raising his voice so he could be heard over the cheering crowds.

The entire town had attended, as well as most of the Vocans staff and servants, a score of battlemages and a few dozen dwarves. Even the grumpy Major Goodwin had attended, though he was now sleeping off a full jug of ale beneath the church altar. It had been a celebration to remember. Fletcher only wished his mother had been there, but she was still too ill to leave the hospital. And Berdon, who had been called away on urgent business in Corcillum.

The guests were gathered along the streets, waiting to cheer the couple as they made their way back to Corcillum, where Harold had prepared a room for them at the palace. Now that Alfric was dead, killed by an orc on the field of battle, the young King had full run of the place.

'Fletcher, stop distracting them,' Othello said, throwing an arm around Fletcher's chest. 'Or they'll be late for their dinner with Harold.'

Fletcher winced. Even after a month, his ribs were still sore.

Sacharissa nudged Arcturus with her snout.

'All right, all right,' Arcturus laughed, allowing himself to be pushed forward. 'We'll come visit soon, Fletcher.'

'You'd better!' Fletcher called after them as Arcturus carried Lovett into the carriage.

Fletcher felt a delicate arm thread through his own as he waved the couple away, the crowds surging past him as they chased the carriage down the cobbled streets.

'Didn't they look happy,' Sylva said, smiling. 'Who would have thought it?'

434

'I had some inkling,' Fletcher said.

'You liar,' Othello butted in. He raised his voice. 'Cress, Fletcher reckons he knew Arcturus and Lovett fancied each other.'

'Liar,' Cress called, eating a fistful of cake in the church's doorway.

Fletcher grinned and began to walk Sylva down the street.

'Come on, I haven't shown you yet,' he said, beckoning the dwarves to follow.

As they walked, Fletcher could see some gremlins lurking at the town's borders, though few of them had summoned the courage to enter and take part in the festivities. Blue had set up a new colony beside Watford Bridge, where food was plentiful and the soil was stable enough to dig a new Warren. They traded their fish with the people of Raleightown, and a budding friendship had sprung up between the two peoples. Still, most of the gremlins were timid things, and watched the celebrations from the safety of the savannah.

The four trudged past the statue that Fletcher had erected over the old passage in front of the town hall. It had been installed that very morning, much to the admiration of his guests. A dwarf, a man and an elf, standing side by side. And beneath, a plaque, with the names of all who had died in defence of Raleighshire.

Names like Atilla, Rory, Dalia, Sir Caulder, Rotherham and more than a dozen others. Too many. Othello paused at the plaque, a hint of pain passing across his face.

'They died, so that we could live,' was all he said, tracing his finger along Atilla's name.

'Heroes, one and all,' Fletcher replied solemnly. He stared up at the dwarf's face, and Atilla's own stared back at him.

'I wish you'd put up a statue of Didric, maybe outside the latrines,' Cress said, kicking a clod of earth. 'With what he did underneath, so his cowardice lives on for ever.'

'I think the King's solution was far more eloquent,' Othello said, a smile touching the edges of his lips.

Didric's refusal to fight had not gone unnoticed by King Harold. In his new position as ruler, he had punished not only Didric, but the rest of the Triumvirate as well. Great fines had been levied against the three families, and the money used to rebuild what the orcs had destroyed.

From what Fletcher had heard, the Cavells were left penniless, and had last been seen on a ship to Swazulu, carrying nothing more than the clothes on their backs.

Better still, the Beartooth Mountains, which covered half of Lord Faversham's lands and all of Didric's, had been gifted to the dwarves as compensation for the Triumvirate's crimes against them. Already, dwarven colonies were springing up along its peaks, with new homes carved deep into the rock.

As for Lord Forsyth and Inquisitor Rook, both were imprisoned in Corcillum's dungeons, to live out the rest of their lives in captivity. Fletcher considered it a fitting end for the pair, though far better than they deserved.

Othello's smile turned into a grin, and he put an arm around Fletcher's shoulders as they walked towards the Foxes' old training ground.

But something was different now, emerging from the landscape beyond it. The ruin of the Raleigh mansion had been transformed, rebuilt by the townsfolk of Raleighshire while Fletcher had recovered from his wounds. Even the lawns had been cleared of debris.

'Bloody hell, nice to see how the other half lives, eh, Othello?' Cress joked.

'I haven't actually been in there yet,' Fletcher said.

'Why not?' Sylva asked.

'It doesn't feel right,' he replied, shrugging. 'Not yet, anyway.'

'He's mad,' Cress said. 'I'll have it if you don't want it.'

'As his best mate, I get first rights to it,' Othello joked.

'Bugger that,' Cress said. 'I'm gonna go choose my room.'

Fletcher grinned as Othello and Cress raced towards the old mansion.

'You'd better hurry, before all the good ones are gone,' Fletcher joked, turning to Sylva.

She smiled faintly, her eyes on the horizon.

'You know, I should get going,' she said, unrolling a summoning scroll from a pocket in her dress. 'My father needs me on the southern border. The elves are holding it while Hominum rebuilds its army.'

'So soon?' Fletcher asked, his heart sinking. 'The whole orc army fled when they saw Khan's Dragon fall. They don't believe in the prophecy any more.'

'They've started raiding again,' Sylva replied, shaking her head regretfully. 'There's an army of leaderless orcs across the frontier. They don't know anything else – they've been raised to fight. This war isn't over.'

She caught Fletcher's crestfallen expression, and paused. She leaned in, and kissed him on the lips.

Fletcher was so surprised, he didn't even have time to react. Not before Lysander materialised, and she had jumped astride the Griffin with an agile leap.

'I'll come visit you,' she said softly.

Then she was gone, disappearing into the sky.

Fletcher watched her ruefully, not allowing himself to hope, yet grinning all the same. She was unreadable, but time would tell. For now, he was just happy to be alive. To be free of the weight of Hominum's future.

A horse neighed. Fletcher turned and saw a carriage wheeling its way on to the lawn, leaving deep tracks in the neatly trimmed grass.

'That's going to leave a mark,' Fletcher groaned.

He jogged up to it.

'You're too late,' Fletcher called to the driver on the coach box. 'If you're quick you might catch them on their way to Corcillum.'

He pointed down the street as the carriage door swung open. Berdon stepped out, a bashful grin on his face.

'Sorry, son,' Berdon said, giving him a friendly hug. 'Forgot they'd done up the place.'

'I don't care about the lawn; I care that you've missed the whole thing,' Fletcher said. 'You know, whatever business you had could've waited. There's not even any cake left – Cress ate it all.'

'Well, that's the thing,' Berdon said, smiling down at him. 'It couldn't wait, actually. There's someone who wants to meet you.'

But Fletcher wasn't listening. Because a woman had stepped out of the carriage.

Alice. His mother.

He stared, not understanding. Her eyes. It was as if she was looking straight at him. He took a hesitant step forward.

'Fletcher?' she said, hesitantly.

'Go on, son,' Berdon said, giving him a gentle push.

Then tears were running down Fletcher's face, and she was there, hugging him to her chest. It was as if a dam had burst within him, flooding him with joy. After all these years, everything he had been through . . . he had his mother back.

'I'm sorry,' she said, sobbing. 'I'm so sorry.'

Fletcher pulled away and looked at her. He touched her cheek, hardly able to believe she was real.

'Don't be sorry,' Fletcher said. 'I'm here now. You're here now.'

She smiled through her tears.

'Come on,' she said, taking him by the hand.

They walked towards the mansion, Berdon waving him on with a booming laugh that filled the air.

Fletcher had never been so happy.

Because, finally, he was home.

FIND OUT WHERE IT ALL BEGAN IN

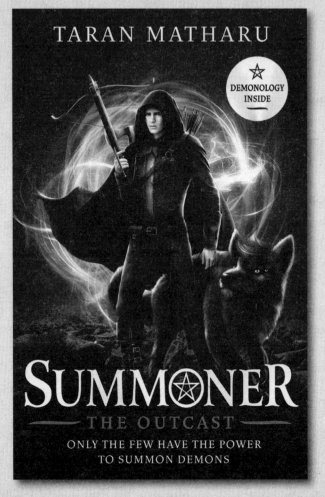

READ ON FOR A SNEAK PEEK OF
THE FIRST CHAPTER...

1

Arcturus shrank deeper into the stable's shadows, waiting for the dead of night. The clamour of the tavern next door had reduced to a gentle murmur, but it was not safe to come out yet.

If all went as planned, his master would ring the midnight bell soon, announcing to patrons that it was time to wend their drunken way home, or if they were lucky, to a room in the inn upstairs. Only then would Arcturus make his move.

It was a plan ten years in the making; almost two thirds of his young life. He was going to escape the beatings, the endless hours of toil and the meagre rations that were his only reward.

As an orphan, Arcturus's value was determined by the yield of his work, rather than the quality of his character. The ox in the stock next to him was fed better than he was; after all, it had been purchased at several times the price his master had paid for him at the local workhouse. He was worth less than a beast of burden.

The bell chimed, disturbing Arcturus from his thoughts. There was a creak as the tavern door swung open, then the crunch of gravel signalled the departure of the drinkers, their coarse laughter fading until silence reigned once again. Even so, it was a full ten minutes before Arcturus padded from the shadows and into the night air of the stables. He adjusted his pack and wondered if he had everything he needed.

Escaping was not as simple as running away, something that Arcturus had learned from bitter experience. In the early days, before he was sold to the innkeeper, children often ran away from the workhouse. They always returned a few days later, starving, beaten or worse.

There was no work for scrawny, uneducated children who had nowhere to go. Arcturus knew that if he ran away unprepared, he would end up begging for scraps before returning, hat in hand, to the inn. In all likelihood he would be sent back to the workhouse. Back to hell on earth.

Arcturus knelt in the straw and checked his pack one more time. Forty-two shillings: his life savings from tips, loose coins and charity. It would last him a few weeks, until he found a new source of income. A thick fur, discarded by a passing trader for the wine stain that adorned its centre, but still fit for Arcturus's purposes; he would not freeze if he needed to camp overnight. A serrated knife, stolen from the tavern kitchen at great risk. Although it was not much of a weapon against a brigand, it gave him peace of mind. Two candles, some bread, salted pork and a few spare garments completed his supplies. Just enough to give him a fighting chance.

The neigh of a horse in the darkness reminded him why he had chosen that night. An opportunity unlike any he had seen before. A young noble had arrived only a few hours earlier, exhausted from a long day's riding. He had not even bothered to unpack his saddlebags, simply throwing the reins disdainfully to Arcturus and trudging into the inn to book a bed for that night. Rude enough that Arcturus only felt a twinge of guilt about robbing the young man.

Arcturus knew where the noble was going. When they came of age, first born children attended Vocans Academy, to learn the art of summoning demons. The academy was all the way in the capital city of Corcillum, on the other side of the Hominum Empire. With any luck, the saddlebags would contain everything Arcturus might need for a similar journey, not to mention the fact that the wealthy young noble's possessions might be extremely valuable.

He sidled up to the horse, clucking his tongue to calm it. As a stable boy, he had a way with horses. This one was no different, nuzzling his palm as if searching for a handful of feed. He stroked it on its muzzle and unclipped the saddlebags, letting them fall to the ground.

Arcturus searched through each pocket, his heart dropping as he discovered that the vast majority of them were empty. No wonder the noble had left without them.

Still, the noble's steed was the real prize. Many horses passed through here, but this was a fine stallion, with long legs, muscled haunches and clear, intelligent eyes. It could outpace any riders who might follow him, be they thieves, brigands or even Pinkertons, Hominum's police force. It was not unknown for them to chase down a runaway orphan if the reward was high enough.

Arcturus rummaged in the last pocket and smiled as he

grasped something solid. It was hard to see in the dim light of the stable, but he could tell by touch it was a roll of leather. He unravelled it on the ground and felt the dry touch of a scroll within.

A thin stream of moonlight cutting through the slats in the roof allowed Arcturus to see printed black letters on the page. He held it up to the light and examined them more closely.

Arcturus's reading ability was poor; his education had been limited to the one year of learning at the workhouse. Fortunately, the books that travellers abandoned in their rooms often found their way into his possession, allowing him to practise over the years. His reading was now better than most, but he still had to sound the words out as he read.

'Do rah lo fah lo go . . .' He whispered the syllables. They made no sense, yet he could not stop, his eyes glued to the page. As he spoke, a strangely familiar sensation suffused his body, starting as a dull giddiness and gradually growing in intensity as word after word rolled off his tongue. The grey of the stable seemed to become brighter, the colours intensifying in his vision.

'Sai lo go mai nei go . . .' The words droned on. His eyes roved back and forth across the page as if they had a mind of their own.

Heart pounding, Arcturus felt something within him stir. There was a flicker in the darkness of the stable. Beneath his feet, the leather wrapping glimmered with violet light, patterns flaring along its surface. Out of the corner of his eye, Arcturus saw the outline of a pentacle, surrounded by symbols on each point of the star. The glow pulsed like a beating heart, accompanied by a low hum.

As he reached the last line of the page, a spinning ball of light formed in the air, growing into a brilliant orb that seared his vision. His ears popped as the humming turned into a roar, growing louder with every second.

Arcturus spoke the last words, then tore his eyes away and dove to the ground, clamping his hands over his ears. He could feel a fiery heat washing over him, as if he were lying beside a great bonfire. Then, as sudden as a lightning strike, Arcturus's world went still.

The new silence fell upon the stable like a cloak, only broken by Arcturus's deep, sobbing breaths. He shut his eyelids tightly, shrinking into a ball on the ground. He knew he should be moving, gathering his things and riding away before anyone arrived to investigate. Yet the ice of fear had taken hold, leaving him petrified on the cold soil of the stable.

There was a snap as the noble's horse broke its tether, then the thunder of hooves as it bolted into the night. The light, heat and noise had been too much for the well-trained beast. Realising his best chance at escape had just galloped out of the door, Arcturus's terror turned to despair.

Straw rustled in the darkness, followed by a low growl. Arcturus froze and held his breath. He kept his eyes shut and remained perfectly still. If he played dead, perhaps whatever it was would move on in search of more interesting prey.

The noise intensified, moving closer and closer, until he could feel the hot, moist breath of the creature in his ear. A tongue slid across his face, leaving a trail of saliva as it tasted him. Arcturus tensed, knowing he would have to fight.

With a yell, he leaped to his feet, striking out with a clenched fist. It met a furry muzzle, rewarding him with a yelp as the creature fell back. Emboldened, Arcturus struck out again, sending the creature skittering into the shadows. It was clumsy, stumbling and tripping over itself as it ran.

Arcturus grabbed his pack and sprinted to the door. The inn was dark still, with no signs of movement. He grinned with relief, realising he might still have a chance to escape. If he was lucky, the horse might not be far away.

But as he began to leave, a strange feeling came over him. Pain and . . . betrayal. He shook his head and took another step, but the feeling intensified. On the edge of his consciousness, Arcturus felt something stir. The creature was connected to him somehow, as if by a mental umbilical cord. Suddenly, Arcturus was overcome with an immense feeling of loneliness and abandonment, emotions that were all too familiar to him.

He turned and stared into the darkness of the stables. In the light of the moon, the entrance yawned like a cave mouth, shrouded in shadow. The creature was whining, like a dog whose master had kicked it. He felt guilty, for the demon had only been licking his face. Of course . . . a demon. The noble was on his way to Vocans Academy to learn the art of summoning them after all. Had Arcturus just done that? Summoned this demon? But that was something only nobles could do . . . wasn't it?

As if it could sense his guilt, the demon tumbled out of the stable, blinking in the moonlight. It was not as huge as he had thought, only the size of a large dog. In fact, it had the head of a dog too, with a pair of large blue eyes, followed by a second, smaller pair behind them. It was entirely black, with a shaggy ridge of hair along its spine. This ridge continued on to a bushy, fox-like tail, though it swished back and forth much like an eager pet. Strangest of all was its body, muscled like a jungle cat with sharp, dangerous claws and powerful limbs.

'What are you?' Arcturus whispered, holding a calming hand out. He could feel the demon's fear dissipating, replaced with an eager desire to please. The demon took a wary step forward, and licked his hand with a rough, wet tongue.

Arcturus examined it more closely, stroking its head. Despite its size, the creature looked young, with an overlarge head and clumsy, thick limbs that gave it a puppy-like mien.

'Do you want to come with me?' Arcturus asked, rubbing the creature under its chin. It closed its four eyes and nuzzled back, panting with pleasure. With each scratch Arcturus felt a keen sense of satisfaction on the edge of his consciousness.

'I bet any passing brigands would think twice before attacking us, eh?' Arcturus murmured, smiling. 'Let's just hope you don't scare the horse too. We're going to need him tonight.'

He turned, just in time to see a cudgel lashing towards his face.

Pain.

Then nothingness.

DON'T MISS THE REST OF THE AMAZING SUMMONER SERIES...

THE ULTIMATE BATTLE FOR
SURVIVAL IS ABOUT TO BEGIN ...

CONTENDER
THE CHOSEN
TARAN MATHARU

DON'T MISS THE EPIC NEW TRILOGY FROM
BESTSELLING AUTHOR, TARAN MATHARU

DEMONOLOGY

JACKALOPE

This demon is one of the most common prey animals in the ether and is not a popular choice among summoners. It appears as a hare with a pair of antlers on its forehead. Known for its speed and sharp incisors, this demon can hold its own in a fight, although it is more likely to flee unless cornered.

SUMMONER MASTER: None

CLASSIFICATION: Caprid
SUMMONING LEVEL: 1
BASE MANA LEVEL: 6
MANA ABILITIES: None
NATURAL SKILLS: Acute hearing, Agility
RARITY: Very Common
DIET: Herbivore
ATTACK/DEFENCE 1: Antlers 2: Bite

PYRAUSTA

SUMMONER MASTER: *Othello*

CLASSIFICATION: *Arthropidae, Reptilia*
SUMMONING LEVEL: *2*
BASE MANA LEVEL: *17*
MANA ABILITIES: *None*
NATURAL SKILLS:
*Flying, Colour Change,
Heat Vision, Sonar*
RARITY: *Endangered*
DIET: *Omnivore*
ATTACK/DEFENCE
1: Paralytic Sting

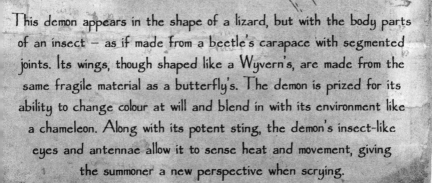

This demon appears in the shape of a lizard, but with the body parts
of an insect — as if made from a beetle's carapace with segmented
joints. Its wings, though shaped like a Wyvern's, are made from the
same fragile material as a butterfly's. The demon is prized for its
ability to change colour at will and blend in with its environment like
a chameleon. Along with its potent sting, the demon's insect-like
eyes and antennae allow it to sense heat and movement, giving
the summoner a new perspective when scrying.

KAPPA

The Kappa is one of the more common Aquarine demons. Appearing in a humanoid shape as an overgrown toad with a turtle's beak and shell, this demon's most unusual feature is the hollow indentation at the top of its head. It is theorized that this bowl is used to store water when the Kappa travels overland, allowing it to breathe with the Kappa's large gill at the bottom. Other than its shell, this demon is a weak species and serves as a prey animal to the Nanaues and Akhluts of the ether's oceans.

SUMMONER MASTER: None

CLASSIFICATION: Aquarine, Reptilia
SUMMONING LEVEL: 3
BASE MANA LEVEL: 21
MANA ABILITIES: None
NATURAL SKILLS: Amphibious

RARITY: Uncommon
DIET: Omnivore
ATTACK/DEFENCE 1: Beak 2: Shell

Coatl

The Coatl is a serpent with multi-coloured plumage instead of scales. Although not capable of flight, the Coatl uses its feathers to glide down from the ether's trees and on to unsuspecting prey below. The Coatl will use its venom to paralyse a victim and then constrict it to death, before swallowing the carcass whole.

SUMMONER MASTER: None

CLASSIFICATION: Reptilia, Aves
SUMMONING LEVEL: 4
BASE MANA LEVEL: 28
MANA ABILITIES: None
NATURAL SKILLS: Gliding

RARITY: Uncommon
DIET: Carnivore
ATTACK/DEFENCE
1: Poison Fangs 2: Constrict

GUNNI

This demon is relatively common in the ether and is considered an acquired taste by some summoners. It appears similar to a bear-sized wombat, with a pair of small antlers on its head. Its claws, teeth and horns are not particularly sharp, but the demon's size and muscle more than make up for this shortfall.

SUMMONER MASTER: None

CLASSIFICATION: Megafauns
SUMMONING LEVEL: 4
BASE MANA LEVEL: 27
MANA ABILITIES: None
NATURAL SKILLS: Digging

RARITY: Common
DIET: Herbivore
ATTACK/DEFENCE
1: Bite 2: Scratch
3: Antlers

ROPEN

The Ropen appears as a hybrid between bat and bird. It has no feathers; its wings are made from a stretched membrane between clawed wing joints. When hunting, it uses its powerful talons to snatch smaller prey. Its most birdlike appendages are a long pelican beak and an elongated crest on the back of its head.

SUMMONER MASTER: *None*

CLASSIFICATION: *Reptilia, Aves*
SUMMONING LEVEL: *4*
BASE MANA LEVEL: *27*
MANA ABILITIES: *None*
NATURAL SKILLS: *Flying*
RARITY: *Common*
DIET: *Carnivore*
ATTACK/DEFENCE *1: Beak 2: Talons*

CATOBLEPAS

The Catoblepas has a powerful bovine body and horns, a horse's mane and a head similar to that of a warthog. This herbivorous demon has a penchant for eating poisonous plants, leaving its breath toxic. Although immune to their own Catoblepas's noxious fumes, summoners avoid this demon for fear of inadvertently injuring others. These demons are one of the more dangerous prey animals that the ether's larger carnivores feed upon.

SUMMONER MASTER: *None*

CLASSIFICATION: *Caprids*
SUMMONING LEVEL: *5*
BASE MANA LEVEL: *35*
MANA ABILITIES: *None*

NATURAL SKILLS:
Immunity to Poison
RARITY: *Rare*
DIET: *Herbivore*
ATTACK/DEFENCE
1: Toxic Breath
2: Horns
3: Tusks

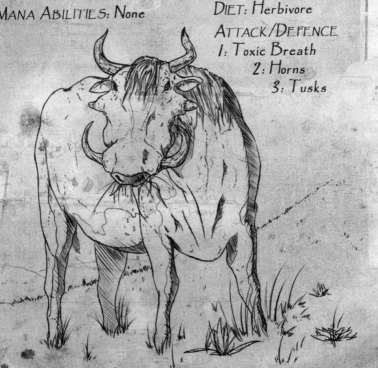

LEUCROTTA

The Leucrotta is a zebra-striped demon that prefers to hunt at
dusk. It is an unusual creature with cloven hooves, a lion-like tail
and the head and body shape of an overgrown badger. It is not
unknown for this demon to follow Shrike migrations across the
ether, eating the carrion left behind. These solitary demons were
once popular with Hominum's summoners, but have
since fallen out of favour.

SUMMONER MASTER: *None*

CLASSIFICATION: *Megafauns*

SUMMONING LEVEL: *5*

BASE MANA LEVEL: *33*

MANA ABILITIES: *None*

NATURAL SKILLS: *Night-vision*

RARITY: *Uncommon*

DIET: *Carnivore*

ATTACK/DEFENCE 1: *Bite*

HIPPALECTRYON

This demon bears the front half of a horse and the back half of a cockerel, with a curved beak and red wattle instead of a muzzle. The male's red and green blend of fur and plumage culminates in a fan of bright tail feathers that it uses to attract its equally deadly, fawn-coloured female counterpart. The hooked talons of its hind legs can easily disembowel an attacker, yet that does not prevent a Hippalectryon's higher-level predators from trying to eat them.

SUMMONER MASTER: *Arcturus*

CLASSIFICATION: *Equine, Aves*

SUMMONING LEVEL: *6*

BASE MANA LEVEL: *43*

MANA ABILITIES: *None*

NATURAL SKILLS: *None*

RARITY: *Uncommon*

DIET: *Omnivore*

ATTACK/DEFENCE
1: *Beak* 2: *Talons*

SOBEK

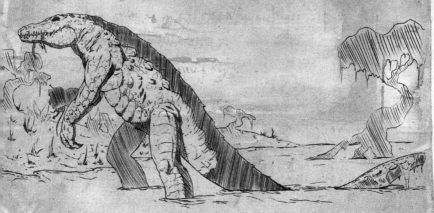

Sobeks are native to swamps, rivers and lakes, avoiding the wider seas and oceans of the ether. These thick-skinned bipedal crocodilians use their claws and jaws to tear apart their opponents, if their large tails haven't battered them to the ground first. Hunched over at five feet tall, this demon could stand toe-to-toe with its natural adversary, the Nanaue.

SUMMONER MASTER: None

CLASSIFICATION: Reptilia
SUMMONING LEVEL: 9
BASE MANA LEVEL: 45
MANA ABILITIES: None
NATURAL SKILLS: Swimming, Camouflage
RARITY: Common
DIET: Carnivore
ATTACK/DEFENCE 1: Bite 2: Claws
3: Tail Swipe 4: Thick-skinned

AHOOL

Appearing as a giant bat with the musculature of a mountain gorilla, the Ahool is a solitary demon that is rarely found in the known ether. Ahools are occasionally used as a mount for more powerful orc shamans. Known for their acute sense of hearing and smell, they make excellent trackers on air and land alike. With sharp claws on its winged forelimbs and fangs as thick as elephant tusks, an Ahool is capable of taking on a Griffin.

SUMMONER MASTER: Khan

CLASSIFICATION: Rodentia
SUMMONING LEVEL: 10
BASE MANA LEVEL: 65
MANA ABILITIES: None

NATURAL SKILLS: Flying, Sonar, Night Vision, Hearing, Smell

RARITY: Very Rare
DIET: Omnivore
ATTACK/DEFENCE
1: Fangs 2: Claws

ZARATAN

This amphibious demon could be described as a hybrid between a tortoise and a turtle, with webbed claws, a sharp beak and a protective shell. Their newborns appear the same size as a sea turtle, but they can grow to the dimensions of a small archipelago. In fact, they are often mistaken for islands, given the amount of vegetation that forms on their rugged shells. Considered the most long-living demons in the ether, these demons are said to live as long as two millennia.

SUMMONER MASTER: *None*

CLASSIFICATION: *Reptilia*
SUMMONING LEVEL: *15*
BASE MANA LEVEL: *120*
MANA ABILITIES: *None*
NATURAL SKILLS: *Swimming*

RARITY: *Rare*
DIET: *Herbivore*
ATTACK/DEFENCE
1: Beak 2: Shell

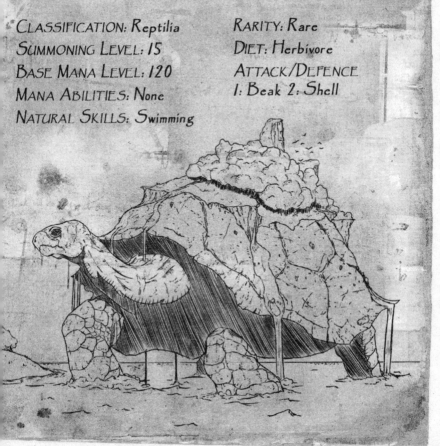

DRAKE

The Drake is something of a mystery to researchers at Vocans, since it is yet to be examined or tested against a fulfilmeter. From the descriptions of the only known specimen, it is clearly the first stage in the metamorphosis of a Salamander, facilitated by the extreme heat of a volcano. Marginally larger than a Griffin, the Drake is similarly proportioned to that of a Salamander, with the addition of a long, sinuous neck, two back facing horns on its head and a pair of large leathery wings. As with their smaller counterparts, Drakes have the ability to breathe fire, self-heal and heal others with their saliva. Rumours have circulated that a Drake's summoner becomes immune to fire, but the veracity of these claims is yet to be determined.

SUMMONER MASTER: *Fletcher*

CLASSIFICATION: *Reptilia*

SUMMONING LEVEL: *Unknown*

BASE MANA LEVEL: *Unknown*

MANA ABILITIES:
Fire Breathing, Healing

NATURAL SKILLS:
Flying, Agility,
Fire Proof

RARITY: *Extremely Rare*

DIET: *Carnivore*

ATTACK/DEFENCE
1: Fire Breath 2: Tail Spike
3: Claws 4: Beak

DRAGON

SUMMONER
MASTER: *Khan*

CLASSIFICATION: *Reptilia*
SUMMONING LEVEL: *Unknown*
BASE MANA LEVEL: *Unknown*
MANA ABILITIES:
Fire Breathing, Healing
NATURAL SKILLS:
Flying, Agility, Fire Proof

RARITY: *Extremely Rare*
DIET: *Carnivore*
ATTACK/DEFENCE
1: Fire Breath 2: Tail Spike
3: Claws 4: Beak
5: Armour Plating

It is believed the Dragon is the final stage in the metamorphosis of the Salamander species. Appearing as a giant Drake, this demon is complimented by larger horns and scaly skin that is extremely difficult to penetrate. Only one specimen is thought to have existed, belonging to Khan, the religious leader of the orcs. It is theorised that only an albino orc is capable of summoning a demon of such power, stemming from the hypothesis that a quirk of evolution has given the albinos of the orc species immensely high fulfilment levels.

LAVELLAN

WILL-O'-THE-WISP

BAKU

ENCANTADO

SLEIPNIR

MUSIMON

KIRIN

YALE

INDRIK

AKHLUT

BEHEMOTH

TRUNKO

Illustrations by David North

TARAN MATHARU

was born in London in 1990 and found a passion for reading at a very early age. His love for stories developed into a desire to create his own, writing his first book at nine years old. At twenty-two, while taking time off to travel, Taran began to write *Summoner*, which became an online sensation, reaching over three million reads in less than six months. Taran is now a full-time author, and spends his time travelling the world and writing. The Summoner series has been translated into 15 languages and is a *New York Times* Bestseller.